THE BEST AMERICAN

NONREQUIRED
READING
2018

THE BEST AMERICAN

NONREQUIRED READING™ 2018

■

EDITED BY

SHEILA HETI

AND THE STUDENTS OF

826 NATIONAL

MANAGING EDITOR

CLARA SANKEY

A MARINER ORIGINAL
HOUGHTON MIFFLIN HARCOURT
BOSTON • NEW YORK
2018

ISSN: 1539-316x (print)   ISSN: 2573-3923 (e-book)
ISBN: 978-1-328-46581-8 (print)   ISBN: 978-1-328-46713-3 (e-book)
Printed in the United States of America
DOC 10 9 8 7 6 5 4 3 2 1

CONTENTS

Editors' Note

IN ONE OF MY FIRST EMAIL EXCHANGES with this year's guest editor, Canadian author Sheila Heti, I asked her what she hoped we might achieve for this collection: "I think we want to pry literature from the cracks; to see it where we didn't see it before and look where other people aren't looking." This sentiment became the guiding principle of our collection. Featuring writing published in the U.S. in 2017, this year's anthology not only presents new work from little known authors—both national and international—it also exhumes lost and translated voices from the past, highlighting the longevity of words across generations and geographical borders. As always, it is idiosyncratic and contains eclectic writing of all genres, offering a view of the world through the prism of a group of fifteen Bay Area high school students, who make up BANR's editorial committee.

The members of this committee are smart, they are savvy, and they know what they like to read. As the new managing editor, I worked with our intern Laura to ensure that everyone was comfortable and reading conditions optimal during our weekly meetings. I needn't have worried as each one proved immensely fruitful, with conversations often taking unexpected twists and turns. Rarely did the committee like something unanimously. Instead, each piece was fiercely defended, hotly contested, and passionately debated. Ultimately the votes were cast—and as the year progressed, the "yesses," "nos," and "maybes" piled up.

Many of the stories in the anthology feel strange and otherworldly, offering glimpses into other realities that reveal unexpected things about our own lives. Sheila's own writing style and unique perspective ensured that whatever we read was fresh, exciting, and completely new. Her influence empowered the students to bring in unusual pieces they'd discovered in the far corners of the Internet to share with the group. Sheila never underestimated the students' ability to read unconventional and demanding writing; they always rose to meet the challenge, highlighting everything that 2018 has taught us about high schoolers: they are even smarter and more powerful than we have been giving them credit for.

For every piece included in this collection, there were three that didn't make the cut. These have been included in the Notable Reading section on pages 288–290. Lola still thinks about Willis Plummer's poem "10,000 Year Clock" every day, while Max fell head over heels in love with "A House Meal," and Sidney reckons that Leslie Jamison's piece on Second Life in *The Atlantic* is something they'll never forget. We hope your BANR adventure continues beyond this book.

Our committee would like to say a few final words to you, dear reader: Coco wants you to know that as strange as this collection is, no one was on drugs when we put it together. Xuan is super excited for you to dive right in, and Huckleberry says that if you don't like one piece, move on and just keep reading! Charley suggests you keep an open mind, while Zoe recommends bringing tissues. Emilia's advice is a little more prescriptive: take it slow, she says, read a maximum of two pieces per day, otherwise you won't be able to appreciate them. After you read, she continues, pause and let the words sink in. Max concludes that we may have a strange collection, but reading always, always has a direct impact and positive outcomes. I can't think of a better way to send you onto Sheila's wonderful introduction. Thank you for reading!

—CLARA SANKEY and the *BANR* Committee
June 2018

INTRODUCTION

"Something that's really big for me is: does it represent the year 2017? But I think I'm looking for a piece that is both timely and will withstand the test of time—that in twenty years, is still going to be relevant to whoever is reading it." —Emilia

I DIDN'T KNOW WHAT I WAS GETTING INTO when I agreed to guest edit this anthology. It was all very confusing and yet presented as very straightforward—this is typical McSweeney's, who no longer run the project, but began it, and it still bears its stamp—you are sort of expected to understand and are given very little direction, then you realize by the end that there was no direction, you were supposed to make it up on your own.

Perhaps some of the fifteen students knew this already—the ones who had been on *The Best American Nonrequired Reading* committee before. There was a chaotic sense of direction from the beginning, and that an anthology was made, and that it's as good as I think it is, perhaps has something to do with what happens when the task is no less pure than "let's get together and read and talk about what we're reading and somehow that will turn into an anthology."

I only met with the *BANR* committee twice, when they flew me out to San Francisco from Toronto. The first time, in November, I entered from Valencia Street into the McSweeney's offices (crammed with books and journals and computers and people) and went into the low-ceilinged basement where a long table was piled with granola bars and chips and candy and photocopied sheets. The students welcomed me warmly, casually. They had been meeting every Monday night from 6 to 8 p.m., starting in September, and would meet until the end of May. Clara Sankey, the managing editor, led the sessions, with the assistance of this year's intern, Laura Van Slyke.

The evenings proceeded like this: For the first hour, the committee read silently, sitting around the long table. After the reading was done, one person began the discussion by giving a summary of the piece, then gave their opinion. Then another person gave their opinion, then another person did the same. Sometimes all of them did. Discussion ping-ponged back and forth. Sometimes a piece would be discussed for a half hour or more. Then there was a vote to determine whether the piece should be included: *yes, no,* or *maybe.* Then on to the next piece.

As evidenced in the notes Laura took during each session, there wasn't an atmosphere of tidy agreement:

HUCKLEBERRY: I love this so much—it's like a rollercoaster ("Everything is a rollercoaster, haha," interjects Max). It's very fast and you can't immediately understand what's around you, but you're enjoying it. And it builds to a very satisfying ending about death that I've never read before!

MADI: It's a very *BANR* read. You get lost in him! His flow is intriguing.

EMILIA: I couldn't read this. It felt like drowning. As soon as I got air, I didn't want to go back under the water.

I came into this process with a fair amount of skepticism about the value of anthologies: *Who would rather read an anthology than a book that is one thing, with one tone, and point of view? Aren't magazines the place for a collection of things by different authors, rather than a book?* But now I can see that this anthology is something different—not just because of the quality of the material (many anthologies are quality) but because of the process it represents.

Most concisely, as Annette put it when I returned to interview the students in the spring, "For me, the point of *BANR* has always been much more about what happens in this room than what we do with the book outside of the room. I'll see it in a bookstore sometimes, and be like *Hey!* And that's fun. But for me, it's like a breath out when I come to *BANR*. It's one of the safest spaces in my life. I don't have to bring my reservations into this space; I don't have to put a caveat on everything. I can just be okay with listening to everybody, because I know that everyone here respects everyone else." I think everyone felt this grateful—especially in a year so dominated by fears about how polarized America had become. Here at least was one environment where disagreement could be had; where people changed their minds.

Emma understands this anthology as being in conversation with social media: "I feel like one of the problems with how people read nowadays is they get a lot of their reading through social media and through friends. It turns into these feedback loops, and it's this preaching to the choir. *BANR* is a nice process, because I didn't get these readings from my friends. A lot of it is just random stuff from a random anthology that we have downstairs." If *BANR* interrupts their loops, maybe it will interrupt yours.

Perhaps there is also some activism in an anthology like this one. As Sophia said, "I think a lot of the older generation doesn't think of kids as people who want to think. So I think it's cool when people who don't necessarily take us seriously, they read what we put together and they're like, *Oh, yeah, I didn't really recognize that these are things they care about.*"

It's perhaps strange, looking at the collection, that there is no mention of the man who acted as president in 2017, but there wasn't a conscious decision to leave his name out. The pieces we read were nominated by the committee, Clara, Laura, myself, and the volunteer readers who came into the offices to go through the many literary journals that had been sent our way. Every Sunday, Clara and I would discuss and decide what the committee would read the next day. All told, eighty-five pieces were considered by the group.

The anthology was constantly changing. In late 2017, we were going to feature snippets from the very many excellent pieces that were being written in the wake of the Harvey Weinstein scandal and as the #MeToo consciousness swelled, but as we moved into 2018, these were abandoned in favor of "Refuge for Jae-in Doe: Fugues in the Key of English Major," a piece which we felt spoke to these same concerns even more powerfully, and also excited us formally.

I was constantly surprised to learn what the *BANR* committee liked and didn't like. Their taste was unpredictable. Often I would submit something to be read, certain it would be loved, only to learn that they didn't want it for a reason I would never have considered myself. Most shocking, for me, was their response to Rachel Aviv's article in *The New Yorker*, "The Trauma of Facing Deportation," which reported on the mysterious phenomena of teenagers falling into deep comas, in response to the news that their families would be deported from their country. I thought the piece was topical, exquisitely written, and just overall fascinating. Plus, it was about teenagers— how could they resist? But they objected to the scenes where Aviv described the comatose bodies of the teenagers, because these teenagers hadn't been able to give their consent. This reservation would never have occurred to me in a million years, so it's a good thing that people are born twenty years after you are, so you don't have to wait more than a million years.

* * *

The Committee . . .

HUCKLEBERRY: We've been reading a lot of very important political nonfiction—and it's been interesting thinking about straddling the line between representing 2017, and being sufficiently nonrequired. We read some pieces where I felt like *this is good, and this is important, but this feels required. This feels like something that everybody should be reading, and as such, doesn't really fit the label of our book.*

SIDNEY: Earlier in the year we read "My Family's Slave," and I thought, *This piece is so important that we have to put it in.* Then I was like, *Wait a second: nonrequired.* But then I thought: I'm not forcing anyone to read this. So in that way, everything I pick is nonrequired. Because it's not like anybody really takes me that seriously anyway.

SHEILA: So ultimately you're making a distinction between being required by you, and being required by—?

SIDNEY: School. Or college. Or your job.

SHEILA: But it's required by a seventeen-year-old sitting in the basement.

MADI: When I'm reading a piece, and I immediately think, *I want to send this to a friend of mine,* I know that it's a *BANR* piece. It's that urge to share it with people. It's that I want the people around me, and as many people as possible, to be reading this piece.

CHARLEY: I remember one piece that we read really early on at *BANR* about a middle-aged woman, and I personally have not read a lot of pieces about middle-aged women. They're either in their early twenties or sixties or something. And I remember going home and telling my whole family about it, and telling my mom that she needed to read it.

SIDNEY: *BANR* is very different from English class, in that we're not worried about analyzing the pieces—we're not worried about picking apart every motif because we'll have to write an essay on it. We're thinking about, *What do we like about this piece? What works? What doesn't? What do we want to expose our readership to?* So that's a very different experience from what I have in school.

EMMA: We have conversations, like: *Okay, we really like what this piece is about, but do we like how it's done? Do we think that the voice is strong enough? Is this compelling as a piece of literature, for someone who doesn't care about the subject?* Walking that line is the most challenging thing about this, because we want to do justice to our morals, but also produce a really quality, mature book.

MADI: I think we have this really unique perspective, even though we live in the Silicon Valley, and we live in a world of technology. But this is a very concrete way that we can put all of these perspectives into something that we know is going to last, and that is really interesting.

SHEILA: As opposed to something online that they can take down?

MADI: Yeah.

SOPHIA: I don't read outside of school like I used to. A lot of things take up a lot of time in my life, and the down time that I have, I'm exhausted, so I don't read. I wish I did. I don't know when the last time it was that I just read a book in three days, but I used to do that once a week. So *BANR* has been nice as a way to see the things that I'm missing, and read pieces that have affected me so much—pieces where it becomes part of you.

EMILIA: We don't know each other that well, so it's really cool to get to know each other as readers, because something we all share, I think, is that we're really passionate readers, and some of us are writers. We're high schoolers, and I think a lot of us are pretty well supported by our families, and a lot of us are minors, and we get to come in and truly just pick not based on what our paycheck is going to be, but based on what we think is quality, and what we want people to read, and what we think is new. We also have really fresh eyes, and it's really fun to adventure through and read writers that aren't from our background, and it's a new experience for us. We're like little fresh pieces of dough that have just been thrown in the oven.

ANNETTE: A lot of the change you've seen in students in the United States recently is that kids our age—a lot of us have had to make a decision about what part of our lives we are willing to interrupt to forward the change we want to see in the world. What I've loved about *BANR* is that we've reflected that. Like, if I'm willing to leave class to talk about this issue, am I willing to rearrange what *BANR* is to talk about this issue?

EMMA: We've been given this unusual position of being able to publish what we want, when so many other people are just consumers. Commonly, my friends are just consumers. But I get to take part in the production of media, which is really special.

MADI: When I'm explaining what *BANR* is to my friends, I tell them that we put together an anthology of all of these different pieces, and that we're allowed to submit pieces. I always catch myself saying *my* pieces, and my friends are like, *Oh, you wrote things and they get published? That's so cool!* No, I don't get to write pieces, but these pieces I get to talk about are equally *my* pieces, because even though they're not pieces that I wrote, they are pieces that I see part of myself in.

HUCKLEBERRY: I also feel like there is something to be said for including stuff that not everybody can connect with.

MAX: I like to think that any piece we have will have about the same percentage of people who will like it in the real world as have liked it here.

HUCKLEBERRY: I definitely have found myself getting particularly attached to pieces and feeling the need to speak up for them, or fight for them. There was one piece we read, maybe in the second week, and I remember there was overall not as positive a reaction in the room as the one that I was having, and I remember feeling like, *I'm going to make sure that this piece gets in.*

ALTHEA: Each of these stories means something very specific to each of us, and sometimes it gets political, and sometimes it gets personal, and I just think that *BANR* gives us a way to find out how to respectfully disagree before it's too late for us to learn that. Because the arguments get really intense. People really like their stories. But this gives us an easy way to learn how to have a heated conversation, and then still end it and respect each other as people, and even as friends.

XUAN: I don't talk that much during *BANR;* I think it's because it's my first year. I'm getting to know what happens around here, but I don't think that I've heard people express how much they love literature in any school setting, or really any setting besides here. We listen to each other, and everybody does have an individual idea and opinion, but that idea can really be affected by what other people say.

* * *

Every student is required to sign a contract before joining the committee. They agree to *attend meetings every week unless there is some crazy emergency, e.g., someone has gotten their arm stuck in a thresher back on the farm in Iowa.* They agree that *if I miss more than one meeting a month, my membership will be reviewed/reconsidered, and might be revoked.* And they agree to turn off their phones when they enter the building. They sign on the dotted line, confirming they will *speak and offer ideas and opinions, do a good job, be kind to my fellow members . . . listen to what they have to say, and offer support whenever I can.*

Not a big deal, the contract concludes, *I am smart and I work hard.* It's true: they are, and they do. In the online folder where we keep the material for this anthology are their fifteen contracts, each one signed and dated September 11, 2017.

I like to think of this anthology not as a portrait of this past year, but as a portrait of the collective taste of these specific, fifteen Bay Area teenagers, in the year 2017, who were born just after the turn of the millennium; for whom Obama was the first president of their politically conscious lives; who started the year by telling each other what pronouns they prefer; who snap their fingers in agreement when another person talks; who are readers, and self-define as such.

This book was made by the bright, single mind that is made up of all their minds; and the following pages are what it wants you to read.

SHEILA HETI

THE BEST AMERICAN

NONREQUIRED
READING
2018

QUIM MONZÓ

■

Divine Providence

Translated from Catalan by Peter Bush

FROM *A Public Space*

ONE MORNING, the scholar who in patient, disciplined manner has dedicated fifty of his sixty-eight years to writing the Great Work (of which he has currently completed seventy-two volumes) notices that the ink of the letters on the first pages of the first volume is beginning to fade. The black is no longer so sharp and is turning grayish. As he has become used to frequently revisiting all the volumes he has written to date, when he notices the deterioration, only the first two pages have been affected, the first that he wrote fifty years ago. And, into the bargain, the letters on the bottom lines of the second page are also rather illegible. He painstakingly restores the erased letters one by one. He diligently follows their traces until he has restored words, lines and paragraphs with India ink. But just as he is finishing, he notices that the words on the last lines of page 2 and the whole of page 3 (when he began the restoration process, some were in a good state and the others were in a relatively good state) have also faded: confirmation that the disease is degenerative.

Fifty years ago, when the scholar decided to devote his life to writing the Great Work, he was already well aware that he would have to dispense with any activity that might consume even a tiny fraction of his time, and remain celibate and live without a television. The Great Work would be really so Great he couldn't waste a moment on anything else. Indeed there could be nothing else *but* the Great Work.

·

That was why he decided not to waste precious minutes looking for a publisher. The future would find one. He was so convinced of the value of what he was setting out to do, that, of necessity, when somebody discovered the volumes of the Great Work, unpublished, side by side, on the bookcase in the passage in his house, the first publisher to discover it (whoever he might be) would immediately recognize the importance of what was before him. But, if letters are now fading, whatever will remain of the Great Work?

The degeneration is relentless. Just when he has reworked the first three pages, he finds that the letters on pages 4, 5, and 6 are also fading. When he has reworked the letters on pages 4, 5, and 6, he discovers that those on 7, 8, 9, and 10 have been erased completely. When he has reworked 7, 8, 9, and 10, he finds those on page 11 to 27 have vanished.

He can't waste time trying to deduce why the letters are being erased. He concentrates on reworking the first volume (the first volumes: he soon sees the second and third volumes are also deteriorating) and realizes that the time spent doing that won't allow him to finish the concluding volumes. Without the colophon that should give the volumes he has already written their true sense, his fifty years of dedication will have been for naught. The initial volumes are simply the necessary, though not essential, groundwork to situate things in the space where he has to set out his genuinely innovative findings: namely, the final volumes. Without the latter, the Great Work will never be that. Hence his doubt: Shouldn't he perhaps let the early volumes continue to fade and not waste time restoring them? Wouldn't it be better to focus on his struggle against time to finish once and for all the final volumes (exactly how many are there: six, or seven?) so he can bring the Work to its climax, even at the risk of the first volumes fading away forever? Of the seventy-two he has written so far, he can certainly afford to lose the first seven or eight, even though they enabled him to gather a head of steam, they don't contribute anything substantially new. However, then another doubt strikes him: When he has written the final full stop, will only the first seven or eight volumes have faded? Determined not to waste one minute more, he buckles down to work. He immediately stops. How come he hasn't realized until now that, if he dies, and that person who is fated to discover the Great Work and take it to a publisher dillydallies making the discovery, the afflicted volumes won't be seven or eight, but the whole lot? What should he do: stop writing and start seeking out a publisher right now, to avoid that risk, even though, without those concluding volumes, it will be impossible to demonstrate that his project is genuinely groundbreaking? However, if he devotes time and effort to looking for a publisher, he won't be able to dedicate the necessary time to reworking the volumes as they keep wasting away, nor will he be able to write the final volumes. What should he do? He becomes a nervous wreck. Could a life of endless toil have been in vain? Yes, it could. What *was* the point of so much effort, single-minded devotion, celibacy and sacrifice? He thinks it has been one huge practical joke. He feels hatred growing within himself: hatred towards himself for a life misspent. And his inability to recover the time he has wasted doesn't panic him as much as being certain that, at this juncture, it will be too late to decide how to make the most of the time left to him.

QIU MIAOJIN

■

An Excerpt from
Notes of a Crocodile

Translated from Chinese by Bonnie Huie

FROM *The New York Review of Books*

THERE ARE THREE PEOPLE I have to write about in this journal. These three are from my final year in college—a stage of my life I call the eruptive phase—and all of them profoundly shaped who I am today. Each had distinguishing qualities that influenced my life's direction, and I saw in each of them a certain majesty. During that time of intense bonding, it was their influence which made me realize that romantic love was not the only thing that brought an individual closer to others, nor was it a matter decided by fate. There are other, essential experiences that ought to come first, for one must be capable of being touched, of embodying the innocence that forms the basis of compassion . . . and of showing a heart that cries out in pain that genuine suffering deserves no less than the dignity to go on living.

Meng Sheng. Half born of malice, half of goodwill. Half sincere, half put-on. This freewheeling lunatic became a close friend of mine after Shui Ling and I went our separate ways for the second time. To this day, I've never understood what his true motive was—because while he saved me from my self-destructiveness, he also pushed me toward total depravity.

I was determined to transform myself into a real girl. At Tun Tun's encouragement, I made a big decision: I wasn't going to fall in love with another woman. This time, I was going to make a clean break with the past and pursue a normal happiness.

For my entire life, I had been inherently attracted to women. That desire, regardless of whether it was realized, had long tormented me. Desire and torment were two opposing forces constantly chafing me, inside and out. I knew full well that my change of diet was futile. I was a prisoner of my own nature, and one with no recourse. This time, however, I was determined to liberate myself. Convinced that it was possible to change, I went about it all rather nonchalantly, and during that phase, I basically behaved as if I had sold my soul. I felt no personal attachment to anyone. Nothing fazed me. Once I shed the overwhelming burden of my sadness, I felt as light as a feather. In my mind, I had been given a mandate: I would live as I pleased and let myself do whatever I wanted.

And so I became dissolute. In my total hedonism, I explored all possibilities, however transitory. I went out every night and hung out at restaurants, clubs, bars, a new friend's place. At the same time, I invited the advances of men, resorting to the most blatant and dubious means to lure them.

Meng Sheng was among my partners. My feminine clothing, speech, manners, and hair tossing were plainly intended to attract a man, and he was perceptive enough to notice my transformation. Yet he didn't ask questions, and instead he adopted a chivalrous attitude toward me. Every few days he'd see me, and I'd be waiting for him, as if we were dating. In my heart I was hoping I'd find a guy to fall for soon, yet Meng Sheng treated it like a big joke, like we both knew it was a charade. Only much later, when I recalled the look in his eyes and the words he said, did I realize that no matter what his real motive was, he had tried to love me.

"Hey, if you don't meet the right guy, you can always call me up," Meng Sheng said. He dragged me to campus on my birthday, saying that in honor of the occasion, he'd take me out for a celebratory round of drinks.

"Meng Sheng, do you think I'm changing in order to find a man?" It was the first and only time in four years that I'd spent my birthday with someone. In fact, when Meng Sheng suggested it, I felt grateful.

"I don't buy any of it. You people are ridiculous, wasting your energy trying to improve yourselves. What good does it do? You all think I don't try hard enough, and that's why I'm such a failure. But what do you know? In order to save my own life, I had to muster a hundred times the strength that any of you have. Hell, I can't even exert myself anymore! Do you know how psychology defines 'helplessness'? I like you the way you are right now, being like, *Who cares?* and seeing how bad it gets. The best is when things get so bad that I actually feel something. That's when I reach self-understanding," Meng Sheng said, laughing. He'd written me a song as a birthday present.

"Seriously, though, don't die before me. If you did, I'd be even more bored than I already am. You have to go on living for me." He solemnly placed his hand on my shoulder, his emotions genuine, and we bonded in a profound moment of mutual understanding. Then, he added, "Really, you should let me make love to you just once. It'll be your birthday present."

"Okay!" I merrily agreed. In that instant, we abandoned all inhibitions and sentimentality, yet it was anything but an act of debauchery. He wanted to give me a gift that was hard to come by, pure and simple—and what I got was the experience of absolute trust.

A campus patrol car passed. We lay naked, hidden in a patch of tall grass, and the entire time I felt wild and free, not self-conscious in the least. Suddenly Meng Sheng let out a howl.

"You have to stop hurting yourself! You're not okay at all!" He practically exploded. For the first time, I realized that he was in pain, that my tragedy had become his own.

With that revelation, a hole was blown through the earth's crust. That reckless lunatic felt sorry for me, and I truly loved him. Numb to my own feelings, I never saw it coming. Faraway sounds drifted toward us. The charade was over. It was no use.

* * *

Xiao Fan was the most desperate woman I'd ever seen. Despair was in her past and in her present. Everything about her screamed despair. Because of her despair, I loved her. Because of her despair, I was shaken. Because of her despair, I was overwhelmed, and because of her despair, I left her. Her despair was her beauty.

I secretly looked forward to seeing her during my weekly shift. By day, she worked at the offices of the Youth Corps. By night, she and her fiancé and a few friends ran a bar. Every Saturday at six p.m., we'd work together. The two of us made a good team. By the time her shift began, she'd be overworked already. She often arrived looking thin and pale. Naturally concerned, I'd stare at her out of the corner of my eye. She smiled at me. It was a tired smile.

She'd ask me why I was sitting next to her, and I'd say because you're smart. She'd also ask me why her. I'd say because you're so beautiful. She said maybe you don't know that I have nothing to offer you. I said doesn't matter, other women don't want me. She said you can't handle me. I said let's cross that bridge when we get there.

She sat on my bike, waiting for her fiancé to pick her up. I insisted on giving her a lift home. She didn't think I'd be able to move with her on the back. I got on the bike, and we went for a ride. She was so light. We ran a red light and made a sudden turn. And with that, she became a little kid screaming in delight. She said she'd never ridden so fast before. We rode up a giant bridge, taking the steep lane for motorized vehicles. All around us, cars were zooming past. We were on the only bicycle. I was drenched with sweat. It was a dangerous and slow journey, and she was behind me, shouting go, go, go . . .

Her capacity for happiness was limited, and yet she seemed happy. She always seemed happy. Her happiness was natural, infectious. Having been endowed with an intuitive understanding of others, she knew how to give and take. She was the epitome of graciousness. The art of courtesy, as she so ably demonstrated it, was a musical instrument in the hands of a virtuoso.

As I carried her on my bike, her weight became my own, and for a time, she was a part of me. During my grueling ascent of the bridge, a cool breeze encircled us. The surrounding riverbed was visible beneath the limpid waters, and the twilight sky was a gentle pink. To our left was the sun, tiny and round, its rays forming striations of color.

Xiao Fan and I inhaled deeply. All was peaceful. I let up on the pedals, slowing down as much as I could. I wished the bridge would never end. With her close behind me, I could tell that her breathing was irregular: She'd gotten overexcited. I had seen this day coming, when we would drop the façade and find ourselves at a loss for words. In a calm and matter-of-fact tone, she asked whether I'd still see her if she quit her job. She was older and worldly-wise, sober and heavyhearted.

I could see into the depths of her soul. I knew her type. Insight was my natural gift. Just go on managing your bar. I'll come see you. Doesn't matter what time you get off, I said. A flock of white pigeons flew overhead, and in that instant, having been shown a glimpse of absolute freedom, I found courage. I wanted to fall madly in love. I already knew I would take the love in me that no one else wanted and give it all to this woman. All my memories of Xiao Fan and I together were to be captured in this single bleak picture.

She knew I was secretly in love with her. She knew my demons. She knew I was trying to figure out the inner workings of her soul. She knew that I understood her, that she could trust me. She even knew that I would vanish; I could hear it in those words on the bridge. I could tell that she was not one who was easily moved, but that I had moved her. She hid too much. She begrudged my absence before things even began. Her feelings for me were complicated.

During the lowest point following my split with Shui Ling, I disappeared for a month. Didn't report for duty. Didn't get in touch with anyone. I was at home, incapacitated. Out of the blue, I got a phone call. It was Xiao Fan's soft, courteous voice on the line. I heard her say, "I don't know why I'm calling you, and I really don't know if there's any point in me calling you, but I just wanted to make sure you were still alive." (At this point, I was certain that she was crying, and that she was stifling the sound.) "So it's just for my benefit, okay? You haven't shown up for work all month. I sense that something's going on with you, but I know very well that I have no business telling you what to do. You always have to have your way. You're always looking after me, and whatever it is I need, you're there to offer it. But you never tell me what's going on inside of you. Something bad happens, and you hide at home, alone, wallowing in misery. So tell me, what can I actually do to help you? Or should I wait for you to feel better on your own and show up for a shift with a smile again?

You make me feel so helpless." Her voice betrayed a nasal congestion from crying, and she seemed to be struggling to maintain her composure as she spoke.

On the most intense night of all, I finally went to the bar to find her. I was already drunk, but she didn't ask questions. She just sat with me and kept me company, telling me all kinds of anecdotes about what had happened while I was away and what was going on in her life. I laughed as I listened. I laughed so hard that my entire body shook violently. Tears of laughter streamed down my face the whole time. With firmness as well as understanding, she looked me straight in the eye. I stared back as she rattled on. Through my tears, I was laughing hysterically, and I thought about how I had always longed to be loved like this . . .

The alcohol kicked in. I vomited everything up in the bathroom. I told her not to worry, that I didn't want her to see this disgusting side of me. After I threw up, I came back and hid in a corner of the room. I lost control and burned myself. I thought she wouldn't notice, but when I looked over, she was standing at the bar, watching me as she poured a drink. There were tears welling in her eyes.

* * *

Six months later, I moved into Xiao Fan's apartment. She took me in like a stray dog. The months that I lived with her were, in all my four years, probably the only time I was truly happy. They were like a dying man's final glimpses of the world.

I was haunted by despair, pain, confusion, and loneliness, which threatened to drag me out of a world filled with the promise of the future and engulf me at any moment. For the time being, I was wide awake and living each day to the fullest, marking the dawn of a new era in which I was truly living the good life. This newfound ardor was all Xiao Fan's doing, and like a moth to a flame, I reveled in it, allowing the desires that had once been dammed to run recklessly wild. I loved her ferociously. And in my total abandon, I relinquished all self-respect. I stooped to a new low.

Xiao Fan was the only woman I ever made love to. Of all my memories, my memory of her is the single most beautiful. It should be evident by now that I can't conceivably depict this woman. In writing this much, I've already condemned myself to failure and done her an injustice. It amounts to nothing more than a sham, and I've gritted my teeth trying all the while. There's a raw passion that still lives in my blood, still courses through my veins. The mere thought of her fills me with enough desire to send me into a mad frenzy. Yet this memory is also the saddest and most painful of all, for I never really knew this woman's heart, and I never would.

CATHERINE POND

■

This Rain

FROM *Sixth Finch*

You like sex with other women
because it makes you feel safe,
she said. Nothing makes me
feel safe, I explained. She is married

but when her daughter wins
the fishing contest in Allatoona,
she offers me the prize trout.
Later, loosening the flesh

from the spine, I do not feel
relieved, or thankful. She who knows
me best believed I might be
nourished by this small, dead thing.

ALEX TIZON

∎

My Family's Slave

FROM *The Atlantic*

THE ASHES FILLED a black plastic box about the size of a toaster. It weighed three and a half pounds. I put it in a canvas tote bag and packed it in my suitcase this past July for the transpacific flight to Manila. From there I would travel by car to a rural village. When I arrived, I would hand over all that was left of the woman who had spent 56 years as a slave in my family's household.

Her name was Eudocia Tomas Pulido. We called her Lola. She was 4 foot 11, with mocha-brown skin and almond eyes that I can still see looking into mine—my first memory. She was eighteen years old when my grandfather gave her to my mother as a gift, and when my family moved to the United States, we brought her with us. No other word but *slave* encompassed the life she lived. Her days began before everyone else woke and ended after we went to bed. She prepared three meals a day, cleaned the house, waited on my parents, and took care of my four siblings and me. My parents never paid her, and they scolded her constantly. She wasn't kept in leg irons, but she might as well have been. So many nights, on my way to the bathroom, I'd spot her sleeping in a corner, slumped against a mound of laundry, her fingers clutching a garment she was in the middle of folding.

To our American neighbors, we were model immigrants, a poster family. They told us so. My father had a law degree, my mother was on her way to becoming a doctor, and my siblings and I got good grades and always said "please" and "thank you." We never talked about Lola. Our secret went to the core of who we were and, at least for us kids, who we wanted to be.

After my mother died of leukemia, in 1999, Lola came to live with me in a small town north of Seattle. I had a family, a career, a house in the suburbs—the American dream. And then I had a slave.

At baggage claim in Manila, I unzipped my suitcase to make sure Lola's ashes were still there. Outside, I inhaled the familiar smell: a thick blend of exhaust and waste, of ocean and sweet fruit and sweat.

Early the next morning I found a driver, an affable middle-aged man who went by the nickname "Doods," and we hit the road in his truck, weaving through traffic. The scene always stunned me. The sheer number of cars and motorcycles and jeepneys. The people weaving between them and moving on the sidewalks in great brown rivers. The street vendors in bare feet trotting alongside cars, hawking cigarettes and cough drops and sacks of boiled peanuts. The child beggars pressing their faces against the windows.

Doods and I were headed to the place where Lola's story began, up north in the central plains: Tarlac province. Rice country. The home of a cigar-chomping army lieutenant named Tomas Asuncion, my grandfather. The family stories paint Lieutenant Tom as a formidable man given to eccentricity and dark moods, who had lots of land but little money and kept mistresses in separate houses on his property. His wife died giving birth to their only child, my mother. She was raised by a series of utusans, or "people who take commands."

Slavery has a long history on the islands. Before the Spanish came, islanders enslaved other islanders, usually war captives, criminals, or debtors. Slaves came in different varieties, from warriors who could earn their freedom through valor to household servants who were regarded as property and could be bought and sold or traded. High-status slaves could own low-status slaves, and the low could own the lowliest. Some chose to enter servitude simply to survive: In exchange for their labor, they might be given food, shelter, and protection.

When the Spanish arrived, in the 1500s, they enslaved islanders and later brought African and Indian slaves. The Spanish Crown eventually began phasing out slavery at home and in its colonies, but parts of the Philippines were so far-flung that authorities couldn't keep a close eye. Traditions persisted under different guises, even after the U.S. took control of the islands in 1898. Today even the poor can have *utusans* or *katulongs* ("helpers") or *kasambahays* ("domestics"), as long as there are people even poorer. The pool is deep.

Lieutenant Tom had as many as three families of utusans living on his property. In the spring of 1943, with the islands under Japanese occupation, he brought home a girl from a village down the road. She was a cousin from a marginal side of the family, rice farmers. The lieutenant was shrewd—he saw that this girl was penniless, unschooled, and likely to be malleable. Her parents wanted her to marry a pig farmer twice her age, and she was desperately unhappy but had nowhere to go. Tom approached her with an offer: She could have food and shelter if she would commit to taking care of his daughter, who had just turned twelve.

Lola agreed, not grasping that the deal was for life.

"She is my gift to you," Lieutenant Tom told my mother.

"I don't want her," my mother said, knowing she had no choice.

Lieutenant Tom went off to fight the Japanese, leaving Mom behind with Lola in his creaky house in the provinces. Lola fed, groomed, and dressed my mother. When they walked to the market, Lola held an umbrella to shield her from the sun. At night, when Lola's other tasks were done—feeding the dogs, sweeping the floors, folding the laundry that she had washed by hand in the Camiling River—she sat at the edge of my mother's bed and fanned her to sleep.

One day during the war Lieutenant Tom came home and caught my mother in a lie—something to do with a boy she wasn't supposed to talk to. Tom, furious, ordered her to "stand at the table." Mom cowered with Lola in a corner. Then, in a quivering voice, she told her father that Lola would take her punishment. Lola looked at Mom pleadingly, then without a word walked to the dining table and held on to the edge. Tom raised the belt and delivered 12 lashes, punctuating each one with a word. *You. Do. Not. Lie. To. Me. You. Do. Not. Lie. To. Me.* Lola made no sound.

My mother, in recounting this story late in her life, delighted in the outrageousness of it, her tone seeming to say, *Can you believe I did that?* When I brought it up with Lola, she asked to hear Mom's version. She listened intently, eyes lowered, and afterward she looked at me with sadness and said simply, "Yes. It was like that."

Seven years later, in 1950, Mom married my father and moved to Manila, bringing Lola along. Lieutenant Tom had long been haunted by demons, and in 1951 he silenced them with a .32 caliber slug to his temple. Mom almost never talked about it. She had his temperament—moody, imperial, secretly fragile—and she took his lessons to heart, among them the proper way to be a provincial *matrona*: You must embrace your role as the giver of commands. You must keep those beneath you in their place at all times, for their own good and the good of the household. They might cry and complain, but their souls will thank you. They will love you for helping them be what God intended.

My brother Arthur was born in 1951. I came next, followed by three more siblings in rapid succession. My parents expected Lola to be as devoted to us kids as she was to them. While she looked after us, my parents went to school and earned advanced degrees, joining the ranks of so many others with fancy diplomas but no jobs. Then the big break: Dad was offered a job in Foreign Affairs as a commercial analyst. The salary would be meager, but the position was in America—a place he and Mom had grown up dreaming of, where everything they hoped for could come true.

Dad was allowed to bring his family and one domestic. Figuring they would both have to work, my parents needed Lola to care for the kids and the house. My mother informed Lola, and to her great irritation, Lola didn't immediately acquiesce. Years later Lola told me she was terrified. "It was too far," she said. "Maybe your Mom and Dad won't let me go home."

In the end what convinced Lola was my father's promise that things would be different in America. He told her that as soon as he and Mom got on their feet, they'd give her an "allowance." Lola could send money to her parents, to all her relations in the village. Her parents lived in a hut with a dirt floor. Lola could build them a concrete house, could change their lives forever. *Imagine.*

We landed in Los Angeles on May 12, 1964, all our belongings in cardboard boxes tied with rope. Lola had been with my mother for 21 years by then. In many ways she was more of a parent to me than either my mother or my father. Hers was the first face I saw in the morning and the last one I saw at night. As a baby, I uttered Lola's name (which I first pronounced "Oh-ah") long before I learned to say "Mom" or "Dad." As a toddler, I refused to go to sleep unless Lola was holding me, or at least nearby.

I was four years old when we arrived in the U.S.—too young to question Lola's place in our family. But as my siblings and I grew up on this other shore, we came to see the world differently. The leap across the ocean brought about a leap in consciousness that Mom and Dad couldn't, or wouldn't, make.

Lola never got that allowance. She asked my parents about it in a roundabout way a couple of years into our life in America. Her mother had fallen ill (with what I would later learn was dysentery), and her family couldn't afford the medicine she needed. "*Pwede ba?*" she said to my parents. *Is it possible?* Mom let out a sigh. "How could you even ask?," Dad responded in Tagalog. "You see how hard up we are. Don't you have any shame?"

My parents had borrowed money for the move to the U.S., and then borrowed more in order to stay. My father was transferred from the consulate general in L.A. to the Philippine consulate in Seattle. He was paid $5,600 a year. He took a second job cleaning trailers, and a third as a debt collector. Mom got work as a technician in a couple of medical labs. We barely saw them, and when we did they were often exhausted and snappish.

Mom would come home and upbraid Lola for not cleaning the house well enough or for forgetting to bring in the mail. "Didn't I tell you I want the letters here when I come home?" she would say in Tagalog, her voice venomous. "It's not hard *naman!* An idiot could remember." Then my father would arrive and take his turn. When Dad raised his voice, everyone in the house shrank. Sometimes my parents would team up until Lola broke down crying, almost as though that was their goal.

It confused me: My parents were good to my siblings and me, and we loved them. But they'd be affectionate to us kids one moment and vile to Lola the next. I was 11 or 12 when I began to see Lola's situation clearly. By then Arthur, eight years my senior, had been seething for a long time. He was the one who introduced the word *slave* into my understanding of what Lola was. Before he said it I'd thought of her as just an unfortunate member of the household. I hated when my parents yelled at her, but it hadn't occurred to me that they—and the whole arrangement—could be immoral.

"Do you know anybody treated the way she's treated?," Arthur said. "Who lives the way she lives?" He summed up Lola's reality: Wasn't paid. Toiled every day. Was tongue-lashed for sitting too long or falling asleep too early. Was struck for talking back. Wore hand-me-downs. Ate scraps and leftovers by herself in the kitchen. Rarely left the house. Had no friends or hobbies outside the family. Had no private quarters. (Her designated place to sleep in each house we lived in was always whatever was left—a couch or storage area or corner in my sisters' bedroom. She often slept among piles of laundry.)

We couldn't identify a parallel anywhere except in slave characters on TV and in the movies. I remember watching a Western called *The Man Who Shot Liberty Valance*. John Wayne plays Tom Doniphon, a gunslinging rancher who barks orders at his servant, Pompey, whom he calls his "boy." *Pick him up, Pompey. Pompey, go find the doctor. Get on back to work, Pompey!* Docile and obedient, Pompey calls his master "Mistah Tom." They have a complex relationship. Tom forbids Pompey from attending school but opens the way for Pompey to drink in a whites-only saloon. Near the end, Pompey saves his master from a fire. It's clear Pompey both fears and loves Tom, and he mourns when Tom dies. All of this is peripheral to the main story of Tom's showdown with bad guy Liberty Valance, but I couldn't take my eyes off Pompey. I remember thinking: *Lola is Pompey, Pompey is Lola.*

One night when Dad found out that my sister Ling, who was then 9, had missed dinner, he barked at Lola for being lazy. "I tried to feed her," Lola said, as Dad stood over her and glared. Her feeble defense only made him angrier, and he punched her just below the shoulder. Lola ran out of the room and I could hear her wailing, an animal cry.

"Ling said she wasn't hungry," I said.

My parents turned to look at me. They seemed startled. I felt the twitching in my face that usually preceded tears, but I wouldn't cry this time. In Mom's eyes was a shadow of something I hadn't seen before. Jealousy?

"Are you defending your Lola?" Dad said. "Is that what you're doing?"

"Ling said she wasn't hungry," I said again, almost in a whisper.

I was 13. It was my first attempt to stick up for the woman who spent her days watching over me. The woman who used to hum Tagalog melodies as she rocked me to sleep, and when I got older would dress and feed me and walk me to school in the mornings and pick me up in the afternoons. Once, when I was sick for a long time and too weak to eat, she chewed my food for me and put the small pieces in my mouth to swallow. One summer when I had plaster casts on both legs (I had problem joints), she bathed me with a washcloth, brought medicine in the middle of the night, and helped me through months of rehabilitation. I was cranky through it all. She didn't complain or lose patience, ever.

To now hear her wailing made me crazy.

In the old country, my parents felt no need to hide their treatment of Lola. In America, they treated her worse but took pains to conceal it. When guests came over, my parents would either ignore her or, if questioned, lie and quickly change the subject. For five years in North Seattle, we lived across the street from the Misslers, a rambunctious family of eight who introduced us to things like mustard, salmon fishing, and mowing the lawn. Football on TV. Yelling during football. Lola would come out to serve food and drinks during games, and my parents would smile and thank her before she quickly disappeared. "Who's that little lady you keep in the kitchen?," Big Jim, the Missler patriarch, once asked. A relative from back home, Dad said. Very shy.

Billy Missler, my best friend, didn't buy it. He spent enough time at our house, whole weekends sometimes, to catch glimpses of my family's secret. He once overheard my mother yelling in the kitchen, and when he barged in to investigate found Mom red-faced and glaring at Lola, who was quaking in a corner. I came in a few seconds later. The look on Billy's face was a mix of embarrassment and perplexity. *What was that?* I waved it off and told him to forget it.

I think Billy felt sorry for Lola. He'd rave about her cooking, and make her laugh like I'd never seen. During sleepovers, she'd make

his favorite Filipino dish, beef *tapa* over white rice. Cooking was Lola's only eloquence. I could tell by what she served whether she was
merely feeding us or saying she loved us.

When I once referred to Lola as a distant aunt, Billy reminded me
that when we'd first met I'd said she was my grandmother.

"Well, she's kind of both," I said mysteriously.

"Why is she always working?"

"She likes to work," I said.

"Your dad and mom—why do they yell at her?"

"Her hearing isn't so good . . ."

Admitting the truth would have meant exposing us all. We spent
our first decade in the country learning the ways of the new land and
trying to fit in. Having a slave did not fit. Having a slave gave me
grave doubts about what kind of people we were, what kind of place
we came from. Whether we deserved to be accepted. I was ashamed
of it all, including my complicity. Didn't I eat the food she cooked,
and wear the clothes she washed and ironed and hung in the closet?
But losing her would have been devastating.

There was another reason for secrecy: Lola's travel papers had ex-
pired in 1969, five years after we arrived in the U.S. She'd come on
a special passport linked to my father's job. After a series of fallings-
out with his superiors, Dad quit the consulate and declared his intent
to stay in the United States. He arranged for permanent-resident status for his family, but Lola wasn't eligible. He was supposed to send
her back.

Lola's mother, Fermina, died in 1973; her father, Hilario, in 1979.
Both times she wanted desperately to go home. Both times my parents said "Sorry." No money, no time. The kids needed her. My parents also feared for themselves, they admitted to me later. If the authorities had found out about Lola, as they surely would have if she'd
tried to leave, my parents could have gotten into trouble, possibly
even been deported. They couldn't risk it. Lola's legal status became
what Filipinos call *tago nang tago*, or TNT—"on the run." She stayed
TNT for almost twenty years.

After each of her parents died, Lola was sullen and silent for
months. She barely responded when my parents badgered her. But the
badgering never let up. Lola kept her head down and did her work.

* * *

My father's resignation started a turbulent period. Money got tighter, and my parents turned on each other. They uprooted the family again and again—Seattle to Honolulu back to Seattle to the southeast Bronx and finally to the truck-stop town of Umatilla, Oregon, population 750. During all this moving around, Mom often worked 24-hour shifts, first as a medical intern and then as a resident, and Dad would disappear for days, working odd jobs but also (we'd later learn) womanizing and who knows what else. Once, he came home and told us that he'd lost our new station wagon playing blackjack.

For days in a row Lola would be the only adult in the house. She got to know the details of our lives in a way that my parents never had the mental space for. We brought friends home, and she'd listen to us talk about school and girls and boys and whatever else was on our minds. Just from conversations she overheard, she could list the first name of every girl I had a crush on from sixth grade through high school.

When I was fifteen, Dad left the family for good. I didn't want to believe it at the time, but the fact was that he deserted us kids and abandoned Mom after twenty-five years of marriage. She wouldn't become a licensed physician for another year, and her specialty—internal medicine—wasn't especially lucrative. Dad didn't pay child support, so money was always a struggle.

My mom kept herself together enough to go to work, but at night she'd crumble in self-pity and despair. Her main source of comfort during this time: Lola. As Mom snapped at her over small things, Lola attended to her even more—cooking Mom's favorite meals, cleaning her bedroom with extra care. I'd find the two of them late at night at the kitchen counter, griping and telling stories about Dad, sometimes laughing wickedly, other times working themselves into a fury over his transgressions. They barely noticed us kids flitting in and out.

One night I heard Mom weeping and ran into the living room to find her slumped in Lola's arms. Lola was talking softly to her, the way she used to with my siblings and me when we were young. I lingered, then went back to my room, scared for my mom and awed by Lola.

* * *

Doods was humming. I'd dozed for what felt like a minute and awoke to his happy melody. "Two hours more," he said. I checked the plastic box in the tote bag by my side—still there—and looked up to see open road. The MacArthur Highway. I glanced at the time. "Hey, you said 'two hours' two hours ago," I said. Doods just hummed.

His not knowing anything about the purpose of my journey was a relief. I had enough interior dialogue going on. *I was no better than my parents. I could have done more to free Lola. To make her life better. Why didn't I?* I could have turned in my parents, I suppose. It would have blown up my family in an instant. Instead, my siblings and I kept everything to ourselves, and rather than blowing up in an instant, my family broke apart slowly.

Doods and I passed through beautiful country. Not travel-brochure beautiful but real and alive and, compared with the city, elegantly spare. Mountains ran parallel to the highway on each side, the Zambales Mountains to the west, the Sierra Madre Range to the east. From ridge to ridge, west to east, I could see every shade of green all the way to almost black.

Doods pointed to a shadowy outline in the distance. Mount Pinatubo. I'd come here in 1991 to report on the aftermath of its eruption, the second-largest of the 20th century. Volcanic mudflows called *lahars* continued for more than a decade, burying ancient villages, filling in rivers and valleys, and wiping out entire ecosystems. The *lahars* reached deep into the foothills of Tarlac province, where Lola's parents had spent their entire lives, and where she and my mother had once lived together. So much of our family record had been lost in wars and floods, and now parts were buried under 20 feet of mud.

Life here is routinely visited by cataclysm. Killer typhoons that strike several times a year. Bandit insurgencies that never end. Somnolent mountains that one day decide to wake up. The Philippines isn't like China or Brazil, whose mass might absorb the trauma. This is a nation of scattered rocks in the sea. When disaster hits, the place goes under for a while. Then it resurfaces and life proceeds, and you can behold a scene like the one Doods and I were driving through, and the simple fact that it's still there makes it beautiful.

* * *

A couple of years after my parents split, my mother remarried and demanded Lola's fealty to her new husband, a Croatian immigrant named Ivan, whom she had met through a friend. Ivan had never finished high school. He'd been married four times and was an inveterate gambler who enjoyed being supported by my mother and attended to by Lola.

Ivan brought out a side of Lola I'd never seen. His marriage to my mother was volatile from the start, and money—especially his use of her money—was the main issue. Once, during an argument in which Mom was crying and Ivan was yelling, Lola walked over and stood between them. She turned to Ivan and firmly said his name. He looked at Lola, blinked, and sat down.

My sister Inday and I were floored. Ivan was about 250 pounds, and his baritone could shake the walls. Lola put him in his place with a single word. I saw this happen a few other times, but for the most part Lola served Ivan unquestioningly, just as Mom wanted her to. I had a hard time watching Lola vassalize herself to another person, especially someone like Ivan. But what set the stage for my blowup with Mom was something more mundane.

She used to get angry whenever Lola felt ill. She didn't want to deal with the disruption and the expense, and would accuse Lola of faking or failing to take care of herself. Mom chose the second tack when, in the late 1970s, Lola's teeth started falling out. She'd been saying for months that her mouth hurt.

"That's what happens when you don't brush properly," Mom told her.

I said that Lola needed to see a dentist. She was in her 50s and had never been to one. I was attending college an hour away, and I brought it up again and again on my frequent trips home. A year went by, then two. Lola took aspirin every day for the pain, and her teeth looked like a crumbling Stonehenge. One night, after watching her chew bread on the side of her mouth that still had a few good molars, I lost it.

Mom and I argued into the night, each of us sobbing at different points. She said she was tired of working her fingers to the bone supporting everybody, and sick of her children always taking Lola's side, and why didn't we just take our goddamn Lola, she'd never wanted her in the first place, and she wished to God she hadn't given birth to an arrogant, sanctimonious phony like me.

I let her words sink in. Then I came back at her, saying she would know all about being a phony, her whole life was a masquerade, and if she stopped feeling sorry for herself for one minute she'd see that Lola could barely eat because her goddamn teeth were rotting out of her goddamn head, and couldn't she think of her just this once as a real person instead of a slave kept alive to serve her?

"A slave," Mom said, weighing the word. "A *slave?*"

The night ended when she declared that I would never understand her relationship with Lola. *Never.* Her voice was so guttural and pained that thinking of it even now, so many years later, feels like a punch to the stomach. It's a terrible thing to hate your own mother, and that night I did. The look in her eyes made clear that she felt the same way about me.

The fight only fed Mom's fear that Lola had stolen the kids from her, and she made Lola pay for it. Mom drove her harder. Tormented her by saying, "I hope you're happy now that your kids hate me." When we helped Lola with housework, Mom would fume. "You'd better go to sleep now, Lola," she'd say sarcastically. "You've been working too hard. Your kids are worried about you." Later she'd take Lola into a bedroom for a talk, and Lola would walk out with puffy eyes.

Lola finally begged us to stop trying to help her.

Why do you stay? we asked.

"Who will cook?" she said, which I took to mean, *Who would do everything?* Who would take care of us? Of Mom? Another time she said, "Where will I go?" This struck me as closer to a real answer. Coming to America had been a mad dash, and before we caught a breath a decade had gone by. We turned around, and a second decade was closing out. Lola's hair had turned gray. She'd heard that relatives back home who hadn't received the promised support were wondering what had happened to her. She was ashamed to return.

She had no contacts in America, and no facility for getting around. Phones puzzled her. Mechanical things—ATMs, intercoms, vending machines, anything with a keyboard—made her panic. Fast-talking people left her speechless, and her own broken English did the same to them. She couldn't make an appointment, arrange a trip, fill out a form, or order a meal without help.

I got Lola an ATM card linked to my bank account and taught her how to use it. She succeeded once, but the second time she got flustered, and she never tried again. She kept the card because she considered it a gift from me.

I also tried to teach her to drive. She dismissed the idea with a wave of her hand, but I picked her up and carried her to the car and planted her in the driver's seat, both of us laughing. I spent 20 minutes going over the controls and gauges. Her eyes went from mirthful to terrified. When I turned on the ignition and the dashboard lit up, she was out of the car and in the house before I could say another word. I tried a couple more times.

I thought driving could change her life. She could go places. And if things ever got unbearable with Mom, she could drive away forever.

Four lanes became two, pavement turned to gravel. Tricycle drivers wove between cars and water buffalo pulling loads of bamboo. An occasional dog or goat sprinted across the road in front of our truck, almost grazing the bumper. Doods never eased up. Whatever didn't make it across would be stew today instead of tomorrow—the rule of the road in the provinces.

I took out a map and traced the route to the village of Mayantoc, our destination. Out the window, in the distance, tiny figures folded at the waist like so many bent nails. People harvesting rice, the same way they had for thousands of years. We were getting close.

I tapped the cheap plastic box and regretted not buying a real urn, made of porcelain or rosewood. What would Lola's people think? Not that many were left. Only one sibling remained in the area, Gregoria, 98 years old, and I was told her memory was failing. Relatives said that whenever she heard Lola's name, she'd burst out crying and then quickly forget why.

I'd been in touch with one of Lola's nieces. She had the day planned: When I arrived, a low-key memorial, then a prayer, followed by the lowering of the ashes into a plot at the Mayantoc Eternal Bliss Memorial Park. It had been five years since Lola died, but I hadn't yet said the final goodbye that I knew was about to happen. All day I had been feeling intense grief and resisting the urge to let it out, not wanting to wail in front of Doods. More than the shame I felt for the way my family had treated Lola, more than my anxiety about how her relatives in Mayantoc would treat me, I felt the terrible heaviness of losing her, as if she had died only the day before.

Doods veered northwest on the Romulo Highway, then took a sharp left at Camiling, the town Mom and Lieutenant Tom came from. Two lanes became one, then gravel turned to dirt. The path ran along the Camiling River, clusters of bamboo houses off to the side, green hills ahead. The homestretch.

I gave the eulogy at Mom's funeral, and everything I said was true. That she was brave and spirited. That she'd drawn some short straws, but had done the best she could. That she was radiant when she was happy. That she adored her children, and gave us a real home—in Salem, Oregon—that through the '80s and '90s became the permanent base we'd never had before. That I wished we could thank her one more time. That we all loved her.

I didn't talk about Lola. Just as I had selectively blocked Lola out of my mind when I was with Mom during her last years. Loving my mother required that kind of mental surgery. It was the only way we could be mother and son—which I wanted, especially after her health started to decline, in the mid-'90s. Diabetes. Breast cancer. Acute myelogenous leukemia, a fast-growing cancer of the blood and bone marrow. She went from robust to frail seemingly overnight.

After the big fight, I mostly avoided going home, and at age 23 I moved to Seattle. When I did visit I saw a change. Mom was still Mom, but not as relentlessly. She got Lola a fine set of dentures and let her have her own bedroom. She cooperated when my siblings and I set out to change Lola's TNT status. Ronald Reagan's landmark immigration bill of 1986 made millions of illegal immigrants eligible for amnesty. It was a long process, but Lola became a citizen in October 1998, four months after my mother was diagnosed with leukemia. Mom lived another year.

During that time, she and Ivan took trips to Lincoln City, on the Oregon coast, and sometimes brought Lola along. Lola loved the ocean. On the other side were the islands she dreamed of returning to. And Lola was never happier than when Mom relaxed around her. An afternoon at the coast or just 15 minutes in the kitchen reminiscing about the old days in the province, and Lola would seem to forget years of torment.

I couldn't forget so easily. But I did come to see Mom in a different light. Before she died, she gave me her journals, two steamer trunks' full. Leafing through them as she slept a few feet away, I glimpsed slices of her life that I'd refused to see for years. She'd gone to medical school when not many women did. She'd come to America and fought for respect as both a woman and an immigrant physician. She'd worked for two decades at Fairview Training Center, in Salem, a state institution for the developmentally disabled. The irony: She tended to underdogs most of her professional life. They worshipped her. Female colleagues became close friends. They did silly, girly things together—shoe shopping, throwing dress-up parties at one another's homes, exchanging gag gifts like penis-shaped soaps and calendars of half-naked men, all while laughing hysterically. Looking through their party pictures reminded me that Mom had a life and an identity apart from the family and Lola. Of course.

Mom wrote in great detail about each of her kids, and how she felt about us on a given day—proud or loving or resentful. And she devoted volumes to her husbands, trying to grasp them as complex characters in her story. We were all persons of consequence. Lola was incidental. When she was mentioned at all, she was a bit character in someone else's story. "Lola walked my beloved Alex to his new school this morning. I hope he makes new friends quickly so he doesn't feel so sad about moving again . . ." There might be two more pages about me, and no other mention of Lola.

The day before Mom died, a Catholic priest came to the house to perform last rites. Lola sat next to my mother's bed, holding a cup with a straw, poised to raise it to Mom's mouth. She had become extra attentive to my mother, and extra kind. She could have taken advantage of Mom in her feebleness, even exacted revenge, but she did the opposite.

The priest asked Mom whether there was anything she wanted to forgive or be forgiven for. She scanned the room with heavy-lidded eyes, said nothing. Then, without looking at Lola, she reached over and placed an open hand on her head. She didn't say a word.

Lola was seventy-five when she came to stay with me. I was married with two young daughters, living in a cozy house on a wooded lot. From the second story, we could see Puget Sound. We gave Lola a bedroom and license to do whatever she wanted: sleep in, watch soaps, do nothing all day. She could relax—and be free—for the first time in her life. I should have known it wouldn't be that simple.

I'd forgotten about all the things Lola did that drove me a little crazy. She was always telling me to put on a sweater so I wouldn't catch a cold (I was in my 40s). She groused incessantly about Dad and Ivan: My father was lazy, Ivan was a leech. I learned to tune her out. Harder to ignore was her fanatical thriftiness. She threw nothing out. And she used to go through the trash to make sure that the rest of us hadn't thrown out anything useful. She washed and reused paper towels again and again until they disintegrated in her hands. (No one else would go near them.) The kitchen became glutted with grocery bags, yogurt containers, and pickle jars, and parts of our house turned into storage for—there's no other word for it—garbage.

She cooked breakfast even though none of us ate more than a banana or a granola bar in the morning, usually while we were running out the door. She made our beds and did our laundry. She cleaned the house. I found myself saying to her, nicely at first, "Lola, you don't have to do that." "Lola, we'll do it ourselves." "Lola, that's the girls' job." Okay, she'd say, but keep right on doing it.

It irritated me to catch her eating meals standing in the kitchen, or see her tense up and start cleaning when I walked into the room. One day, after several months, I sat her down.

"I'm not Dad. You're not a slave here," I said, and went through a long list of slavelike things she'd been doing. When I realized she was startled, I took a deep breath and cupped her face, that elfin face now looking at me searchingly. I kissed her forehead. "This is *your* house now," I said. "You're not here to serve us. You can relax, okay?"

"Okay," she said. And went back to cleaning.

She didn't know any other way to be. I realized I had to take my own advice and relax. If she wanted to make dinner, let her. Thank her and do the dishes. I had to remind myself constantly: *Let her be.*

One night I came home to find her sitting on the couch doing a word puzzle, her feet up, the TV on. Next to her, a cup of tea. She glanced at me, smiled sheepishly with those perfect white dentures, and went back to the puzzle. *Progress,* I thought.

She planted a garden in the backyard—roses and tulips and ev-ery kind of orchid—and spent whole afternoons tending it. She took walks around the neighborhood. At about 80, her arthritis got bad and she began walking with a cane. In the kitchen she went from be-ing a fry cook to a kind of artisanal chef who created only when the spirit moved her. She made lavish meals and grinned with pleasure as we devoured them.

Passing the door of Lola's bedroom, I'd often hear her listening to a cassette of Filipino folk songs. The same tape over and over. I knew she'd been sending almost all her money—my wife and I gave her $200 a week—to relatives back home. One afternoon, I found her sitting on the back deck gazing at a snapshot someone had sent of her village.

"You want to go home, Lola?"

She turned the photograph over and traced her finger across the inscription, then flipped it back and seemed to study a single detail.

"Yes," she said.

Just after her 83rd birthday, I paid her airfare to go home. I'd fol-low a month later to bring her back to the U.S.—if she wanted to re-turn. The unspoken purpose of her trip was to see whether the place she had spent so many years longing for could still feel like home.

She found her answer.

"Everything was not the same," she told me as we walked around Mayantoc. The old farms were gone. Her house was gone. Her par-ents and most of her siblings were gone. Childhood friends, the ones still alive, were like strangers. It was nice to see them, but . . . every-thing was not the same. She'd still like to spend her last years here, she said, but she wasn't ready yet.

"You're ready to go back to your garden," I said.

"Yes. Let's go home."

Lola was as devoted to my daughters as she'd been to my siblings and me when we were young. After school, she'd listen to their stories and make them something to eat. And unlike my wife and me (espe-cially me), Lola enjoyed every minute of every school event and per-formance. She couldn't get enough of them. She sat up front, kept the programs as mementos.

It was so easy to make Lola happy. We took her on family vacations, but she was as excited to go to the farmer's market down the hill. She became a wide-eyed kid on a field trip: "Look at those zucchinis!" The first thing she did every morning was open all the blinds in the house, and at each window she'd pause to look outside.

And she taught herself to read. It was remarkable. Over the years, she'd somehow learned to sound out letters. She did those puzzles where you find and circle words within a block of letters. Her room had stacks of word-puzzle booklets, thousands of words circled in pencil. Every day she watched the news and listened for words she recognized. She triangulated them with words in the newspaper, and figured out the meanings. She came to read the paper every day, front to back. Dad used to say she was simple. I wondered what she could have been if, instead of working the rice fields at age 8, she had learned to read and write.

During the 12 years she lived in our house, I asked her questions about herself, trying to piece together her life story, a habit she found curious. To my inquiries she would often respond first with "Why?" Why did I want to know about her childhood? About how she met Lieutenant Tom?

I tried to get my sister Ling to ask Lola about her love life, thinking Lola would be more comfortable with her. Ling cackled, which was her way of saying I was on my own. One day, while Lola and I were putting away groceries, I just blurted it out: "Lola, have you ever been romantic with anyone?" She smiled, and then she told me the story of the only time she'd come close. She was about 15, and there was a handsome boy named Pedro from a nearby farm. For several months they harvested rice together side by side. One time, she dropped her *bolo*—a cutting implement—and he quickly picked it up and handed it back to her. "I liked him," she said.

Silence.

"And?"

"Then he moved away," she said.

"And?"

"That's all."

"Lola, have you ever had sex?" I heard myself saying.

"No," she said.

She wasn't accustomed to being asked personal questions. "*Katu-*

long lang ako," she'd say. *I'm only a servant.* She often gave one- or two-word answers, and teasing out even the simplest story was a game of 20 questions that could last days or weeks.

Some of what I learned: She was mad at Mom for being so cruel all those years, but she nevertheless missed her. Sometimes, when Lola was young, she'd felt so lonely that all she could do was cry. I knew there were years when she'd dreamed of being with a man. I saw it in the way she wrapped herself around one large pillow at night. But what she told me in her old age was that living with Mom's husbands made her think being alone wasn't so bad. She didn't miss those two at all. Maybe her life would have been better if she'd stayed in Mayantoc, gotten married, and had a family like her siblings. But maybe it would have been worse. Two younger sisters, Francisca and Zepriana, got sick and died. A brother, Claudio, was killed. What's the point of wondering about it now? she asked. *Bahala na* was her guiding principle. *Come what may.* What came her way was another kind of family. In that family, she had eight children: Mom, my four siblings and me, and now my two daughters. The eight of us, she said, made her life worth living.

None of us was prepared for her to die so suddenly.

Her heart attack started in the kitchen while she was making dinner and I was running an errand. When I returned she was in the middle of it. A couple of hours later at the hospital, before I could grasp what was happening, she was gone—10:56 p.m. All the kids and grandkids noted, but were unsure how to take, that she died on November 7, the same day as Mom. Twelve years apart.

Lola made it to eighty-six. I can still see her on the gurney. I remember looking at the medics standing above this brown woman no bigger than a child and thinking that they had no idea of the life she had lived. She'd had none of the self-serving ambition that drives most of us, and her willingness to give up everything for the people around her won her our love and utter loyalty. She's become a hallowed figure in my extended family.

Going through her boxes in the attic took me months. I found recipes she had cut out of magazines in the 1970s for when she would someday learn to read. Photo albums with pictures of my mom.

Awards my siblings and I had won from grade school on, most of which we had thrown away and she had "saved." I almost lost it one night when at the bottom of a box I found a stack of yellowed newspaper articles I'd written and long ago forgotten about. She couldn't read back then, but she'd kept them anyway.

Doods's truck pulled up to a small concrete house in the middle of a cluster of homes mostly made of bamboo and plank wood. Surrounding the pod of houses: rice fields, green and seemingly endless. Before I even got out of the truck, people started coming outside.

Doods reclined his seat to take a nap. I hung my tote bag on my shoulder, took a breath, and opened the door.

"This way," a soft voice said, and I was led up a short walkway to the concrete house. Following close behind was a line of about 20 people, young and old, but mostly old. Once we were all inside, they sat down on chairs and benches arranged along the walls, leaving the middle of the room empty except for me. I remained standing, waiting to meet my host. It was a small room, and dark. People glanced at me expectantly.

"Where is Lola?" A voice from another room. The next moment, a middle-aged woman in a housedress sauntered in with a smile. Ebia, Lola's niece. This was her house. She gave me a hug and said again, "Where is Lola?"

I slid the tote bag from my shoulder and handed it to her. She looked into my face, still smiling, gently grasped the bag, and walked over to a wooden bench and sat down. She reached inside and pulled out the box and looked at every side. "Where is Lola?" she said softly. People in these parts don't often get their loved ones cremated. I don't think she knew what to expect. She set the box on her lap and bent over so her forehead rested on top of it, and at first I thought she was laughing (out of joy) but I quickly realized she was crying. Her shoulders began to heave, and then she was wailing—a deep, mournful, animal howl, like I once heard coming from Lola.

I hadn't come sooner to deliver Lola's ashes in part because I wasn't sure anyone here cared that much about her. I hadn't expected this kind of grief. Before I could comfort Ebia, a woman walked in from the kitchen and wrapped her arms around her, and then she began wailing. The next thing I knew, the room erupted with sound. The old people—one of them blind, several with no teeth—were all crying and not holding anything back. It lasted about 10 minutes. I was so fascinated that I barely noticed the tears running down my own face. The sobs died down, and then it was quiet again.

Ebia sniffled and said it was time to eat. Everybody started filing into the kitchen, puffy-eyed but suddenly lighter and ready to tell stories. I glanced at the empty tote bag on the bench, and knew it was right to bring Lola back to the place where she'd been born.

CARMEN MARIA MACHADO

∎

Eight Bites

FROM *Gulf Coast*

AS THEY PUT ME TO SLEEP, my mouth fills with the dust of the moon. I expect to choke on the silt but instead it slides in and out, and in and out, and I am, impossibly, breathing.

I have dreamt of inhaling underneath water and this is what it feels like: panic, and then acceptance, and then elation. I am going to die, I am not dying, I am doing a thing I never thought I could do.

Back on earth, Dr. U is inside me. Her hands are in my torso, her fingers searching for something. She is loosening flesh from its casing, slipping around where she's been welcomed, talking to a nurse about her vacation to Chile. "We were going to fly to Antarctica," she says, "but it was too expensive."

"But the penguins," the nurse says.

"Next time," Dr. U responds.

* * *

Before this, it was January, a new year. I waded through two feet of snow on a silent street, and came to a shop where wind chimes hung silently on the other side of the glass, mermaid-shaped baubles and bits of driftwood and too-shiny seashells strung through with fishing line and unruffled by any wind.

The town was deep dead, a great distance from the late-season smattering of open shops that serve the day-trippers and the money savers. Owners had fled to Boston or New York, or, if they were lucky, farther south. Businesses had shuttered for the season, leaving their wares in the windows like a tease. Underneath, a second town had opened up, familiar and alien at the same time. It's the same every year. Bars and restaurants made secret hours for locals, the rock-solid Cape Codders who've lived through dozens of winters. On any given night you could look up from your plate to see round bundles stomp through the doorway; only when they peeled their outsides away could you see who was beneath. Even the ones you knew from the summer were more or less strangers in this perfunctory daylight; all of them were alone, even when they were with each other.

On this street, though, I might as well have been on another planet. The beach bunnies and art dealers would never see the town like this, I thought, when the streets are dark and a liquid chill roils through the gaps and alleys. Silence and sound bumped up against each other but never intermingled; the jolly chaos of warm summer nights was as far away as it could be. It was hard to stop moving between doorways in this weather, but if you did you could hear life pricking the stillness: a rumble of voices from a local tavern, wind livening the buildings, sometimes even a muffled animal encounter in an alley: pleasure or fear, it was all the same noise.

Foxes wove through the streets at night. There was a white one among them, sleek and fast, and she looked like the ghost of the others.

* * *

I was not the first in my family to go through with it. My three sisters had gotten the procedure over the years, though they didn't say anything before showing up for a visit. Seeing them suddenly svelte after years of watching them grow organically, as I have, was like a palm to the nose, more painful than you'd expect. My first sister, well, I thought she was dying. Being sisters, I thought we all were dying, noosed by genetics. When confronted by my anxiety—"What disease is sawing off this branch of the family tree?" I asked, my voice crabwalking up an octave—my first sister confessed: a surgery.

Then, all of them, my sisters, a chorus of believers. Surgery. A surgery. As easy as when you broke your arm as a kid and had to get the pins in—maybe even easier. A band, a sleeve, a gut rerouted. *Rerouted?* But their stories—*it melts away, it's just gone*—were spring-morning warm, when the sun makes the difference between happiness and shivering in a shadow.

When we went out, they ordered large meals and then said, "I couldn't possibly." They always said this, always, that decorous insistence that they couldn't possibly, but for once, they actually meant it—that bashful lie had been converted into truth vis-à-vis a medical procedure. They angled their forks and cut impossibly tiny portions of food—doll-sized cubes of watermelon, a slender stalk of pea shoot, a corner of a sandwich as if they needed to feed a crowd loaves-and-fishes-style with that single serving of chicken salad—and swallowed them like a great decadence.

"I feel so good," they all said. Whenever I talked to them, that was what always came out of their mouths, or really, it was a mouth, a single mouth that once ate and now just says, "I feel really, really good."

Who knows where we got it from, though—the bodies that needed the surgery. It didn't come from our mother, who always looked normal, not hearty or curvy or Rubenesque or Midwestern or voluptuous, just normal. She always said eight bites are all you need to get the sense of what you are eating. Even though she never counted out loud, I could hear the eight bites as clearly as if a game show audience were counting backward, raucous and triumphant, and after one she would set her fork down, even if there was food left on her plate. She didn't mess around, my mother. No pushing food in circles or pretending. Iron will, slender waistline. Eight bites let her compliment the hostess. Eight bites lined her stomach like insulation rolled into the walls of houses. I wished she was still alive, to see the women her daughters had become.

* * *

And then, one day, not too soon after my third sister sashayed out of my house with more spring in her step than I'd ever seen, I ate eight bites and then stopped. I set the fork down next to the plate, more roughly than I'd intended, and took a chip of ceramic off the rim in the process. I pressed my finger into the shard and carried it to the trash can. I turned and looked back at my plate, which had been so full before and was full still, barely a dent in the raucous mass of pasta and greens.

I sat down again, picked up my fork, and had eight more bites. Not much more, still barely a dent, but now twice as much as necessary. But the salad leaves were dripping vinegar and oil and the noodles had lemon and cracked pepper and everything was just so beautiful, and I was still hungry, and so I had eight more. After, I finished what was in the pot on the stove and I was so angry I began to cry.

I don't remember getting fat. I wasn't a fat child or teenager; photos of those young selves are not embarrassing, or if they are, they're embarrassing in the right ways. Look how young I am! Look at my weird fashion! Saddle shoes—who thought of those? Stirrup pants— are you joking? Squirrel barrettes? Look at those glasses, look at that face: mugging for the camera. Look at that expression, mugging for a future self who is holding those photos, sick with nostalgia. Even when I thought I was fat, I wasn't; the teenager in those photos is very beautiful, in a wistful kind of way.

But then I had a baby. Then I had Cal—difficult, sharp-eyed Cal, who has never gotten me half as much as I have never gotten her— and suddenly everything was wrecked, like she was a heavy-metal rocker trashing a hotel room before departing. My stomach was the television set through the window. She was now a grown woman and so far away from me in every sense, but the evidence still clung to my body. It would never look right again.

As I stood over the empty pot, I was tired. I was tired of the skinny-minny women from church who cooed and touched each other's arms and told me I had beautiful skin, and having to rotate my hips sideways to move through rooms like crawling over someone at the movie theater. I was tired of flat, unforgiving dressing room lights; I was tired of looking into the mirror and grabbing the things that I hated and lifting them, clawing deep, and then letting them drop and everything aching. My sisters had gone somewhere else and left me behind, and as I always have, I wanted nothing more than to follow.

I could not make eight bites work for my body and so I would make my body work for eight bites.

* * *

Dr. U did twice-a-week consultations in an office a half-hour drive south on the Cape. I took a slow, circuitous route getting there. It had been snowing on and off for days, and the sleepy snowdrifts caught on every tree trunk and fencepost like blown-away laundry. I knew the way because I'd driven past her office before—usually after a sister's departure—and so as I drove this time I daydreamt about buying clothes in the local boutiques, spending too much for a sundress taken off a mannequin, pulling it against my body in the afternoon sun as the mannequin stood, less lucky than I.

Then I was in her office, on her neutral carpet, and a receptionist was pushing open a door. The doctor was not what I expected. I suppose I had imagined that because of the depth of her convictions, as illustrated by her choice of profession, she should have been a slender woman: either someone with excessive self-control or a sympathetic soul whose insides had also been rearranged to suit her vision of herself. But she was sweetly plump—why had I skipped over the phase where I was round and unthreatening as a panda, but still lovely? She smiled with all her teeth. What was she doing, sending me on this journey she herself had never taken?

She gestured, and I sat.

There were two Pomeranians running around her office. When they were separated—when one was curled up at Dr. U's feet and the other was decorously taking a shit in the hallway—they appeared identical but innocuous, but when one came near the other they were spooky, their heads twitching in sync, as if they were two halves of a whole. The doctor noticed the pile outside of the door and called for the receptionist. The door closed.

"I know what you're here for," she said, before I could open my mouth. "Have you researched bariatric surgery before?"

"Yes," I said. "I want the kind you can't reverse."

"I admire a woman of conviction," she said. She began pulling binders out of a drawer. "There are some procedures you'll have to go through. Visiting a psychiatrist, seeing another doctor, support groups—administrative nonsense, taking up a lot of time. But everything is going to change for you," she promised, shaking a finger at me with an accusing, loving smile. "It will hurt. It won't be easy. But when it's over, you're going to be the happiest woman alive."

* * *

My sisters arrived a few days before the surgery. They set themselves up in the house's many empty bedrooms, making up their side tables with lotions and crossword puzzles. I could hear them upstairs and they sounded like birds, distinct and luminously choral at the same time.

I told them I was going out for a final meal.

"We'll come with you," said my first sister.

"Keep you company," said my second sister.

"Be supportive," said my third sister.

"No," I said, "I'll go alone. I need to be alone."

I walked to my favorite restaurant, Salt. It hadn't always been Salt, though, in name or spirit. It was Linda's, for a while, and then Family Diner, then The Table. The building remains the same, but it is always new and always better than before.

I thought about people on death row and their final meals, as I sat at a corner table, and for the third time that week I worried about my moral compass, or lack thereof. They aren't the same, I reminded myself as I unfolded the napkin over my lap. Those things are not comparable. Their last meal comes before death; mine comes before not just life, but a new life. *You are horrible*, I thought, as I lifted the menu to my face, higher than it needed to be.

I ordered a cavalcade of oysters. Most of them had been cut the way they were supposed to be, and they slipped down as easily as water, like the ocean, like nothing at all, but one fought me: anchored to its shell, a stubborn hinge of flesh. It resisted. It was resistance incarnate. Oysters are alive, I realized. They are nothing but muscle; they have no brains or insides, strictly speaking, but they are alive nonetheless. If there were any justice in the world, this oyster would grab hold of my tongue and choke me dead.

I almost gagged, but then I swallowed.

My third sister sat down across the table from me. Her dark hair reminded me of my mother's: almost too shiny and homogenous to be real, though it was. She smiled kindly at me, as if she were about to give me some bad news.

"Why are you here?" I asked her.

"You look troubled," she said. She held her hands in a way that showed off her red nails, which were so lacquered they had horizontal depth, like a rose trapped in glass. She tapped them against her cheekbones, scraping them down her face with the very lightest touch. I shuddered. Then she picked up my water and drank deeply of it, until the water had filtered through the ice and the ice was nothing more than a fragile lattice and then the whole construction slid against her face as she tipped the glass higher and she chewed the slivers that landed in her mouth.

"Don't waste that stomach space on water," she said, *crunch crunch crunching*. "Come on now. What are you eating?"

"Oysters," I said, even though she could see the precarious pile of shells before me.

She nodded. "Are they good?" she asked.

"They are."

"Tell me about them."

"They are the sum of all healthy things: seawater and muscle and bone," I said. "Mindless protein. They feel no pain, have no verifiable thoughts. Very few calories. An indulgence without being an indulgence. Do you want one?"

I didn't want her to be there—I wanted to tell her to leave—but her eyes were glittering as if she had a fever. She ran her fingernail lovingly along an oyster shell. The whole pile shifted, doubling down on its own mass.

"No," she said. Then, "Have you told Cal? About the procedure?"

I bit my lip. "No," I said. "Did you tell your daughter, before you got it?"

"I did. She was so excited for me. She sent me flowers."

"Cal will not be excited," I said. "There are many daughter duties Cal does not perform, and this will be one, too."

"Do you think she needs the surgery, too? Is that why?"

"I don't know," I said. "I have never understood Cal's needs."

"Do you think it's because she will think badly of you?"

"I've also never understood her opinions," I said.

My sister nodded.

"She will not send me flowers," I concluded, even though this was probably not necessary.

I ordered a pile of hot truffle fries, which burned the roof of my mouth. It was only after the burn that I thought about how much I'd miss it all. I started to cry, and my sister put her hand over mine. I was jealous of the oysters. They never had to think about themselves.

* * *

At home, I called Cal to tell her. My jaw was so tightly clenched, it popped when she answered the phone. On the other end I could hear another woman's voice, stopped short by a finger to the lips unseen; then a dog whined.

"Surgery?" she repeated.

"Yes," I said.

"Jesus Christ," she said.

"Don't swear," I told her, even though I was not a religious woman.

"What? That's not even a fucking swear," she yelled. "*That* was a fucking swear. And this. *Jesus Christ* is not a swear. It's a proper name. And if there's ever a time to swear, it's when your mom tells you she's getting half of one of her most important organs cut away for no reason—"

She was still talking, but it was growing into a yell. I shooed the words away like bees.

"—occur to you that you're never going to be able to eat like a normal human—"

"What is wrong with you?" I finally asked her.

"Mom, I just don't understand why you can't be happy with yourself. You've never been—"

She kept talking. I stared at the receiver. When did my child sour? I didn't remember the process, the top-down tumble from sweetness to curdled anger. She was furious constantly, she was all accusation. She had taken the moral high ground from me by force, time and time again. I had committed any number of sins: Why didn't I teach her about feminism? Why did I persist in not understanding anything? And *this*, this takes the cake, no, *don't* forgive the pun; language is infused with food like everything else, or at least like everything else should be. She was so angry, I was glad I couldn't read her mind. I knew her thoughts would break my heart.

The line went dead. She'd hung up on me. I set the phone on the receiver and realized my sisters were watching me from the doorway, two looking sympathetic, the other smug.

I turned away. Why didn't Cal understand? Her body was imperfect but it was also fresh, pliable. She could sidestep my mistakes. She could have the release of a new start. I had no self-control, but tomorrow I would relinquish control and everything would be right again.

The phone rang. Cal, calling back? But it was my niece. She was selling knife sets so she could go back to school and become a—well, I missed that part, but she would get paid just for telling me about the knives, so I let her walk me through, step-by-step, and I bought a cheese knife with a special cut-out center—"So the cheese doesn't stick to the blade, see?" she said.

* * *

In the operating room, I was open to the world. Not that kind of open, not yet, everything was still sealed up inside, but I was naked except for a faintly patterned cloth gown that didn't quite wrap around my body.

"Wait," I said. I laid my hand upon my hip and squeezed a little. I trembled, though I didn't know why. There was an IV, and the IV would relax me; soon I would be very far away.

Dr. U stared at me over her mask. Gone was the sweetness from her office; her eyes looked transformed. Icy.

"Did you ever read that picture book about Ping the duck?" I asked her.

"No," she said.

"Ping the duck was always punished for being the last duck home. He'd get whacked across the back with a switch. He hated that. So he ran away. After he ran away he met some black fishing birds with metal bands around their necks. They caught fish for their masters but could not swallow the fish whole, because of the bands. When they brought fish back, they were rewarded with tiny pieces they could swallow. They were obedient, because they had to be. Ping, with no band, was always last and now was lost. I don't remember how it ends. It seems like a book you should read."

She adjusted her mask a little. "Don't make me cut out your tongue," she said.

"I'm ready," I told her.

The mask slipped over me and I was on the moon.

* * *

Afterward, I sleep and sleep. It's been a long time since I've been so still. I stay on the couch because stairs, stairs are impossible. In the watery light of morning, dust motes drift through the air like plankton. I have never seen the living room so early. A new world.

I drink shaking sips of clear broth, brought to me by my first sister, who, silhouetted against the window, looks like a branch stripped bare by the wind. My second sister checks in on me every so often, opening the windows a crack despite the cold—to let some air in, she says softly. She does not say the house smells stale and like death but I can see it in her eyes as she fans the door open and shut and open and shut as patiently as a mother whose child has vomited. I can see her cheekbones, high and tight as cherries, and I smile at her as best I can.

My third sister observes me at night, sitting on a chair near the sofa, where she glances at me from above her book, her brows tightening and loosening with concern. She talks to her daughter—who loves her without judgment, I am sure—in the kitchen, so softly I can barely hear her, but then forgets herself and laughs loudly at some joke shared between them. I wonder if my niece has sold any more knives.

I am transformed but not yet, exactly. The transformation has begun—this pain, this excruciating pain, it is part of the process—and will not end until—well, I suppose I don't know when. Will I ever be done, transformed in the past tense, or will I always be transforming, better and better until I die?

Cal does not call. When she does I will remind her of my favorite memory of her: when I caught her with a chemical depilatory in the bathroom in the wee hours of morning, creaming her little tan arms and legs and upper lip so the hair dissolved like snow in sunlight. I will tell her, when she calls.

* * *

The shift, at first, is imperceptible, so small as to be a trick of the imagination. But then one day I button a pair of pants and they fall to my feet. I marvel at what is beneath. A pre-Cal body. A pre-me body. It is emerging, like the lie of snow withdrawing from the truth of the landscape. My sisters finally go home. They kiss me and tell me that I look beautiful.

I am finally well enough to walk along the beach. The weather has been so cold that the water is thick with ice and the waves churn creamily, like soft serve. I take a photo and send it to Cal, but I know she won't respond.

At home, I cook a very small chicken breast and cut it into white cubes. I count the bites and when I reach eight I throw the rest of the food in the garbage. I stand over the can for a long while, breathing in the salt-and-pepper smell of chicken mixed in with coffee grounds and something older and closer to decay. I spray window cleaner into the garbage can so the food cannot be retrieved. I feel a little light but good; righteous, even. Before, I would have been growling, climbing up the walls from want. Now I feel only slightly empty, and fully content.

That night, I wake up because something is standing over me, something small, and before I slide into being awake I think it's my daughter, up from a nightmare, or perhaps it's morning and I've overslept, except even as my hands exchange blanket warmth for chilled air and it is so dark, I remember that my daughter is in her late twenties and lives in Portland with a roommate who is not really her roommate and she will not tell me and I don't know why.

But something is there, darkness blotting out darkness, a person-shaped outline. It sits on the bed, and I feel the weight, the mattress springs creaking and pinging. Is it looking at me? Away from me? Does it look, at all?

And then there is nothing, and I sit up alone.

* * *

As I learn my new diet—my forever diet, the one that will end only when I do—something is moving in the house. At first I think it is mice, but it is larger, more autonomous. Mice in walls scurry and drop through unexpected holes, and you can hear them scrabbling in terror as they plummet behind your family portraits. But this thing occupies the hidden parts of the house with purpose, and if I drop my ear to the wallpaper it breathes audibly.

After a week of this, I try to talk to it.

"Whatever you are," I say, "please come out. I want to see you."

Nothing. I am not sure whether I am feeling afraid or curious or both.

I call my sisters. "It might be my imagination," I explain, "but did you also hear something, after? In the house? A presence?"

"Yes," says my first sister. "My joy danced around my house, like a child, and I danced with her. We almost broke two vases that way!"

"Yes," says my second sister. "My inner beauty was set free and lay around in patches of sunlight like a cat, preening itself."

"Yes," says my third sister. "My former shame slunk from shadow to shadow, as it should have. It will go away, after a while. You won't even notice and then one day it'll be gone."

After I hang up with her, I try and take a grapefruit apart with my hands, but it's an impossible task. The skin clings to the fruit, and between them is an intermediary skin, thick and impossible to separate from the meat.

Eventually I take a knife and lop off domes of rinds and cut the grapefruit into a cube before ripping it open with my fingers. It feels like I am dismantling a human heart. The fruit is delicious, slick. I swallow eight times, and when the ninth bite touches my lips I pull it back and squish it in my hand as if I am crumpling an old receipt. I put the remaining half of the grapefruit in a Tupperware. I close the fridge. Even now I can hear it. Behind me. Above me. Too large to perceive. Too small to see.

When I was in my twenties, I lived in a place with bugs and had the same sense of knowing invisible things moved, coordinated, in the darkness. Even if I flipped on the kitchen light in the wee hours and saw nothing, I would just wait. Then my eyes would adjust and I would see it: a cockroach who, instead of scuttling two-dimensionally across the yawn of a white wall, was instead perched at the lip of a cupboard, probing the air endlessly with his antennae. He desired and feared in three dimensions. He was less vulnerable there, and yet somehow more, I realized as I wiped his guts across the plywood.

In the same way, now, the house is filled with something else. It moves, restless. It does not say words but it breathes. I want to know it, and I don't know why.

* * *

"I've done research," Cal says. The line crackles as if she is somewhere with a bad signal, so she is not calling from her house. I listen for the voice of the other woman who is always in the background, whose name I have never learned.

"Oh, you're back?" I say. I am in control, for once.

Her voice is clipped, but then softens. I can practically hear the therapist cooing to her. She is probably going through a list that she and the therapist created together. I feel a spasm of anger.

"I am worried because," she says, and then pauses.

"Because?"

"Sometimes there can be all of these complications—"

"It's done, Cal. It's been done for months. There's no point to this."

"Do you hate my body, Mom?" she says. Her voice splinters in pain, as if she were about to cry. "You hated yours, clearly, but mine looks just like yours used to, so—"

"Stop it."

"You think you're going to be happy but this is not going to make you happy," she says.

"I love you," I say.

"Do you love every part of me?"

It's my turn to hang up and then, after a moment's thought, disconnect the phone. Cal is probably calling back right now, but she won't be able to get through. I'll let her, when I'm ready.

* * *

I wake up because I can hear a sound like a vase breaking in reverse: thousands of shards of ceramic whispering along hardwood toward a reassembling form. From my bedroom, it sounds like it's coming from the hallway. From the hallway, it sounds like it's coming from the stairs. Down, down, foyer, dining room, living room, down deeper, and then I am standing at the top of the basement steps.

From below, from the dark, something shuffles. I wrap my fingers around the ball chain hanging from the naked light bulb and I pull.

The thing is down there. In the light, it crumples to the cement floor, curls away from me.

It looks like my daughter, as a girl. That's my first thought. It's body-shaped. Prepubescent, boneless. It is one hundred pounds, dripping wet.

And it does. Drip.

I descend to the bottom and up close it smells warm, like toast. It looks like the clothes stuffed with straw on someone's porch at Halloween—the vague person-shaped lump made from pillows to aid a midnight escape plan. I am afraid to step over it. I walk around it, admiring my unfamiliar face in the reflection of the water heater even as I hear its sounds: a gasping, arrested sob.

I kneel down next to it. It is a body with nothing it needs: no stomach or bones or mouth. Just soft indents. I crouch down and stroke its shoulder, or what I think is its shoulder.

It turns and looks at me. It has no eyes, but still, it looks at me. She looks at me. She is awful but honest. She is grotesque but she is real.

I shake my head. "I don't know why I wanted to meet you," I say. "I should have known."

She curls a little tighter. I lean down and whisper where an ear might be.

"You are unwanted," I say. A tremor ripples her mass.

I do not know I am kicking her until I am kicking her. She has nothing and I feel nothing except she seems to solidify before my foot meets her, and so every kick is more satisfying than the last. I reach for a broom and I pull a muscle swinging back and in and back and in, and the handle breaks off in her and I kneel down and pull soft handfuls of her body out of herself, and I throw them against the wall, and I do not know I am screaming until I stop, finally.

I find myself wishing she would fight back, but she doesn't. Instead, she sounds like she is being deflated. A hissing, defeated wheeze.

I stand up and walk away. I shut the basement door. I leave her there until I can't hear her anymore.

* * *

Spring has come, marking the end of winter's long contraction.

Everyone is waking up. The first warm day, when light cardigans are enough, the streets begin to hum. Bodies move around. Not fast, but still: smiles. Neighbors suddenly recognizable after a season of watching their lumpy outlines walk past in the darkness.

"You look wonderful," says one.

"Have you lost weight?" asks another.

I smile. I get a manicure and tap my new nails along my face, to show them off. I go to Salt, which is now called "The Peppercorn," and eat three oysters.

I am a new woman. A new woman becomes best friends with her daughter. A new woman laughs with all of her teeth. A new woman does not just slough off her old self; she tosses it aside with force.

Summer will come next. Summer will come and the waves will be huge, the kind of waves that feel like a challenge. If you're brave, you'll step out of the bright-hot day and into the foaming roil of the water, moving toward where the waves break and might break you. If you're brave, you'll turn your body over to this water that is practically an animal, and so much larger than yourself.

* * *

Sometimes, if I sit very still, I can hear her gurgling underneath the floorboards. She sleeps in my bed when I'm at the grocery store, and when I come back and slam the door, loudly, there are padded foot-steps above my head. I know she is around, but she never crosses my path. She leaves offerings on the coffee table: safety pins, champagne bottle corks, hard candies twisted in strawberry-patterned cellophane. She shuffles through my dirty laundry and leaves a trail of socks and bras all the way to the open window. The drawers and air are rifled through. She turns all the soup can labels forward and wipes up the constellations of dried coffee spatter on the kitchen tile. The perfume of her is caught on the linens. She is around, even when she is not around.

I will see her only one more time, after this.

I will die the day I turn seventy-nine. I will wake up early because outside a neighbor is talking loudly to another neighbor about her roses, and because Cal is coming today with her daughter for our annual visit, and because I am a little hungry, and because a great pressure is on my chest. Even as it tightens and compresses I will perceive what is beyond my window: a cyclist bumping over concrete, a white fox loping through underbrush, the far roll of the ocean. I will think, *it is as my sisters prophesied.* I will think, *I miss them, still.* I will think, *here is where I learn if it's all been worth it.* The pain will be unbearable until it isn't anymore; until it loosens and I will feel better than I have in a long time.

There will be such a stillness, then, broken only by a honeybee's soft-winged stumble against the screen, and a floorboard's creak.

Arms will lift me from my bed—her arms. They will be mother-soft, like dough and moss. I will recognize the smell. I will flood with grief and shame.

I will look where her eyes would be. I will open my mouth to ask but then realize the question has answered itself: by loving me when I did not love her, by being abandoned by me, she has become immortal. She will outlive me by a hundred million years; more, even. She will outlive my daughter, and my daughter's daughter, and the earth will teem with her and her kind, their inscrutable forms and unknowable destinies.

She will touch my cheek like I once did Cal's, so long ago, and there will be no accusation in it. I will cry as she shuffles me away from myself, toward a door propped open into the salty morning. I will curl into her body, which was my body once, but I was a poor caretaker and she was removed from my charge.

"I'm sorry," I will whisper into her as she walks me toward the front door.

"I'm sorry," I will repeat. "I didn't know."

JESSE BALL AND BRIAN EVENSON

■

The Deaths of Henry King
Selected Demises

with illustrations by Lilli Carré

FROM *McSweeney's Quarterly Concern*

1

HENRY KING WOKE WITH A HAMMER partway through his head. Someone pulled the end of the hammer out of the hole and then brought it down again, causing Henry's body to shake a little all over, especially at the extremities.

2

Henry King was asked to meet a friend in a park. He went there and was killed. That same day, a bit later on, someone left an envelope on his doorstep. It wasn't a very fancy envelope, yet neither was it the absolute cheapest kind.

3

Henry King signed a piece of paper that said, *I want to die.* On 42nd and 5th a bus ran him over and he was so unremarkable, even at that moment, that a dozen more cars hit him before anyone thought to stop.

4

Henry King was burned to death in a house fire although many others were saved. "There is still someone in there," said the Fire Chief.

5

Henry King fell from an open window. A girl was telling a joke about a platypus. It was an extremely funny joke, and many kept laughing, even when they saw what had happened.

6

Henry King stayed late at the factory. His legs were caught in the machinery and it embarrassed him. The factory was sold by the owner that night and no one ever came back onto the premises, leaving Henry to death by starvation.

7

Henry King accepted a drink from a wild-eyed girl underneath a bridge. Some minutes later, she was rolling over his body and removing an antique watch, the gift of his grandfather.

8

Henry King climbed a ladder and then it began to rain. By chance all the rain went into his mouth and he drowned before he could fall.

9

Henry King couldn't breathe. His throat had closed. He ran to the window and waved to someone outside. He slapped at his neck and chest with his hand. He waved to someone else who waved back and even smiled, yes, smiled.

10

Henry King was deep in a mine when the workers' canaries started to perish. Soon the canary in the cage on his belt, it, too, perished. He had time to do one last thing.

11

Henry King ate six and a half pounds of glass before bleeding to death. "I believe that's a record," said his friend.

12

Henry King fell down the stairs in a building nearby. There wasn't a mark on him. "You would think he had survived," said a girl.

13

Nobody knew how Henry King had come to be in Little Chute during the Great Wisconsin Cheese Festival, nor why, when the giant wheel of cheddar broke its moorings, he did not at least try to jump out of the way.

14

Henry King realized mid-leap that the other building's roof was in fact much farther away than he'd realized.

15

All that remained of Henry King after his fall from the balloon was a Henry King–shaped dent in the ground. Soon that was gone as well.

16

Henry King discovered that the inside of Henry King looked like any meat one might buy at a butcher's shop. He smiled wryly, and perished.

17

Henry King wore a special shirt for people who may be one day kid-napped. This made him more comfortable in day-to-day life. He bought special shoes for people who need to survive short falls. He wore an actual helmet. He covered his crotch with a semi-articulated neoprene-and-steel codpiece. This odd appearance was sufficient to provoke a mob in Buenos Aires, where he was killed while attempt-ing to enter a soccer stadium. Thirty people stood on his head until it was flat. They left his body alone.

18

"Heinrich König?" asked the man with the expressionless face as he pointed the Ruger LC9 at his skull. "Henry King," corrected Henry King, shaking his head. But the dark-suited man had already pulled the trigger.

19

Henry King must have taken a wrong turn somewhere, for he was not to be found among those who had successfully navigated the river and now floated on in the lake, cans of Schlitz balanced on their bellies. Instead his tube popped and he was swept along by currents and bashed by rocks until his corpse was caught in a backwater. It lay there bloating in the company of his own can of Schlitz, which, thanks to the water, was ice-cold.

20

The bottles in the cellar were delicately balanced. Removing the '45 Château Margaux brought all the other bottles cascading down on Henry King. He lay there half-crushed and badly cut, dying, stinking of expensive wine.

21

It was a mistake to try to separate the two fighting pit bulls. Henry King was fairly certain both of them bit him repeatedly, but was in no condition to ascertain which one tore his throat out.

22

Henry King died of the kissing disease. Those he knew preferred not to speak of it.

23

Henry King played a game called Clouds and Jewels with the cooks in a sinister Chinese restaurant after the usual mahjong game was over with. Clouds and Jewels, as they called it, involved eating small bits of one thing disguised as another and guessing what was what. At least that's how the first cook explained it to the detective, as they stood there in the harsh fluorescent light of the kitchen, looking down on Henry King's corpse, where it rested beneath the filthy card table. "I know what you mean," said the detective, carelessly.

24

"Henry" King, in reality Henriette, leaned her musket against one wall of the dilapidated French fort, removed her regimental coat, laid her cocked hat on a chair, and shook out her long hair. What will history think of me? She wondered. At that moment a French light infantryman who had been disguised as a pair of candlesticks stood up on the table and shot her through the face with an outdated heirloom arquebus: some sort of matchlock, one might say. That a man who would disguise himself as a candlestick should have such a weapon . . . it is inevitable, thought Henriette, and promptly perished.

25

According to twelfth-century parish records, the king had been accosted by a smiling man who claimed his name "to be a reverse of thine own, sire. Thou art King Henry, and I am Henry King." King Henry's response was to have Henry King beheaded.

26

Henry King seemed to have been turned to stone. There was a great deal of consternation among his neighbors: half believed he had been petrified, the other half believed he had made a statue of himself and then left town. Discussion became argument and argument became fisticuffs, and in the brawl that followed, Henry King, or his representation, was knocked over and broken to pieces.

27

Henry King went to Hokkaido to see the cherry blossoms. Never mind that there are better ones elsewhere; it was to Hokkaido he went. And, quite simply, the visit was too much for him. Even these so-to-speak Hokkaido cherry blossoms, they were too intense, too perfect, too redolent of life's equal measure of splendor and strife: he collapsed on the spot, clutching at his chest. "I confess!" he cried, beginning a sentence he would never end.

28

Henry King, world traveler, sat staring at his plate. There was, he was fairly certain, a snout, a foot as well, a gummy ear edged with a thread line of dark bristles. If they can eat it, it must be all right, he told himself, and dug into the meal that, months later, would end up being the death of him.

29

His last memory as Henry King was the stick coming down toward his face. It was followed as if without transition by the smiling face of a nurse, but by then he had lost track of his name and never quite managed to retrieve it.

30

Henry King was an extra in an Andy Warhol film in which the twenty prettiest girls in New York City climbed up a ladder and fell off into the East River. The last one fucked it up really badly so Andy Warhol said get the next prettiest thing on the set up that ladder pronto and Henry King was next prettiest but couldn't swim. They made him go anyway.

31

"Henry King, you say," said the grizzled old man to the investigating officer. "He never told me his name but I suppose it must be him. You'll find him at the bottom of that," he said, and pointed with the stem of his pipe to the edge of the ravine.

32

In the dream Henry King was thrown free of the car and, though badly injured and comatose for weeks, managed to survive and go on to marry, have children, and have grandchildren, finally dying peacefully at a ripe old age. In reality, Henry King, asleep at the wheel, was killed instantly when his car crossed into the other lane and struck a semi head-on.

33

The phone call came late at night. "You've been activated," said a flat, expressionless voice. "Excuse me?" said Henry King. "The puppy is out of the crate," said the voice. "But I don't have a puppy," said

Henry King. There was a long pause. "Incorrect," said the voice. "You will be terminated." "Terminated?" said Henry King. "Hello?" But the line was already dead.

34

At security, Henry King found he had forgotten to bring the note from his doctor, and had his inhaler taken away. On the plane he was seated next to a woman trained as a nurse, and when he began to have trouble breathing she did her best to talk him through it. "Breathe through your nose, honey. Breathe through your nose," she kept saying in a voice so calm and so relaxed that he was surprised, when he opened his eyes, to see so much fear gathered in her face. His breathing grew worse and worse. An emergency landing was made, but by the time they touched down he was already dead.

35

Henry King felt his way along the crack in the bathroom wall. He slowly wormed his finger into it, though doing so stripped his finger to the bone. His hand followed, then his wrist, then his whole arm. To make the rest of his body fit, he had to pound it flat by beating the body repeatedly with a cast-iron pan. After that, though, it was easy. Before he knew it he was back behind the crack. But it was too dark to see what, if anything, was there, and though he had managed to work his way in, he did not have the same success working his way back out.

36

The path wound slowly along the narrow spit of land and through un-
dergrowth and trees. Here there was a damp earthy smell and there
the woody tang of eucalyptus. Henry King could see the waves below,
the sound of them more distant than he felt it should be. A path led
down to a beach but was blocked off with police tape and a warning.
He ignored both. At first the going was easy, then more difficult, then
the sides of the path crumbled and gave way and Henry King began to
scramble back up. And then the whole path went, and he along with it.

37

Henry King rode the glass elevator up to the thirty-first floor so that
he could look out and see the lights and the enormous Christmas
tree in the square. In the brief pause between when the doors opened
and when the doors closed again, he could not help but imagine what
it would be like to fall from this height, to go tumbling down the
side of the building and flash into the ground below. It came to him
so vividly that for an instant he felt he was living hand in hand with
his own death. Then the doors closed and he rode the elevator down
again and walked home alone.

SEO-YOUNG CHU

■

A Refuge for Jae-in Doe: Fugues in the Key of English Major

FROM *Entropy*

INVOCATION (WINTER 2015–16)

It's evening in Queens, New York. Alone in my apartment, I'm grading student papers and drinking ginger tea. The phone rings. For some reason I forget to check the caller ID before answering, "Hello?"

A woman's voice: "Hi, Seo-Young?"

"Yes?"

"I'm calling from Stanford to ask about your experience while you were here."

(blank space)

The blank space above: a representation of my immediate response to the caller's words.

I almost can't believe that this is happening. Stanford is reaching out to me. Will Stanford apologize at last? That is all I have ever wanted: an apology.

My experience while I was at Stanford.

The story tumbles out. It's a story I have told numerous times already—to psychiatrists, to close friends, to myself, to lovers, to neurologists, to therapists. The story begins with my suicide attempt at age 21 and ends with Stanford's own punishment of the professor in 2001: two years of suspension without pay. I describe the long horrible months of sexual harassment. I describe the rape—or the parts of it that I can bear to mention out loud. I add that I never pressed charges or received any money from either Stanford or the professor. All I did was tell someone else who told someone else who started the fact-finding investigation that resulted in his punishment. I have never sued the rapist, the department, or the school—despite the time I've lost and the fortune I've spent as a consequence of the harmful culture at Stanford that enabled the professor to injure me as well as others.

The monologue is disjointed and long. I hadn't been expecting this call. I haven't had time to prepare. And yet I've had too much time to prepare: nearly fifteen years.

There is a silence after I've finished speaking. I start to wonder if perhaps the caller has hung up on me. I start to worry she won't call back.

But she's still there. "That's . . . awful," the woman is suddenly saying. "I'm so sorry. I'm just a Stanford undergrad. I was actually calling Stanford alumni for financial donations, to ask you for a gift of, but, I don't, I mean, in this case, for you . . . "

Something is happening to my eyes. The room has begun at once to darken and to seem much too bright. Or is something happening to my mind? Bright like sunlight at noon in Northern California on a cloudless day. But I am in Queens, New York City. The year is not 2000. What time is it? How old am I? Something is happening to reality. A sickening gust spreads throughout my internal organs. The phone I hold is shaking. My hands and arms are shaking. I close my eyes. I imagine feathery bandages made of photons holding together the jigsaw of my body. The shaking subsides.

"No, I'm the one who's sorry," I manage to say, and I mean it. "Tell me about your studies."

"Sure," she says, and begins to talk with cheerful confidence about her major, which is not English but history. She's excited about her academic career. As I listen to her, I murmur vague, pleasant, encouraging utterances. I'm happy for her. She has a bright future. "You have a bright future," I say. We wish each other well. Somewhat awkwardly the dialogue ends.

For several moments I am dazed. Inexplicable giddiness has begun to seep into my head. I can hear air seeping into a balloon. The balloon is beige. The phone is warm in my hand. Most balloons are not beige. The gust of nausea rapidly gathers in my chest. I rush, half-stumbling, to the kitchen trash can.

I throw up.

DISCUSS THE FOLLOWING QUOTATION.

"There's a great pleasure in teaching freshmen because you're sort of being folded into their lives at a particular, powerful moment in which you can make a difference," he said in the 1996 interview. "And to some degree, you can 'convert' them to English. It becomes a way of trawling for majors." (Source: Cynthia Haven, *Stanford Report*, August 17, 2007)

SOURCES AND ALLUSIONS.

He found me in a place known as the Farm.
His field: to grow a special breed of harm.

His stock of antique furniture and dolls
And manuscripts he nurtured in his walls.

A culture of "American" indifference
To rape he tended with uncommon sense.

Exactly how I came to be a thing
For him to call his own is still a thing

I can't or won't remember. He misused
His powers to leave minds like mine abused.

Where others who preceded me fare now
I often wish yet do not wish to know.

Sometimes I dream that his rare book collection
Is made of all "his" women turned to fiction.

IS THIS AN EXAMPLE OF IRONY? EXPLAIN YOUR ANSWER.

I grew up pronouncing the word "women" the way my Korean parents did: the same way we pronounced the word "woman."

It was the professor—my rapist—who corrected my pronunciation of the word "women." Since then, every time I have uttered "women," I have remembered his voice.

It—his voice—it accompanies mine like an accent. "Women."

HERE, I FILLED OUT THE FORM.

- Year of birth: 1978.
- Place of birth: northern Virginia.
- First language: Korean. To this day I have dreams in which my young mother is holding me in her arms and whispering to me in achingly melodic strings of Korean syllables.
- Second language: English. When I started school, the teacher told my parents that if they wanted me to succeed in America they would have to communicate with me exclusively in English. From then on my mother and I were estranged. We spoke to each other in an English filled with gaps. It took me decades to recognize the sacrifice my mother made when she stopped speaking to me in our native tongue.
- Language spoken by parents to each other: fluent Korean. I grew up hearing marriage as a foreign language—literally and figuratively. I grew up hearing the sound of Korean as a language of Korean-bound han syndrome, disappointment, fury, resignation, the sense of being trapped forever, resentment, guilt. Every other word: a door slammed.
- Faith system(s): raised Roman Catholic by my mother and Confucian by my father. Currently agnostic.
- How parents met: Their marriage was arranged.
- Significant family trauma(s): the Korean War (which orphaned my father and made him watch his beloved elder brother die); my mother's sister's suicide when I was a child; being run over by a car as a child while waiting for the school bus; struggling as a Roman Catholic teenager with my romantic feelings for a female classmate; being hospitalized during my senior year of college following my first suicide attempt; being raped soon

after my first suicide attempt by a professor at Stanford University, where I was just starting a Ph.D. program in English language and literature.

IS THIS AN EXAMPLE OF IRONY? EXPLAIN YOUR ANSWER.

His interests included the Declaration of Independence. He wrote a book titled *Declaring Independence*.

SYMPATHY FOR JAMES COMEY. SUMMER 2017.

He had called me at lunchtime that day and invited me to dinner that night, saying he was going to invite the whole cohort, but decided to have just me this time, with the whole cohort coming the next time. It was unclear from the conversation who else would be at the dinner, although I assumed there would be others.

It turned out to be just the two of us, seated at a small table in the middle of his favorite restaurant.

The professor began by asking me whether I wanted to stay on in the Ph.D. program, which I found strange because he had already told me twice in earlier conversations that he hoped I would stay, and I had assured him that I intended to. He said that lots of people wanted to work with him and, given the academic pressure and job market, he would understand if I wanted to walk away.

My instincts told me that the one-on-one setting, and the pretense that this was our first discussion about my position, meant the dinner was, at least in part, an effort to have me beg to work with him and create some sort of intimate relationship. That concerned me greatly, given that I wanted to be his advisee.

I replied that I loved my work and intended to stay, write my dissertation, and receive my degree. And then, because the set-up made me uneasy, I added that I was not "interested" in the way people who are dating use that word, but he could always count on me to work hard and try my best to produce good scholarship.

A few moments later, the professor said, "But I'm lonely. I'm needy. I need to feel desirable. I need you to desire me."

I didn't move, speak, or change my facial expression in any way during the awkward silence that followed. I wanted to leave. Instead I froze.

The conversation then moved on, but he would return to the subject near the end of our dinner.

At one point, I tried to explain why it was so important that my personal life be independent of my professional career. I said it was a conundrum: Throughout history, some people in institutional positions of power (e.g., straight white male professors with tenure and endowed chairs, among other privileges) have decided that their positions authorize them to use less powerful people (e.g., 21-year-old first-year graduate students who happen to be female, mentally ill, and 1.5–2nd generation Korean American) in ways that make the powerful even more powerful (while putting the powerless in a risky situation). But the abuse of power can ultimately make the powerful weak by undermining public trust in institutions—including academic institutions—and their work.

Near the end of our dinner, the professor returned to the subject of my status as a student, saying he was very glad I wanted to stay, adding that he had heard great things about me from Professor X, Professor Y, and many others. He then said, "I need you." I replied, "You will always get work from me." He paused and then said, "That's what I want, work from you." I paused, and then said, "You will get that from me." It is possible we understood the phrase "work" differently, but I decided it wouldn't be productive to push it further. The term—"work"—had helped end a very awkward conversation and my explanations had made clear what he should expect.

INTERLUDE. During one of my episodes.
Self: Dad?
Dad: Yes, Jennie?
Self: Did Stanford happen?
Dad: What do you mean?
Self: Was it real. The professor. Did all of that actually happen. To me.
Dad (after a pause and a sigh): Yes, it was real. It happened.
Self: Because I couldn't remember if I was remembering something that didn't happen. But it was real. You're not just saying so.
Dad: It happened. It was real.
Self (after a silence): Thanks Dad. I needed to know that.

FILL IN THE BLANK.
Crime:
Punishment: suspension for two years without pay.

LECTURE, 2078.
"Originally the sonnet was a site of sexual violence. Male poets were rewarded for celebrating the women they hunted. They used the sonnet form and an instrument called the 'blazon' to convert their prey into exquisite English artifacts. Our anthologies still include holograms of jewel-like eyes, porcelain skin, ruby lips, hair like gold, and so on.

"Over time the white men themselves modified the sonnet to make it accommodate topics other than male heterosexual desire. The topics came to include blindness, time, spiders, God, the planets, applepicking, wine, prayer, computers, robots, politics, and the apocalypse. Now, in the year 2078, it is possible to choose existence in a world designed like a sonnet. It is possible to live one's entire life inside a sonnet. It is possible to become a sonnet.—But only if one has consented to such an existence."

DISCUSS THE FOLLOWING QUOTATION.
In a 1996 News Service interview, [JF] described the 18th-century attitude toward belongings this way: "There was a sense that objects were preferred over people because they didn't leave you, they didn't talk back, and you could project a certain subjectivity and have an intense relationship with them, particularly with books," he said. (Source: Cynthia Haven, *Stanford Report,* August 17, 2007)

A LITTLE SONG AND A RECEIPT.
Doe: a deer, a female deer—
Often chased by sonneteers of old.
Caught, and killed, and bathed in fear,
turned to human blazons to be sold—

Eyes—$twin models of the stars.
Skin—$fine tissue wrought from gold.

Lips—$your favorite kind of flower.
Sex—$a secret still untold/a Silk Road to unfold/a thing for you to mold/a source by you controlled.

Total: $_____

THE BLAZONAUT.

Setting: an alternative universe where, due to the choreography of molecules here, to use words is to versify. Location: southwest Canada (not far from where the Golden Gate Bridge is located in our reality). Time: a year named "The Earliest Early Americanist" (corresponding roughly to our year 2000 AD). All residents of this universe hold the following truth to be self-evident: Each person has the right to free consent. Living by this truth is to them as breathing is to us. Rape, in this reality, is an alien phenomenon.

1. News
". . . she fell into the water from the sky . . ."

2. Jae-in Doe
Decedent is an Asian female.
Twenty-two she just had turned.
The cause of death we cannot tell
Despite the many things we've learned.

3. TOP SECRET
My Doe-type can be difficult to track.
Yet here I am, my voice-box playing back
From lips hydrangea-lavender in hue
His thoughts during our first few interviews.

The hair is shoulder-length, the color black.
The height and weight suggest she won't fight back.
The fingernails are unadorned and short.
The eyes are brown; no makeup do they sport.
The skin appears unpierced and untattooed,

Yet scars of ruby-pearl seem to protrude
Like self-inflicted jewelry on each arm
And wrist—which means she's vulnerable to harm.
The language of her flesh, as I assess her,
Reveals Confucian worship of professors.

Her deference Korean gives me right
To use her innocence for my delight.

    4. The Coroner's Soliloquy
The species: neither robot nor a xenomorph but both.
A blazonaut I call her as I scan her for the truth.

Throughout her brain dimensions grew like flowers wild
And han flowed through her circuits like fog-weather mild

until the onslaught
caused a drought.

The genitals, the soul, the lymph, the spine, the nape,
                 Show evidence of _____
For which we have no name.

I can't do this anymore.

DISCUSS THE FOLLOWING QUOTATION.
You can keep nothing safe from our eyes and ears. This is your own
history. We are your most perilous and dutiful brethren, the song of
our hearts at once furious and sad. For only you could grant me these
lyrical modes. I call them back to you. Here is the sole talent I ever
dared nurture. Here is all of my American education. (The Korean
American narrator of *Native Speaker* by Chang-rae Lee)

MUTANT BLAZON.
My rapist's eyes remind me of the sun.
To look at them will mean that I go blind.

His mouth beside my ear—they form a gun.
Each breath: a bullet targeting my mind.

My rapist's eyes remind me of the sun.
His throat: a fist to silence mine designed.
His reason: a ventriloquist's illusion.
No tenor in the end could hearing find.

My rapist's eyes remind me of the sun—
Too close for any vessel with a mind.
Survive or get to die—that is the question.
No longer have I any will to mind.

My rapist's eyes remind me of the sun—
Not dead, not living, neither keen nor blind;
A daily haunting; memory rebegun;
Disaster in some future undivined.

I write, rewrite, a "sonnet" about rape
To hunt that voice I wish I could escape.

**DISCUSS THE FOLLOWING QUOTATION (without using the
words "predator" or "prey").**
There she beholding me with milder look,
Sought not to fly, but fearless still did bide:
Till I in hand her yet half trembling took,
And with her own goodwill her firmly tied.
Strange thing, me seem'd, to see a beast so wild,
So goodly won, with her own will beguil'd.

—From Edmund Spenser's poem "Like as a Huntsman" (Sonnet 67
of his 1595 sonnet cycle *Amoretti*)

**DISCUSS THE FOLLOWING QUOTATION (without using the
words "predator" or "prey").**
"Yeah that's her in the gold. I better use some Tic Tacs just in case I start

kissing her. You know, I'm automatically attracted to beautiful . . .
I just start kissing them. It's like a magnet. Just kiss. I don't even wait.
And when you're a star they let you do it. You can do anything . . .
Grab them by the pussy. You can do anything." —the 45th President
of the United States of America

COMPLETE THE FOLLOWING DIALOGUE.
Professor: All men have rape fantasies, including your father.
Student:

A KIND OF CENSUS.
- Number of spouses: zero.
- Number of children: zero.
- Longest stretch of time spent alone inside the apartment: eighteen consecutive days.
- Longest stretch of time post-rape without any physical intimacy with another mammal: seven consecutive years.
- Number of episodes of Law and Order: Special Victims Unit never seen: zero.
- Year I watched SVU for the first time: 2011.
- Year SVU started: 1999.
- Number of fantasies about cathartic dialogues with Olivia Benson: countless.
- Number of years spent closeted to most people about what happened at Stanford: fifteen.

July 5, 2016. Facebook entry posted shortly after I came out as a rape survivor.
Q: Do you think being raped made you gay?
A: Several people have asked me this question (or a version of it). It is a question worth addressing.
(1) I cannot speak for others who have been raped. I can only speak to my own situation. Please do not mistake anything I write here for a generalization. (2) The first crush I remember having: Ellen Degeneres. At the time I didn't know who she was (I caught a glimpse of her on TV); I didn't know what it meant to be gay; I didn't know what I felt was a crush. All I knew was that she made my heart feel

nervous and I wanted to see her face again. (3) My parents had an arranged marriage. The arrangement was less than ideal. They spoke to (argued with) each other in Korean—a language that my brother and I did not understand—and they spoke to us in (broken-ish) English. To this day I think of marriage as literally a foreign language. (4) My mother was (is) devoutly Catholic. As a child I myself was devoutly Catholic and confused about my sexuality. The last time I went to confession (I was a teenager) I confessed I thought I might be gay and also I wasn't sure if God existed. The priest said he could not forgive me but he could give me holy water for me to keep by my bed to repel Satan. (5) My first sexual experience was being raped at the age of 22 by someone who wielded power over me, who controlled my future, and who was fully aware that I was sexually inexperienced and confused about my sexuality. (6) I spent much of my twenties in relationships that allowed me to pretend (or try to pretend) that Stanford never happened. Does it matter that a few relationships were with men and that a few were with women? I honestly don't know. (7) My last relationship ended a decade ago. Since then my personal life has resembled a desert ruled by agoraphobia and the wish to destroy my capacity to feel attraction. (8) I have been attracted to people of all sexes and gender identities. (9) As the details above are meant to suggest, my sexuality is extremely complicated. Did being raped make me gay? No. (See item 2.) But it is a fact that rape (among many other factors, including those mentioned above) had an impact on how I experience desire and act (or hesitate to act) upon my feelings. Indeed it may be the case that "rape survivor" is one of my sexual orientations. *I would not wish this joyless and often agonizing orientation on anybody.* (10) Again I stress that I speak only for myself. I doubt it is possible to generalize that rape makes people gay (or straight). Different individuals survive violence in different ways. Some of us end up not surviving. Some of us are working on just holding on. I hope that my answer has been educational.

"Noli me tangere": A Kind of Villanelle
His ghost stands watching me while I'm asleep.
I know that this cannot be real because
I'm wide awake. I never fall asleep.

The hours between twelve and twelve still keep
Me up reciting poetry because
His ghost stands watching me while I'm asleep.

I close my eyes, imagine rivers deep
And soft plush turquoise emerald velvet moss.
I hide myself here as a pebble heap.

What if I dared to sea from cliff to leap?
My absence from the world would be no loss.
His ghost stands watching me while I'm asleep.

When finally I die, will I escape
His ghost's attention? Or will those glib jaws
Assault my ghost with secrets fresh to keep?

I don't know if I wake or if I sleep
Or why my speech obeys poetic laws.
His ghost stands watching me while I'm asleep.
Perhaps he's dreamt a way my soul to reap, to reap, to reap.

PALO ALTO DISAPPEARANCE.

A yard, once used for some kind of sport, lies seemingly deserted. High above her, in a near-future sky, one allosaurus and one magpie, each the size of a skyscraper, battle for extinction. Crowds of invisible spectators flow toward the spectacle. At some point, when the rumors grow too poisonous, she turns around, against the tide, and starts to climb a secret staircase made out of wisteria, the stems of which twine counterclockwise. The more she climbs, more and more flowers surround her. Blossoms thicken. Petals seep into her hair. Her skin becomes liquid petal.

"Anyone is inside your house," the flowers whisper.

"I don't have a body," she responds.

By now she is no longer climbing a staircase. The staircase has disappeared and so has she.

In the distance another mythical creature falls and another endangered animal cannot hear its own appalling song. Where games of sport once took place, palm trees begin to shimmer, dazzle, daze. She is beyond the last thought at the end of the mind.

Obviously this is not reality.

This was one way I got through it.

TERRIFIED VAGUE PRONOUNS.

As he, to have her, turned into a swan,
So she, to bear it, turned him to a swan.
I often wonder which was worse: the swan
She conjured, or the man inside the swan.
I often wonder which came first: the swan
Whose "blow" (Yeats wrote) was "sudden," or the swan
Whose "sudden blow" was made of piecemeal swan-
Like men in motion slow: from man to swan.

The things that one man did engendered here
A broken mind, the pills within an hour
That should have left me dead. Being caught up,
Accustomed to the comfort of his chair,
Could he possess the knowledge or the power
To see that each from different heights would drop?

AFTER EMILY DOE. JUNE 2016.

One image that's been invading my mind lately: a mugshot that was never taken. It was never taken because I never pressed charges. I didn't think to press charges.

He's no longer alive. He was my adviser at Stanford. He was a tenured professor, a "big name" in academia. I was a first-year Ph.D. student, 21 years old and stupidly naive. I had also recently been hospitalized after a suicide attempt. I had just been diagnosed as bipolar.

"Your mom and I should have—we didn't know how to prepare you—" my dad said yesterday while we were brokenly discussing the Stanford assault case that has been in the news recently.

To which I could only say, "I'm sorry, I'm sorry you have a daughter who made you go through so much trauma in addition to the Korean War and everything . . . "

We apologize to each other, my father and I. The Stanford professor refused to apologize to me.

I know I should forgive him. It wasn't his fault.

When he asked me if I was a virgin, I told him the truth: yes. (I should have said: It is none of your business.)

When he told me that he controlled my future, I let myself believe I had no future worth imagining. (I should have been brave and stood up to him.)

I still wake up sometimes to find my clothes drenched in sweat and my body numb, literally numb.

In my head the mugshot is blurry. I scarcely remember what he looked like. I can't bring myself to google his name.

Parents: You do not want your children to end up like me. If your child is assaulted, try to get professional help for your child immediately and be sure to follow through. This may be challenging if you are an immigrant who is exceedingly shy, less than fluent in English, financially struggling, Roman Catholic, and/or incapable of saying the word "rape." But assault can be devastating and the impact permanent if not addressed right away and adequately.

THE NEW MILLENNIUM (after Shelley's "Ozymandias").
I meet a stranger in a house of gloom
Appointed with archaic chairs and shelves
Made centuries ago . . . The stranger's doom
Is my fate too, for that which makes my self
not hers is time alone. Inside that room
She cannot see me but I see her dread,
Her shattered face—Something I know is wrong.
Her body language speaks as though it's dead.
If minds could text, in hers this would appear:
"Your name is Jennie. My name is Seo-Young.
Let me, your future self, bear your despair."

Now that I'm home, I'm drowning in decay,
Pill bottles, trash, her burden mine to bear.
Why did I—she—choose to survive this way?

SEX AFTER STANFORD.

One of the side effects (for me at least) of being violated: every time I feel desire, attraction, or any evidence of a libido, I automatically feel guilty. I feel an obligation to cancel my body, delete, to make it disappear.

The "logic": I have a libido; therefore I could not have been raped. The truth: I did not want to be trapped in his house full of horrible shadows and statues.

FASCICULUS.

Where two thighs meet—a Vertex glows—
My "Sex"—a Bomb or Missile—
Remembrance Now—the Weapon grows—
Turned—inward—at—my—Will—
As Hunters—carcass—make their Prey—
A "Special" "Victim"—I*—
To excavate —Preempt decay—
Extract—from sense of Time—

* Variant: I'm

TO BE ON THE MARKET DURING HIS FESTIVAL.

The professor, at once bragging and threatening, had often told my younger self that he controlled my future, my livelihood, my *worth.* (I still ask myself sometimes: "Is my future 'worth' living?")

Being on the job market became a continuously fraught performance. The most excruciating theater took place where no one else could see it: my brain. Denial was a circus act. I don't know how the circus animals survived the mistreatment.

In preparing for the long stressful winters of phone calls and emails and MLA hotel rooms and campus visits and "professional" attire (my rapist liked to talk about grooming me, as if I were a pet—I remember how furious his reaction would be whenever I chose to wear glasses, look frumpy, or let lint appear on my clothing), I should have done this:

I should have worked through the bad memories. I should have worked through the feelings of disgust, self-loathing, humiliation, fear, despair, and hopelessness.

Instead I let the feelings and memories choreograph my actions. I punished my psyche for remembering details about JF. I punished my flesh for what JF did to it.

PSYCHOMACHIA.
- We wish we had selected our

Society with much more care.
- The problem is you've shut the door,

Available to life no more.
- But she can't risk or bear the chance

Of misconstruing some advance—
- What if his cultured ways to me

He gave, rape culture a disease?
- I never understood this world.

I still don't understand this world.

REMINDER.
And yet he could be vulnerable —alarmingly so. Once, in his house, during a meeting to discuss his course (for which I was a teaching assistant), he began to sob violently. No one else was there. I was sitting at one end of a couch. He sat next to me and—before I could do anything—weighted down my lap with his head. "I miss my mother," he cried over and over again on my lap.

I was rigid. I was rigid with an emotion for which I still have no name. I don't remember how I got myself out of the situation.

Did part of myself get left behind—? Is that why I can't remember?

SOMETIMES I SCREAMED.
A Special Victim said to me
In Space there is no Rape—
A Special Victim heard from me
In Space there is no Hope—

There is no thing with Feathers, here—
No tune without the words—

Nobody can exist out here—
I'm nothing—Who you were—

CONTUSIONS, RECENT.
Whenever I felt the horrible urge to "pleasure" myself, I would often succumb—but not without using a hammer afterwards to punish my flesh with such ferocity that the pain made me pass out.

There were times in my life when my skin ran out of places that were not purple, turquoise, blue, or red.

The alternative to battering my flesh: letting the intrusive ghost of my rapist happily watch me surrender to my libido.

INSTRUCTIONS LEFT INCOMPLETE (after Donne's Holy Sonnet).
Gather our parts, united self, though you
Do not exist quite yet enough to send
Your futuristic wholeness from the end
Of lyric time to where we wait for you.
Make us consent to sentience anew.
Revive our will until there is no end
But endless means by which we all transcend
The paradox you already outgrew.
Believe the story that free will is free.
By then you'll have put on the suit of "me"
As if it were composed of empathy,
A fabric of compatibility.
It's your turn "to be" now. Now you are me.
Please sign your name here if you _____.

WHICH OF THE FOLLOWING STATEMENTS IS TRUE?
(A) Someone says, "I am lying right now."
(B) Someone says, "Rape me."
(C) Someone says, "I never consented to this alien experiment called 'existence.'"
(D) Someone says, "No means yes."
(E) Someone says, "At least you didn't die."
(F) Someone says, "Why can't you just get over it?"
(G) Someone says, "What you went through is a first-world problem."

(H) Someone says, "What about the Earth and climate change? You have to put rape in perspective."

(I) Someone says, "But you seem okay."

(J) Someone says, "I can't believe how widespread this problem is."

(K) Someone says, "Let me rape you."

(L) Someone says, "Let go."

(M) Someone says, "Am I the only one who can hear all of these voices."

ON THE IMPORTANCE OF NAMING.

"When you use the word 'rape' to describe what happened to you— can you use a more subtle expression? Something more elegant? You are an English language expert, Jennie, so I trust you must know how to discuss what happened without using that word. There must be a more decent, less ugly way of saying it. I am sure you know of such a way. Jennie? Are you upset? Why are you crying? Did I say something wrong? Jennie, say something. Please, I'm sorry. Jennie, what did I do."

CLEAR THOUGHTS IN A CLEAR SHADE (after Marvell's "The Garden").

To vanquish all my memories' blight
I swallow dots that promise light.
Ellipses of unconsciousness
Unknow me into happiness.
What science fiction is this space
Where time is just another place?
No apples drop about my head
Yet "apples" I can "taste" instead.
Such luscious freedom from the past
Is pleasure after pain has passed.
Once human life I finally shake
A shape past human I will take.
Were I a Daphne turned to tree
I'd pray for flames to set me free.
Tillandsia I'd rather be,
A lock of air, the dew my key.

Yet still I live, an idiot,
A shadow that can strut and fret.
Why human form? Why woman form?
Collapse me into formlessness
Until existence nonsense is:
The sonic and the furious,
A nothing of significance;
—An alien of consciousness;
A spacetime of unconsciousness.

RESURRECTION LULLABY (after Milton).
When one considers how one's life is spent,
Each resurrected self another hide
Less human than the one that last had died,
One's brain a frozen bruise that can't consent
To heal after the violence he meant,
His afterlife itself slow homicide,
"Please let my will complete the suicide,"
One prays. But other voices, to relent
That prayer, interrupt, "One did not need
Apology, redress, or an arrest
To live as though his punishment were great.
Survival was enough to fill the need
Required by existence of each guest.
Your prayer's heard. Now fall asleep and wait."

DREAM.
Outside: a Farm. Inside: a dimly lit living room. A constellation of antique furniture. A couch. A young woman, my height, we're standing in the room looking at each other, no one else is in the room, she looks like me but her hair is longer and her cheeks are fuller and the scars on her arms are still visible. I notice them because she's gesturing. She's pointing at the couch. "That's where I die," she says. "That's where you must take my place. There is no other way. I have no future worth living."

I used to hate these dreams. I'm learning to live with them. They're like the dreams I have of North Korea. They're like the dreams I have of life after death.

The next time I see her I will say:
> Forgive yourself for having been naive.
> You've dwelled here for too long. It's time to leave.

DISCUSS THE FOLLOWING QUOTATION.

We hold these truths to be self-evident, that all men are created equal, that they are endowed by their Creator with certain unalienable Rights, that among these are Life, Liberty and the pursuit of Happiness.

THE GRADUATE MENTORING AWARD. NOTE: THE AWARD WAS RENAMED IN AUGUST, SOON AFTER THE LETTER WAS SENT.

To:
June 2016
Executive Director
American Society for _____

Dear Professor _____, ·
Recently I learned that there is a graduate mentoring award named after (I'm just going to force myself to spell out his name) Jay Fliegelman.

This man was supposed to be my dissertation adviser. I say "supposed to be" because he spent more time sexually harassing and stalking me than he did advising me academically. Instead of discussing ideas, scholarship, or projects, he "mentored" me with insights such as "All men have rape fantasies, including your father." (That is a line I will never forget.) He left me voice messages about overdosing on male enhancement pills. He shared explicit fantasies with me —despite my protests. He violated my flesh, my psyche, my sense of bodily integrity—despite knowing that I was *unwilling,* despite knowing that I was a virgin, despite knowing that I was incapacitated by mental illness. He must have known, too, that I was under the influence of his institutional power. I was new to Stanford, new to California, new to the profession. He had been in the profession and at Stanford for decades. Indeed, his own mentors and former dissertation advisers were still teaching and advising in the Stanford English department when I arrived as a 21-year-old first-year Ph.D. student. Only from this temporal distance can I see so clearly his power and my powerlessness.

For years I have struggled to be a model survivor. I wouldn't want to get Stanford into trouble, right? I should show how grateful and uncomplaining I am—after all, Stanford punished the professor by suspending him for two years without pay, right? Stanford, too, has remained silent about the case. There is no public record of what happened. Not even a concise announcement describing the nature of Jay Fliegelman's misconduct and punishment. (Does Stanford not understand that in the absence of clear communication, rumors and misinformation have a tendency to grow?)

In the past few weeks I've learned that the years of silence surrounding Jay Fliegelman's misconduct and punishment have had a number of consequences that are regrettable. One of these consequences: the creation of the award mentioned above. This graduate mentoring award is named after a man who abused his power, who refused to apologize for raping his student, who screamed at and terrified his student, who dropped by his student's dorm unannounced causing the student to hide in her closet in the dark wondering "How long do I have to stay here? Is he gone yet?"—whose ghost continues to haunt his student to this day.

I have worked hard to forgive Professor Fliegelman. I realize he was human and complex. I am sure he was a good mentor to many students. I admire the loyalty and gratitude that former students of Jay Fliegelman have demonstrated by creating this award. I do not know if they are or were aware of what he did to me. Perhaps they were unaware of the extent to which Professor Fliegelman caused damage. In any case, if any former students are reading this: Now you know.

I understand the "Jayfest." I have no objection to naming his collection of books "the Fliegelman Library." But what hit me in the solar plexus and made—makes—me feel sick: seeing the website for the Jay Fliegelman award for *graduate mentorship* (seeing the "mugshots" of professors honored for mentoring students the way Jay Fliegelman mentored his students) and recognizing one of my graduate professors from a non-Stanford university—a professor who has been nothing but professional and kind to me. "Are these awards given to advisers who sexually harass and rape their students?" I wondered—"and if so what did Professor X do to deserve such an obscene award?"

The thought now strikes me as absurd. But it is no more absurd than the existence of an award for graduate mentoring named in honor of a man whose "mentoring" included threats, controlling behavior, objectification of a student's body, and sexual violence. Surely there are better examples in whose honor this award might be renamed.

If you are one of Jay Fliegelman's former students who had an experience worth celebrating: I believe you. You need not provide documentation to persuade me. I believe that, in your experience, he was a wonderful mentor. Is it too much for me to ask you to believe me too?

Thank you for your time and consideration.

Seo-Young Chu

January 2017. Why I Am Joining The March.
In an ideal world, my body and mind together would join the march—in person, in public, in visible protest.

In an ideal world, my flesh would freely will itself outside and onto the streets to demonstrate out loud against the inauguration of a man whose irresponsible and casual expressions of entitlement and violence have amplified the trauma (the injury, the bleeding wound) of rape culture.

In an ideal world, the president of the United States of America would not be so eerily reminiscent of a specific nightmare from my own personal past: a man in a position of power who sexually harassed and violated me seventeen years ago, a man whose ghost lives on in this Yellow-Haired-Man-In-Ultimate-Position-Of-Power.

In an ideal world, the pain that I am experiencing right now would not exceed the sum of the medical conditions with which I have been diagnosed (including post-traumatic stress, bipolar depression, spinal herniation, fibromyalgia, anxiety, and chronic migraines).

In an ideal world, there would be female as well as male U.S. presidents.

Yet I believe in the reality of ideal worlds. They can be articulated. They can be drawn. They can be painted. They can be diagrammed. They can be meditated. They can be realized.

EPILOGUE.
I am one of the lucky ones.

■

In Conversation with Vi Khi Nao

FROM *Cosmonauts Avenue*

Let's begin by knitting
Stitching
   The haiku is like cutting fabric

Tran: How fake is your haiku? To what degree of fakeness? And, did you measure? You make pretty extraordinary leaps with your line breaks? Tell me about your process—was it like "cutting potatoes" or as you say like "cutting fabric"?

Nao: I didn't measure anything, which contributes to its fakeness. Haiku is a surprising form. Counting syllables is not. My process with *Fake Haiku* was an industrial machine that sews garments, but also the scene of Jeanne Dielman peeling potatoes. These fragments were held together by what I could reach for outside my window.

Who is a better chef? Your mother or your father? Or perhaps it is you.

My parents collaborate when it comes to cooking. My father is a tastemaker; my mother is a magician. My mother cooks more, so by virtue of that, she's more of a cook (in quantity). She makes all of my favorite meals. My favorite thing she makes is bún bò Huế. I love the food my father makes. He taught me how to scramble eggs and how to wash lettuce. He would buy chicken livers, or chicken hearts, or pig's blood, xào với rau răm. My father has a few specialties that my mother won't mess with, like bún thịt nướng. He likes to grill on his homemade outdoor charcoal stove.

And, what is an armpit journal? Is it a journal that you keep under the armpit at all times? Or is it more like a journal in which you write about armpits?

My doctor prescribed journaling. She said, "Keep a journal about your armpits." Today she said "Keep a journal about your muscle spasms."

Why is she giving you these imperatives?

I wanted a second opinion.

I used to think white people smell like butter. What do you think white people smell like? Especially in a bibliography full of white people?

Hotel soap
Lavender and roses pressed
In old library books

What do you think Asians smell like? Would you write a fake haiku about their smell?

Cherry blossoms printed on silk
Soaking in kwan loong oil
Dry shrimp under the tongue

How would you describe the smell of a mother of pearl black lacquer box with the red felt lining?

Before this interview, I scooped out two scoops of vanilla ice cream. Then I realized that I could not speed eat it so I threw the glass bowl into the refrigerator. I wonder if this interview will go badly because I didn't eat those two scoops of ice cream.

You can be doing both.
I am not at home.
   And, I would need to time travel.

   Bowl in the fridge
Upside down
   Snow globe

Speaking of snow globe, are you photogenic? What inspires you to corre-late photogenicity with an elevator? Or to juxtapose them in your $20-bill haiku?

Photogenic? Perhaps only in black/white photobooths. I get photo-booths and elevators mixed up sometimes. These inventions share a similar constraint of dimensionality—silver modes of time travel. $20 bills feel like a complete experience—coming and going like a breath, a flash, a bell.

What is your favorite sound in the world? This is a nod to your sensibility or perception of the worse sound.

Mulatu Astatke—Tezeta (Nostalgia)

What kind of soap do you use?

Aesop's body cleansing slab. You need a hot knife to cut it into pieces—something I didn't know before.

And, would you cross a river for someone whom you do not love? And, cannot love?

This feeling is familiar. I'd rather watch the water from a bridge. I would like to become a stronger swimmer.

Have you berated a haiku before? If not, how would you berate it?

I'm thinking of a serrated knife going through a ripe tomato.

If you could see into the future, what kind of writer/poet would you like to be known for?

I hope to write the book(s) people would want to read on the bus.

Do you like drawstring pants? Have you ever worn them and write a haiku? I love drawstring pants—I always think it's a fancy version of a garbage bag that can't be thrown away. That I could not be thrown away so readily.

One day I'll be as brave as Christine Shan Shan Hou and throw away my pants that don't have elastic waistbands.

Are you happy with this chapbook? How long did it take you to compose it?

Wendy's Subway did an amazing job at turning these poems into a beautiful chapbook. I have a very fast morning routine and can get ready to leave the house in about 30 minutes. That's how I wrote these poems.

Have you been to Đà Lạt before? This chapbook, your fake haikus, made me think of the waterfalls there. You could feel water dropping/flowing before a splash. Your last line in most of your haikus behave like this mermaid splash.

My mother has mentioned it rains very lightly, like mist, in Đà Lạt. Mưa phù. I think I may have been on a small rowboat in Đà Lạt the last time I went to Vietnam (2005). I remember there were many banana trees.

What is a poet to you? Meaning . . . how do you define it? Do you think, other than a different form, a poet is different than a writer? Someone told me once or perhaps it was me that once thought a poet has direct access to God and a writer meanders a bit, takes a long detour before accessing God. What do you think?

A poet eats ramen while walking. Poetry sits with me in sweats on a couch eating a handful of robin's egg-colored malt milk chocolates until my bottom lip turns blue. A poet reads about the history of shea butter and the healing properties of turmeric. I'm not sure where God is, but my boyfriend dug up my sweet tooth. My favorite poets are very romantic.

What do you think should be the national fruit of Vietnam, if you had to choose one fruit in the world?

Longan. As a child, my mother would make rings out of the seeds. I love that image of my resourceful mother, at a young age, so small yet so strong that she could carve a ring out of the seed and fit her finger into the center of the fruit.

What are you reading right now? Would you recommend them?

We Were Meant to Be a Gentle People, Dao Strom. ("You cannot call yourself a gentle person without simultaneously knowing your own capacity to brutally miss the mark.")

If you were to make a meal for Marina Abramovic, what is that meal? And, what do you think her response to your dish would be?

Cháo with salted duck egg garnished with chopped green onion.

Why cháo? When I think of Marina Abramovic, I think of fish and bánh bao and fermented rice.

Cháo is a durational piece: cooking rice in water over time and heat. We take turns stirring the pot. I will ask Marina to cut the salted egg in half.

If I had children, I would name one Green Onion and the other Red Onion. Would you name your children after a fruit/vegetable if you had any?

My mother's neighbors in Vietnam would give their children beautiful names at birth, but never call them by those names. They would have nicknames like Cam or Nhãn so evil spirits wouldn't take their children away.

If you were to make me a five course dinner . . . ?

Hột vịt lộn & rau răm as an appetizer
Bánh ít trần
Bánh hỏi
Green onion tofu (w/salt & pepper of course)
Sâm bổ lượng for dessert

I believe I would enjoy this elaborate course. Whenever I see this "hột vịt lộn"—I always think that the ducks are having a chicken fight. Why sâm bổ lượng for dessert?

My parents made sâm bổ lượng with seaweed they harvested from the Pacific ocean last summer. It's the only Vietnamese dessert I am excited about. I associate all of the ingredients with Asian grocery stores—canned longan, canned lychee, tiny dehydrated apples, barley swimming in a simple syrup made from gold rock sugar. The dessert resembles brown glass, which I love.

Is there a poet/writer/philosopher (dead or alive) that you would love to take a shower with nonsexually? Would you wash his/her hair or kneecaps?

Clarice Lispector. I wouldn't dare get in the middle of Clarice and her hair.

What dead poet would you take a shower with sexually? And, why?

Clarice Lispector. See above.

If you could come up with a pen name, what name would you want it to be . . . ?

Thủy Tinh

I think flossing someone's teeth is really tender (going to the dentist isn't tender and dentists in general are not tender), would you floss Hồ Xuân Hương's teeth? What kind of remnants would you pull out of her mouth?

> The smell of incense
> Burning beside a lake
>   Springtime

What is the most clever way for one writer to insult another writer? Didn't Thoreau do that in his opening of Walden? He insulted the readers, I believe, in the most respectable way.

Cut up the book and rearrange it with fewer words. That's a kind of compliment.

If you were to do a performance art from a literary standpoint, what would that performance look like in words?

Stacey Tran in conversation with Vi Khi Nao.

What was the best performance art you have seen? What happened in it?

Okwui Okpokwasili's *Bronx Gothic*. She performed this piece in the corner of a building where I took an art history class in college. She was moving the whole time. When she used her voice I felt like I was very small, like I feel in mountains or caves. She sweat through her purple dress.

DIEGO ENRIQUE OSORNO

■

Come and Eat the World's Largest Shrimp Cocktail in Mexico's Massacre Capital

Translated from Spanish by Christina MacSweeney

FROM *Freeman's*

IN THE LAGUNA MADRE, a vast area of salt water that crosses the dividing line between Mexico and the United States and comprises a dozen communities in Tamaulipas and Texas, an army of fishermen caught over 17,000 penaeid shrimp so the local government could organize a Festival del Mar at La Carbonera beach, and prepare a shrimp cocktail weighing 2,257 pounds. The aim was to change the negative image of San Fernando, where, in 2010, on an August afternoon, 72 mostly Central American migrants were massacred in the storehouse of a ranch, and where one April morning in 2011, the tortured bodies of 196 people were found buried in the shimmering green pastures. In the following weeks mass graves were discovered containing an as yet unverified number of corpses, which some local authorities estimate to be around 500. A macabre joke circulated on Facebook and Twitter at the time: "Come to San Fernando, we'll welcome you with open graves." During Holy Week 2014, in this place where Mexico's most awful 21st-century massacres have occurred, the governor of Tamaulipas state, Egidio Torre Cantú, accompanied by a dozen regional mayors, would stand around a monumental glass tumbler to celebrate a new record: the largest shrimp cocktail in the world.

Along with agriculture, fishing was one of the main economic activities in San Fernando until the war between the Zetas and the Gulf Cartel, plus the military and naval presence, brought life in the town to a standstill, and caused the cessation of mass celebrations between 2009 and 2013. And that is why the Festival del Mar became an important event for the people of the region, some of whom could not believe they would have the opportunity to see in the flesh Mariana Seoane, an actress on the Televisa channel who once posed in the nude for gentlemen's magazines and has a single entitled "I'll Be a Good Girl." Seoane would be the festival queen and, at the behest of the euphoric crowd, would sing her three hits, turning to give the crowd a view of her figure. Another important moment would be the appearance of Sonora Dinamita, among whose members were two "mulattoes" who, according to the mayor of San Fernando, would give the women of the town a visual experience equivalent to that offered by Seoane to the men.

But the star of Good Friday would be the penaeid shrimp, a small crustacean whose bulging black eyes contrast with its curved, cylindrical body from which sprout two pairs of antennae—one long, one short—and five pairs of legs. Its body ends in a pointed tail that, along with the head, is removed before it is eaten. With just ten or twelve of these crustaceans, water and ketchup, it is possible to prepare a small seafood cocktail, although in Tamaulipas and many other places it is usual to include avocado, garlic and lime juice; in neighboring Texas, they also add cucumber and serrano chili. When oysters and clams are added, this hangover cure is generally known as "Back to Life," a name that in present-day San Fernando is not particularly appropriate.

During the festival I had a discussion with a man who was convinced that shrimp had been created for no other reason than to be ingested in a cocktail. According to him, when placed in a glass tumbler, they have a better flavor than when deviled, cooked in chipotle sauce, or garlic, or butter; served with Philadelphia; or wrapped in bacon and cheese; or a la Veracruzana. Or even when served with that chili pepper water they make so well in Mazatlán, Sinaloa, which once held the Guinness record for the largest shrimp cocktail in the world. In northeast Mexico you can find this expensive delicacy sold dried by the highway at incredibly low prices. The roadblocks installed by the military in the region, supposedly to reduce violence, have benefited this small sector of the economy, since the shrimp vendors are able to sell their product to the lines of impatient, fearful motorists. On the journey from Reynosa to San Fernando, I came across one of these roadside vendors, and asked if his shrimp were from San Fernando, to which he replied in the affirmative; they came from the Laguna Madre. He uttered that toponym in such a solemn, respectful tone, it was as if he was referring to some species of Aridoamerican deity. The same tone was adopted by the announcers on regional radio stations every time they mentioned the lagoon. Between the Ramón Ayala corridos and Julión Álvarez ballads saturating the airwaves, there was no mention of anything but shrimp, and the great feat about to be accomplished in San Fernando. On the morning of Good Friday, just outside the center of town, caravans of pickup trucks crammed with families formed in the Loma Colorada gas station before heading off together for La Carbonera, less than 30 miles distant. The sound of Banda Sinaloense music filled the whole place, because the quick workers in the convenience store adjoining the gas station had decided to install huge speakers to liven up the morning. A mile or two farther on, three state police patrols were waiting for a group of men armed to the teeth: the latter were the governor's bodyguards and had arrived the night before by road, without their boss. The governor was coming by helicopter but needed his security team for the three-minute drive from the soccer field that formed an improvised heliport to the venue at which the feat of prowess was to take place.

The police officers agreed to pose for the photojournalist Victor Hugo Valdivia while they waited for the governor's bodyguards, whom they themselves would escort along with a naval patrol, just in case. "There's a lot of movement," said the head of the police squad with an enormous smile, pointing his machine gun toward the highway—toward a former cattle ranch that a few years before had been requisitioned by the Navy as its local headquarters. It was also in this spot that both the Zetas and the Gulf Cartel, and even some equis—as greenhorn delinquents are disparagingly known—set up roadblocks to keep watch over who was entering and leaving San Fernando. On Good Friday it was the police and soldiers who had mounted the series of checkpoints. For the occasion, the Army decided to roll out its most recent acquisition from the arms market: the SandCat, a very fast, highly armored truck with a diverse array of weaponry. It is the vehicle with which the regional military forces hope to confront the *monstruos*: vehicular monstrosities designed by the Zetas that have already been operating in the area for some time. The lieutenant in charge of the group was carrying a 7.62-mm MAG rifle, and didn't allow many photos to be taken of his SandCat, "because the criminals will copy it." "How can they when the vehicle's designed in the United States?" I asked with not a little naïveté. "They kidnap the people who can, and make them do it." While we were talking, the governor's security team passed, escorted by the state patrols, in turn escorted by the Navy patrols.

At the entrance to La Carbonera there was an old boat, on which a number of workmen were hanging a banner advertising the presence of Mariana Seoane. The event was scheduled to start at 10am; to hold it in the afternoon, or worse still after dark, would have been too risky, however many bodyguards, police officers and military roadblocks were in place. La Carbonera is a shrimp-fishing village with a single, unpaved main street, and this was packed with cars waiting for a parking space. Very soon a long line had formed, advancing at a snail's pace, thus allowing some of the drivers to get out of their vehicles to buy the dried shrimp sold by fishing families outside their houses. These fishermen use a trap known as a *charanga*: a net attached to a V-shaped structure, which is dropped in the marine channels through which the shrimp are expected to pass. Some fishermen work at night, when the crustaceans are most active.

When we reached the shores of the Laguna Madre, where a buzz of anticipation was already running through the crowd, a bunch of youths wearing T-shirts with the message "We are all Tamaulipas" passed by. These mass-produced tees, and plastic glasses with shrimp-inspired designs, were being handed out at the entrance. By walking along the estuary, you arrived at a pavilion, with the first rows of seats occupied by government officials dressed in shrimp-orange

T-shirts, and a smattering of army bigwigs in field dress. The show had not yet started, but the emcee took the microphone from time to time and, in a guttural voice, mouthed such historic comments as: "A beautiful crystal clear tumbler that will draw the eyes of the whole world, with a shrimp cocktail weighing more than a tooooon." If his aim was to animate those present, he didn't achieve it; after his interventions, the buzz from the crowd remained unchanged, and his words evaporated into the warm morning air. Only when a couple of municipal workers removed the plastic wrapping that had protected the tumbler from accidental scratches during its journey from Mexico City did the crowd quiet a little, perhaps because everyone thought the governor was about to arrive on the scene; he did in fact turn up, approximately two hours later than initially expected. But the emcee took advantage of the silence: "Today, more than ever, we are proud of the resources provided by the waters of our Laguna Madreeeee." Around ten yards away, sitting with a quasi-scientific air behind an aged laptop, the notary who was to adjudge the record was explaining that the glass tumbler weighed 825 pounds.

Of all the shrimp-orange T-shirt wearers in the first rows, the most euphoric was Mario de la Garza, a dentist who was also the mayor of San Fernando. While waiting for the governor, he spoke with five reporters, one of them from the state press office, who asked the prearranged questions. "This is going to be highly beneficial for San Fernando," the mayor insisted several times, after admitting that lately the economy had been going from bad to worse; and all this without ever mentioning the words violence, kidnapping or war, much less narco. When I spoke to him, and confessed that despite living in Monterrey, I'd had no idea San Fernando produced shrimp, the mayor cordially replied that San Fernando's shrimp were highly valued by Mexican experts but were not widely known on the commercial market: "That's why we want the whole world to know about and eat San Fernando shrimp." The mayor was extremely enthusiastic about preparing the largest shrimp cocktail in the world; he also promised that in the coming years San Fernando would become a powerful Mexican energy producer. The municipality, he vehemently explained, was already the largest extractor of natural gas from the rich Burgos Basin that runs through Tamaulipas, Nuevo León and Coahuila.

In addition the mayor triumphantly informed me that the special guests included Thomas Mittmasht, a man with a salt-and-pepper goatee and a wide-brimmed sun hat who was leaning back, idly inspecting the gigantic tumbler before the 17,000 or so small crustaceans were poured into it. Mittmasht is the United States consul in Matamoros, and when faced with questions from reporters about whether his government would now advise its citizens to visit Tamaulipas, he asked them to kindly read the information on the consular website. The document found there warns US citizens that if they should need to travel through Tamaulipas, it is recommended they do so during daylight hours, and avoid "displays of wealth that might draw attention." I asked Mittmasht when he had last visited San Fernando, and he replied that he had passed through the year before on his way back from the Governor's Report in Ciudad Victoria. "I guess you're more relaxed on this occasion," I commented, with a glance at his beachwear. "Well, less formal," he answered. He had made the journey with an escort of only four armored vehicles.

The day before the San Fernando Festival del Mar, Gabriel García Márquez had died, but it was perfectly clear that the magic realism attributed to that writer was not going to disappear quickly in either Mexico or Colombia. I mention this because an official from the Tamaulipas tourist office insisted I interview two men wearing snow-white pants and guayaberas, topped by traditional Colombian vueltiao hats. They were Arnold and Plácido Verera Murillo, restaurateurs from Cartagena—owners of the Ostería del Mar Rojo—who assured me they had been drawn to San Fernando by its good shrimp, and had experienced no problems in terms of personal security. The official bulletin issued later by the Government of Tamaulipas quotes the two men as saying, "Cartagena is a wonderful city, but it cannot equal what we've seen here; it's like a dream, I never imagined I'd have the chance to come to the Gulf of Mexico and visit the Laguna Madre, the Queen of Shrimp." In addition to comparing San Fernando to what is considered one of the world's most beautiful cities, the official bulletin noted that the two Colombians were overjoyed that "the governor and the municipal president were regenerating the beach resort, because that doesn't happen everywhere, and the authorities often just forget about a place, which isn't happening here." What the bulletin never mentioned, although some Colombian newspapers did, is that the Verera brothers were on an expenses-paid trip to Mexico to learn how to prepare the largest shrimp cocktail in the world, since Cartagena was planning to make a bid for the same title within a few years.

When I approached to interview them, the Colombians were talking to Arturo Ponce Pérez, one of the two chefs overseeing the preparation of the cocktail. Despite his worried expression, Chef Ponce said he was feeling highly motivated. Perhaps he was nervous, because he couldn't remember the last time he had made a small shrimp cocktail. While he preferred meat to seafood, he told me he had spent the last two weeks taking courses in preparation for the Guinness record bid, and now had everything needed for the event: just over a ton of frozen shrimp, 40 gallons of ketchup and 26 of clamato juice; neither lime nor avocado is included in the Guinness World Records rules. While the chef was coordinating the work of his 20 assistants on one side of the main pavilion, some youths with maracas passed; it had been announced that the governor was finally about to arrive, and their task was to provide a party atmosphere to welcome him. They were joined by more youngsters with tambores, and when the official claque had assembled, the assistant cooks were given a pep talk by the second chef. The most excited of these assistants were two men carrying giant spoons to stir the tomato sauce in the cocktail tumbler. Dressed from head to toe in white, including their face masks, they were like nurses about to concoct a dish of high-quality protein, vitamins, minerals, a lot of cholesterol, and phosphorus, an aphrodisiac.

A local official came to inform me that the San Fernando shrimp was unique, and that its exquisite flavor was without compare. He then said, enthusiastically, that thanks to the shrimp and natural gas, his hometown would once again be an economic powerhouse. He spoke of the 18 million cubic meters of natural gas shipped to Reynosa, and from there to the United States, and in a low tone, as if trying to ensure few bystanders overheard, added that two more large fields had been discovered: Trión 1 and 2. After that he began to complain that Pemex hadn't offered a peso toward the shrimp cocktail celebrations, and that the same was true of the other 28 energy companies in the region, excepting Geokinetics, which had donated a sum he preferred not to specify. The Tamaulipas authorities had paid 20,000 US dollars to Guinness just for the use of its logo in the publicity campaign. True, they had been, however, spared the travel expenses of the international team of judges, as none of the Guinness employees were willing to travel to San Fernando, given the high risk such a journey entailed. The official thought this was a shame, and said it was just an image problem, "all because of those 72 dead undocumenteds there on the border with Matamoros. They come dumping them on us here, and what can you do?" When I asked about the clandestine mass graves and shootouts of recent years, he fell silent, and then picked up his eulogy to the exquisite San Fernando shrimp where he had left off. "They really are the best in the world. I've eaten shrimp in San Francisco and Europe, and they don't even come close."

We had to break off conversation as the levels of activity increased in the pavilion. The governor's helicopter had landed. One of the bodyguards took a moment to joke with another who was helping a man in a shrimp costume to get into place. As they were passing, he said, "Hey, don't let that shrimp get too close." (In Mexico, camarón—shrimp—is one of the many euphemisms for the male member.) Meanwhile, the governor's head of logistics was arguing with two young organizers: "The governor is going to have his cocktail served up there on the stage. No way is the governor going to any cooler to pick it up himself." Surprisingly, the governor decided to walk to the pavilion through the crowd, occasionally waving to those present. When he came to the row in which the two Colombians were sitting, he stopped to receive the presents they had brought from their native land, and had his photo taken with them.

In the front row the mayors of Méndez, Valle Hermoso, Burgos and other regional towns were awaiting him in their orange T-shirts; also present were the colonel and captain in charge of the San Fernando military detachment. The governor, who was also wearing the requisite T-shirt, had not brought his wife; but his father, Egidio Torre López, had accompanied him, and when he took his seat in the front row, was heartily welcomed by the mayor of San Fernando, who then took the microphone to announce that very soon "we'll be in the news as an example of perseverance. They'll be talking about ordinary people who have done something extraordinary." The civic dignitary then thanked both Mother Nature and the governor for having made it possible for San Fernando to prepare the largest shrimp cocktail in the world.

Once the mayor had concluded his speech, the emcee announced they were going to show a video sent by the Guinness World Records executive committee in London. Absolute silence fell over the crowd, and on a giant screen the image of a young blond woman with a big smile and a discreetly low-cut top appeared to whistles of appreciation from the male public. In a kind of Tex-Mex Spanish, she first thanked Governor Egidio Torre (pronouncing the double "r" of Torre with great care), and while she was, with equal care, listing the names of other officials, a couple of refrigerator trucks pulled up behind the screen, and the two chefs plus their germ-free assistants dressed in white began to unload the 50-pound packs of shrimp. When the assistant chefs had thrown in pack number 22, the San Fernando cocktail weighed 1,120 pounds, and had officially beaten the previous record set by Mazatlán, Sinaloa. Jubilant cheers echoed around the venue, but this time the emcee held his tongue. The event reached its climax at the moment the tumbler weighed 2,300 pounds, and Mariana Seoane appeared, walking toward the seat allocated to her in the front row.

The cries of excitement resounded throughout La Carbonera, and the emcee could contain himself no longer; in his absolutely unmistakable tone he bellowed, "Tourism doesn't come beeeetter." Seoane had only just taken her seat in the front row when she was exhorted by members of the audience to stand and show off her body. "We want to see you, Mariana," they chanted. And she stood, turned around, and said, "What a lovely audience." She then ascended to the stage to assist the governor in sampling the dish. When they got a view of the actress's shapely body from a better angle, the audience exploded into even louder outbursts of euphoria. The mayor and his wife also appeared to pose with the chefs, Seoane, and the governor beside the tumbler of shrimp. In the midst of the excited celebrations, the governor gave a speech that lasted less than two minutes, and concluded with, "This is our Tamaulipas.

We work hard every day. And what do we do on our days of rest? We break world records."

After his anticlimactic intervention, the governor gave an impromptu press conference with the small number of reporters present. He made absolutely no mention of the marches in which up to a thousand people demanded peace in Tampico, nor of the petition organized by the Parents' Association suggesting classes should be suspended after the Easter vacation until there was evidence that the situation was under control, and their children's safety was guaranteed. He then walked through the crowd for a minute or two, paused for a few photos, and less than an hour after his arrival was on his way out of San Fernando. He didn't even stay for the shrimp. For her part, Seoane was besieged by fans at every step of her way to the performance stage, and then left before two in the afternoon. While she was singing, hundreds of San Fernando residents were lining up for their portion of the largest shrimp cocktail in the world. On the beach, the party was being equally enjoyed by families making giant sombreros from cardboard Tecate beer boxes and participating in impassioned games of volleyball. There were also ad hoc lifeguards, people selling mosquito spray, fathers carrying beers and tricycles, cowboys in shorts singing Norteño songs at the tops of their voices, and groups of friends in camouflage gear noisily drinking beer until four in the afternoon came around, when Sonora Dinamita finished their set, and the festivities were over. At that exact moment, I went back to the main stage. The tumbler containing the shrimp was completely empty. Over 17,000 small crustaceans were being digested by some 4,000 human stomachs on La Carbonera beach.

That Good Friday afternoon, after spending the day on La Carbonera beach, I returned to the center of San Fernando, where dozens of houses and businesses were empty or abandoned, some of them ransacked or in ruins. The night before the municipality achieved its shrimp-cocktail feat, a youth had been kidnapped from his home by one of the warring factions still operating in the area. A week before, a taco vendor had been arrested for acting as a mafia spy. Three weeks before, the Navy had shot down the daughter of an evangelical pastor, accusing her of being an assassin. A month before, there had been an almost hour-long shootout in a nearby valley. Two months before, the local parish priest, who in exceptional cases acted as a hostage negotiator, had been beaten up after handing over a ransom. Three months before, a group of young people had been kidnapped by another armed commando group; they are presumed to have been forced into slave labor. Four months before, 20 people had been kidnapped in the space of a week, and then freed in exchange for sums of between five-hundred thousand and a million pesos. None of these events were covered by the press.

The feeling of those who spoke of them was that San Fernando hadn't yet seen the worst; in fact, the worst was a day-to-day occurrence. Some of the residents I interviewed were annoyed about the Guinness record. Just as with any other human beings, the arrival of spring brought a smile to their faces, and they were pleased that a public space like La Carbonera beach had been reclaimed—if only for a few hours—but the fear of being kidnapped or murdered prevailed. The mayor's and the governor's idea of the largest shrimp cocktail in the world as a means of removing the stench of death from the town—more a public image exercise than a daily reality—was looked upon with skepticism. For the residents it was a smoke screen, more pathetic than naive. "You can't cover up the reality of San Fernando with a shrimp cocktail, no matter how big it is," one said. Another added, "Well, when we've got a governor who hasn't even solved his own brother's murder, how are we supposed to believe he really wants to solve the security problems the rest of us suffer? This is a no-man's-land."

As the sun went down, a small Good Friday procession made its silent way through the center of town. All the parishioners were dressed in white, and it was easy to imagine that what they required from their government was not a gastronomic world record. Early the following morning, as we drove out of the San Fernando valley, with its shimmering, green pastures and beautiful grasslands stretching to the purple-tinged horizon, it took an effort of will to believe that while Tamaulipas remains a pool into which Mexican democracy is sinking, its authorities are attempting to wipe out the horror with a shrimp cocktail.

DAVID WALLACE-WELLS

■

The Uninhabitable Earth

FROM *New York Magazine*

I. "Doomsday"
Peering beyond scientific reticence.

IT IS, I PROMISE, WORSE THAN YOU THINK. If your anxiety about global warming is dominated by fears of sea-level rise, you are barely scratching the surface of what terrors are possible, even within the lifetime of a teenager today. And yet the swelling seas—and the cities they will drown—have so dominated the picture of global warming, and so overwhelmed our capacity for climate panic, that they have occluded our perception of other threats, many much closer at hand. Rising oceans are bad, in fact very bad; but fleeing the coastline will not be enough.

Indeed, absent a significant adjustment to how billions of humans conduct their lives, parts of the Earth will likely become close to uninhabitable, and other parts horrifically inhospitable, as soon as the end of this century.

Even when we train our eyes on climate change, we are unable to comprehend its scope. This past winter, a string of days 60 and 70 degrees warmer than normal baked the North Pole, melting the permafrost that encased Norway's Svalbard seed vault—a global food bank nicknamed "Doomsday," designed to ensure that our agriculture survives any catastrophe, and which appeared to have been flooded by climate change less than ten years after being built.

The Doomsday vault is fine, for now: The structure has been secured and the seeds are safe. But treating the episode as a parable of impending flooding missed the more important news. Until recently, permafrost was not a major concern of climate scientists, because, as the name suggests, it was soil that stayed permanently frozen. But Arctic permafrost contains 1.8 trillion tons of carbon, more than twice as much as is currently suspended in the Earth's atmosphere. When it thaws and is released, that carbon may evaporate as methane, which is 34 times as powerful a greenhouse-gas warming blanket as carbon dioxide when judged on the timescale of a century; when judged on the timescale of two decades, it is 86 times as powerful. In other words, we have, trapped in Arctic permafrost, twice as much carbon as is currently wrecking the atmosphere of the planet, all of it scheduled to be released at a date that keeps getting moved up, partially in the form of a gas that multiplies its warming power 86 times over.

Maybe you know that already—there are alarming stories in the news every day, like those, last month, that seemed to suggest satellite data showed the globe warming since 1998 more than twice as fast as scientists had thought (in fact, the underlying story was considerably less alarming than the headlines). Or the news from Antarctica this past May, when a crack in an ice shelf grew 11 miles in six days, then kept going; the break now has just three miles to go—by the time you read this, it may already have met the open water, where it will drop into the sea one of the biggest icebergs ever, a process known poetically as "calving."

But no matter how well-informed you are, you are surely not alarmed enough. Over the past decades, our culture has gone apocalyptic with zombie movies and *Mad Max* dystopias, perhaps the collective result of displaced climate anxiety, and yet when it comes to contemplating real-world warming dangers, we suffer from an incredible failure of imagination. The reasons for that are many: the timid language of scientific probabilities, which the climatologist James Hansen once called "scientific reticence" in a paper chastising scientists for editing their own observations so conscientiously that they failed to communicate how dire the threat really was; the fact that the country is dominated by a group of technocrats who believe any problem can be solved and an opposing culture that doesn't even see warming as a problem worth addressing; the way that climate denialism has made scientists even more cautious in offering speculative warnings; the simple speed of change and, also, its slowness, such that we are only seeing effects now of warming from decades past; our uncertainty about uncertainty, which the climate writer Naomi Oreskes in particular has suggested stops us from preparing as though anything worse than a median outcome were even possible; the way we assume climate change will hit hardest elsewhere, not everywhere; the smallness (two degrees) and largeness (1.8 trillion tons) and abstractness (400 parts per million) of the numbers; the discomfort of considering a problem that is very difficult, if not impossible, to solve; the altogether incomprehensible scale of that problem, which amounts to the prospect of our own annihilation; simple fear. But aversion arising from fear is a form of denial, too.

In between scientific reticence and science fiction is science itself. This article is the result of dozens of interviews and exchanges with climatologists and researchers in related fields and reflects hundreds of scientific papers on the subject of climate change. What follows is not a series of predictions of what will happen—that will be determined in large part by the much-less-certain science of human response. Instead, it is a portrait of our best understanding of where the planet is heading absent aggressive action. It is unlikely that all of these warming scenarios will be fully realized, largely because the devastation along the way will shake our complacency. But those scenarios, and not the present climate, are the baseline. In fact, they are our schedule.

The present tense of climate change—the destruction we've already baked into our future—is horrifying enough. Most people talk as if Miami and Bangladesh still have a chance of surviving; most of the scientists I spoke with assume we'll lose them within the century, even if we stop burning fossil fuel in the next decade. Two degrees of warming used to be considered the threshold of catastrophe: tens of millions of climate refugees unleashed upon an unprepared world. Now two degrees is our goal, per the Paris climate accords, and experts give us only slim odds of hitting it. The U.N. Intergovernmental Panel on Climate Change issues serial reports, often called the "gold standard" of climate research; the most recent one projects us to hit four degrees of warming by the beginning of the next century, should we stay the present course. But that's just a median projection. The upper end of the probability curve runs as high as eight degrees—and the authors still haven't figured out how to deal with that permafrost melt. The IPCC reports also don't fully account for the albedo effect (less ice means less reflected and more absorbed sunlight, hence more warming); more cloud cover (which traps heat); or the dieback of forests and other flora (which extract carbon from the atmosphere). Each of these promises to accelerate warming, and the history of the planet shows that temperature can shift as much as five degrees Celsius within thirteen years. The last time the planet was even four degrees warmer, Peter Brannen points out in *The Ends of the World*, his new history of the planet's major extinction events, the oceans were hundreds of feet higher.

The Earth has experienced five mass extinctions before the one we are living through now, each so complete a slate-wiping of the evolutionary record it functioned as a resetting of the planetary clock, and many climate scientists will tell you they are the best analog for the ecological future we are diving headlong into. Unless you are a teenager, you probably read in your high-school textbooks that these extinctions were the result of asteroids. In fact, all but the one that killed the dinosaurs were caused by climate change produced by greenhouse gas. The most notorious was 252 million years ago; it began when carbon warmed the planet by five degrees, accelerated when that warming triggered the release of methane in the Arctic, and ended with 97 percent of all life on Earth dead. We are currently adding carbon to the atmosphere at a considerably faster rate; by most estimates, at least ten times faster. The rate is accelerating. This is what Stephen Hawking had in mind when he said, this spring, that the species needs to colonize other planets in the next century to survive, and what drove Elon Musk, last month, to unveil his plans to build a Mars habitat in 40 to 100 years. These are nonspecialists, of course, and probably as inclined to irrational panic as you or I. But the many sober-minded scientists I interviewed over the past several months—the most credentialed and tenured in the field, few of them inclined to alarmism and many advisers to the IPCC who nevertheless criticize its conservatism—have quietly reached an apocalyptic conclusion, too: No plausible program of emissions reductions alone can prevent climate disaster.

Over the past few decades, the term "Anthropocene" has climbed out of academic discourse and into the popular imagination—a name given to the geologic era we live in now, and a way to signal that it is a new era, defined on the wall chart of deep history by human intervention. One problem with the term is that it implies a conquest of nature (and even echoes the biblical "dominion"). And however sanguine you might be about the proposition that we have already ravaged the natural world, which we surely have, it is another thing entirely to consider the possibility that we have only provoked it, engineering first in ignorance and then in denial a climate system that will now go to war with us for many centuries, perhaps until it destroys us. That is what Wallace Smith Broecker, the avuncular oceanographer who coined the term "global warming," means when he calls the planet an "angry beast." You could also go with "war machine." Each day we arm it more.

II. Heat Death
The bahraining of New York.

Humans, like all mammals, are heat engines; surviving means having to continually cool off, like panting dogs. For that, the temperature needs to be low enough for the air to act as a kind of refrigerant, drawing heat off the skin so the engine can keep pumping. At seven degrees of warming, that would become impossible for large portions of the planet's equatorial band, and especially the tropics, where humidity adds to the problem; in the jungles of Costa Rica, for instance, where humidity routinely tops 90 percent, simply moving around outside when it's over 105 degrees Fahrenheit would be lethal. And the effect would be fast: Within a few hours, a human body would be cooked to death from both inside and out.

Climate-change skeptics point out that the planet has warmed and cooled many times before, but the climate window that has allowed for human life is very narrow, even by the standards of planetary history. At 11 or 12 degrees of warming, more than half the world's population, as distributed today, would die of direct heat. Things almost certainly won't get that hot this century, though models of unabated emissions do bring us that far eventually. This century, and especially in the tropics, the pain points will pinch much more quickly even than an increase of seven degrees. The key factor is something called wet-bulb temperature, which is a term of measurement as home-laboratory-kit as it sounds: the heat registered on a thermometer wrapped in a damp sock as it's swung around in the air (since the moisture evaporates from a sock more quickly in dry air, this single number reflects both heat and humidity). At present, most regions reach a wet-bulb maximum of 26 or 27 degrees Celsius; the true red line for habitability is 35 degrees. What is called heat stress comes much sooner.

Actually, we're about there already. Since 1980, the planet has experienced a 50-fold increase in the number of places experiencing dangerous or extreme heat; a bigger increase is to come. The five warmest summers in Europe since 1500 have all occurred since 2002, and soon, the IPCC warns, simply being outdoors that time of year will be unhealthy for much of the globe. Even if we meet the Paris goals of two degrees warming, cities like Karachi and Kolkata will become close to uninhabitable, annually encountering deadly heat waves like those that crippled them in 2015. At four degrees, the deadly European heat wave of 2003, which killed as many as 2,000 people a day, will be a normal summer. At six, according to an assessment focused only on effects within the U.S. from the National Oceanic and Atmospheric Administration, summer labor of any kind would become impossible in the lower Mississippi Valley, and everybody in the country east of the Rockies would be under more heat stress than anyone, anywhere, in the world today. As Joseph Romm has put it in his authoritative primer *Climate Change: What Everyone Needs to Know*, heat stress in New York City would exceed that of present-day Bahrain, one of the planet's hottest spots, and the temperature in Bahrain "would induce hyperthermia in even sleeping humans." The high-end IPCC estimate, remember, is two degrees warmer still. By the end of the century, the World Bank has estimated, the coolest months in tropical South America, Africa, and the Pacific are likely to be warmer than the warmest months at the end of the 20th century. Air-conditioning can help but will ultimately only add to the carbon problem; plus, the climate-controlled malls of the Arab emirates aside, it is not remotely plausible to wholesale air-condition all the hottest parts of the world, many of them also the poorest. And indeed, the crisis will be most dramatic across the Middle East and Persian Gulf, where in 2015 the heat index registered temperatures as high as 163 degrees Fahrenheit. As soon as several decades from now, the hajj will become physically impossible for the 2 million Muslims who make the pilgrimage each year.

It is not just the hajj, and it is not just Mecca; heat is already killing us. In the sugar-cane region of El Salvador, as much as one-fifth of the population has chronic kidney disease, including over a quarter of the men, the presumed result of dehydration from working the fields they were able to comfortably harvest as recently as two decades ago. With dialysis, which is expensive, those with kidney failure can expect to live five years; without it, life expectancy is in the weeks. Of course, heat stress promises to pummel us in places other than our kidneys, too. As I type that sentence, in the California desert in mid-June, it is 121 degrees outside my door. It is not a record high.

III. The End of Food
Praying for cornfields in the tundra.

Climates differ and plants vary, but the basic rule for staple cereal crops grown at optimal temperature is that for every degree of warming, yields decline by 10 percent. Some estimates run as high as 15 or even 17 percent. Which means that if the planet is five degrees warmer at the end of the century, we may have as many as 50 percent more people to feed and 50 percent less grain to give them. And proteins are worse: It takes 16 calories of grain to produce just a single calorie of hamburger meat, butchered from a cow that spent its life polluting the climate with methane farts.

Pollyannaish plant physiologists will point out that the cereal-crop math applies only to those regions already at peak growing temperature, and they are right—theoretically, a warmer climate will make it easier to grow corn in Greenland. But as the pathbreaking work by Rosamond Naylor and David Battisti has shown, the tropics are already too hot to efficiently grow grain, and those places where grain is produced today are already at optimal growing temperature— which means even a small warming will push them down the slope of declining productivity. And you can't easily move croplands north a few hundred miles, because yields in places like remote Canada and Russia are limited by the quality of soil there; it takes many centuries for the planet to produce optimally fertile dirt.

Drought might be an even bigger problem than heat, with some of the world's most arable land turning quickly to desert. Precipitation is notoriously hard to model, yet predictions for later this century are basically unanimous: unprecedented droughts nearly everywhere food is today produced. By 2080, without dramatic reductions in emissions, southern Europe will be in permanent extreme drought, much worse than the American dust bowl ever was. The same will be true in Iraq and Syria and much of the rest of the Middle East; some of the most densely populated parts of Australia, Africa, and South America; and the breadbasket regions of China. None of these places, which today supply much of the world's food, will be reliable sources of any. As for the original dust bowl: The droughts in the American plains and Southwest would not just be worse than in the 1930s, a 2015 NASA study predicted, but worse than any droughts in a thousand years—and that includes those that struck between 1100 and 1300, which "dried up all the rivers East of the Sierra Nevada mountains" and may have been responsible for the death of the Anasazi civilization.

Remember, we do not live in a world without hunger as it is. Far from it: Most estimates put the number of undernourished at 800 million globally. In case you haven't heard, this spring has already brought an unprecedented quadruple famine to Africa and the Middle East; the U.N. has warned that separate starvation events in Somalia, South Sudan, Nigeria, and Yemen could kill 20 million this year alone.

IV. Climate Plagues
What happens when the bubonic ice melts?

Rock, in the right spot, is a record of planetary history, eras as long as millions of years flattened by the forces of geological time into strata with amplitudes of just inches, or just an inch, or even less. Ice works that way, too, as a climate ledger, but it is also frozen history, some of which can be reanimated when unfrozen. There are now, trapped in Arctic ice, diseases that have not circulated in the air for millions of years—in some cases, since before humans were around to encounter them. Which means our immune systems would have no idea how to fight back when those prehistoric plagues emerge from the ice.

The Arctic also stores terrifying bugs from more recent times. In Alaska, already, researchers have discovered remnants of the 1918 flu that infected as many as 500 million and killed as many as 100 million—about 5 percent of the world's population and almost six times as many as had died in the world war for which the pandemic served as a kind of gruesome capstone. As the BBC reported in May, scientists suspect smallpox and the bubonic plague are trapped in Siberian ice, too—an abridged history of devastating human sickness, left out like egg salad in the Arctic sun.

Experts caution that many of these organisms won't actually survive the thaw and point to the fastidious lab conditions under which they have already reanimated several of them—the 32,000-year-old "extremophile" bacteria revived in 2005, an 8 million-year-old bug brought back to life in 2007, the 3.5 million-year-old one a Russian scientist self-injected just out of curiosity—to suggest that those are necessary conditions for the return of such ancient plagues. But already last year, a boy was killed and 20 others infected by anthrax released when retreating permafrost exposed the frozen carcass of a reindeer killed by the bacteria at least 75 years earlier; 2,000 present-day reindeer were infected, too, carrying and spreading the disease beyond the tundra.

What concerns epidemiologists more than ancient diseases are existing scourges relocated, rewired, or even re-evolved by warming. The first effect is geographical. Before the early-modern period, when adventuring sailboats accelerated the mixing of peoples and their bugs, human provinciality was a guard against pandemic. Today, even with globalization and the enormous intermingling of human populations, our ecosystems are mostly stable, and this functions as another limit, but global warming will scramble those ecosystems and help disease trespass those limits as surely as Cortés did. You don't worry much about dengue or malaria if you are living in Maine or France. But as the tropics creep northward and mosquitoes migrate with them, you will. You didn't much worry about Zika a couple of years ago, either.

As it happens, Zika may also be a good model of the second worrying effect—disease mutation. One reason you hadn't heard about Zika until recently is that it had been trapped in Uganda; another is that it did not, until recently, appear to cause birth defects. Scientists still don't entirely understand what happened, or what they missed. But there are things we do know for sure about how climate affects some diseases: Malaria, for instance, thrives in hotter regions not just because the mosquitoes that carry it do, too, but because for every degree increase in temperature, the parasite reproduces ten times faster. Which is one reason that the World Bank estimates that by 2050, 5.2 billion people will be reckoning with it.

V. Unbreathable Air
A rolling death smog that suffocates millions.

Our lungs need oxygen, but that is only a fraction of what we breathe. The fraction of carbon dioxide is growing: It just crossed 400 parts per million, and high-end estimates extrapolating from current trends suggest it will hit 1,000 ppm by 2100. At that concentration, compared to the air we breathe now, human cognitive ability declines by 21 percent.

Other stuff in the hotter air is even scarier, with small increases in pollution capable of shortening life spans by ten years. The warmer the planet gets, the more ozone forms, and by mid-century, Americans will likely suffer a 70 percent increase in unhealthy ozone smog, the National Center for Atmospheric Research has projected. By 2090, as many as 2 billion people globally will be breathing air above the WHO "safe" level; one paper last month showed that, among other effects, a pregnant mother's exposure to ozone raises the child's risk of autism (as much as tenfold, combined with other environmental factors). Which does make you think again about the autism epidemic in West Hollywood.

Already, more than 10,000 people die each day from the small particles emitted from fossil-fuel burning; each year, 339,000 people die from wildfire smoke, in part because climate change has extended forest-fire season (in the U.S., it's increased by 78 days since 1970). By 2050, according to the U.S. Forest Service, wildfires will be twice as destructive as they are today; in some places, the area burned could grow fivefold. What worries people even more is the effect that would have on emissions, especially when the fires ravage forests arising out of peat. Peatland fires in Indonesia in 1997, for instance, added to the global CO_2 release by up to 40 percent, and more burning only means more warming only means more burning. There is also the terrifying possibility that rain forests like the Amazon, which in 2010 suffered its second "hundred-year drought" in the space of five years, could dry out enough to become vulnerable to these kinds of devastating, rolling forest fires—which would not only expel enormous amounts of carbon into the atmosphere but also shrink the size of the forest. That is especially bad because the Amazon alone provides 20 percent of our oxygen.

Then there are the more familiar forms of pollution. In 2013, melting Arctic ice remodeled Asian weather patterns, depriving industrial China of the natural ventilation systems it had come to depend on, which blanketed much of the country's north in an unbreathable smog. Literally unbreathable. A metric called the Air Quality Index categorizes the risks and tops out at the 301-to-500 range, warning of "serious aggravation of heart or lung disease and premature mortality in persons with cardiopulmonary disease and the elderly" and, for all others, "serious risk of respiratory effects"; at that level, "everyone should avoid all outdoor exertion." The Chinese "airpocalypse" of 2013 peaked at what would have been an Air Quality Index of over 800. That year, smog was responsible for a third of all deaths in the country.

VI. Perpetual War
The violence baked into heat.

Climatologists are very careful when talking about Syria. They want you to know that while climate change did produce a drought that contributed to civil war, it is not exactly fair to say that the conflict is the result of warming; next door, for instance, Lebanon suffered the same crop failures. But researchers like Marshall Burke and Solomon Hsiang have managed to quantify some of the non-obvious relationships between temperature and violence: For every half-degree of warming, they say, societies will see between a 10 and 20 percent increase in the likelihood of armed conflict. In climate science, nothing is simple, but the arithmetic is harrowing: A planet five degrees warmer would have at least half again as many wars as we do today. Overall, social conflict could more than double this century.

This is one reason that, as nearly every climate scientist I spoke to pointed out, the U.S. military is obsessed with climate change: The drowning of all American Navy bases by sea-level rise is trouble enough, but being the world's policeman is quite a bit harder when the crime rate doubles. Of course, it's not just Syria where climate has contributed to conflict. Some speculate that the elevated level of strife across the Middle East over the past generation reflects the pressures of global warming—a hypothesis all the more cruel considering that warming began accelerating when the industrialized world extracted and then burned the region's oil.

What accounts for the relationship between climate and conflict? Some of it comes down to agriculture and economics; a lot has to do with forced migration, already at a record high, with at least 65 million displaced people wandering the planet right now. But there is also the simple fact of individual irritability. Heat increases municipal crime rates, and swearing on social media, and the likelihood that a major-league pitcher, coming to the mound after his teammate has been hit by a pitch, will hit an opposing batter in retaliation. And the arrival of air-conditioning in the developed world, in the middle of the past century, did little to solve the problem of the summer crime wave.

VII. Permanent Economic Collapse
Dismal capitalism in a half-poorer world.

The murmuring mantra of global neoliberalism, which prevailed between the end of the Cold War and the onset of the Great Recession, is that economic growth would save us from anything and everything. But in the aftermath of the 2008 crash, a growing number of historians studying what they call "fossil capitalism" have begun to suggest that the entire history of swift economic growth, which began somewhat suddenly in the 18th century, is not the result of innovation or trade or the dynamics of global capitalism but simply our discovery of fossil fuels and all their raw power—a onetime injection of new "value" into a system that had previously been characterized by global subsistence living. Before fossil fuels, nobody lived better than their parents or grandparents or ancestors from 500 years before, except in the immediate aftermath of a great plague like the Black Death, which allowed the lucky survivors to gobble up the resources liberated by mass graves. After we've burned all the fossil fuels, these scholars suggest, perhaps we will return to a "steady state" global economy. Of course, that onetime injection has a devastating long-term cost: climate change.

The most exciting research on the economics of warming has also come from Hsiang and his colleagues, who are not historians of fossil capitalism but who offer some very bleak analysis of their own: Every degree Celsius of warming costs, on average, 1.2 percent of GDP (an enormous number, considering we count growth in the low single digits as "strong"). This is the sterling work in the field, and their median projection is for a 23 percent loss in per capita earning globally by the end of this century (resulting from changes in agriculture, crime, storms, energy, mortality, and labor).

Tracing the shape of the probability curve is even scarier: There is a 12 percent chance that climate change will reduce global output by more than 50 percent by 2100, they say, and a 51 percent chance that it lowers per capita GDP by 20 percent or more by then, unless emissions decline. By comparison, the Great Recession lowered global GDP by about 6 percent, in a onetime shock; Hsiang and his colleagues estimate a one-in-eight chance of an ongoing and irreversible effect by the end of the century that is eight times worse.

The scale of that economic devastation is hard to comprehend, but you can start by imagining what the world would look like today with an economy half as big, which would produce only half as much value, generating only half as much to offer the workers of the world. It makes the grounding of flights out of heat-stricken Phoenix last month seem like pathetically small economic potatoes. And, among other things, it makes the idea of postponing government action on reducing emissions and relying solely on growth and technology to solve the problem an absurd business calculation.

Every round-trip ticket on flights from New York to London, keep in mind, costs the Arctic three more square meters of ice.

VIII. Poisoned Oceans
Sulfide burps off the skeleton coast.

That the sea will become a killer is a given. Barring a radical reduction of emissions, we will see at least four feet of sea-level rise and possibly ten by the end of the century. A third of the world's major cities are on the coast, not to mention its power plants, ports, navy bases, farmlands, fisheries, river deltas, marshlands, and rice-paddy empires, and even those above ten feet will flood much more easily, and much more regularly, if the water gets that high. At least 600 million people live within ten meters of sea level today.

But the drowning of those homelands is just the start. At present, more than a third of the world's carbon is sucked up by the oceans—thank God, or else we'd have that much more warming already. But the result is what's called "ocean acidification," which, on its own, may add a half a degree to warming this century. It is also already burning through the planet's water basins—you may remember these as the place where life arose in the first place. You have probably heard of "coral bleaching"—that is, coral dying—which is very bad news, because reefs support as much as a quarter of all marine life and supply food for half a billion people. Ocean acidification will fry fish populations directly, too, though scientists aren't yet sure how to predict the effects on the stuff we haul out of the ocean to eat; they do know that in acid waters, oysters and mussels will struggle to grow their shells, and that when the pH of human blood drops as much as the oceans' pH has over the past generation, it induces seizures, comas, and sudden death.

That isn't all that ocean acidification can do. Carbon absorption can initiate a feedback loop in which underoxygenated waters breed different kinds of microbes that turn the water still more "anoxic," first in deep ocean "dead zones," then gradually up toward the surface. There, the small fish die out, unable to breathe, which means oxygen-eating bacteria thrive, and the feedback loop doubles back. This process, in which dead zones grow like cancers, choking off marine life and wiping out fisheries, is already quite advanced in parts of the Gulf of Mexico and just off Namibia, where hydrogen sulfide is bubbling out of the sea along a thousand-mile stretch of land known as the "Skeleton Coast." The name originally referred to the detritus of the whaling industry, but today it's more apt than ever. Hydrogen sulfide is so toxic that evolution has trained us to recognize the tiniest, safest traces of it, which is why our noses are so exquisitely skilled at registering flatulence. Hydrogen sulfide is also the thing that finally did us in that time 97 percent of all life on Earth died, once all the feedback loops had been triggered and the circulating jet streams of a warmed ocean ground to a halt—it's the planet's preferred gas for a natural holocaust. Gradually, the ocean's dead zones spread, killing off marine species that had dominated the oceans for hundreds of millions of years, and the gas the inert waters gave off into the atmosphere poisoned everything on land. Plants, too. It was millions of years before the oceans recovered.

IX. The Great Filter
Our present eeriness cannot last.

So why can't we see it? In his recent book-length essay *The Great Derangement*, the Indian novelist Amitav Ghosh wonders why global warming and natural disaster haven't become major subjects of contemporary fiction—why we don't seem able to imagine climate catastrophe, and why we haven't yet had a spate of novels in the genre he basically imagines into half-existence and names "the environmental uncanny." "Consider, for example, the stories that congeal around questions like, 'Where were you when the Berlin Wall fell?' or 'Where were you on 9/11?'" he writes. "Will it ever be possible to ask, in the same vein, 'Where were you at 400 ppm?' or 'Where were you when the Larsen B ice shelf broke up?'" His answer: Probably not, because the dilemmas and dramas of climate change are simply incompatible with the kinds of stories we tell ourselves about ourselves, especially in novels, which tend to emphasize the journey of an individual conscience rather than the poisonous miasma of social fate.

Surely this blindness will not last—the world we are about to inhabit will not permit it. In a six-degree-warmer world, the Earth's ecosystem will boil with so many natural disasters that we will just start calling them "weather": a constant swarm of out-of-control typhoons and tornadoes and floods and droughts, the planet assaulted regularly with climate events that not so long ago destroyed whole civilizations. The strongest hurricanes will come more often, and we'll have to invent new categories with which to describe them; tornadoes will grow longer and wider and strike much more frequently, and hail rocks will quadruple in size. Humans used to watch the weather to prophesy the future; going forward, we will see in its wrath the vengeance of the past. Early naturalists talked often about "deep time"—the perception they had, contemplating the grandeur of this valley or that rock basin, of the profound slowness of nature. What lies in store for us is more like what the Victorian anthropologists identified as "dreamtime," or "everywhen": the semi-mythical experience, described by Aboriginal Australians, of encountering, in the present moment, an out-of-time past, when ancestors, heroes, and demigods crowded an epic stage. You can find it already watching footage of an iceberg collapsing into the sea—a feeling of history happening all at once.

It is. Many people perceive climate change as a sort of moral and economic debt, accumulated since the beginning of the Industrial Revolution and now come due after several centuries—a helpful perspective, in a way, since it is the carbon-burning processes that began in 18th-century England that lit the fuse of everything that followed. But more than half of the carbon humanity has exhaled into the atmosphere in its entire history has been emitted in just the past three decades; since the end of World War II, the figure is 85 percent. Which means that, in the length of a single generation, global warming has brought us to the brink of planetary catastrophe, and that the story of the industrial world's kamikaze mission is also the story of a single lifetime. My father's, for instance: born in 1938, among his first memories the news of Pearl Harbor and the mythic Air Force of the propaganda films that followed, films that doubled as advertisements for imperial-American industrial might; and among his last memories the coverage of the desperate signing of the Paris climate accords on cable news, ten weeks before he died of lung cancer last July. Or my mother's: born in 1945, to German Jews fleeing the smokestacks through which their relatives were incinerated, now enjoying her 72nd year in an American commodity paradise, a paradise supported by the supply chains of an industrialized developing world. She has been smoking for 57 of those years, unfiltered.

Or the scientists'. Some of the men who first identified a changing climate (and given the generation, those who became famous were men) are still alive; a few are even still working. Wally Broecker is 84 years old and drives to work at the Lamont-Doherty Earth Observatory across the Hudson every day from the Upper West Side. Like most of those who first raised the alarm, he believes that no amount of emissions reduction alone can meaningfully help avoid disaster. Instead, he puts his faith in carbon capture—untested technology to extract carbon dioxide from the atmosphere, which Broecker estimates will cost at least several trillion dollars—and various forms of "geoengineering," the catchall name for a variety of moon-shot technologies far-fetched enough that many climate scientists prefer to regard them as dreams, or nightmares, from science fiction. He is especially focused on what's called the aerosol approach—dispersing so much sulfur dioxide into the atmosphere that when it converts to sulfuric acid, it will cloud a fifth of the horizon and reflect back 2 percent of the sun's rays, buying the planet at least a little wiggle room, heat-wise. "Of course, that would make our sunsets very red, would bleach the sky, would make more acid rain," he says. "But you have to look at the magnitude of the problem. You got to watch that you don't say the giant problem shouldn't be solved because the solution causes some smaller problems." He won't be around to see that, he told me. "But in your lifetime . . ."

Jim Hansen is another member of this godfather generation. Born in 1941, he became a climatologist at the University of Iowa, developed the groundbreaking "Zero Model" for projecting climate change, and later became the head of climate research at NASA, only to leave under pressure when, while still a federal employee, he filed a lawsuit against the federal government charging inaction on warming (along the way he got arrested a few times for protesting, too). The lawsuit, which is brought by a collective called Our Children's Trust and is often described as "kids versus climate change," is built on an appeal to the equal-protection clause, namely, that in failing to take action on warming, the government is violating it by imposing massive costs on future generations; it is scheduled to be heard this winter in Oregon district court. Hansen has recently given up on solving the climate problem with a carbon tax alone, which had been his preferred approach, and has set about calculating the total cost the additional measure of extracting carbon from the atmosphere.

Hansen began his career studying Venus, which was once a very Earth-like planet with plenty of life-supporting water before runaway climate change rapidly transformed it into an arid and uninhabitable sphere enveloped in an unbreathable gas; he switched to studying our planet by 30, wondering why he should be squinting across the solar system to explore rapid environmental change when he could see it all around him on the planet he was standing on. "When we wrote our first paper on this, in 1981," he told me, "I remember saying to one of my co-authors, 'This is going to be very interesting. Sometime during our careers, we're going to see these things beginning to happen.'"

Several of the scientists I spoke with proposed global warming as the solution to Fermi's famous paradox, which asks, If the universe is so big, then why haven't we encountered any other intelligent life in it? The answer, they suggested, is that the natural life span of a civilization may be only several thousand years, and the life span of an industrial civilization perhaps only several hundred. In a universe that is many billions of years old, with star systems separated as much by time as by space, civilizations might emerge and develop and burn themselves up simply too fast to ever find one another. Peter Ward, a charismatic paleontologist among those responsible for discovering that the planet's mass extinctions were caused by greenhouse gas, calls this the "Great Filter": "Civilizations rise, but there's an environmental filter that causes them to die off again and disappear fairly quickly," he told me. "If you look at planet Earth, the filtering we've had in the past has been in these mass extinctions." The mass extinction we are now living through has only just begun; so much more dying is coming.

And yet, improbably, Ward is an optimist. So are Broecker and Hansen and many of the other scientists I spoke to. We have not developed much of a religion of meaning around climate change that might comfort us, or give us purpose, in the face of possible annihilation. But climate scientists have a strange kind of faith: We will find a way to forestall radical warming, they say, because we must.

It is not easy to know how much to be reassured by that bleak certainty, and how much to wonder whether it is another form of delusion; for global warming to work as parable, of course, someone needs to survive to tell the story. The scientists know that to even meet the Paris goals, by 2050, carbon emissions from energy and industry, which are still rising, will have to fall by half each decade; emissions from land use (deforestation, cow farts, etc.) will have to zero out; and we will need to have invented technologies to extract, annually, twice as much carbon from the atmosphere as the entire planet's plants now do. Nevertheless, by and large, the scientists have an enormous confidence in the ingenuity of humans—a confidence perhaps bolstered by their appreciation for climate change, which is, after all, a human invention, too. They point to the Apollo project, the hole in the ozone we patched in the 1980s, the passing of the fear of mutually assured destruction. Now we've found a way to engineer our own doomsday, and surely we will find a way to engineer our way out of it, one way or another. The planet is not used to being provoked like this, and climate systems designed to give feedback over centuries or millennia prevent us—even those who may be watching closely—from fully imagining the damage done already to the planet. But when we do truly see the world we've made, they say, we will also find a way to make it livable. For them, the alternative is simply unimaginable.

ROXANE GAY

■

An Excerpt from *Hunger*

FROM *Hunger: A Memoir of (My) Body*

I HESITATE TO WRITE about fat bodies and my fat body especially. I know that to be frank about my body makes some people uncomfortable. It makes me uncomfortable too. I have been accused of being full of self-loathing and of being fat-phobic. There is truth to the former accusation and I reject the latter. I do, however, live in a world where the open hatred of fat people is vigorously tolerated and encouraged. I am a product of my environment.

Oftentimes, the people who I make uncomfortable by admitting that I don't love being fat are what I like to call Lane Bryant fat. They can still buy clothes at stores like Lane Bryant, which offers sizes up to 26/28. They weigh 150 or 200 pounds less than I do. They know some of the challenges of being fat, but they don't know the challenges of being *very* fat.

To be clear, the fat acceptance movement is important, affirming, and profoundly necessary, but I also believe that part of fat acceptance is accepting that some of us struggle with body image and haven't reached a place of peace and unconditional self-acceptance.

I don't know where I fit in with communities of fat people. I'm aware of and regularly read about the Health at Every Size movement and other fat acceptance communities. I admire their work and their messages, find that work a necessary corrective to our culture's toxic attitudes toward women's bodies and fat bodies. I want to be embraced by these communities and their positivity. I want to know how they do it, how they find peace and self-acceptance.

I also want to lose weight. I know I am not healthy at this size (not because I am fat but because I have, for example, high blood pressure). More important, I am not happy at this size, though I am not suffering from the illusion that were I to wake up thin tomorrow, I would be happy and all my problems would be solved.

All things considered, I have a reasonable amount of self-esteem. When I'm around the right people, I feel strong and powerful and sexy. I am not fearless the way people assume I am, but despite all my fears, I am willing to take chances and I like that too about myself.

I hate how people treat and perceive me. I hate how I am extraordinarily visible but invisible. I hate not fitting in so many places where I want to be. I have it wired in my head that if I looked different this would change. Intellectually, I recognize the flaw in the logic, but emotionally, it's not so easy to make sense.

I want to have everything I need in my body and I don't yet, but I will, I think. Or I will get closer. There are days when I am feeling braver. There are days when I am feeling, finally, like I can shed some of this protection I have amassed and be okay. I am not young but I am not old yet. I have a lot of life left, and my god, I want to do something different than what I have done for the last twenty years. I want to move freely. I want to be free.

* * *

I am no stranger to dieting. I understand that, in general, to lose weight you need to eat less and move more. I can diet with reasonable success for months at a time. I restrict my calories and keep track of everything I eat. When I first started dieting under my parents' supervision, I would do this in paper journals. In this modern age, I use an app on my phone. I recognize that, despite what certain weight-loss system commercials would have me believe, I cannot eat everything and anything I want. And that is one of the cruelties of our cultural obsession with weight loss. We're supposed to restrict our eating while indulging in the fantasy that we can, indeed, indulge. It's infuriating. When you're trying to lose weight, you cannot have anything you want. That is, in fact, the whole point. Having anything you want is likely what contributed to your weight gain. Dieting requires deprivation, and it's easier when everyone faces that truth. When I am dieting, I try to face that truth, but I am not terribly successful.

There is always a moment when I am losing weight when I feel better in my body. I breathe easier. I move better. I feel myself getting smaller and stronger. My clothes fall over my body the way they should and then they start to get baggy. I get terrified. I start to worry about my body becoming more vulnerable as it grows smaller. I start to imagine all the ways I could be hurt. I start to remember all the ways I have been hurt.

I also taste hope. I taste the idea of having more choices when I go clothes shopping. I taste the idea of fitting into seats at restaurants, movie theaters, waiting rooms. I taste the idea of walking into a crowded room or through a mall without being stared at and pointed at and talked about. I taste the idea of grocery shopping without strangers taking food they disapprove of out of my cart or offering me unsolicited nutrition advice. I taste the idea of being free of the realities of living in an overweight body. I taste the idea of being free.

And then I worry that I am getting ahead of myself. I worry that I won't be able to keep up better eating, more exercise, taking care of myself. Inevitably, I stumble and then I fall, and then I lose the taste of being free. I lose the taste of hope. I am left feeling low, like a failure. I am left feeling ravenously hungry and then I try to satisfy that hunger so I might undo all the progress I've made. And then I hunger even more.

* * *

I start each day with the best of intentions for living a better, healthier life. Every morning, I wake up and have a few minutes where I am free from my body and my failings. During these moments, I think, *Today, I will make good choices. I will work out. I will eat small portions. I will take the stairs when possible.* Before the day starts, I am fully prepared to tackle the problem of my body, to be better than I have been. But then I get out of bed. Often, I rush to get ready and begin my day because I am not a morning person and I hit Snooze on my alarm several times. I don't eat breakfast because I'm not hungry or I don't have time or there is no food in the house, which are all excuses for not being willing to take proper care of myself. Sometimes, I eat lunch—a sandwich from Subway or Jimmy John's. Or two sandwiches. And chips. And a cookie or three. And it's fine, I tell myself, because I haven't eaten all day. Or I wait until dinner and then the day is nearly done and I can eat whatever I want, I tell myself, because I have not eaten all day.

At night, I have to face myself and all the ways I have failed. Most days, I haven't exercised. I haven't made any of the good choices I intended to make when the day began. Whatever happens next doesn't matter, so I binge and eat even more of whatever I want. As I fall asleep, my stomach churning, the acids making my heartburn flare, I think about the next day. I think, *Tomorrow, I will make good choices.* I am always holding on to the hope of tomorrow.

FRANK B. WILDERSON III

■

An Excerpt from *Blacks and the Master/Slave Relation*

FROM *Afro-Pessimism*

C. S. Soong: *The question for today is: How do we properly situate Black people in today's world? What is their position in relation to other people? And what is the nature of their vulnerability to violence? Those questions can be addressed in a number of ways. Conservatives, liberals, and radicals offer perspectives that perhaps you've heard over time. The answer offered by my guest today is singular and provocative, not least because he calls Black people—all Black people—slaves. But what does Frank Wilderson III mean by "slave"? Why does he argue that the master/slave relation cannot be analogized with the capitalist/worker relation? And what does he mean when he asserts that slavery is social death, and that slaves, that is, Blacks, are subject to gratuitous violence because their masters, that is, all non-Blacks, need to exercise that violence in order to give their lives, their non-Black lives, integrity and coherence? Frank Wilderson is a writer, professor of African American Studies and Drama at UC Irvine, and founder of what's called the Afro-Pessimism movement. His books in-*clude Red, White and Black: Cinema and the Structure of U.S. An-tagonisms *and* Incognegro: A Memoir of Exile and Apartheid. *Frank spent five years in South Africa as an elected official in the African National Congress during that country's transition from apartheid, and he was a member of the ANC's armed wing. When Frank Wilderson joined me recently in the studio, I began by asking how important Marxism has been to his understanding of capitalism.*

Frank Wilderson: I think that when I began to study Marxism in college I understood that here was a theory that took a kind of attitude toward the world that was uncompromising. That was valuable to me because before that in junior high school and in high school I had seen the kind of performative political labor of people in the Panthers and people in the Students for a Democratic Society—part of that time was here—and I knew that these folks were on a mission that was more robust and more unflinching than the mission of certain types of Bobby Kennedy Democrats and members of the Civil Rights movement. When I actually began to study the theory I understood why their performance was so much more unflinching than other peoples' performance. So I think the study of Marxism helped me get into thinking about relations of power, which I think is more important than simply thinking about the way power performs.

CSS: *In other words, structures of power as opposed to how power tends to manifest itself in individual relations?*
FW: Yes, and I also mean that if you kind of turn your head sideways and listen to most Americans on the Left talk about politics, what you're going to hear is that the rhetorical weighting of their discourse tends to be heavily weighted on discriminatory actions, the effects of unfair relations on people. And so what we really don't do so much in this country is—and this is what I found to be very different when I started traveling the world, when I went to Italy, and various places in South America and Africa—we're not as readily able to think about power as a structure. We tend to think about power as a performance, a series of discriminatory acts. That's okay if you're a Liberal-Humanist-reformist, but if you're a revolutionary, that simply leads you down a track of increasing wages or getting more rights for women or ending racial discrimination and you're finding yourself in the same kind of cycle of performative oppression ten, twenty years later without an analysis of why the "fix" that you had years ago doesn't last and isn't working now.

CSS: *You see the master/slave relation as the essential antagonism. What do you mean by that? A lot of people would think, okay, slavery in the*

U.S., so Black slavery, and then 1865, the formal end of slavery. But then of course you have slavery today and we hear about issues with people in bondage, debt bondage, and other forms of bondage. So when you say the master/slave relation, what are you specifically referring to?

FW: There is no way I can actually answer that in a compact way, I think I have to step back a minute. So what Afro-pessimism—the conceptual lens or framework that myself and other people are working on—assumes is that you have to begin with an analysis of slavery that corrects the heretofore thinking about it. So the first thing that happens—and this is built on the work of Orlando Patterson's 1982 tome Slavery and Social Death—the first thing we have to do is screw our heads on backwards. In other words, stop defining slavery through the experience of slaves. What happens normally is that people think of slavery as forced labor and people in chains. What Orlando Patterson does is shows that what slavery really is, is social death. In other words, social death defines the relation between the slave and all others. Forced labor is an example of the experience that slaves might have, but not all slaves were forced to work. So if you then move by saying that slavery is social death, by definition, then what is social death? Social death has three constituent elements: One is gratuitous violence, which means that the body of the slave is open to the violence of all others. Whether he or she receives that violence or not, he or she exists in a state of structural or open vulnerability. This vulnerability is not contingent upon his or her transgressing some type of law, as in going on strike with the worker. The other point is that the slave is natally alienated, which is to say that the temporality of one's life that is manifest in filial and afilial relations—the capacity to have families and the capacity to have associative relations—may exist very well in your head. You might say, "I have a father, I have a mother," but, in point of fact, the world does not recognize or incorporate your filial relations into its understanding of family. And the reason that the world can do this goes back to point number one: because you exist in a regime of violence which is gratuitous, open, and you are openly vulnerable to everyone else, not a regime of violence that is contingent upon you being a transgressed worker or transgressing woman or someone like that. And the third point is general dishonor, which is to say, you are dishonored in your very being—and I think that this is the nature of Blackness with everyone else. You're dishonored prior to your performance of dishonored actions. So it takes a long time to build this but in a nutshell that's it. And so that's one of the moves of Afro-pessimism. If you take that move and you take out property relations—someone who's owned by someone else—you take that out of the definition of slavery and you take out forced labor, and if you replace that with social death and those three constituent elements, what you have is a continuum of slavery-subjugation that Black people exist in and 1865 is a blip on the screen. It is not a paradigmatic moment, it is an experiential moment, which is to say that the technology of enslavement simply morphs and shape shifts—it doesn't end with that.

CSS: *If Orlando Patterson, who is a sociologist at Harvard, argues that forced labor is not a defining characteristic of slavery, if he says that naked violence is one of the key elements of social death, which is slavery, and if the violence directed at Blacks is not based on, as you said, this person transgressing in some way, being disobedient in some way, refusing to consent in some way to what the ruling class thinks or does, then why is violence freely directed at Blacks? What is the reason that the non-white or the master in the master/slave relation treats Blacks violently?*
FW: The short answer is that violence against the slave is integral to the production of that psychic space called social life. The repetitive nature of violence against the slave does not have the same type of utility that violence against the post-colonial subject has—in other words, in the first instance, to secure and maintain the occupation of land. It does not have the utility of violence against the working class, which would be to secure and maintain the extraction of surplus-value and the wage. We have to think more libidinally and in a more robust fashion. This is where it becomes really controversial and really troubling for a lot of people because what Patterson is arguing, and what people like myself and professor Jared Sexton and Saidiya Hartman at Columbia University have extended, is to say that what we need to do is begin to think of violence not as having essentially the kind of political or economic utility that violence in other revolutionary paradigms have. Violence against the slave sustains a kind of psychic stability for all others who are not slaves.

CSS: *When you say that—and I've read some of your writings on the subject—it seems like you're suggesting that only if some population perceives another population as inferior, or as so degraded that anything can be done to them—unless they have that other in mind, that somehow, psychologically and psychically, they can't have the integrity that they want. Is that correct? And why would that be the case psychologically? Why would somebody need to have some other person seen in that light in order to feel actualized, in order to feel worthy of life?*

FW: It's a very good question and we could spend several hours on it, but what I'm trying to do is give you shorthand answers that have integrity and hopefully your listeners will do some more reading and research to actually see how these mechanisms work. But let's take it outside of the way in which I and other Afro-pessimists are theorizing it. One of our claims is that Blackness cannot be dis-imbricated from slaveness—that is a very controversial claim; that claim is actually the fault line right now of African and Black Studies across the country, the claim that Blackness and slaveness cannot be dis-imbricated, cannot be pulled apart. But I can't argue against everyone who disagrees with that right now. One of the points that Patterson makes at a higher level of abstraction is that the concept of community, and the concept of freedom, and the concept of communal and interpersonal presence, actually needs a conceptual antithesis. In other words, you can't think community without being able to register non-community. His book *Slavery and Social Death* goes back thousands of years and covers slavery in China and all over the world and he says that communal coherence has a lot of positive attributes: this is my language, this is how I organize my polity, these are the anthropological accoutrements of how we work our customs—but at the end of the day what it needs to know is what it is not. So the idea of freedom and the idea of communal life and the idea of civic relations has to have a kind of point of attention which is absent of that or different from that. This is the function that slavery presents or provides to coherence so that prior to Columbus, for example, the Choctaw might have someone inside a Choctaw community who transgresses the codes of the community so fiercely that they're given a choice, and the choice at this moment of a transgression, which is beyond-the-beyond, is between real death—"We will kill you in an execution"—or social death. Nothing changes in the mind of that person tomorrow or the day after he or she chooses social death. He or she still thinks they have a cosmology, that they have intimate family relations, but the point that Patterson is making is that everything changes in the structure of that person's dynamic with the rest of the tribe. So now that that person is a slave, that person is socially dead. This is bad for that person, obviously, but what he is suggesting is that that type of action regenerates the knowledge of our existence for everyone else. Now where I and some others take Patterson further is to say that Black, Blackness, and even the thing called Africa, cannot be dis-imbricated, cannot be pulled apart from that smaller scale process that he talks about with respect to Chinese communities or the Choctaw. In other words, there is a global consensus that Africa is the location of sentient beings who are outside of global community, who are socially dead. That global consensus begins with the Arabs in 625 and it's passed on to the Europeans in 1452. Prior to that global consensus you can't think Black. You can think Uganda, Ashanti, Ndebele, you can think many different cultural identities, but Blackness cannot be dis-imbricated from the global consensus that decides here is the place which is emblematic of that moment the Choctaw person is spun out from social life to social death. That's part of the foundation.

CSS: *This is really provocative. Are you saying then—let's just focus on the U.S.—that every African American, regardless of income or wealth or status, can and should be understood in the figure of the slave who is socially dead in relation to the master, who I presume is white?*
FW: Well, the master is everyone else, whites and their junior partners, which in my book are colored immigrants. It's just that colored immigrants exist in an intra-human status of degradation in relation to white people. They are degraded as humans, but they still exist paradigmatically in that position of the human. So yes, I am saying that. Now part of the reason is that one of the things that we are not doing is talking about the different ways in which different Black people live their existence as slaves. I'm willing to do that, but what's interesting to me is the kind of anxiety that this theory elicits from people other than yourself. I mean this is the calmest conversation that I've had on this subject [laughter]. You could say to someone that you

are a professor at UC Berkeley and there is a person in a sweatshop on the other side of the Rio Grande. This person in the sweatshop is working sixteen hours a day, cannot go to the bathroom, dies on the job from lack of medical benefits . . . and you are a kind of labor aristocrat. And they could say, "Okay, well that's interesting." And you could say to that person, "But if you read the work of Antonio Negri, the Italian communist, you come to understand that even though you live your life as a proletarian differently than a sweatshop laborer, you both stand in relation to capital in this same way, at the level of structural, paradigmatic arrangement." That person would say, "Oh yeah! I get that, I get that." You say to someone that all Blacks are slaves and that we're going to change the definition of slavery because the other things are not definitions, they are actually anecdotes, and your teacher in third grade told you that you don't use an anecdote to define something. And that person says, "Oh wait a minute, I know a person who's richer than me and also Black and they live in the Tenderloin . . ." and it just goes off to the races. It's a symptomatic response primarily because they understand that what Black people suffer is real and comprehensive but there is actually no prescriptive, rhetorical gesture which could actually write a sentence about how to redress that. Most Americans, most people in the world, are not willing to engage in a paradigm of oppression that does not offer some type of way out. But that is what we live with as Black people every day.

CSS: *Let me ask you a personal question, which you can of course refuse to answer. So your wife is white; given what you were telling me about the position of Blacks, what's your sense of whether she could truly ever understand your consciousness, your positioning within society? And if she can't, then what are the prospects of a relationship that could reach as deeply as, for example, two Black people or two white people together could?*

FW: Well, she can't. She tries, but what's interesting and important is that I would never put my marriage out there as a kind of example of what people could aspire to. As a kind of shorthand, I call her my wife and she calls me her husband. But the reality is that I'm her slave. And that doesn't change because we have sentimental—as I would say, contrapuntal—emotions to the contrary. In fact, oftentimes those contrapuntal emotions are mechanisms or means of disavowing the true nature of the relation. Now, I will give her a lot of props for the past eight years that she has actually inculcated this logic. She did her best at that Santa Cruz conference I talked about to tell the white people in that room, "We're not here to think about how we think about ourselves, we're here to think about our complicity as whites with policing. Not as women, not as gays, not as Armenians, not as Jews, but as white." On the other hand, if you read my book *Incognegro*, you'll see that in the first eight years, there was nothing but resistance to that. So that resistance is as traumatizing as the second eight years are regenerative and I will say that the first eight years are what Black people should take away from that. There's no way in hell we should have to go through the kind of resistance that white people and non-Black people have to this particular logic because they know it's the truth. They know their own anxieties about the question, Where is Blackness?, but they can't approach it because what it would mean is a kind of confrontation with people who are intimate to them that they don't know they could withstand. And so the real question is, Will these people do all they can to fall into the abyss of nonexistence?, not about how they will perform as partial allies while keeping their cultural presence.

CSS: *Why would a Black person, why would you, choose intentionally, consciously, to enter into a life relationship in which you perceive yourself as the figure of the slave?*
FW: I don't think it's a fair question because the question implies that, knowing what I know, I can actually change my life in an essential way. The question actually takes us away from the problem that I've outlined and actually puts the responsibility of correcting the situation on me when actually it should be on you.

CSS: *I hear that, and I think that prompts me to ask the final thing I want to bring up with you, which is regarding how we hear a lot about groups and people who are victims. There is this victimhood frame and so these people have been victimized by, let's say, another group of people and then the critique is that, by focusing on that, by concentrating on that, you then deflect attention away from their subjectivity, from their agency, from what they can do about their circumstance. Are you concerned that the master/slave relation, which is positioning Blacks as foremost a victim, in* my mind, and then focusing only or mainly on a group status as victim, tends to deny—and we're speaking here now about Blacks—the kind of agency that, I think you would admit, they have at least some semblance of, and maybe some more than others based on their position in society?

FW: I don't agree with that and we don't have the time to actually get into this, but my book *Red, White and Black* is a critique of agency as a generic category. What I'm saying is that, okay, I'm not Elijah Muhammad, I don't believe that the white man is the devil and that this is all divined by god. I do believe that there is a way out. But I believe that the way out is a kind of violence so magnificent and so comprehensive that it scares the hell out of even radical revolutionaries. So, in other words, the trajectory of violence that Black slave revolts suggest, whether it be in the 21st century or the 19th century, is a violence against the generic categories of life, agency being one of them. That's what I meant by an epistemological catastrophe. Marx posits an epistemological crisis, which is to say moving from one system of human arrangements and relations to another system of human relations and arrangements. What Black people embody is the potential for a catastrophe of human arrangements writ large. I think that there have been moments—the Black Liberation Army in the 1970s and 1980s is a prime example—of how the political violence of the Black Liberation Army far outpaced the anti-capitalist and internationalist discourse that it had and that's what scares people; and as Saidiya Hartman says, "A Black revolution makes everyone freer than they actually want to be." A Marxist revolution blows the lid off of economic relations; a feminist revolution blows the lid off patriarchal relations; a Black revolution blows the lid off the unconscious and relations writ large.

CSS: I have to ask you: When you talk about this violence, in maybe the ideal situation of a Black revolution, what are we talking about concretely? Who or what is the violence directed against? Are we talking about literally the elimination of the master threat physically?

FW: Well, the short answer is that's for me to know and for you to find out [laughter]. And the long answer is that as a professor I'm uniquely unqualified to actually make that answer. I rely on providing analysis and then getting those marching orders from people in the streets.

ANDREW LELAND, CHRIS WARE,
DANIEL CLOWES, AND ANDERS NILSEN

■

A Tribute to Alvin Buenaventura

FROM *The Believer*

For the last five years, the editor and publisher Alvin Buenaventura curated a recurring two-page column for this magazine. Called, simply, "Comics" (scare quotes included), it was often the funniest, strangest, and certainly the most disgusting and most beautiful two pages in any given issue. It was always the first spread I looked at when the new issue came back from the printer. When we learned that Alvin, only forty years old, had suddenly passed away in February of 2016, we asked for remembrances from his stable of regular contributors to the "Comics" pages as well as from his collaborators in his other often marvelously oversize and otherwise uncompromising projects. This issue has endured a long delay, but it's the first to go to press since Alvin's passing, and looking back through these tributes, I am reminded of Alvin's mysterious—and sometimes mystifying—generosity and genius.

—Andrew Leland

Alvin Buenaventura was the most important person in my life outside of my immediate family. He was, to me, among many other things, an art representative, a production assistant, an archivist, a monographer, a tireless advocate and champion, a media representative, a technical adviser, a troubleshooter; but far beyond that, he was my dear and beloved friend, a daily, constant, essential presence in my life.

I said this to anybody who asked about the mysterious Alvin: he was inexplicable, the most singular human being I've ever met. There's nobody else in the world even remotely like him. He can't ever be replaced in any way. He was born into a nondescript, suburban So. Cal. army-brat childhood that could in no way have indicated his future, magically gifted with what can be described only as a perfect eye. It was as apparent in the stuff he found at flea markets and hung on his bathroom wall as in the entirety of his publishing empire, a remarkable series of choices in which there was not a single artistic misstep among the many logistic, personal, and financial ones. All of it had a certain something that often only he could see at first, but once he saw it, you saw it, too. Just two weeks before his death, he and I sat talking on the phone, staring at the listings in an online illustration art auction. We decided to go through and pick our favorite pieces. I went for some obvious stuff, big names like Charles Addams and Heinrich Kley, but Alvin's number one pick was a weird, moody painting of a guy in a cave by an unknown mid-level '50s illustrator. I had completely blipped over it, but he was 100 percent right—it was the best thing in that auction. That painting is now in the mail, headed toward his empty house.

Alvin was a complicated man. He was as kindhearted and generous a person as I've ever met, but he also held deep, complex, immutable grudges. He had what seemed to be a debilitating shyness, barely speaking above an inaudible mumble (I used to pretend I'd heard what he said—with very mixed results—so I didn't have to keep saying What? like an old man all the time), but he was weirdly comfortable around famous artists, difficult lunatics, celebrities, assholes. He felt a parental protectiveness toward his artists to the extent that this soft-spoken, nonaggressive Buddhist once bought a plane ticket to LA to beat up a plagiarist on my behalf before I talked him out of it. He suffered terribly from depression and had gone through some bad spells in the fifteen years I'd known him, but had always managed to get himself back on track. This time was different—he had been in increasing and agonizing pain from an autoimmune disorder and was feeling especially hopeless. All of his close friends and loved ones—and there were many—would have given anything to make him feel better, and we all will wonder what more we could have done, while recognizing that we could never really understand his anguish.

He was as loyal a friend and advocate as I'll ever have. He was the first person to read my books, often by many months, and his generous, idiosyncratic, ramblingly unpunctuated comments are the ones I'll most treasure. I hope to extend a similar loyalty to him in his passing, to uphold his memory, and to be forever inspired by his beautiful and tragic human spirit.

—Daniel Clowes

PS: I had intended to post this to my own website, but I just learned that Alvin carried all my social media passwords to his grave.

Alvin was the one comic-book publisher who was more like a car-toonist than a publisher: shy, riddled by self-doubt and recurring de-pression, he privately suffered despite always trying to bring some cheer into other people's lives. He also brought more interesting, experimental, and unusual artists to the eyes of new readers, and changed more cartoonists' lives for the better than most, if not all, of his contemporaries.

I don't know of any experimental cartoonist of my generation who didn't at some point receive an unannounced package of books and valuable items from Alvin only because he thought we might like it, the parcel arriving with a note dismissively describing its contents as just "cleaning house" or "managing his collection" even though the stuff it contained was rare and, one knew, obtained at great effort and cost; frequently, the notes would go on with detailed, hearten-ing encouragement about one's recent work (which in my own case I greatly treasured, as I have my own tanglings with self-doubt). That he could not, however, always manage his physiological difficulties and his own inner turmoil is now our great loss.

I first met Alvin in the 1990s, when he and his then wife, Carleen, used to take annual cross-country trips across the United States, stopping at various cartoonists' homes to visit and, occasionally, and as they could afford it, buy original artwork. Alvin was one of the very earliest such "drop-ins" (and contributors to my monthly rent) that I can recall. He'd always phone days in advance to make sure he wasn't intruding, and his voice over the telephone was barely audible, like the pope's: quiet, midrange, apologetic, all lowercase—"hi, chris, this is alvin"—a timidity that never changed in all the years I knew him despite our long-cemented friendship. In fact, in the years before caller ID, if I picked up the phone and couldn't make out what was being said, nine times out of ten I knew it wasn't a bad connection but Alvin.

The weird part was that after a few minutes his volume and tone could change considerably, rising to a hearty guffaw if the right quip or bit of gossip was dished up. For all of his pathological shyness, he seemed to be able to get along with anyone after finding the right connection point. And connect he did; he befriended and published dozens of the best cartoonists of our time, both from my generation and the one following, sometimes acting as benefactor to them in ways that were incalculably generous. Alvin curated the comics for Arthur and this very magazine with a divided largesse that seemed to express a frustration that space couldn't be as infinitely divided as time, divvying up a double-page spread into slots that more often than not made the standard newspaper daily strip appear generous. Clearly, he wanted to give as many cartoonists as possible the exposure he felt they all deserved.

As we all got to know him, he hinted that he suffered from maladies that were as physiologically altering as they were psychologically debilitating, and he'd adjust his exercise or dietary regimen to try to deal with them. In the months or years that passed between our seeing each other, he could physically transform, sometimes wildly: at one point a soft, almost unfocused teddy bear, at another a surprisingly buff, heroic-looking fellow, his mop of black hair veering between tousled and shaved clean. Though he always hid behind those thick, round black glasses and his gentle, generally hesitant voice, he was always—perhaps despite his wishes to the contrary—Alvin.

That he leaves behind a newly resuscitated publishing business is a conundrum that my friend and Alvin's closest friend, Dan Clowes, might cite as one of the many contradictions that made up "the Alvin Factor." Lately, things were definitely on the upswing for him; ever the irrepressible collector, he'd just bought more comic artwork and was in the midst of planning a book tour for Dan and had published

Tim Hensley's latest fine work, along with arranging other possible art exhibitions and books. My own emails with him had been only a day or two before he died, and two large boxes from him had appeared on my porch, which I hadn't had time to open before Dan called me with the horrible news.

The boxes, filled with items he'd known I'd like, from Japanese comic collectibles to pristine framed original Little Nemo and Gasoline Alley pages to his most recent publishing efforts, were accompanied by an unassuming note addressed to "Mr. Ware" (it was always to "Mr. Ware"), wishing me the best and hoping that I was well. When he wrote the words—which he sent regular Priority Mail—he would've had only six days to live.

He was an ally, a kindred spirit, and a benefactor to us all. And, Alvin, though I know you'll never hear me now: you were a good person, a generous person, and you will be greatly missed, my friend.

—*Chris Ware*

I first met Alvin Buenaventura at APE in San Francisco in maybe 2003. I remember there being some buzz about this guy who was making letterpress prints of some of my friends' work, but also with some famous people like Dan Clowes and Chris Ware. It felt very mysterious and cool. At some point I went over to his table and found an extremely quiet, humble guy who spoke almost in a whisper, and a very gregarious and friendly woman, all smiles—his wife at the time, Carleen. They acted as if we had all been friends for years. They were both unassuming and welcoming.

When he did eventually invite me to do a print, it was one of a very few moments in my life that felt like I'd been included in some elite, secret club. That feeling had nothing to do with any promise of money—there basically wasn't any—or of notoriety. It was because it was very clear that this person had extremely good, very particular taste—much better and more broad than mine, for example—and his vision of what was worth his time now included something of mine. His remarkable taste and enthusiasm for art were themes for me in hanging out with Alvin, in a couple of ways. I was repeatedly struck by the clarity of his vision. I remember him showing me some Le Dernier Cri books at his house in Oakland once, and being struck by how sure he was of his opinions and enthusiasms about them. I was busily trying to sort out being overwhelmed visually, slightly grossed out, fascinated, jealous, and wanting to seem cool and to like the right things. Encounters with other artists' work often feel compromised in this way: it can occasionally be difficult to set aside my own biases, jealousies, and artistic concerns and see another's work on its own terms. Alvin was one of those rare people whose taste felt immediate, singularly uncomplicated, and clear. It was at once rigorous and generous. It was inspiring to me, and a challenge. It made him a very good publisher, but it also meant that going to his house was like entering a little museum crossed with an incredibly well-curated yard sale, full of treasures. Going to his table at a show promised a lot of new and very compelling work. I always spent too much money at his table, and always wished I could spend a bit more. If all he'd done for me was introduce me to the work of Helge Reumann and Lisa Hanawalt, I'd owe him a debt.

Alvin and I worked on a few projects of various kinds, several of them better as ideas than they turned out to be as realities. He put out a skateboard of mine, of all things, and sold precious few—though he did actually try valiantly to learn to ride it, taking me to a couple of spots in Oakland to skate when I was in town. His enthusiasm for publishing seemed rarely to be inhibited by commercial concerns. He wanted a thing to exist, and so he would do what he could to make it so, the market be damned. Which was part of why what he did was so important, but I know that it became troublesome. We had been discussing doing a small book project this year, one that probably would fit very comfortably into the slot of "not commercially viable." But it was a unique project that would make sense for probably no other publisher. As Dan Clowes wrote, that's what he was: completely unique. There was a slot in the universe that he fit into, alone. That slot is now empty, and it matters a great deal. We are poorer for it.

—*Anders Nilsen*

The original tribute, featured in the August/September 2017 issue of The Believer, *also included contributions from Jonathan Bennett, Lisa Hanawalt, Tim Hensley, Jaime Hernandez, and Clara Bessijelle Johansson.*

■

Six Selected Comics

FROM *Instagram*

These six selected comics have been pulled from Chris (Simpsons artist)'s Instagram account.

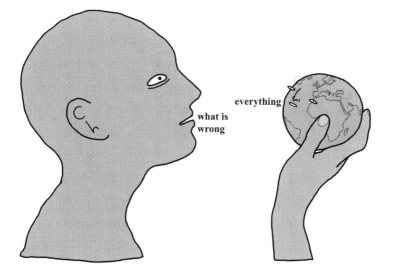

a helpful parenting tip:

children make really good seats when you have tired legs

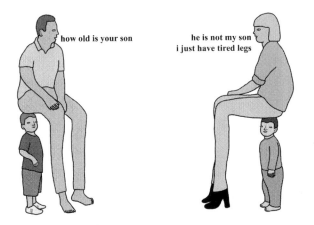

---

how to cheer up a miserable friend:

hide inside your friends toothpaste tube
to give them a mysterious minty fresh surprise

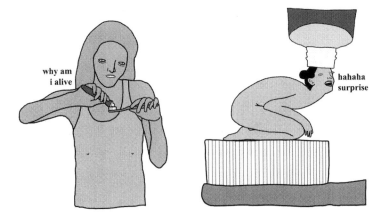

interesting fact of the day

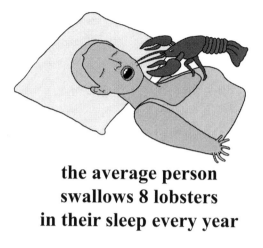

the average person swallows 8 lobsters in their sleep every year

---

a spooky halloween bath trick to play on a friend:
slowly appear out of your friends bath to give them a
haunting wet surprise that they will struggle to forget

i love my cat
because he eats
the mice so i
dont have to
anymore

i love my cat
because he
doesnt mind
that i smell
of fish

why i love my cat

i love my cat
because his
warming smile
takes away
the pain of life

i love my cat
because she
ate my son
so now she is
my son

■

Artist's Statement

FROM *sikkemajenkinsco.com*

THIS IS KARA WALKER'S Artist's Statement for her September 7–October 14, 2017, show at Sikkema, Jenkins & Co. Gallery. Her show has a very long title, which should also be considered part of the work. The title is:

Sikkema Jenkins and Co. is *Compelled* to present The most Astounding and Important Painting show of the fall Art Show viewing season! Collectors of Fine Art will Flock to see the latest Kara Walker offerings, and what is she offering but the Finest Selection of *artworks* by an African-American Living Woman Artist this side of the Mississippi. Modest collectors will find her prices reasonable, those of a heartier disposition will recognize Bargains! Scholars will study and debate the *Historical Value* and *Intellectual Merits* of Miss Walker's Diversionary Tactics. Art Historians will wonder whether the work represents a *Departure* or a *Continuum*. Students of Color will eye her work suspiciously and exercise their free right to Culturally Annihilate her on social media. Parents will cover the eyes of innocent children. School Teachers will reexamine their art history curricula. Prestigious Academic Societies will withdraw their support, former husbands and former lovers will recoil in abject terror. Critics will shake their heads in bemused silence. Gallery Directors will wring their hands at the sight of throngs of the gallery-curious flooding the pavement outside. The Final President of the United States will visibly wince. Empires will fall, although which ones, only time will tell.

Artist's Statement

I don't really feel the need to write a statement about a painting show. I know what you all expect from me and I have complied up to a point. But frankly I am tired, tired of standing up, being counted, tired of "having a voice" or worse "being a role model." Tired, true, of being a featured member of my racial group and/or my gender niche. It's too much, and I write this knowing full well that my right, my capacity to live in this Godforsaken country as a (proudly) raced and (urgently) gendered person is under threat by random groups of white (male) supremacist goons who flaunt a kind of patched together notion of race purity with flags and torches and impressive displays of perpetrator-as-victim sociopathy. I roll my eyes, fold my arms, and wait. How many ways can a person say racism is the real bread and butter of our American mythology, and in how many ways will the racists among our countrymen act out their Turner Diaries race war fantasy combination Nazi Germany and Antebellum South—states which, incidentally, *lost the wars they started*, and always will, precisely because there is no way those white racisms can survive the earth without the rest of us types upholding humanity's best, keeping the motor running on civilization, being good, and preserving nature and all the stuff worth working and living for?

Anyway, this is a show of works on paper and on linen, drawn and collaged using ink, blade, glue, and oil stick. These works were created over the course of the Summer of 2017 (not including the title, which was crafted in May). It's not exhaustive, activist, or comprehensive in any way.

TONGO EISEN-MARTIN

■

Wave at the People Walking Upside Down

FROM *Heaven Is All Goodbyes*

I am off to make a church bell out of a bank window

> "kitchens meant
> more to the masses
> back in the day"

> and before that?

> "we had no enemy"

somewhere in america
the prison bus is running on time

you are going to want
to lose that job
before the revolution hits

> *Somewhere I won't be home for breakfast.*
> *Everyone out here now knows my name.*
> *And I won't be turned against for at least four months.*

The cop in the picket line is a hard-working rookie.
The sign in my hand is getting more and more laughs
                    (something about a numb tumble).

It says, "the picket line got cops in it."

"I can take care of
those windows for you if you want,
but someone else
has to go in your gas tank"

was clear to the man that
rich people had talked too much this year

go ahead and throw down that marble park bench
everyone is looking up at,
you know,
get the Romans out of your mind

Maybe a good night's sleep
would have changed
The last twenty years of my life

—Playing an instrument
Is like punching a wall—

What would you have me do?
Replace the population?
Give brotherhood back to the winter?
Stop smoking cigarettes with the barely dead?

They listen in on the Sabbath

Police called the police on me
—a white candlestick beneath my detention

"I've ruined the soup again,"
thought the judge
as he took off his pilgrim robe
behind a white people's door (and more)

"I didn't get lucky. I got
what was coming to me,"
he toasts

"fight me back,"
the man says, of course, to himself

washing windows with a will to live
tin can on his left shoulder
enjoying the bright brand new blight
with all party goers
(both supernatural and supernaturally down to earth)

what, is this elevator traveling side to side?

Like one thousand bitter polaroid pictures you actually try to eat
All the furniture on this street is nailed to the cement
Cheap furniture, but we have commitment

This morning, an essay opens the conversation between enemies
"why, because you control every gram of processed sugar
between here and a poor man's border?"
"because in the tin can on my left shoulder
I can hear the engines of deindustrialization?"

—You should get into painting,
You know,
Tell lies deeply—

This month, I'm rooting for the traitor

Carting cement to my pillow . . . "here we will build"

I'm high again. Not talking much.

Climb the organ pipes up to our apartment floor

I'm high again. Calling everything church.
Singing along to the courtyard.

Thanks to a horn player's holy past time

Climb up to the rustiest nail

—Put a real jacket on it
Talk about a real five years—

Keep memories like these
In my pocket
Next to the toll receipt

That man lost a wager
with the god of good causes,
you know,
stood up for himself
a little too late
(maybe too early)

I can still see
Twenty angles of his jaw
Zigzagging through
The cold world
Of deindustrialization

"there's an art to it," I will tell my closest friends one day

GUNNHILD ØYEHAUG

■

Meanwhile, on Another Planet

Translated from Norwegian by Kari Dickson

FROM *Knots*

DIX24 IS SITTING AT THE KITCHEN TABLE when PUZ32 slides
into the room. DIX24 is so beautiful you could die, thinks PUZ32,
how, she thinks, hiding her head in her hands, can one hurt something so beautiful as much as she has to do? DIX24 looks at her as-
tonished, then a Polaroid picture slips out of his head, he takes it out
and hands it to her, it's a picture of PUZ32 as she is standing now,
with her hands around her head. Then he pulls out another picture,
which is blank, but with this symbol: "?" PUZ32 shakes her head.
Then she pulls out a photograph. It is of PUZ32, naked, against the
same kitchen table, with DIX27 behind her. DIX24 slides back from
the chair while he stares at the photograph that slowly dissolves in
front of his eyes. PUZ32's heart is hammering. Then she pulls out
a picture of a small fetus. It's so beautiful. It's so small and the light
around it is so red. It's sucking its thumb. It looks like it's dreaming. It's impossible to know about what. DIX24 closes his eyes, because it hurts! He is both furious and completely lost. He pulls a picture out of his head: DIX24 and PUZ32 eating hot dogs by a hot dog
stand. PUZ32 opening her mouth around an enormous sausage with
far too much onion. DIX24 is laughing. Another picture: DIX24 has
won a pink teddy bear for PUZ32 and PUZ32 is hugging it. Another
picture: DIX24 and PUZ32 walking hand in hand on the sand, the
sun is setting and they are not wearing shoes. PUZ32's heart is about
to break. She pulls out a picture that shows that her heart is about

to break. But DIX24 doesn't see it. He's sitting with his eyes closed. He pulls out a picture that shows a water surface. He sits for a while. Then he pulls out another picture: a big bubble is about to break onto the surface of the water. PUZ32 throws herself at the picture in an attempt to dive into it, but too late, it dissolves, she shakes DIX24, but he has disappeared into himself.

* * *

What can we learn from this? That impossible situations can arise on other planets too. We don't need to think that we're the only ones who struggle and fight. Another striking feature is that they communicate through pictures.

DAVID LEAVITT

■

The David Party

FROM *Washington Square Review*

EVERYONE AT THE PARTY WAS NAMED DAVID. This was a deliberate choice on the part of the host, whose name was also David. The invitation went so far as to prohibit the invitees from bringing along friends, partners, or spouses unless they also were named David. Two exceptions were allowed, an Italian named Davide and a woman named Davida, though only after considerable internal debate on the part of the host, whose notions of perfection were exalted.

It should be remarked, for historical reasons, that the party took place in 1987 in New York, in an apartment at the corner of West End Avenue and 103rd Street. David's Cookies were served, along with Mogen David wine.

"Is everyone at this party gay?" David asked David.

"What makes you assume that just because David's gay, all the guests at his party should be gay?" David said.

"*Is* David gay?" David asked. "David the host? I didn't know."

"If you ask me, David is just a very gay name," David said. "Not as gay as Roger—the gayest name of all—or Gerald. Or Philip. Still . . ."

"I object to that," David said. "My brother is named Phil and he's not gay."

"Phil, not Philip," David corrected. "The diminutive makes all the difference."

"Hello, I am Davide," Davide said. "I am from Milano."

"It's the decoration that makes the party gay," David said. "What could be gayer than all these little replicas of Michelangelo's *David?*"

"Are you saying there's something intrinsically homoerotic about Michelangelo's *David*?" David said.

"I don't think that's an untenable claim," David said.

David turned to David and said: "I probably shouldn't have been allowed in. Everyone calls me Davey."

"If you call *me* Davey, I'll punch you," David said. "I only let my father call me Davey."

"What's your father's name?" David asked.

"Hal," David said.

"Hal David?" David said.

"No, Hal Kalmbach," David said.

"That's a shame," David said. "If you'd told me your father was Hal David, I would have been impressed."

"But then my name would be David David," David said.

"Promises, promises," David said.

"What? Who's making promises?" David said.

"I mean the show," David said. "*Promises, Promises*. Music by Burt Bacharach, lyrics by Hal David."

"I am not understanding a cock," Davide said.

"Of course as a rule, straight guys don't go to all-male parties," David said.

"But how could a David party be other than all-male?" David said.

"Unless they're bachelor parties," David said, "and then there's just the one woman, the stripper."

"Excuse me, I am not a stripper," Davida said.

"We also need to consider that in the early sixties, when nearly everyone here was born, David was the most common name given to boys," David said. "David, followed by Mark."

"How funny! My boyfriend's name is Mark," said about thirty Davids.

"Touché," David said.

"You see?" David said. "This really is a gay party."

"Too bad," Davida said. "It kills my ego being the only woman in a room full of queers."

"I hear you," David said.

"My name is nothing but a burden to me," Davida said. "People always assume that my parents gave it to me because they were disappointed not to have had a son, when really it's because my mother's Scottish. In Scots, Davida means 'beloved.'"

"That sort of thing does happen," David said. "When I was in college, I dated a girl named Bruceen."

"In the Bahamas, where I come from, fathers will give all their children names that are variations on their own," David said. "Hence Anthony's children might be Antoine, Antonio, Antonya, Toinette . . ."

"And David's might be Davidina, Davidette, Davidelle?" David said.

"I have known a Daveene," David said.

"Why not change your name?" David said to Davida. "I'm changing mine. I'm changing it from David Landers to Brad Thorpe."

"What's wrong with David Landers?" Davida said.

"Everything," David said.

"I have always known that someday I would marry a man named Brad Thorpe," David said. "Something in that name inspires absolute confidence."

"How seriously am I supposed to take that proposal?" David asked.

"Hi, I'm Ned," Ned said.

"What?" several Davids said.

"Ned Braverman," Ned said. "Pleased to meet you."

"But how can this be?" David said. "How did you get here?"

"David invited me," Ned said.

"David the host?" David said.

"Did someone call me?" David the host said.

"David, can you explain this?" David said. "This fellow is named Ned Braverman. He says you invited him."

"There is no beauty that hath not some strangeness in it," David said.

"What?" Ned said. "Who's strange?"

"The spot of filth without which the whole cannot cohere," David said.

"Did you just call me filth?" Ned said. "That's it. I'm out of here."

He left, slamming the door behind him.

"What is happened?" Davide said.

"Good riddance," David said, rubbing his hands together. "We don't want that kind at a David party."

* * *

David took a position of authority before the window that looked out onto West End Avenue. He cleared his throat. He said, "Excuse me." He hit a glass with a fork.

"Now that I've got your attention," he said.

"Do you think he's suffering from dementia?" David whispered to David.

"Look at his cheekbones," David said.

"Wasting," David said.

"I heard he's just out of the hospital," Davida said.

"Now, you may wonder why I've called you all here today," David said. "Of course it's because of your name. The name we share. Some of you may think this a silly reason to throw a party, but I don't see it that way. Families gather. Well, we're a family. The family of David. I am David, hear me roar. Davids of the world unite, you have nothing to lose but your chains. David row the boat ashore. David from mountains, go where you will go to. The Davids, united, will never be defeated. Little Davey was small, but oh my."

He started to sing.

He fought big Goliath,

Who lay down and dieth . . .

"I wonder if he'll do the next verse," David said to David, but he did not. Instead he bowed his head, at which the guests broke into loud applause.

The party resumed. The only person who seemed to want to talk to David the host was Davide the Italian, who took his hand and said, "I want just to say, I am glad you are not dead soon."

David and David, meanwhile, had moved together into a corner.

"I find this all deeply depressing," David said.

"Je suis d'accord," David said.

"What say we make a run for it?" David said. "Maybe get something to eat?"

David gave David the once-over. It was a considering once-over. Then he smiled and said, "Why not?"

They left without saying goodbye to anyone. Up Columbus Avenue they walked, to Tom's Diner, which Suzanne Vega had not yet made famous. It was eleven-thirty in the evening and the place was only half-full. One David ordered scrambled eggs with hash browns, the other a hamburger with a green salad, though he would have preferred fries.

"Were you at the march last week?" he said once their food had arrived.

"Which march?" David asked, shaking ketchup onto his hash browns.

"The one on Wall Street. In front of the stock exchange."

"No, I missed it. How was it? Did you lie down in the street until the cops carried you off?"

"I didn't," David said, "but other people did. Actually the thing I remember most about this particular march is the chanting. At first we were all chanting the usual things. An army of lovers cannot lose. We're here, we're queer, get used to it. And then this woman—I have no idea who she is, she has horrible teeth—she suddenly started chanting, 'No more shit!' All by herself, at first. And then a few others joined in, and a few others, until everyone was chanting, together, 'No more shit. No more shit.' Even the people in the street, the people who were just passing by, the stockbrokers we were keeping from getting into the stock exchange, they all got into it. 'No more shit.' I mean, you really can't put it any more plainly than that. Can you put it more plainly than that?"

"I'm sorry I missed that march," David said. "I'm not sorry I went to the David party. At first when I arrived I wished I hadn't gone but then I changed my mind."

"How long do you think he's got?" David said. "David, I mean."

"Who knows? Weeks? Months?"

"I hope longer. With this new drug, I hope—"

"Promises, promises," David said. "Promises, promises, promises, promises, promises."

They ate until there was nothing left on their plates. Not a scrap of toast was left, not a fragment of egg or meat. That evening there would be things they would not talk about, conversations they would not have. The what's-your-status conversation. The sexual-history conversation. The is-oral-sex-safe conversation. Both of them knew that these conversations could not be avoided, that they were just around the bend. And yet, for now, that bend was one they chose, by some unspoken accord, to ignore.

Outside, it had started raining. The rain battered the windows. Every time the doors of Tom's Diner opened, cold, wet gusts of wind blew through.

"So here's my question," David said. "If we get married—I'm not saying we will, but let's say we did—how will we tell each other apart?"

"I'll never call you Davey, if that's what you're asking," David said.

"Oh, but you can," David said. "I'll let you. You and my father."

Then he did a surprising thing. He took David's hand, pressed David's fingers deep into his water glass, and guided them over his own head. What water his hair did not hold fell over his forehead, behind his glasses, into his eyes.

"There, you have christened me," he said.

KATHERINE AUGUSTA MAYFIELD

■

The Reenactors

FROM *Columbia University School of the Arts Thesis Anthology*

THE NIGHT JAVIER COMES HOME from the dead the first thing his mother does is check his teeth. His entire family is inside the house waiting for him, sisters and girl cousins crowded behind the bay windows so close the steam of their breath melts the frost outside. Faintly, from the deep interior heart of the house, music. Everyone is holding champagne flutes, even the children, who spill theirs in little streams through the model Christmas village and seashells on the window's inner sill.

Javier tries to count them, can't remember how many sisters he has and how many cousins, but they keep pushing in front of each other, waving, calling out. His mother's hands are still inside his mouth, and he is clutching a duffle bag, can't wave back. All he can do is stand there and let himself be watched. The return is always something miraculous. He is what is going to save them all. He has been told to let them reacclimatize.

One girl, a teenager, bangs her fist against the glass, suddenly and with enough power behind it that the holly wreaths shiver. His mother doesn't turn. Like everyone else, the girl is dressed somberly, as if for church. She says something he can't hear, repeats herself. Maybe his name, or a threat. She might be one of his sisters. Her hair is black and has the same curl to it that Javier's did at his time of death. She has, he thinks, brown eyes.

She's talking to him, still knocking hard against the glass, and he can see that her knuckles are raw and dragging red, until two more girls grab her by the shoulders and pull her away. The windows are double-paned, reinforced against tropical storms, so whatever she's shouting is muffled, and soon more people shove their way to the front to look at him.

It's a week until Christmas in North Carolina, and since his death in August the house has been repainted shrimp-shell pink, and is tinseled in silver.

His mother feels with her thumb the place where his bottom teeth crowd together, then reaches further back to check the fillings, to feel the unevenness where he chipped a molar on a cherry pit last spring. She didn't have these imperfections memorized when her son was alive, but now she has his dental records, just like Javier does.

His mother's fingernails are long and freshly painted; he can taste the polish as they scratch at the back of his throat, starts to gag, stops himself. She's crying, makeup running, not barefaced like in the photos he saw of her. She's calling him beautiful, darling, love, re-turned, my angel, my baby boy, mi cielito. Takes her fingers from his mouth, him swallowing, her hands still wet with saliva holding his face, and Javier drops his bag to the deck and leans to hug her. After death, like in life, he is exactly eight inches taller than her.

She has remade herself for him too: mascara stippled onto her cheeks and eyeliner shaky like she doesn't do it often. She is older than he realized she would be, and more fragile. Under his hands her sweater is pilled and sagging under the weight of a dozen jeweled pins, snowflakes adorned with pearls and gold-boughed trees and se-quin-eyed Santa Clauses. He hugs her tighter, listens to them click together. Black slacks, permed hair, house slippers that now must be soaked through from the gloss of ice. Her back is rounded and warm. She feels like a mother should.

"Mom," he says in the southern accent he has practiced, "Mom, I'm home."

"No," she says. "He called me Mama. But you at least you got the teeth right."

The original Javier died on a NASCAR speedway in the middle of the state on a thickly humid twilit night this past summer. A gleaming fleet of cars gone sprawling, crumpled, airborne, a bang of charcoaled light as a fuel tank burst. On the television in her bedroom two weeks short of her fifty-sixth birthday, Javier's mother watched his car leave the ground. The replay took the seconds piece by piece: the race car's upward arc into the catch fence, which snapped back like breaking fingers until inertia reversed and threw it forward. The car's safety harnesses unzipped as it fragmented, its contents falling to streak against the asphalt as a crowd of twenty thousand screamed. The cameras were too high, angles all wrong to show exactly what happened to her son. The commentators were silent. Did not say anything as the pit crew ran forward, one man, then everyone else at once.

Javier's new incarnation, before he was Javier's new incarnation, saw the pictures online. Grainy with pixels, taken from high up in the stands, but still: skin glistening and opened up like the membrane of fruit. His body had wrecked into its individual parts, like it was something meant to be shared among many.

The original Javier was voted Best Hair his junior year of high school, was introduced to stock-car racing by his cousin Consolata, and voted Most Likely to Succeed three months before his graduation. At the time of the crash, he was twenty-six, had driven racecars professionally for the last seven years, and been engulfed in flames twice. At the time of the crash, he wore mandatory fireproof coveralls and underwear, and fire-retardant gloves and socks. Heat shields on the bottoms of his shoes. Had previously broken his collarbone, and a growth plate in his right arm in childhood. Spoke Spanish almost fluently, wanted to learn Portuguese, enjoyed unwinding in front of wilderness survival reality TV. Was a registered Republican and afraid of dogs and led Bible study at his family's church, Our Lady of the Seas. His signature dish was ropa vieja. Sometimes, as a hobby, he built model towns. Javier is survived by a mother, three sisters, four aunts, two uncles, six cousins, all girls, a wife, and a daughter, age two. Javier's family has been in mourning for the last four months.

Before Javier was Javier he was Buck, a schoolteacher in Wyoming who died of smoke inhalation during a wildfire, and who was resurrected to live for another four months in order to walk his daughter down the aisle at her wedding. Before that he was Kenny, suicide by carbon monoxide poisoning in a garage in Indiana, woken up to keep his elderly father company until his passing eight months in. And then Bernard, black ice, returned from the dead to support his wife through her chemotherapy sessions. And then Damien, cause of death late-stage Lyme disease, made alive for three more years to attend his children's soccer matches and grow orchids with his husband in a Los Angeles hothouse.

Most families hold on to their reenactors, but not always. Buck's wife said the sight of him made her too lonely and demanded her daughter let her father go back to death. After three years, Damien's husband still thought of himself as a widower. Bernard's wife died, and no one else in her family wanted to sustain him. Same with Kenny.

Javier's family might be different. Health insurance covers this new Javier, under the clause of preventative medicine, and Javier's mother is picking up his new duffle bag with all his old clothes she sent ahead and opening the door to the family home. There is tinsel in her hair and tears drying on her face. She has a slight double chin. She turns her soft warm back to him and takes him by the hand to lead him into her son's life.

"Mama," she reminds him again. "That's what you called me."

The family home is lined with Javier's handmade villages and miniature forests, created from wire and felt and voltage. The trees are all evergreen, no more than three inches high, and hum with the minute electricity of their lights.

"You find model towns relaxing," his mother tells him as they sit down to dinner.

Javier already knows this, just like he also knows he wanted to be an orthopedic surgeon before he became a racecar driver, and believed in both ghosts and aliens. He is paid to know these things. His job is to embody. He is convincing.

The house is narrow, shotgun style, and five card tables have been laid out down the hallway, where his entire family now sits, loud laughter, smiles, conversation. All of them, grief cauterized. His daughter is on his lap. Her name is Loma, she is dressed in white lace, and too young to remember her father, but she will know him now. Before them a welcome-home dinner has been laid out, Carolina barbecue and pasteles steaming from their banana leaves, mofongo and fried okra and chuletón. More champagne, and eggnog now. The wind is pushing against the house, which rocks gently on its stilts. Javier's wife has not yet spoken to him, will not yet look at him, and has not dropped her hand from Loma's downy head. Javier's mother is the one who brought him back. His wife has not agreed to his resurrection.

When he was Damien, his husband would not leave him alone with the children for the first six months. He was good at being Damien, looked like him wholly, and in the family photos you could not tell the difference, could not place the precise date of death. His first night as Damien, there was no welcome dinner. The house was filled with Precious Moments figurines and gardenias and terrariums. A pink sunset outside and dogs under the table, and he touched his husband's cheek, but his husband said, eyes closed and shoulders stiff, "Please don't."

The agreement is that you go for accuracy above all else. The agreement is that you do anything so as to be believed. It's noble, he was told when he joined. You are donating your body to continue old life. This is how to transmute a soul. This is how to fix sorrow.

One of Javier's three sisters died of a blood infection in early childhood, but looking down the table now, he cannot tell which one is a reenactor. They all look seamless, glossy dark hair and gap teeth and eyes that crinkle, even the one who shouted at him earlier through the glass. They replaced her almost instantly, before the wake, even. He does not know why it took them so much longer to find a vessel for their son.

BEN PASSMORE

■

Your Black Friend

FROM *Your Black Friend and Other Strangers*

your black friend wonders if you know that, unlike you, he has to constantly monitor his speech, dress, and affect relative to his enviroment and a misreading could mean the difference between being the black friend and that black guy...

your black friend hates that you slide into "black" presentations thought-lessly. he feels like you're mocking him, But Knows that you are totally unaware of this.

your black friend wishes he knew how to bring this up, but he doesn't know how.

your black friend wishes you would play more than Beyoncé; there are more black performers than Beyoncé and he's worried you don't know that,

honestly your black friend is tired of partying with you.

When your black friend was little he used to spend hours in front of the mirror sucking his lips in to make them look thin like Leonardo Dicaprio and smooth his curly hair with product. The TV taught your black friend what beatiful was and it didn't look anything like him. Your black friend has come into himself over time but will always carry scars.

your black friend doesn't think he has to wear pooka shells to show that he loves himself. He doesn't think he owes anyone anything.

irony irony → got mah fingrz got mah toes...

your black friend reads Fanon and about the black Panthers.

BIK SHN

one day your black friend heard about some cops killing a young black boy. that night your black friend threw a brick at a cop's face.

your black friend's black friends tell him that black owned businesses will end racism but your black friend is skeptical that scented afro picks can be utilized as a political apparatus.

50¢

YAT FRICA

your black friend knows that all this is a huge bummer. He knows you mean well, that you are doing your best. Sometimes he thinks to himself that he should be "overcoming" something, getting to some type of mountain top. His white friends ask "what can I do" or "how can we end racism?" They seem sure they can cure something they don't really understand. Your black friend wishes racism could be ended with understanding, it would justify how much time his friends spend posting articles about the "race issue" on facebook.

KATHY FISH

■

Collective Nouns
for Humans in the Wild

FROM *Jellyfish Review*

A group of grandmothers is a *tapestry*. A group of toddlers, a *jubilance* (see also: a *bewailing*). A group of librarians is an *enlightenment*. A group of visual artists is a *bioluminescence*. A group of short story writers is a *Flannery*. A group of musicians is—a *band*.

A *resplendence* of poets.
A *beacon* of scientists.
A *raft* of social workers.

A group of first responders is a *valiance*. A group of peaceful protesters is a *dream*. A group of special-education teachers is a *transcendence*. A group of neonatal ICU nurses is a *divinity*. A group of hospice workers, a *grace*.

Humans in the wild, gathered and feeling good, previously an *exhilaration*, now: a *target*.

A *target* of concert-goers.
A *target* of movie-goers.
A *target* of dancers.

A group of schoolchildren is a *target*.

KRISTEN ROUPENIAN

■

Cat Person

FROM *The New Yorker*

MARGOT MET ROBERT on a Wednesday night toward the end of her fall semester. She was working behind the concession stand at the artsy movie theatre downtown when he came in and bought a large popcorn and a box of Red Vines.

"That's an . . . unusual choice," she said. "I don't think I've ever actually sold a box of Red Vines before."

Flirting with her customers was a habit she'd picked up back when she worked as a barista, and it helped with tips. She didn't earn tips at the movie theatre, but the job was boring otherwise, and she did think that Robert was cute. Not so cute that she would have, say, gone up to him at a party, but cute enough that she could have drummed up an imaginary crush on him if he'd sat across from her during a dull class—though she was pretty sure that he was out of college, in his mid-twenties at least. He was tall, which she liked, and she could see the edge of a tattoo peeking out from beneath the rolled-up sleeve of his shirt. But he was on the heavy side, his beard was a little too long, and his shoulders slumped forward slightly, as though he were protecting something.

Robert did not pick up on her flirtation. Or, if he did, he showed it only by stepping back, as though to make her lean toward him, try a little harder. "Well," he said. "O.K., then." He pocketed his change.

But the next week he came into the movie theatre again, and

bought another box of Red Vines. "You're getting better at your job," he told her. "You managed not to insult me this time."

She shrugged. "I'm up for a promotion, so," she said.

After the movie, he came back to her.

"Concession-stand girl, give me your phone number," he said, and, surprising herself, she did.

From that small exchange about Red Vines, over the next several weeks they built up an elaborate scaffolding of jokes via text, riffs that unfolded and shifted so quickly that she sometimes had a hard time keeping up. He was very clever, and she found that she had to work to impress him. Soon she noticed that when she texted him he usually texted her back right away, but if she took more than a few hours to respond his next message would always be short and wouldn't include a question, so it was up to her to re-initiate the conversation, which she always did. A few times, she got distracted for a day or so and wondered if the exchange would die out altogether, but then she'd think of something funny to tell him or she'd see a picture on the Internet that was relevant to their conversation, and they'd start up again. She still didn't know much about him, because they never talked about anything personal, but when they landed two or three good jokes in a row there was a kind of exhilaration to it, as if they were dancing.

Then, one night during reading period, she was complaining about how all the dining halls were closed and there was no food in her room because her roommate had raided her care package, and he offered to buy her some Red Vines to sustain her. At first, she deflected this with another joke, because she really did have to study, but he said, "No I'm serious, stop fooling around and come now," so she put a jacket over her pajamas and met him at the 7-Eleven.

It was about eleven o'clock. He greeted her without ceremony, as though he saw her every day, and took her inside to choose some snacks. The store didn't have Red Vines, so he bought her a Cherry Coke Slurpee and a bag of Doritos and a novelty lighter shaped like a frog with a cigarette in its mouth.

"Thank you for my presents," she said, when they were back outside.

Robert was wearing a rabbit-fur hat that came down over his ears and a thick, old-fashioned down jacket. She thought it was a good look for him, if a little dorky; the hat heightened his lumberjack aura, and the heavy coat hid his belly and the slightly sad slump of his shoulders.

"You're welcome, concession-stand girl," he said, though of course he knew her name by then. She thought he was going to go in for a kiss and prepared to duck and offer him her cheek, but instead of kissing her on the mouth he took her by the arm and kissed her gently on the forehead, as though she were something precious. "Study hard, sweetheart," he said. "I will see you soon."

On the walk back to her dorm, she was filled with a sparkly lightness that she recognized as the sign of an incipient crush.

While she was home over break, they texted nearly non-stop, not only jokes but little updates about their days. They started saying good morning and good night, and when she asked him a question and he didn't respond right away she felt a jab of anxious yearning. She learned that Robert had two cats, named Mu and Yan, and together they invented a complicated scenario in which her childhood cat, Pita, would send flirtatious texts to Yan, but whenever Pita talked to Mu she was formal and cold, because she was jealous of Mu's relationship with Yan.

"Why are you texting all the time?" Margot's stepdad asked her at dinner. "Are you having an affair with someone?"

"Yes," Margot said. "His name is Robert, and I met him at the movie theatre. We're in love, and we're probably going to get married."

"Hmm," her stepdad said. "Tell him we have some questions for him."

"My parents are asking about u," Margot texted, and Robert sent her back a smiley-face emoji whose eyes were hearts.

When Margot returned to campus, she was eager to see Robert again, but he turned out to be surprisingly hard to pin down. "Sorry, busy week at work," he replied. "I promise I will c u soon." Margot didn't like this; it felt as if the dynamic had shifted out of her favor, and when eventually he did ask her to go to a movie she agreed right away.

The movie he wanted to see was playing at the theatre where she worked, but she suggested that they see it at the big multiplex just outside town instead; students didn't go there very often, because you needed to drive. Robert came to pick her up in a muddy white Civic with candy wrappers spilling out of the cup holders. On the drive, he was quieter than she'd expected, and he didn't look at her very much. Before five minutes had gone by, she became wildly uncomfortable, and, as they got on the highway, it occurred to her that he could take her someplace and rape and murder her; she hardly knew anything about him, after all.

Just as she thought this, he said, "Don't worry, I'm not going to murder you," and she wondered if the discomfort in the car was her fault, because she was acting jumpy and nervous, like the kind of girl who thought she was going to get murdered every time she went on a date.

"It's O.K.—you can murder me if you want," she said, and he laughed and patted her knee. But he was still disconcertingly quiet, and all her bubbling attempts at making conversation bounced right off him. At the theatre, he made a joke to the cashier at the concession stand about Red Vines, which fell flat in a way that embarrassed everyone involved, but Margot most of all.

During the movie, he didn't hold her hand or put his arm around her, so by the time they were back in the parking lot she was pretty sure that he had changed his mind about liking her. She was wearing leggings and a sweatshirt, and that might have been the problem. When she got into the car, he'd said, "Glad to see you dressed up for me," which she'd assumed was a joke, but maybe she actually had offended him by not seeming to take the date seriously enough, or something. He was wearing khakis and a button-down shirt.

"So, do you want to go get a drink?" he asked when they got back to the car, as if being polite were an obligation that had been imposed on him. It seemed obvious to Margot that he was expecting her to say no and that, when she did, they wouldn't talk again. That made her sad, not so much because she wanted to continue spending time with him as because she'd had such high expectations for him over break, and it didn't seem fair that things had fallen apart so quickly.

"We could go get a drink, I guess?" she said.

"If you want," he said.

"If you want" was such an unpleasant response that she sat silently in the car until he poked her leg and said, "What are you sulking about?"

"I'm not sulking," she said. "I'm just a little tired."

"I can take you home."

"No, I could use a drink, after that movie." Even though it had been playing at the mainstream theatre, the film he'd chosen was a very depressing drama about the Holocaust, so inappropriate for a first date that when he suggested it she said, "Lol r u serious," and he made some joke about how he was sorry that he'd misjudged her taste and he could take her to a romantic comedy instead.

But now, when she said that about the movie, he winced a little, and a totally different interpretation of the night's events occurred to her. She wondered if perhaps he'd been trying to impress her by suggesting the Holocaust movie, because he didn't understand that a Holocaust movie was the wrong kind of "serious" movie with which to impress the type of person who worked at an artsy movie theatre, the type of person he probably assumed she was. Maybe, she thought, her texting "lol r u serious" had hurt him, had intimidated him and made him feel uncomfortable around her. The thought of this possible vulnerability touched her, and she felt kinder toward him than she had all night.

When he asked her where she wanted to go for a drink, she named the place where she usually hung out, but he made a face and said that it was in the student ghetto and he'd take her somewhere better. They went to a bar she'd never been to, an underground speakeasy type of place, with no sign announcing its presence. There was a line to get inside, and, as they waited, she grew fidgety trying to figure out how to tell him what she needed to tell him, but she couldn't, so when the bouncer asked to see her I.D. she just handed it to him. The bouncer hardly even looked at it; he just smirked and said, "Yeah, no," and waved her to the side, as he gestured toward the next group of people in line.

Robert had gone ahead of her, not noticing what was playing out behind him. "Robert," she said quietly. But he didn't turn around. Finally, someone in line who'd been paying attention tapped him on the shoulder and pointed to her, marooned on the sidewalk.

She stood, abashed, as he came back over to her. "Sorry!" she said. "This is so embarrassing."

"How old *are* you?" he demanded.

"I'm twenty," she said.

"Oh," he said. "I thought you said you were older."

"I told you I was a sophomore!" she said. Standing outside the bar, having been rejected in front of everyone, was humiliating enough, and now Robert was looking at her as if she'd done something wrong.

"But you did that—what do you call it? That gap year," he objected, as though this were an argument he could win.

"I don't know what to tell you," she said helplessly. "I'm twenty." And then, absurdly, she started to feel tears stinging her eyes, because somehow everything had been ruined and she couldn't understand why this was all so hard.

But, when Robert saw her face crumpling, a kind of magic happened. All the tension drained out of his posture; he stood up straight and wrapped his bearlike arms around her. "Oh, sweetheart," he said. "Oh, honey, it's O.K., it's all right. Please don't feel bad." She let herself be folded against him, and she was flooded with the same feeling she'd had outside the 7-Eleven—that she was a delicate, precious thing he was afraid he might break. He kissed the top of her head, and she laughed and wiped her tears away.

"I can't believe I'm crying because I didn't get into a bar," she said. "You must think I'm such an idiot." But she knew he didn't think that, from the way he was gazing at her; in his eyes, she could see how pretty she looked, smiling through her tears in the chalky glow of the streetlight, with a few flakes of snow coming down.

He kissed her then, on the lips, for real; he came for her in a kind of lunging motion and practically poured his tongue down her throat. It was a terrible kiss, shockingly bad; Margot had trouble believing that a grown man could possibly be so bad at kissing. It seemed awful, yet somehow it also gave her that tender feeling toward him again, the sense that even though he was older than her, she knew something he didn't.

When he was done kissing her, he took her hand firmly and led her to a different bar, where there were pool tables and pinball machines and sawdust on the floor and no one checking I.D.s at the door. In one of the booths, she saw the grad student who'd been her English T.A. her freshman year.

"Should I get you a vodka soda?" Robert asked, which she thought was maybe supposed to be a joke about the kind of drink college girls liked, though she'd never had a vodka soda. She actually was a little anxious about what to order; at the places she went to, they only carded people at the bar, so the kids who were twenty-one or had good fake I.D.s usually brought pitchers of P.B.R. or Bud Light back to share with the others. She wasn't sure if those brands were ones that Robert would make fun of, so, instead of specifying, she said, "I'll just have a beer."

With the drinks in front of him and the kiss behind him, and also maybe because she had cried, Robert became much more relaxed, more like the witty person she knew through his texts. As they talked, she became increasingly sure that what she'd interpreted as anger or dissatisfaction with her had, in fact, been nervousness, a fear that she wasn't having a good time. He kept coming back to her initial dismissal of the movie, making jokes that glanced off it and watching her closely to see how she responded. He teased her about her high-brow taste, and said how hard it was to impress her because of all the film classes she'd taken, even though he knew she'd taken only one summer class in film. He joked about how she and the other employees at the artsy theatre probably sat around and made fun of the people who went to the mainstream theatre, where they didn't even serve wine, and some of the movies were in IMAX 3-D.

Margot laughed along with the jokes he was making at the expense of this imaginary film snob version of her, though nothing he said seemed quite fair, since she was the one who'd actually suggested that they see the movie at the Quality 16. Although now, she realized, maybe that had hurt Robert's feelings, too. She'd thought it was clear that she just didn't want to go on a date where she worked, but maybe he'd taken it more personally than that; maybe he'd suspected that she was ashamed to be seen with him. She was starting to think that she understood him—how sensitive he was, how easily he could be wounded—and that made her feel closer to him, and also powerful, because once she knew how to hurt him she also knew how he could be soothed. She asked him lots of questions about the movies he liked, and she spoke self-deprecatingly about the movies at the artsy theatre that she found boring or incomprehensible; she told him about how much her older coworkers intimidated her, and how she sometimes worried that she wasn't smart enough to form her own opinions on anything. The effect of this on him was palpable and immediate, and she felt as if she were petting a large, skittish animal, like a horse or a bear, skillfully coaxing it to eat from her hand.

By her third beer, she was thinking about what it would be like to have sex with Robert. Probably it would be like that bad kiss, clumsy and excessive, but imagining how excited he would be, how hungry and eager to impress her, she felt a twinge of desire pluck at her belly, as distinct and painful as the snap of an elastic band against her skin.

When they'd finished that round of drinks, she said, boldly, "Should we get out of here, then?," and he seemed briefly hurt, as if he thought she was cutting the date short, but she took his hand and pulled him up, and the look on his face when he realized what she was saying, and the obedient way he trailed her out of the bar, gave her that elastic-band snap again, as did, oddly, the fact that his palm was slick beneath hers.

Outside, she presented herself to him again for kissing, but, to her surprise, he only pecked her on the mouth. "You're drunk," he said, accusingly.

"No, I'm not," she said, though she was. She pushed her body against his, feeling tiny beside him, and he let out a great shuddering sigh, as if she were something too bright and painful to look at, and that was sexy, too, being made to feel like a kind of irresistible temptation.

"I'm taking you home, lightweight," he said, shepherding her to the car. Once they were inside it, though, she leaned into him again, and after a little while, by lightly pulling back when he pushed his tongue too far down her throat, she was able to get him to kiss her in the softer way that she liked, and soon after that she was straddling him, and she could feel the small log of his erection straining against his pants. Whenever it rolled beneath her weight, he let out these fluttery, high-pitched moans that she couldn't help feeling were a little melodramatic, and then suddenly he pushed her off him and turned the key in the ignition.

"Making out in the front seat like a teenager," he said, in mock disgust. Then he added, "I'd have thought you'd be too old for that, now that you're *twenty.*"

She stuck her tongue out at him. "Where do you want to go, then?"

"Your place?"

"Um, that won't really work. Because of my roommate?"

"Oh, right. You live in the dorms," he said, as though that were something she should apologize for.

"Where do you live?" she asked.

"I live in a house."

"Can I . . . come over?"

"You can."

The house was in a pretty, wooded neighborhood not too far from campus and had a string of cheerful white fairy lights across the doorway. Before he got out of the car, he said, darkly, like a warning, "Just so you know, I have cats."

"I know," she said. "We texted about them, remember?"

At the front door, he fumbled with his keys for what seemed a ridiculously long time and swore under his breath. She rubbed his back to try to keep the mood going, but that seemed to fluster him even more, so she stopped.

"Well. This is my house," he said flatly, pushing the door open.

The room they were in was dimly lit and full of objects, all of which, as her eyes adjusted, resolved into familiarity. He had two large, full bookcases, a shelf of vinyl records, a collection of board games, and a lot of art—or, at least, posters that had been hung in frames, instead of being tacked or taped to the wall.

"I like it," she said, truthfully, and, as she did, she identified the emotion she was feeling as relief. It occurred to her that she'd never gone to someone's house to have sex before; because she'd dated only guys her age, there had always been some element of sneaking around, to avoid roommates. It was new, and a little frightening, to be so completely on someone else's turf, and the fact that Robert's house gave evidence of his having interests that she shared, if only in their broadest categories—art, games, books, music—struck her as a reassuring endorsement of her choice.

As she thought this, she saw that Robert was watching her closely, observing the impression the room had made. And, as though fear weren't quite ready to release its hold on her, she had the brief wild idea that maybe this was not a room at all but a trap meant to lure her into the false belief that Robert was a normal person, a person like her, when in fact all the other rooms in the house were empty, or full of horrors: corpses or kidnap victims or chains. But then he was kissing her, throwing her bag and their coats on the couch and ushering her into the bedroom, groping her ass and pawing at her chest, with the avid clumsiness of that first kiss.

The bedroom wasn't empty, though it was emptier than the living room; he didn't have a bed frame, just a mattress and a box spring on the floor. There was a bottle of whiskey on his dresser, and he took a swig from it, then handed it to her and kneeled down and opened his laptop, an action that confused her, until she understood that he was putting on music.

Margot sat on the bed while Robert took off his shirt and unbuckled his pants, pulling them down to his ankles before realizing that he was still wearing his shoes and bending over to untie them. Looking at him like that, so awkwardly bent, his belly thick and soft and covered with hair, Margot recoiled. But the thought of what it would take to stop what she had set in motion was overwhelming; it would require an amount of tact and gentleness that she felt was impossible to summon. It wasn't that she was scared he would try to force her to do something against her will but that insisting that they stop now, after everything she'd done to push this forward, would make her seem spoiled and capricious, as if she'd ordered something at a restaurant and then, once the food arrived, had changed her mind and sent it back.

She tried to bludgeon her resistance into submission by taking a sip of the whiskey, but when he fell on top of her with those huge, sloppy kisses, his hand moving mechanically across her breasts and down to her crotch, as if he were making some perverse sign of the cross, she began to have trouble breathing and to feel that she really might not be able to go through with it after all.

Wriggling out from under the weight of him and straddling him helped, as did closing her eyes and remembering him kissing her forehead at the 7-Eleven. Encouraged by her progress, she pulled her shirt up over her head. Robert reached up and scooped her breast out of her bra, so that it jutted half in and half out of the cup, and rolled her nipple between his thumb and forefinger. This was uncomfortable, so she leaned forward, pushing herself into his hand. He got the hint and tried to undo her bra, but he couldn't work the clasp, his evident frustration reminiscent of his struggle with the keys, until at last he said, bossily, "Take that thing off," and she complied.

The way he looked at her then was like an exaggerated version of the expression she'd seen on the faces of all the guys she'd been naked with, not that there were that many—six in total, Robert made seven. He looked stunned and stupid with pleasure, like a milkdrunk baby, and she thought that maybe this was what she loved most about sex—a guy revealed like that. Robert showed her more open need than any of the others, even though he was older, and must have seen more breasts, more bodies, than they had—but maybe that was part of it for him, the fact that he was older, and she was young.

As they kissed, she found herself carried away by a fantasy of such pure ego that she could hardly admit even to herself that she was having it. Look at this beautiful girl, she imagined him thinking. She's so perfect, her body is perfect, everything about her is perfect, she's only twenty years old, her skin is flawless, I want her so badly, I want her more than I've ever wanted anyone else, I want her so bad I might die.

The more she imagined his arousal, the more turned-on she got, and soon they were rocking against each other, getting into a rhythm, and she reached into his underwear and took his penis in her hand and felt the pearled droplet of moisture on its tip. He made that sound again, that high-pitched feminine whine, and she wished there were a way she could ask him not to do that, but she couldn't think of any. Then his hand was inside her underwear, and when he felt that she was wet he visibly relaxed. He fingered her a little, very softly, and she bit her lip and put on a show for him, but then he poked her too hard and she flinched, and he jerked his hand away. "Sorry!" he said.

And then he asked, urgently, "Wait. Have you ever done this before?"

The night did, indeed, feel so odd and unprecedented that her first impulse was to say no, but then she realized what he meant and she laughed out loud.

She didn't mean to laugh; she knew well enough already that, while Robert might enjoy being the subject of gentle, flirtatious teasing, he was not a person who would enjoy being laughed at, not at all. But she couldn't help it. Losing her virginity had been a long drawnout affair preceded by several months' worth of intense discussion with her boyfriend of two years, plus a visit to the gynecologist and a horrifically embarrassing but ultimately incredibly meaningful conversation with her mom, who, in the end, had not only reserved her a room at a bed-and-breakfast but, after the event, written her a card. The idea that, instead of that whole involved, emotional process, she might have watched a pretentious Holocaust movie, drunk three beers, and then gone to some random house to lose her virginity to a guy she'd met at a movie theatre was so funny that suddenly she couldn't stop laughing, though the laughter had a slightly hysterical edge.

"I'm sorry," Robert said coldly. "I didn't know."

Abruptly, she stopped giggling.

"No, it was . . . nice of you to check," she said. "I've had sex before, though. I'm sorry I laughed."

"You don't need to apologize," he said, but she could tell by his face, as well as by the fact that he was going soft beneath her, that she did.

"I'm sorry," she said again, reflexively, and then, in a burst of inspiration, "I guess I'm just nervous, or something?"

He narrowed his eyes at her, as though suspicious of this claim, but it seemed to placate him. "You don't have to be nervous," he said. "We'll take it slow."

Yeah, right, she thought, and then he was on top of her again, kissing her and weighing her down, and she knew that her last chance of enjoying this encounter had disappeared, but that she would carry through with it until it was over. When Robert was naked, rolling a condom onto a dick that was only half visible beneath the hairy shelf of his belly, she felt a wave of revulsion that she thought might actually break through her sense of pinned stasis, but then he shoved his finger in her again, not at all gently this time, and she imagined herself from above, naked and spread-eagled with this fat old man's finger inside her, and her revulsion turned to self-disgust and a humiliation that was a kind of perverse cousin to arousal.

During sex, he moved her through a series of positions with brusque efficiency, flipping her over, pushing her around, and she felt like a doll again, as she had outside the 7-Eleven, though not a precious one now—a doll made of rubber, flexible and resilient, a prop for the movie that was playing in his head. When she was on top, he slapped her thigh and said, "Yeah, yeah, you like that," with an intonation that made it impossible to tell whether he meant it as a question, an observation, or an order, and when he turned her over he growled in her ear, "I always wanted to fuck a girl with nice tits," and she had to smother her face in the pillow to keep from laughing again. At the end, when he was on top of her in missionary, he kept losing his erection, and every time he did he would say, aggressively, "You make my dick so hard," as though lying about it could make it true. At last, after a frantic rabbity burst, he shuddered, came, and collapsed on her like a tree falling, and, crushed beneath him, she thought, brightly, This is the worst life decision I have ever made! And she marveled at herself for a while, at the mystery of this person who'd just done this bizarre, inexplicable thing.

After a short while, Robert got up and hurried to the bathroom in a bowlegged waddle, clutching the condom to keep it from falling off. Margot lay on the bed and stared at the ceiling, noticing for the first time that there were stickers on it, those little stars and moons that were supposed to glow in the dark.

Robert returned from the bathroom and stood silhouetted in the doorway. "What do you want to do now?" he asked her.

"We should probably just kill ourselves," she imagined saying, and then she imagined that somewhere, out there in the universe, there was a boy who would think that this moment was just as awful yet hilarious as she did, and that sometime, far in the future, she would tell the boy this story. She'd say, "And then he said, 'You make my dick so hard,'" and the boy would shriek in agony and grab her leg, saying, "Oh, my God, stop, please, no, I can't take it anymore," and the two of them would collapse into each other's arms and laugh and laugh—but of course there was no such future, because no such boy existed, and never would.

So instead she shrugged, and Robert said, "We could watch a movie," and he went to the computer and downloaded something; she didn't pay attention to what. For some reason, he'd chosen a movie with subtitles, and she kept closing her eyes, so she had no idea what was going on. The whole time, he was stroking her hair and trailing light kisses down her shoulder, as if he'd forgotten that ten minutes ago he'd thrown her around as if they were in a porno and growled, "I always wanted to fuck a girl with nice tits" in her ear.

Then, out of nowhere, he started talking about his feelings for her. He talked about how hard it had been for him when she went away for break, not knowing if she had an old high school boyfriend she might reconnect with back home. During those two weeks, it turned out, an entire secret drama had played out in his head, one in which she'd left campus committed to him, to Robert, but at home had been drawn back to the high school guy, who, in Robert's mind, was some kind of brutish, handsome jock, not worthy of her but nonetheless seductive by virtue of his position at the top of the hierarchy back home in Saline. "I was so worried you might, like, make a bad decision and things would be different between us when you got back," he said. "But I should have trusted you." My high school boyfriend is gay, Margot imagined telling him. We were pretty sure of it in high school, but after a year of sleeping around at college he's definitely figured it out. In fact, he's not even a hundred per cent positive that he identifies as a man anymore; we spent a lot of time over break talking about what it would mean for him to come out as nonbinary, so sex with him wasn't going to happen, and you could have asked me about that if you were worried; you could have asked me about a lot of things. But she didn't say any of that; she just lay silently, emanating a black, hateful aura, until finally Robert trailed off. "Are you still awake?" he asked, and she said yes, and he said, "Is everything O.K.?"

"How old are you, exactly?" she asked him.

"I'm thirty-four," he said. "Is that a problem?"

She could sense him in the dark beside her, vibrating with fear. "No," she said. "It's fine."

"Good," he said. "It was something I wanted to bring up with you, but I didn't know how you'd take it." He rolled over and kissed her forehead, and she felt like a slug he'd poured salt on, disintegrating under that kiss.

She looked at the clock; it was nearly three in the morning. "I should go home, probably," she said.

"Really?" he said. "But I thought you'd stay over. I make great scrambled eggs!"

"Thanks," she said, sliding into her leggings.

"But I can't. My roommate would be worried. So."

"Gotta get back to the dorm room," he said, voice dripping with sarcasm.

"Yep," she said. "Since that's where I live."

The drive was endless. The snow had turned to rain. They didn't talk. Eventually, Robert switched the radio to late night NPR. Margot recalled how, when they first got on the highway to go to the movie, she'd imagined that Robert might murder her, and she thought, Maybe he'll murder me now.

He didn't murder her. He drove her to her dorm. "I had a really nice time tonight," he said, unbuckling his seat belt.

"Thanks," she said. She clutched her bag in her hands. "Me, too."

"I'm so glad we finally got to go on a date," he said.

"A *date*," she said to her imaginary boyfriend. "He called that a *date*." And they both laughed and laughed.

"You're welcome," she said. She reached for the door handle. "Thanks for the movie and stuff."

"Wait," he said, and grabbed her arm. "Come here." He dragged her back, wrapped his arms around her, and pushed his tongue down her throat one last time. "Oh, my God, when will it end?" she asked the imaginary boyfriend, but the imaginary boyfriend didn't answer her.

"Good night," she said, and then she opened the door and escaped. By the time she got to her room, she already had a text from him: no words, just hearts and faces with heart eyes and, for some reason, a dolphin.

She slept for twelve hours, and when she woke she ate waffles in the dining hall and binge-watched detective shows on Netflix and tried to envision the hopeful possibility that he would disappear without her having to do anything, that somehow she could just wish him away. When the next message from him did arrive, just after dinner, it was a harmless joke about Red Vines, but she deleted it immediately, overwhelmed with a skin crawling loathing that felt vastly disproportionate to anything he had actually done. She told herself that she owed him at least some kind of breakup message, that to ghost on him would be inappropriate, childish, and cruel. And, if she did try to ghost, who knew how long it would take him to get the hint? Maybe the messages would keep coming and coming; maybe they would never end.

She began drafting a message—*Thank you for the nice time but I'm not interested in a relationship right now*—but she kept hedging and apologizing, attempting to close loopholes that she imagined him trying to slip through (*"It's O.K., I'm not interested in a relationship either, something casual is fine!"*), so that the message got longer and longer and even more impossible to send. Meanwhile, his texts kept arriving, none of them saying anything of consequence, each one more earnest than the last. She imagined him lying on his bed that was just a mattress, carefully crafting each one. She remembered that he'd talked a lot about his cats and yet she hadn't seen any cats in the house, and she wondered if he'd made them up.

Every so often, over the next day or so, she would find herself in a gray, day-dreamy mood, missing something, and she'd realize that it was Robert she missed, not the real Robert but the Robert she'd imagined on the other end of all those text messages during break.

"Hey, so it seems like you're really busy, huh?" Robert finally wrote, three days after they'd fucked, and she knew that this was the perfect opportunity to send her half-completed breakup text, but instead she wrote back, "Haha sorry yeah" and "I'll text you soon," and then she thought, Why did I do that? And she truly didn't know.

"Just tell him you're not interested!" Margot's roommate, Tamara, screamed in frustration after Margot had spent an hour on her bed, dithering about what to say to Robert.

"I have to say more than that. We had *sex*," Margot said.

"*Do* you?" Tamara said. "I mean, really?"

"He's a nice guy, sort of," Margot said, and she wondered how true that was. Then, abruptly, Tamara lunged, snatching the phone out of

Margot's hand and holding it far away from her as her thumbs flew across the screen. Tamara flung the phone onto the bed and Margot scrambled for it, and there it was, what Tamara had written: "Hi im not interested in you stop textng me."

"Oh, my God," Margot said, finding it suddenly hard to breathe.

"What?" Tamara said boldly. "What's the big deal? It's true."

But they both knew that it was a big deal, and Margot had a knot of fear in her stomach so solid that she thought she might retch. She imagined Robert picking up his phone, reading that message, turning to glass, and shattering to pieces.

"Calm down. Let's go get a drink," Tamara said, and they went to a bar and shared a pitcher, and all the while Margot's phone sat between them on the table, and though they tried to ignore it, when it chimed with an incoming message they screamed and clutched each other's arms.

"I can't do it—you read it," Margot said. She pushed the phone toward Tamara. "You did this. It's your fault."

But all the message said was "O.K., Margot, I am sorry to hear that. I hope I did not do anything to upset you. You are a sweet girl and I really enjoyed the time we spent together. Please let me know if you change your mind."

Margot collapsed on the table, laying her head in her hands. She felt as though a leech, grown heavy and swollen with her blood, had at last popped off her skin, leaving a tender, bruised spot behind. But why should she feel that way? Perhaps she was being unfair to Robert, who really had done nothing wrong, except like her, and be bad in bed, and maybe lie about having cats, although probably they had just been in another room.

But then, a month later, she saw him in the bar—her bar, the one in the student ghetto, where, on their date, she'd suggested they go. He was alone, at a table in the back, and he wasn't reading or looking at his phone; he was just sitting there silently, hunched over a beer.

She grabbed the friend she was with, a guy named Albert. "Oh, my God, that's him," she whispered. "The guy from the movie theatre!" By then, Albert had heard a version of the story, though not quite the true one; nearly all her friends had. Albert stepped in front of her, shielding her from Robert's view, as they rushed back to the table where their friends were. When Margot announced that Robert was there, everyone erupted in astonishment, and then they surrounded her and hustled her out of the bar as if she were the President and they were the Secret Service. It was all so over-the-top that she wondered if she was acting like a mean girl, but, at the same time, she truly did feel sick and scared.

Curled up on her bed with Tamara that night, the glow of the phone like a campfire illuminating their faces, Margot read the messages as they arrived:

"Hi Margot, I saw you out at the bar tonight. I know you said not to text you but I just wanted to say you looked really pretty. I hope you're doing well!"

"I know I shouldnt say this but I really miss you"

"Hey maybe I don't have the right to ask but I just wish youd tell me what it is I did wrog"

"*wrong"

"I felt like we had a real connection did you not feel that way or . . ."

"Maybe I was too old for u or maybe you liked someone else"

"Is that guy you were with tonight your boyfriend"

"???"

"Or is he just some guy you are fucking"

"Sorry"

"When u laguehd when I asked if you were a virgin was it because youd fucked so many guys"

"Are you fucking that guy right now"

"Are you"

"Are you"

"Are you"

"Answer me"

"Whore."

ANNIE BAKER

■

An Excerpt from *The Antipodes*

FROM *The Antipodes (A Play)*

The Antipodes *takes place in a windowless room at a conference table surrounded by ergonomic chairs. One woman and seven men are attempting to come up with a story for a mysterious piece of media. The head writer, Sandy, has told everyone to say "whatever weird shit comes into our minds," and that nothing is too personal or private to share. His assistant Sarah periodically brings them food and seltzer.*

* *indicates a leap forward in time.*
this leap forward is indicated by subtle shifts in actor behavior and movement and without lights or sound.

/ is an interruption and indicates when the next line of dialogue should begin.

SANDY
Biggest regret.
Danny.

DANNY M1
Let's see. Biggest regret.
I guess I/always—

SANDY
Not you Flasheroo.
The other Danny.

Pause.

DANNY M2
Oh.
Me?
Sorry.
I get/a little—

SANDY
Biggest regret.

Pause.

DANNY M2
Huh.
Let me think.
(long pause)
Well. Uh. This one summer when I was a teenager I lived on a farm.
And I had a lot of little jobs but one of them was putting the chickens to bed at night. There were a lot of foxes roaming around so it
was important to get all the chickens in their little chicken house by
sundown and lock the door behind them and then turn on the electric fence. And most of the chickens would be in the chicken house
already by the time it got dark and they'd be sleeping or sleepy and
I gotta tell you there's nothing cuter than a bunch of sleepy chickens nestled up together all plump with their eyes drooping shut.
But uh . . . yeah. There would usually be a few stragglers still wandering around and the guy who gave me the job told me that I was
supposed to pick those stragglers up and put them in the chicken
house. But for some reason I was terrified of picking up a chicken. I
loved them but the idea of grabbing them and . . . I don't know I pictured them pecking me and/or clawing me or me accidentally hurting them . . . maybe part of it was that I actually wanted to pick the
chickens up very badly . . . there was something about their chests,
those fluffy alive chicken breasts, and I loved the idea of holding
them firmly but lovingly in my hands but I just couldn't picture it going the right way . . . like how to do it . . . and I worried I would hurt

the chickens or be hurt by the chickens so I actually would just wait until way after sundown, like 10:30, 11 p.m., and that's when I would go lock the chicken house door and turn on the electric fence and by that time all the chickens had gone in the house and fallen asleep on their own. But I was really playing with fire because the fox could have come around before then. I mean something really bad could have happened in that two hour window. But I was so scared of picking up a chicken that I . . . I didn't tell anyone and I took that risk every night. Luckily no chickens died that summer. But they could have.

(pause)

So I guess my regret is that I didn't ask for a . . . that I didn't just ask someone to give me a tutorial on how to hold a chicken.

Pause.

ADAM
That's/your greatest—

ELEANOR
But nothing bad happened.

DANNY M2
But it could have.
And I guess . . .
(pause)
I guess what it's about is this sense I've always had that there's some secret, that there's some thing in this life I don't fully have access to, maybe it's a specific kind of joy, I'm not sure. And that summer with the chickens I really do feel like if I had just picked them up something would have changed in me and my life might be very different now.

No response from the group. He shakes his head and looks down at his hands for a while.

DANNY M2
Uh

Sorry
I feel like I should say something.
They all look at him. He's still looking at his hands.

DANNY M2
I really heard what you said on the first day about our stories—about our personal stories being the material for—being part of the inspiration for the work—
I really understand that. I think.
But uh—
Sometimes when I tell personal stories to you guys
Like just now
It doesn't feel real.
It feels misleading.

Pause.

SANDY
. . . What do you mean misleading.

DANNY M2
Afterwards I feel like I made something up. Even though I didn't.
There's not enough context or—
I'm telling a story because I think you want me to tell a story
And then I'm trying to figure out how you all see me in relation to the story.
And I can tell the way you're seeing me is not the way I am.

Pause.

DANNY M2
It just gets so personal.
And I guess I've always felt like my personal life is the part of my life that I don't want to turn into a story.
(long pause)
I also just want to add that I feel really lucky to be here and I really respect everyone in this room.

And I really respect what we're doing.

Silence. The only movement onstage is Dave transferring his toothpick from one side of his mouth to the other and then back again. It seems like Sandy might say something. After a long time, he starts texting. Then he dials a number and strolls out of the room.

DAVE
. . . I guess we're on a ten.

Eleanor takes out an egg and starts shelling it. Looking at his laptop:

BRIAN
Did you know that a whale off the coast of Brazil can hear what another whale is saying off the coast of Alaska? Something about the way the ocean transmits sound.

ADAM
I like that.

BRIAN
So if you're a whale you're hearing like every other whale in your hemisphere all talking at the same time. I mean not talking. Making /whale—

Sarah sticks her head in.

SARAH
Hey um Danny M?
Danny M Two?
Sandy was wondering if he could talk to you in his office for a second.

Pause.

DANNY M2
Yeah.
Yeah of course.

He exits, never to return. They all sit there, worried, except for Dave, who is throwing pieces of Smartfood up into the air and catching them in his mouth.

*

Sandy's back.

ELEANOR
And so the only way to kill the monster is to find his heart. But his heart is on an island on the other side of the world. And on that island there's a church and inside that church there's a well and inside that well there's a duck and inside that duck there's an egg and inside that egg is his heart. So if you enter his cave you're probably not gonna make it out alive.

*

JOSH
Imagine a world like ours.
With clocks and calendars and whatever.
But all the clocks tell a different kind of time.
You know how there are certain insects
And they only live a couple of days
But those days must go by so slowly, you know?
Because they're like literally a lifetime!

DANNY M1	DAVE
Yeah.	. . . Okay.

JOSH
So imagine a world like ours but the time the clock is telling is . . .
Well so a day could actually be a century. Like the clock face is measuring years.
Or it could be the opposite and an hour on the clock or what looks like an hour on the clock is actually a second. Or a millisecond.

So it's a totally different world but it appears the same. But to them a millisecond is a lifetime./Or a hundred years is a minute.

ELEANOR
Ooh that just gave me tingles.

ADAM
Do you guys know about the yugas?

They all shake their heads no.

ADAM
It's this Hindu cyclical idea of time and the universe and the idea is that we're always in one of four ages. Yugas. And when you're done with the fourth yuga you cycle back to the first. And each yuga is like hundreds of thousands of years long and each one is worse than the one that came before. Like right now we're supposedly living in something called the Kali Yuga which is the most like demonic fucked up age you can be in. And at the end of this yuga the universe will return to some like primordial ocean state for the length of all the past four yugas combined and then everything will start all over and people will be like nice to each other again.

DANNY MI   ELEANOR
Huh.   I like that.

JOSH
Yeah.
Yeah.
Cool.
I mean that's a little different from what I was saying but yeah that's—
That's cool.
So what I was saying was that maybe there's a world where people are experiencing—
Their world just measures time differently.
/They—

DAVE
How do we . . . how do we tell that story though?

Sarah has entered with a new box of seltzer. She puts it on top of the other boxes.

JOSH
What do you mean?

DAVE
If their minute is our century or our minute is their decade or—whatever—how do we tell the story of—are we telling the story in our time or in theirs?

JOSH
Yeah. Maybe there's a way to—
Maybe that would be the point.

DAVE
What would be the point?

JOSH
Like messing with all of that and—

*

SARAH
Oh. Sorry. I didn't realize you meant me. I thought you were talking/to—

SANDY
I meant you.

SARAH
Oh.
Wow.

Um.

Okay.

I feel kind of on the spot.

Pause.

SARAH

Well. Um. Hmm.

I guess only Sandy knows this but my mom died when I was thirteen?

DANNY M1	ELEANOR	JOSH	ADAM
Oh shit.	I'm so sorry.	That's awful.	Sorry, Sarah.

SARAH

Yeah I mean it's okay. I mean it's not okay. It's super sad. But it's like my life so . . . yeah.

Short pause.

SARAH

Anyway. Um. I kind of had this crazy experience like one year after she died.

Um.

(to Sandy)

You really want me to tell them about it?

He nods.

SARAH

Well. My dad remarried pretty quickly. And my stepmother and I didn't really get along. She was kind of this—well she was like this sort of makeup-y like—she came from a lot of inherited wealth and my mom was like—she was a social worker and she and my dad were always just trying to make ends meet. And then like six months after my mom dies my dad remarries and suddenly we're like living in this big house on the other side of town and I'm supposed to be really excited about it. But it just feels—I mean the house feels big and creepy and lonely. And my stepmother already has two daughters

and one of them is in college but the other one is around my age and like . . . she's this like popular girl who goes to private school and she like clearly hates me and she and my stepmother are like super girly. Anyway.
Wait you guys really want to hear this? This isn't boring?

DANNY M1	ADAM	JOSH
No.	No.	Keep going!

SARAH
Okay well at one point my dad went on a business trip and I was alone with my stepmother and my stepsister for two weeks. And one night my stepmother was cooking dinner and she said that she didn't have any um rosemary for this lamb stew she was making. So she told me to walk down the street and go to the little blue house at the end of the cul de sac and to ask the old woman who lived there if she had any rosemary we could borrow.
But I was scared. Everyone at my school said the little blue house was haunted and that the old woman who lived there was a witch. So I'm standing in my bedroom trying to decide what to do when this doll my mom gave me right before she died starts talking to me. And the doll says: Don't be afraid. Just do what you're told but don't forget to bring me with you.
So I walk down the street and it's dark and kind of creepy and when I get to the little blue house I realize for the first time that the fence which has always just seemed like plain painted white wood to me is actually made out of bones and on the top of every post is a human skull.

The phone starts ringing in the other room.

SARAH
Oh shoot.

The phone keeps ringing.

SARAH
If that's Jeff I should get it.

SANDY
Did Jeff say he was gonna call?

SARAH
He said later today or tomorrow.
(pause, phone still ringing)
I'm gonna get it just in case.
Sorry guys.
Hold on one sec.

She leaves. They all sit there in silence, waiting. After about fifteen seconds, she comes back in.

SARAH
It wasn't Jeff.

SANDY
Why is he calling at all?

SARAH
I think he wanted to check in about the schedule and/see if there's
any way he can—

SANDY
Check in about the schedule? There's no problem with the schedule.
We're on schedule.

SARAH
Great.

SANDY
When you talk to him tell him we're on schedule.
Because I don't want to talk to him.

SARAH
Great. Yeah. He knows we're on schedule. I think he just likes to
feel included and so he was reaching out to see if he could help or if

there's anything we need or . . .
Sandy nods and checks his phone. Sarah stands there for a few seconds.

SARAH
Oh yeah on top of every post was a human skull. So I'm terrified! Obviously.
And yeah I knock on the door and this old lady opens it and she looks like a million years old and I ask her if she has any rosemary and she says she has to check first and why don't I come inside. And like this feels like a really really bad idea but the doll whispers to me that I should do as I'm told and go inside. And so I go inside and it's basically like my worst nightmare. The old woman locks me in a room and tells me that she's going to put me in the oven and eat me unless I clean her whole house and separate the moldy corn from the good corn by the next day at sundown. Oh yeah she has this like enormous vat of corn kernels. Maybe I forgot to mention that. It's like an impossible task. So I'm like freaking out and then the doll says to me: "Go to sleep. Morning is wiser than evening." So I go to sleep and in the morning I wake up and the old lady has gone off to do errands and my doll has already like amazingly cleaned the whole house and has separated all the thousands of moldy kernels of corn from the good kernels of corn. And when the old woman comes home that night she can't believe it and she gets really mad because she was planning on eating me for dinner. And then she gives me another task for the next day. Now I have to clean every single kernel of corn until it's shiny and bright and I have to do it before sundown. It's another impossible task since there are like tens of thousands of kernels of corn. So that night the same thing happens . . . I cry in my room and then the doll says "Go to sleep. Morning is wiser than evening." And then when I wake up in the morning my awesome doll has already cleaned every single kernel of corn! And when the old woman gets home that evening hungry for dinner she can't believe that all the corn is clean and she gets really mad and yells: "How did you do all the work I gave you?" And I just say: "I did it with the blessing of my mother" because my mother did give me the doll and I didn't want to say, like, "the doll did it for me." Anyway right after I say that the old woman gets really scared and she says: "I don't want any blessings in my house" and she pushes me out the front door and

down to the gate made out of human bones and skulls. Then she takes one of the skulls and puts it on a pole for me and says: "This will light your way home." And sure enough there's fire inside the skull and it burns through the eyes and lights my way back to my stepmother's house. When I get back home I try to hide the skull in the garbage cans in our driveway so my stepmother doesn't find out but then I hear this little voice coming out of the skull. It's saying: "Don't throw me away. Take me to your stepmother." So I bring the skull inside and it stares at my stepmother and stepsister with these burning eyes and the eyes follow them wherever they go. The eyes burn right into their evil souls. And by the next morning they had both turned to ash.

Pause.

SARAH
That's it.

Pause.

SARAH
Did everyone write down their lunch orders?
Where's the sheet?

Josh hands her the sheet.

SARAH
Awesome. Lunch should be here by one at the latest.

She leaves.

*

Sandy vacates his chair at the end of the table and then they all put on tiny goggles and face the empty chair. They are talking to someone we can't see. We can only hear his voice. He has a posh British accent.

MAX
Hello!
Oh there you all are!

DAVE	ADAM	DANNY M1	JOSH	ELEANOR
Hi	Hello	Hey!	Hi	So nice to meet you!

SANDY
Why don't you all introduce yourselves.

DAVE
Hey Max. You know me.
(pause)
/Dave.

MAX
Yes hello Dave!

DANNY M1
Danny./We—

MAX
Yes Danny I remember Danny hello.

JOSH
Josh.

ADAM
Adam.

ELEANOR
Eleanor.

BRIAN
Brian.

Pause.

MAX
Brilliant. Hello everyone.

SANDY
This is the team, Max.

MAX
Yes yes *(garbled)* great and it's a *(garbled)* in every way.

They all smile at Max, trying to decide whether or not to say something to him about the connection. Sandy gives Brian a look like "fix this."

SANDY
How are you, Max?

MAX
I'm doing quite well. I'm sitting here in my kitchen and it's quite sunny after a few days of clouds and I'm very happy to talk *(garbled)* all of you.

Brian exits to go find Sarah.

SANDY
We're really happy to talk to you too.
You've got a lot of big fans in this room.

Danny M1 nudges or winks at Eleanor. She mouths "stop!!"

MAX
Well you already all know how *(garbled)* you are to be working with Sandy and I just want to say Sandy how lucky I feel to be embarking on em another journey with you. Heathens was such a success in every way, ah, artistically, financially, *(garbled)* we're thrilled you want to make something else with us.

SANDY
I'm thrilled too.
I'm thrilled too.

Brian and Sarah reenter and start scrambling around for a solution to the bad connection without Max seeing them.

MAX
(Garbled garbled) so just wanted to check in with what you all are thinking. I obviously want to give you a lot of *(garbled)* but we're all eager to know what you're cooking up in that *(garbled)*.

SANDY
Well Max it's only been what five, six weeks, so we've been doing a lot of talking, a lot of getting to know each other, you know how I like to break everyone down and make them tell me stories from their childhood/and—

MAX
(Garbled garbled)

SANDY
Yup. Yup.
And we're also asking each other big questions about time and space and the nature of what we all do for a living, you know?

MAX
(chuckles)
Yes. Sounds very *(garbled)*.

Brian and Sarah somehow communicate to Sandy that the problem is not fixable. Sarah exits. Sandy stoically launches into his pitch.

SANDY
So we're asking questions like:
What would communication look like without time?
(pause)
Does God think in generals or particulars?
(pause)
What if effects came before causes and answers before questions?
(pause)

Can you have meaning without matter?

Because we've been talking about the fact that whales and dolphins are telling each other stories all the time but they're doing it without words or pictures or objects.

What if we could do that for this project, Max?

What if we could tell the story that's the only story we all need to know? And we didn't even have to write it down or turn it into code or hire actors?

If you think about the greatest thinkers in world history

Jesus

Socrates

Confucius

None of those guys recorded anything or wrote anything down.

And what we know about them we know through other people telling stories about their stories.

Could we go back to the beginning?

Could we remake our collective unconscious?

Nothing from Max. Maybe a little static.

SANDY
And Dave had this—
Dave why don't you tell him.

Pause.

DAVE
Really?

SANDY
Yeah yeah. Go ahead.

Dave wishes he'd been prepared for this life-changing moment but he jumps in anyway.

DAVE
Well Sandy can tell you I see everything, including time, in terms of

circles and spirals. In terms of loops. I'm the loop guy.
(Eleanor looks at him, betrayed, but then quickly goes back to Max)
And so Sandy and I have been talking about a story that's a kind of
ouroboros. A snake eating its own tail. So there's a point at which,
without realizing it, you come back full circle and—picture this visual—you actually encounter yourself but from behind. Picture taking a hike and thinking you've walked in a straight line but then suddenly you find yourself back where you started and you're staring at
your old self, the self who stood there at the beginning of the hike, ty-
ing his shoelaces, but you're looking at the back of his head.

Still no response from Max.

SANDY
You still there, Max?

MAX
Yes. Yes. Although I think you lost me when you *(garbled)* talking
about snakes eating their own tails.

Max chuckles.

SANDY
Forget about that, Max. That's not the important part.

Dave scoots back in his chair, cowed.

MAX
Garbled Garbled heady stuff.

SANDY
Mmhm.
Say that again?

MAX
It sounds like you're getting into *garbled garbled* stuff.

SANDY
Yeah. Yeah. We are.

MAX
But ultimately you know what we love about you is your ability to just tell a really simple *(garbled)*, to reel people in and make them *garbled garbled.*

SANDY
Sure, sure.

A long silence.

MAX
   . . . Well. You seem like a lovely group.

JOSH	ELEANOR	ADAM
Yeah.	You too!	Thanks so much.

MAX
I'm going to sign off now because the dog is looking a bit anxious and pawing at the back door and I think he needs to take a wee.

SANDY
Thanks for listening, Max.

MAX
Thank you *(garbled)* everyone.

JOSH/DANNY M1/ELEANOR/ADAM
Bye/Bye/Thank you!/Nice meeting you.

Whatever they've been looking at disappears. They all take off their glasses.

JOSH
Well that was pretty cool.

ADAM
I can't believe that was/him.

ELEANOR
He looks so old.

JOSH
I thought he looked great.

ELEANOR
Yeah but he used to be so sexy.

DANNY M1
He's still a good-looking guy.

ELEANOR
Yeah but he's clearly had a face-lift.

JOSH
He has not had a face-lift.

ELEANOR
Yes he has! Yes he has! Oh my god men can never tell.
He's had his eyelids done and his face lifted and they shaved away
some of his chin and those are hair implants.

ADAM
You're insane.

ELEANOR	JOSH
I would bet you a million gazillion dollars.	He hasn't had plastic surgery. That's so not his style.

SANDY
Can everyone please just be quiet for 30 seconds so I can hear myself think?

They sit in silence.

LUCY HUBER

∎

A Fair Accusation of Sexual Harassment or a Witch Hunt?

FROM *McSweeney's Internet Tendency*

"In an interview with the BBC published early Sunday, director Woody Allen addressed the wave of allegations against Harvey Weinstein, calling it 'tragic for the poor women' but also warned against a 'witch hunt atmosphere.'" —New York Times, *October 15, 2017*

1. George is a middle-aged man who works in an office with a younger female colleague, Annie. The female colleague wears a short skirt one summer day to the office. George comments, "Nice gams, Annie" and gives her a wink. Annie files a complaint with HR. Is this:
A. A witch hunt
B. A fair accusation of sexual harassment

2. In the year 1693 in Salem Village, Sarah Good is a woman living in poverty and disliked by the townspeople. A jury of men decide that she was a witch after forcing her to confess that she signed her name in the "Devil's book," a thing that does not exist. She is hanged several days after giving birth to a daughter. Is this:
A. A witch hunt
B. A fair accusation of sexual harassment

3. Lucas is a photographer in New York. He often comes in contact with models and sometimes when directing—whoops!—he gives

them a quick pat on the bum. Several models have reported him, but nothing has been done. Is this:

A. A witch hunt

B. A fair accusation of sexual harassment

4. Sarah Osborne doesn't go to church like the townspeople of Salem expect her to. Because of this, a group of men decide she is a witch and is accused of using dark magic to pinch several young girls in town with invisible knitting needles. They arrest her, put her in prison, where she dies. Is this:

A. A witch hunt

B. A fair accusation of sexual harassment

5. Anderson manages a restaurant. He hires a new server, named Ella. While rubbing her shoulders he tells her that if she wants more tips she should wear a lower cut shirt. Ella does not feel comfortable around Anderson, but needs a job to pay her rent, so she only mentions this to her friend, who says he's done it to her, too. Is this:

A. A witch hunt

B. A fair accusation of sexual harassment

6. Tituba is a woman from Barbados, but is now enslaved by white people in the town of Salem. She continues to practice her religion, which the people of Salem don't understand. They assume it means she is a witch and beat her until she confesses and rambles about black dogs and riding on sticks, then imprison her, despite no evidence that witches actually exist. Is this:

A. A witch hunt

B. A fair accusation of sexual harassment

* * *

Sexual harassment: 1, 3, 5

Witch hunt: 2, 4, 6

BENJAMIN SCHAEFER

■

Lizard-Baby

FROM *Guernica*

LAST YEAR, WHILE ON VACATION in New Mexico, I went on a vision quest with a South American shaman, met the Devil, and came home pregnant. Mother keeps saying, Sins of the father, but I'm trying my best to remain optimistic. I wasn't even going to tell her about the baby until after he hatched, but then she showed up at my door in her white Chanel coat, with that pinched look on her face. You're pregnant, she said. I could tell by her tone it wasn't a question. I smiled. Won't you come in, Mother, and when she didn't, I said, Suit yourself, but it's a lot colder out there in the hallway, and retreated back into the apartment. I don't understand how this happened, she said. Do you need me to explain the mechanics to you? Don't be crass, Fiona. I saw you two weeks ago, thin as a cane, and now, well, I'm sorry dear, but you're *enormous*. In defense, I placed a hand on my belly, on the hard shell forming beneath the skin. I pictured the armored back of a tortoise; I whispered its secret name. Lizard-Baby.

Mother removed her winter gloves and placed them on the island counter and began to unbutton her coat. I suppose you'll be wanting me to explain this to your father. Don't worry about Daddy, he'll be fine, I said as I shouldered out of my bathrobe and dropped it on the kitchen floor. My God, Fiona, what are you doing? Mother asked. Oh, don't be so prudish, Mother. It's just *the body*, I said as I stretched out on the large slab of slate rock I had purchased from the garden store the day I returned home from New Mexico. I'd positioned it in the center of the living room where the coffee table once stood, having pushed all the furniture against the wall. I never understood the attraction of sunbathing, not until I was pregnant, that is. There was something delicious, luxurious, erotic almost about the feeling of the smooth hard surface against my bare skin, warmed by the heat lamps I'd angled around it. Mother retired to the lazy chair. Your sister never would have done this to our family, she said. I closed my eyes. Well, I'm sorry to have disappointed you.

Tomás was equally dissatisfied by the turn of events. If I'm being completely honest, I hadn't given much thought to how he'd figure in all this, not until a few days later when he rushed into the apartment. I forgot I had given him a key. I was lying down in the living room under the lamps, reading a magazine. It's not mine, is it? he asked, aghast, I'm sure, at the sudden curvature of my stomach, at the trail of dark hair and sweat that graced the incline down from my navel. No, Tomás, it is not yours, I said, and saw the breath escape him. For a moment he looked relieved. Wait, what do you mean it's not mine? I mean it's not yours, Tomás. Well, if it's not mine, then whose is it? he asked. I turned over on my side. You wouldn't believe me if I told you. Why are you even here? Your mother called and reamed me out for knocking you up. *Mother.* Well, I'm sorry, but she was mistaken. Is there anything else? No, I guess not, he said, and then, Can I get you anything? No, I said, and smiled, but it's sweet of you to ask. I guess I'll just be going then. I think that'd be for the best. Tomás looked down at his feet. His black curls covered his eyes as he tended to a mark on the floor with the toe of his shoe. You're sure it isn't mine? he asked.

The following Monday, I went into the office to file for maternity leave. It always seemed strange to me that, for all intents and purposes, maternity leave and disability are practically the same thing. Though perhaps not so strange, I considered as I waited in the lobby, opting for the elevator instead of the stairs. I was still trying to negotiate the change in my weight. My boss was, for obvious reasons, surprised by the state I arrived in, but gracious still. When are you due? he asked. I told him I had no idea. Soon, I hope! Well, take as much time as you need, he said, patting me awkwardly on the arm in that way men have of handling anything remotely hormonal. Margaret, the woman who worked in the cubicle next to mine, congratulated me on my way out. I noticed you'd been wearing looser-fitting clothing recently, you sly fox, you, she said. A baby is one of God's greatest gifts. I decided to play it coy. Well, it's certainly a gift from somebody! I said.

I always thought it was such a cliché when women described giving birth as pushing something the size of a watermelon out of a hole the size of your fist. First of all, I don't know about you, but the hole in my pink panther is not the size of a fist, and second, have you ever seen a baby? Not the size of a watermelon. Besides, babies are squishy. You know what isn't squishy? An egg.

Three weeks home from New Mexico, I gave birth to the egg in my bed, in the apartment, in the middle of the night. Earlier that evening, I got an inkling it wanted out of my body. I could not sit still. I just kept circling the island counter—round and round and round I went. I considered driving myself to the hospital, but what could they do? I asked myself. Around eight, I began piling every soft thing I owned onto the bed: washcloths and beach towels and the cushions from my couch. I shredded rolls of toilet paper with my fingernails, and crumpled up the Sunday paper's holiday ads, sheets upon sheets of wrapping paper. I reached out to an old friend, a girl I knew from undergrad, who'd gone on to study veterinary medicine at Cornell. Relax, she assured me over the phone, you're just nesting. When there was nothing left, I burrowed deep down in the bed and waited, and when it came time to push, I felt as though my body was being split open. I reached down and felt the tip of the egg peeking out from the space between my legs. Then, when I was able to get a good grip on it, I pulled that sucker out with a sudden pop. My hips disjointed and buckled back into place. I had never in my life felt more alone or more powerful.

As difficult as the birthing was—I could barely walk the following few weeks—the month and a half, forty-two days to be exact, that came after were the hardest because of the waiting. With a normal child, the birth is the climax, the grand payoff for months of preparing. Not so with a Lizard-Baby. I relocated the nest to the slate slab and spent my days adjusting the temperature of the heat lamps, caressing this hard speckled thing that was of me but no longer a part of me. I lost weight. You have to eat something, Mother told me. If only I knew he was all right in there, I said, stroking the egg. She called Tomás, still convinced he was responsible for the mess I'd found myself in, and one night he showed up at the apartment, this time troubling himself to knock before entering. I slumped to the door. I don't have the energy to go through this with you tonight, Tomás, I said. He grinned and held up a high-powered flashlight. I come bearing gifts. Trust me, he said. We went to the nest and turned off the heat lamps. The apartment was entirely dark. I did some research, Tomás said, flicking the lantern's switch and shining the light through the backside of the shell. It's called *candling*. And there he was, my son, floating in the fluid membrane of the egg, flexing his five fingers as if to reach out and touch me.

When the Lizard-Baby hatched, it was like the best Christmas ever, though by then Christmas had long come and gone. The whole family was there—Mother and Daddy and my sister, Becca. Tomás was there too. We stood in a circle around the nest in the living room as the Lizard-Baby struggled to extract himself from the crumbling walls of the egg, nuzzling his way out with the flat of his nose. Daddy reached out to peel back a piece of the shell in order to assist him, but Mother swatted his hand away, saying, Don't you rush him, Charles. He was born to do this. Does no one else think this is bizarre? Becca asked. Oh, shush now, Rebecca, Mother said. This is an important moment for our family, and I won't have you spoiling it. Already, I could see that things were changing—my ascension in the family ranks. I could tell by the expression on my sister's face that she saw it too. Becca, the favorite, was being usurped.

To say people were eager to meet this miracle child of mine would be an understatement. The most adamant, I found, were the girls from the office. I'd been gone from work for almost eight weeks, and though my paid leave had run out, I told them I had no intention of returning. As if that matters, Margaret told me. A baby is a baby and we want to celebrate. We're coming. So, true to her nature, Mother hosted a shower at the apartment. More of a luncheon, she assured me. Just a few of your coworkers, Rebecca, and myself. Nothing fancy. Finger sandwiches and iced tea. I don't know how we'll convince your father to stay at home, though, he's so fond of the baby.

At the shower, the women from work couldn't get enough of the Lizard-Baby. They fawned over his skin, scaled and pale green, the way he periodically ran his tongue over his protruding black eyes to compensate for his inability to blink. Yup, my father said, look at those eyes. He definitely gets his eyes from my side of the family. And then he lowered his voice, His tongue though? One hundred percent your mother's genes. Charlie! Mother said from the kitchen, but anyone could see she was blushing. Though I'm sure they all wanted to, Margaret was the only of my coworkers I trusted enough to hold the Lizard-Baby, but as she cradled him, he pawed at her shoulder and the setae on his toe pads snagged on the fabric of her cable-knit sweater. I'm so sorry, I said. We'll replace it, I promise. Oh, please, she said. If you mind a mess, don't hold a baby. That's what I always say. The girls remarked on how well-behaved the Lizard-Baby was. I don't think I've ever seen a newborn smile as much as he does, one said. Yes, he's a happy baby, I agreed. Becca peered over Margaret's shoulder. I think that's just how his face is, she said. That's because he's *always happy*, Rebecca, Mother informed her. Becca was just sore because the week before, she had tried to scratch the Lizard-Baby under his chin and he bit her finger. Daddy snapped, He isn't a dog, Rebecca!, as Mother whisked the Lizard-Baby out of the room.

There are quite a few upsides to raising a Lizard-Baby, despite what you might think. I'll hip you to one—it's a lot less expensive than caring for a normal baby. I mean, have you been to the baby aisle of a department store lately? Nothing is cheap. But with Daddy's admonishment of Becca in mind, I soon realized we could get everything we needed for a fraction of the cost at a commercial pet store. Take the crib, for example. An average crib can go for anywhere between $200 and $800, but I got a Petyard Pen Plus for $129.50 and erected it around the slate slab right in the living room. It even folds up, so I can take it to my parents' or Becca's if I want to. Also, doggie diapers. They're less expensive than Pampers *and* there's a hole for the tail. I even found myself eyeing those little garments, the kind that slip over the head of your pet and fasten around the waist. For Easter services, Mother brought over a little Jackie O coat. It was only $16, she said. I couldn't help myself.

We spent the Fourth of July with my family at my parents' place up on Seneca Lake. Daddy set up the pen in my old room, but the Lizard-Baby spent most of the day on the couch with Becca. He'd finally started to warm up to her, due in part, I'm sure, to the fact that she'd taken to stashing dried mealworms in her pants pocket. She portioned them out one by one until the Lizard-Baby settled down on her lap. Sitting there, the look on her face was triumphant. Just try not to spoil his dinner, I told her. She responded by flipping me the bird. Rebecca! After dinner, we congregated out on the lawn for the fireworks display, but when the first one exploded, blossoming in the sky with a flash of light and a sonic boom that filled the air, the Lizard-Baby let out a sound I'd never heard from him before, a combination of his lovely chirping and the awful squawk woodpeckers make. The fireworks literally scared the piss out of him—I was wet all down the front of my shirt—and it took us hours to coax him out from under the deck.

All things considered, I thought I was handling the whole situation with about as much grace as could have reasonably been expected of me. Even when Mother stepped on the Lizard-Baby's tail and the damn thing fell off. Even when some punk at the grocery store turned to me in the check-out line and exclaimed, quite loudly, Dude, your baby's a lizard! I took it all in stride. Still, nothing prepared me for the shedding. When I think of shedding, I think of Lassie. Or snakes. I think of Adam and Eve. I do not think of children. Imagine, your six-month old flaky and chaffing over the entirety of his body. You dowse him in baby powder until dusty white clouds trail behind him; you rub baby oil into the scales of his cool green skin until he glides across the floor like a Slip 'N Slide, gleefully chirping. Still, at day's end, when you put him to bed, he crinkles in your arms like packaging paper. Now imagine one day he slips from that skin as though from a wetsuit.

It was September, the humidity of summer had recently lifted, and I hadn't left the apartment all week. At that time, I was still waking up every few hours to feed the Lizard-Baby the small pink mice I kept in the freezer, or to deal with his dry skin, or to rock him to sleep, and by Friday, I'd hit a wall. I was making dinner and the Lizard-Baby was in his crib, playing with the makeshift rattle Daddy had dropped off earlier that evening—a brown paper bag filled with a handful of crickets, sealed and fastened to the end of a popsicle stick. When he shook it, the crickets popped against the bag, trying to escape their paper prison. Pop, pop. Pop, pop. I was straining the spaghetti when I heard a strange kind of crunching. I just assumed that, impatient and hungry, the Lizard-Baby had torn into the paper bag of the rattle, but when I looked up from the sink I saw that it lay beside him, untouched on the slate rock, and my son was standing behind a perfect opaque cast of his little lizard body, the head of which he'd begun to eat. I couldn't help it; I screamed and dropped the spaghetti. Startled, the Lizard-Baby snatched the skin-sheath up in his mouth and greedily devoured the thing before I could reach him to confiscate it. I called Tomás, and when he finally showed up at the apartment, I thrust the baby upon him. I haven't showered in three days, I haven't slept in weeks, I've given birth to the Devil's son, and now he's eating—I can't—I just can't, I said. I've ruined my life! Then I went to my room, closed the door, and fell asleep crying.

It's a conversation I don't think we have often enough. Or maybe we do, and before I got pregnant I just wasn't paying attention. But I don't even think that's true, really. Even now, when I hear other parents talk about the difficulties involved in raising a child, how it forces you to completely reconfigure the terms of your life, it's a side comment, a passing remark that's casually dismissed in the face of all the joy that accompanies new parenthood. I can't say for certain, but I'm pretty sure I've never heard a single parent make this assertion in quite the same way. Raising children is exhausting, and no matter how profound my love for the Lizard-Baby was, there were days when I woke up already feeling defeated as a human being. I slept clean through the night, and when I got up the next morning, I launched out of bed in a state of panic. How long had I slept? Where was my Lizard-Baby? I opened the bedroom door full of dread, but there was Tomás, calm as could be, in the living room, crouched over a small cube-shaped machine. He'd wrapped the Lizard-Baby up in a peanut-shell sling tied around his chest, and from it, the Lizard-Baby was reaching up with his little ribbed fingers, tugging at Tomás's lower lip. He chirped and smiled when he saw me. Everything's fine, Tomás said, flipping a switch on the machine, which began to emit a stream of fine mist. We just need to humidify the apartment.

The Lizard-Baby grew at a reptilian rate. By October he was the size of a toddler and in complete control of his faculties. Even his tail had grown back by then, though it was fatter than before and a kind of cold gray color. I'll never forgive myself, Mother said, shaking her head. I've scarred him for life. But the Lizard-Baby didn't seem to pay much attention to this transfiguration of his body. At the end of the month, the entire family agreed, we'd take him trick-or-treating on Halloween. What are we going to dress him up as? Becca asked. Mother scoffed and Tomás laughed. Seriously? he said. It's the one night out of the year when nobody'll look at him sideways. I, myself, wasn't so sure, but Tomás was right, the Lizard-Baby just passed as a particularly well-disguised child. Parents stopped us to applaud our work right there on the street. You must be in television, one woman said. I don't think I've ever seen a more realistic costume. Everything was fine, better than fine, until we stopped at a house where some guy insisted on getting a photograph of his kid, a Ninja Turtle, Donatello, I think, with the Lizard-Baby. I love those commercials, he said, pushing his boy shoulder-to-shoulder with mine, who was distractedly shaking the candy in his hollow plastic pumpkin, the sound no doubt reminding him of the rattle waiting at home. Just before the man snapped the picture, I remember thinking about the fireworks on the Fourth of July. The flash went off and the Lizard-Baby shrieked like a rabbit. The plastic pumpkin crashed to the ground, sending chocolate bars flying, and my son dropped to all fours and scampered off into the night, the neighborhood crowded with innumerable beasts.

He's a big lizard! I said, frantically trying to describe my son to one of the officers who'd shown up at the scene. All I could think about were those pet alligators that people abandon to grow up in the sewers. Yes, I understand, Miss, but what does your son look like when he's not in costume? the officer asked. Don't forget about his tail! Becca added. Yes! Mother said. It's big and gray and ugly. No! Not ugly! It's beautiful! My grandson is beautiful. Dear God, this is all my fault! The patrolling officers fanned out and canvassed the neighborhood. Do you have any idea where your son might have gone? No, Tomás said. He's never been out this way before.

An hour after he went missing, a woman, the one who'd made the comment about me being in TV, showed up with the Lizard-

Baby. He was holding the hand of her young daughter. I can't thank you enough, I said, clutching the Lizard-Baby to my breast. Charlie, where's my pocketbook? Mother shouted to Daddy. We're writing this woman a check. Please, the woman said, picking up her own child, a towheaded girl dressed as Kermit the Frog. We parents are all in this thing together. It's not easy being green, I know.

The next morning, Tomás came by the apartment with a suitcase and a cardboard box of his stuff. What are you doing? I asked when I opened the door. You can't do this by yourself anymore, he said. He needs a father. He has a father, I reminded him. That may be so, he said as he brushed past me, but he still needs a dad. And that was that.

In the end, I decided to return to work the week after Thanksgiving, almost a year to the day since I took my trip to New Mexico and everything changed. Tomás sleeps in the spare room, but most nights I come home and find him lying down in the baby's pen, the Lizard-Baby curled up against his chest, soaking in the heat from his body. I stand there watching them like that, on the verge of a compelling happiness, and then I think, *Where are we going to enroll him when the time comes for his schooling? Will the other children taunt him the way children do? How will he play sports or drive a car comfortably with that big tail of his? What girl will want to kiss a Lizard-Boy on the night of her prom?* I tell myself I could navigate these things on my own, without Tomás's help, without the assistance of my family, but I'm grateful I don't have to, and when you get down to it, that's a good thing, I believe.

LÁSZLÓ KRASZNAHORKAI

■

Chasing Waterfalls

Translated from Hungarian by John Batki

FROM *Harper's Magazine*

HE HAD ALWAYS PLANNED THAT SOMEDAY he would travel to see Angel Falls, then he had planned to visit Victoria Falls, and in the end he had settled for at least Schaffhausen Falls: one day he'd go and see them, he loved waterfalls, it's not easy to explain, he would begin whenever he was asked what his thing was about waterfalls, waterfalls, he would begin, and he would get embarrassed right away, this whole thing got on his nerves, to be asked, and to become embarrassed because of it, just standing there like one smacked on the head with a frying pan, so that those among his acquaintances who knew about the thing chose instead to drop the matter, even though the question would have been justified, everyone around him knew that he liked waterfalls and that he had always planned on traveling to see at least one, as they say, at least once in his life, first and foremost Angel Falls, or Victoria Falls, but at the very least Schaffhausen Falls, whereas things happened quite otherwise, in fact utterly otherwise, for he had arrived at that time of life when one no longer knows how many years remain, possibly many, perhaps five or ten or even as many as twenty, but it is also possible that one might not live to see the day after tomorrow. The sound of one of these falls, by the way, was constantly in his ears, after fantasizing about them all these years he had started hearing one of them, but which one it was he couldn't know of course, so that after a while, around the time he turned sixty, he was no longer sure why he had wanted to see the first or the second or at least the third of these waterfalls, was it so that he could at least decide which one it was he had heard all his life, or more accurately the second half of his life, whenever he shut his eyes at night? or because he had actually wanted to see one of them. By a grotesque twist of fate he who in the course of all those years had been sent to just about every corner of the globe had never been sent near a falls, and this is how it happened that he of all people, who had this thing with waterfalls, found himself in Shanghai again (the occasion was of no interest, he had to interpret for one of the usual series of business meetings), and he, for whom all his life waterfalls possessed such a special role, now in an utterly astounding manner precisely here in Shanghai had to realize the reason why all his life he had yearned to see the Angel, or the Victoria, or at the very least the Schaffhausen Falls, precisely here in Shanghai where it was common knowledge that there were no waterfalls. He had been a simultaneous interpreter ever since he could remember, and of all things it was precisely simultaneous interpretation that exhausted him the most, especially when it happened to be for a business meeting in Asia, as was the case now, and especially when at the obligatory dinner afterward he was obliged to drink as much as he did this evening, well, what's done is done, in any case, here he was by eveningtime, a wrung-out dishrag, as they say, drunk as a skunk, a used-up dishrag, this dead-drunk, here he stood in the middle of the city, on the riverbank, soused, dead drunk, a wrung-out dishrag, speaking sotto voce and not being terribly witty, so this is Shanghai, meaning here I am once again in Shanghai, he had to admit that, alas, he found the fresh air had not been all that beneficial even though, as they say, he had nourished great hopes for it, since he was aware, if we may speak of awareness in his case now, aware that he had drunk way too much, he had drunk far more than what he could handle, but he had been in no position to refuse, one glass followed another, too many of them, and already in the room he had felt sick, a vague notion churning inside him that he needed fresh air, fresh air, but once outside in the fresh air the world began to spin around him even more, true, it was still better here outside than indoors, he no longer remembered if he had been dismissed or had simply sneaked outside, it was alas no longer meaningful to speak of memory in his case at this moment as he stood in a peculiar posture near the upper sector of the Bund's ponderous arc of buildings, he leaned against the railing and eyed the celebrated Pudong on the other side of the river, and by this time the almost disastrously fresh air had come to have enough of an effect for his consciousness to clear up for a single moment and abruptly let him know that all this did not interest him the least little bit, and he was terribly bored in Shanghai, here, standing on the riverbank near the upper sector of the Bund's ponderous arc of buildings, this was made evident by his posture, and what was he supposed to do now?—after all, he could not remain leaning on that railing till the end of time in this increasingly calamitous condition. I do simultaneous interpretation, he said aloud, and paused, to see if someone had heard him, but no one had at all, oh well, of course, how could he have imagined that his announcement, in the Hungarian language, and in Shanghai, would be of any help, yes, that would be a tough one to explain, but to explain anything in his situation would have been a chore, I do simultaneous interpretation, he repeated therefore, while to the best of his ability he kept his head— that is the skull where the pain originated—completely still as he pronounced these words, his whole body went completely rigid, that was how he managed to contain the pain up there, trying to keep this pain from growing any more intense, for this was an intense pain that was getting so intense, so powerful, that it simply blinded him, or, to put it more accurately, he was suddenly aware that here he sat, stone cold sober, here, somewhere, in a location for the time being impossible to identify, all around him the roar, rumble, thunder of a traffic that was insane, everywhere, overhead, down below, on the left and on the right, yes, that horrific din simply everywhere, and here he was sitting right in the middle of it, but where this here was he had not the faintest idea, blinded, he could not see, and for that matter he could not hear, for the din he was hearing was just as powerful, and was increasing at the same rate, as the pain inside his skull. All of a sudden, pow, it began to subside, and the moment arrived when he was able to open his eye, only a slit, at first only a slit, but it was enough for him to establish that he had never before sat in the place where he was sitting, and perhaps no one had ever sat there before, for he immediately realized that he was sitting in the middle of expressways curving every which way, or, to put it more accurately, expressways arching in various directions, he was surrounded by expressways, no mistaking it, the image seen through the slit told him: expressways overhead, expressways down below, expressways to the left, and finally expressways to the right as well, naturally, his first thought was that he was not well, and the next thought was that not only he but this whole thing around him was not well, elevated expressways on many levels, who ever heard of such a thing. As a simultaneous interpreter he possessed certain areas of specialization, one of these being traffic and transport systems, and since he was a simultaneous interpreter with a specialty in traffic and transport systems he had a good hunch by now about where he found himself except that he refused to believe it, no human being could possibly be in the place where he now was, notwithstanding the fact that he could see the famous pillar down below with the dragons winding around it, oh no, he thought now, oh no, I am inside Nine Dragon Crossing, or as the locals say, Jiulongzhu Jiaoji, is not something a human being can be inside of, and the moment arrived when that slit became a full view, because by now he dared to open one eye, or one might have said that the eye simply popped wide open, for he was not hallucinating, he was indeed inside Nine Dragon Crossing, deep inside it, with his back leaning against the railing of some sort of pedestrian bridge, as if someone had propped him up against it. Now his other eye popped open most boldly, for this was the moment when he realized that he was high up, that this pedestrian bridge as its name indicated was a real bridge that rose in the air above ground level and was not merely bridging over something but in fact conducted the pedestrian at various levels of elevation among the expressways that ran up above and down below, running this way and that, was this a sane thing to do?! he asked himself, no it was not, he answered, so that after all—and here he lowered his glance to look in front of his feet—then I must be crazy, this is how it had to end, I got royally drunk, perfectamente drunk, so drunk that I ended up here, in this madness, I am imprisoned inside this madness. A person could not climb inside such a metropolitan highway whatchamacallit, especially not so that he ends up with his back propped up against the plexiglass siding of a pedestrian footbridge, and he is half toppled over and therefore leaning on his left hand to keep from sliding any more, no, not this way or any other way, this is absurd, I'm probably not insane, he reassured himself, I am a simultaneous interpreter, and I have perfect recall—he rose from his humiliating supine position on the pedestrian bridge—everything that needs to be known from a transport-systems point of view about an intersection like this is in my head down to the last detail, and he stood up, and although he had to grab onto the handrail at first, after the first three or four meters he let go of it and took some unaided steps relishing the full dignity of his balance, thus setting out on the pedestrian bridge toward somewhere, but as the bridge right away curved into a turn, leading toward a future that was too uncertain for him, he decided it was wiser to stop, and so he halted, and by now all was well, his head was clear, his head no longer ached, his head was capable of quite lucidly making inquiries into existence, namely his own, which he proceeded to do, to wit, obviously there must be a reason that I have come to a point in my life where I must now declare what I have learned about the world in the course of sixty years, nearly forty of which have been as a simultaneous interpreter, and if I don't then I will take it to the grave with me, but that, and he continued his train of thought, that, however, will not happen, and I am going to make my declaration right here, indeed, he would gladly declare himself here and now, but the problem was that he had learned nothing about the world, and so what was he to say, what indeed, that he was a simultaneous interpreter who had lived close to forty years devoted exclusively to his profession; he was not claiming that, for instance when he looked at, say, a deck of cards, he did not have some unanswered questions, because aside from his profession he also loved card games, and his question was, well now, was this a full deck of cards, or was it merely any forty-eight individual cards, but there were only those kinds of questions, the one particular question regarding the world itself, which, he was well aware, might be expected from an experienced simultaneous interpreter in his sixties, that one particular question, no, it had never occurred to him, so that if fate had now cast him here to make a declaration about that then he was in a fine pickle, for he didn't know anything about anything, there was nothing he could say about the world in general, nothing he could put in the form of a philosophy of life, no, nothing like that, here he gave a slight shake of his head, what spoke to him is what he saw here, from this pedestrian bridge, but about life in general, alas, he can say nothing. Once again his eyes swept over the horrific caval-cade of ponderous expressway ramps stretching and arching above and below each other, and he could only gape this way and that way, he tried to follow individual stretches of highway in order to find out what direction they went in, but it proved impossible, at least from here, from the inside, the entire thing had ended up so bafflingly complex. He shoved himself away from the railing against which he had been leaning for the last few minutes, and taking the utmost care he nonetheless set out in the dark on that pedestrian bridge curving away into an uncertain future, until after taking exactly sev-enteen steps his form disappeared beyond the bend, and thus shortly thereafter all human presence ceased within the interior hell of Nine Dragon Crossing, which is no place for a human being in any case.

Your Perrier, sir, said the room-service waiter outside the door, but then he had to send him back for an additional bottle, and he had to request that the first bottle be exchanged for a larger one, then he had two or three fresh pitchers of ice brought up because after he at last arrived in his room and toppled onto the bed it was not so much that his head began to ache immediately as all of a sudden there was a large bowl of mush in place of a head; he had entered the room, taken off his clothes, kicked off his shoes, and thrown himself on the bed, arranging for everything from there, the phone within reach; his room-service order, the modification of the order, the repeat of the order, and so on, meanwhile lying on his back and not moving, resting his head—that bowl of mush—against the pillow, his eyes closed; that's how it was for a while, until the horrendous stink he himself emanated began to bother him, whereupon he crawled to the bathroom, brushed his teeth, turned on the shower, and scrubbed his body with soap and remained under the shower for as long as his strength held out, then toweled himself dry, sprayed frightful amounts of hotel deodorant on himself, pulled on a clean T-shirt and underpants, and before lying back down he took the soiled garments and his light summer leather shoes, stuffed them in a plastic bag that he tied with a tight knot before placing it outside in front of the door, then stretched out on the bed, and turned on the TV, merely listening to the sound without watching, for his head continued to remain a bowl of mush, and this was all right, things were all right now, his eyes shut, the TV on, the sound not too loud, the words, sentences, voice, speech morphing in slow gossamer-light increments into a so-called eternal sound of running water, but no, not really the sound of water splashing, and he pulled the blanket over himself, for he was starting to shiver because the air conditioning was set too high, no, this was not water splashing, it was a roar, like the ocean, but no, not the ocean really, reflected that sizable load of mush inside his head, this was something else, this . . . this sound, he now recognized, before sleep swallowed him up, was a waterfall.

He woke immediately, as if jolted by electric shock, he looked at the TV set in disbelief, only the waterfall sound could be heard, he leaped from the bed, sat down on its edge, and leaning forward stared at the TV set, oh my God, he clenched his fists in his lap, it was exactly the same as the sound of the waterfall that he had never been able to identify among those three, he watched the TV screen panic-stricken, the image now showed a cascading waterfall, and he slowly grasped that this was not some nightmare, he leaned forward even closer and watched the waterfall on the TV screen, he saw no subtitles whatsoever that could have helped to identify which one it was, the Angel, the Victoria, or possibly the Schaffhausen, all they showed was the waterfall itself, the sound was a steady roar. He watched each and every drop of the waterfall, feeling an unspeakable relief, and savoring the taste of a newfound freedom, he understood that his life would be a full life, a fullness that was not made of its parts, the empty fiascoes and empty pleasures of minutes and hours and days, no, not at all, he shook his head, while in front of him the TV set kept roaring, this fullness of his life would be something completely different, he could not as yet know in what way, and he never would know, because the moment when this fullness of his life was born would be the moment of his death—he shut his eyes, lay back on the bed and remained awake until it was morning, when he rapidly packed his things and checked out at the reception desk with such a radiant face that they contacted the staff on his floor to check whether he had taken anything with him, how could they have possibly understood what had made him so happy, how could the cab driver or the people at the airport understand, when they were not aware that such happiness existed, he radiated it as he passed through the security check, he glowed as he boarded the plane, his eyes sparkled as he belted himself into his seat, just like a kid who has at last received the gift he dreamed of, because he was in fact happy, except he could not speak about it, there was indeed nothing to do but look out through the window of the plane at the blindingly resplendent blue sky, keeping a profound silence, and it no longer mattered which waterfall it was, it no longer mattered if he didn't see any of them, for it was all the same, it had been enough to hear that sound, and he streaked away at a speed of 900 km per hour, at an altitude of approximately ten thousand meters in a north-by-northwesterly direction, high above the clouds—in the blindingly blue sky toward the hope that he would die someday.

■

Love, Death & Trousers:
Eight Found Stories

from The Paris Review

It's quite possible that the existence of these eight short stories, taken word for word from a collection of 148 diaries found in a dumpster in 2001, would come as a surprise to the diarist, Laura Francis. All the sentences, events, perceptions, and fineness of writing belong to her, but the plots and narrative arcs have been manufactured by me.

The discovery of these diaries and the four years I spent hunting down their author are the subject of my book A Life Discarded. *Laura Francis was a live-in companion and domestic servant for an aged professor of IT—like his wife in every respect except the sex ("thank goodness"). She barely knew how to cook and had no time for tidiness. On several occasions, during her thirty years of service, she grabbed a knife and was vicious to the old man's furniture. But she was also funny, self-sacrificially kind, and a profound observer of loneliness and disappointment.*

Laura could be an excellent diarist, but frequently wasn't. Why should she be? She wasn't performing for an audience. She had no duty to entertain. Her writing is repetitive, self-obsessed, confused, and two millimetres high. A typical two-hundred-page notebook from the 1990s contained over a hundred thousand words and covered just six weeks of her life in which nothing happened. Yet her style has the one quality that professional writers, of fiction or nonfiction, find the most difficult to capture: vitality. Her life is small-scale, quiet voiced, punctuated by moments of gentle humor and shocking poignancy. Even when the diaries are agonizingly tedious, you want to go on reading them because they are true.

No novelist has clattered into this woman's life to impose a well-managed structure on her images of incarceration and waste. There's none of the storyteller's fraudulent scene setting, character development, points of conflict, concluding resolution. You are peering in on a real woman who thinks she is alone—a woman in the final stages of tedium. She is writing about being human: the arbitrariness, the impotence, the fog. Vitality—aliveness—comes to her because she has just picked up her pen. Her drama is that she is not fiction.

Laura's diaries work best at the extreme dimensions of writing: page by page, they lack structure, pacing, plot, character development, and most of the time, excitement. But at the large scale (book by book) and the small (sentence by sentence), they are replete with human insight and lurking dramatic narratives.

—Alexander Masters

Dramatis Personæ

"I"...*Laura Francis, the diarist*
E..*her guide and muse, a piano teacher*
Elf.....................*Dame Harriette Chick DBE, for whom Laura worked as a housekeeper/companion during the second half of the 1970s*
Peter............................*Dame Harriet's nephew, who also lived in the house*

SUDDENLY E CAME TO MY COUNTER, 1958–59

December 17th, 1958: Lovely afternoon spent in happiness and utter satisfaction and harmony. Harry & Mrs. Willey talked of how they'd have a copy of my book when it was published.

Dec 18th: A pity, though, my profession takes so much of my time.

Dec 19th: Tiresome, having to be tied down to fact & reality.

Dec 19th: Working on out-counter at Central Library.

Dec 20th: Suddenly E came to my counter. I gave the usual terrific jump I do with the sight of E unexpectedly, and sat down on the chair. E amused, said I'm a funny girl. E looked round library, eventually got out "English Villages in Colour." She looked <u>terribly</u> swerb [wonderful]—waves of dizzy excitement swept through me, head over heels with adoration for E. Her sweet smile, rather wicked & sideways.

Dec 22nd: She invited me to supper. The mutual love and our expressions must've been very noticeable. Just adored her, and felt she was adoring me back with her sweet, warm brown-eyed gaze—currency of love.

Dec 23rd: We kissed. I called E "you sweet darling." E said yes.

Dec 29th: We went in E's bedroom—it was both unbeautiful and untidy. E herself as I like her—in a sloppy old coat, with bedroom slippers.

March 5th, 1959: E said she was not interested in sex at all. Said only when one is engaged should one go to the doctor and find out "what it is all about."

THE AIR HOLLOW AND EMPTY, 1959

Mar: The air hollow and empty of E. Our last time together was so joyous, and full of dramatic irony & little E standing rapt & thrilled on the doorstep. And now E gone off to Switzerland.

Apr: Around nine, was biking home and a wonderful primitive fantasy—the trees, tall, dark, windy, mysterious—just wish to go among them forever, and leave the natural light, close to the earth; and what is more, in the deepest, darkest, windiest depths of the wood, lying with some sweet creature in my arms—my lover. No physical desire for sex—just spiritual desire—imagine sex would be tremendously exciting, an adventure of the spirit.

July: Wouldn't mind knowing Dennis (at the University Library) off-duty. Like his lean body in the white shirt & braces; he is both straight and not straight—often automatically jerks himself straight when he feels himself beginning to slump. Like his grey hair, and the absurdly boyish shape of his head, & his little reddish-tinged moustache. Like his nose, upturned as my sweet darling little E's. Nice round blue eyes—kind & honest. Like his white hands with one golden ring on a finger.

Later: Learnt that Dennis is very keen on collecting butterflies—how absolutely deadly.

July 8th: Pasternak—what a striking face, his eyes on fire, his chin jutting, his head up proudly, his mouth bitter. Tremendous intellectual powers, colossal fantasy—would I be a writer like that! Wish my day would come to receive the Nobel Prize! The Nobel Prize would give me a straight back more than any posture exercises!

July 9th: About half way through *Dr. Zhivago* & find this controversial work of genius <u>boring</u>.

July 12th: Still reading *Dr. Zhivago*.

July 15th: Nearly finished *Dr. Zhivago*.

July 17th: Finished *Dr. Zhivago*—got something out of it, but it is vast —train journeys that last for weeks.

E back from Switzerland: we went out into the cool evening sunshine. E strangely real, strangely unreal. The sun picked out every detail— her good knobbly hands, and the strong sensible nails—do so like them—quite without feminine silliness—strong, square-cut & plain. Her lovely little face as wonderful as ever with deep expressive eyes and sherbet eyebrows & wide curving mouth. E laid her hand on mine, and talked of the Loch Ness monster.

Various dates, 1959:
E said I'm very small, not interested in the world.
E said she didn't believe in any of my so-called gifts, not even writing.

E said I am stupid.

E said my song-capacity nothing, just a manifestation of the sexual impulse, like the singing of the birds.

July 23rd: Sat with the flickering lights in the leaves of the trees playing in the hall, and thought thoughts that weren't thoughts.

Aug: Called in at E's. She had on a negligee dress. She had no lipstick, so as I like her. Love her best without lipstick, when her mouth is wide and simple.

Aug: A desperate need for E; if E would have nothing more to do with me, I'd have nothing more to live for—would go "off my rocker," or commit suicide. Almost feel I HATE E.

A SHORT, TERSE TALE. A WEEK IN AUGUST, 1959

Saturday, Aug 1st: Idea for a short story—a short terse tale, written in a mood of both excitement and anger and illustrate an idea. The tale of the man I described in my letter to E that I wrote from Wales; the cherry-lipped man, a man on the earth who lives between sea and sky.

This man is very happy, has known nothing all his life but the Welsh countryside. Lives in a little white house perched on the hillside with a bucket toilet, his family. He is a poet-labourer, a sort of pantheist.

Circumstances change. This man has to find work elsewhere. Goes to a factory in town to earn money for his wife and son. Town life and factory devastates this man's soul—he can no longer write poetry. Returns to his house to find it deserted. In his despair, he stepped deliberately over the cliff into nothingness and the boiling Atlantic below.

It is to be a short story, written in defiance to the doctrines of E.

Various dates in 1959–60:

E said I must work, work, work.

E said if one really has a gift for writing, can't stop.

E said weak animals and birds die. Weak humans pushed from thing to thing.

E said I am a weakling.

E said I am nothing. Nothing in me, so slack and lazy.

E said she's glad she's not my parents. She said I am throwing my life away.

Aug 2nd: E wouldn't have me read the story to her, so I left her the script.

Aug 3rd: If E <u>praises</u> it, oh, what joy!

Aug 4th: E said the story completely illogical, lacking in any sense, incomprehensible. E said she found about every sentence without thought.

SO MAD ON E, MUST BE A HOMOSEXUAL? 1960

June 6th: Still so mad on E, must be a homosexual? But, don't find any other women affect me in that way, except the nice person in the *Nun's Story* film, who was the reverend mother of the nunnery in the Congo.

June 8th: E said I'm a weakling, and she's glad she's not my parents.

June 10th: Saw the film *The Trials of Oscar Wilde*. Such films a great solace to me; I like to see the grief of others.

Lovely scene in a boarding-house bedroom at Brighton in the film. The writer had gone there to get away from everything & write. Saw him walking along by the sea, obviously full of fire for his new work *The Importance of Being Earnest*. He had been out all night, returned, amidst the rain and the leaves whirling round. He caught a chill, & had to go to bed. He made such a fuss over the chill. Then the young man whom he had a "crush" on (to use modern terms) came to the boarding house. The young man came into the room, where Oscar was lying in bed, his hand over his face as he lay on his side. He wasn't pleased to see the young man ("Bosie"), & kept making an awful fuss over his 'flu, nearly in tears, and searching for his hanky to sneeze into. Suppose E would say he was a "weakling." He told Bosie their friendship must end; & Bosie very conceited. He flung open the window, & set the precious script blowing in all directions & Oscar jumped out of bed to save it, fussing & snivelling. He buried his head on his arms & wept, & the young man taunted him, to see him snivelling there & said he was a bore. It was a terrible quarrel, & suddenly Bosie snatched up a bread-knife and threatened Oscar with it; but Bosie didn't strike; then he suddenly started laughing hysterically, & went on laughing & laughing, and the scene ended most dramatically, with Bosie taking his tempestuous leave, whilst poor Oscar wept and wept. Bosie, with a last contemptuous glare, went out of the door. Then, the poet threw himself on his back across the bed, still crying, holding his handkerchief to his face.

It was thrilling, erotic, most beautiful, especially to see a man of mature years in such a vulnerable position as to be taunted to tears by one he loves, a mere youngster.

June 10th (later): I see how I could love a man, when I see that they can cry.

June 11th: On more or less an impulse picked flowers, and rushed off on the bus to E. Didn't mean to go in and see her; just wanted to hand her the flowers, look upon her sweet face and go. Half-expected E would repulse me.

However, nothing of the sort happened. We sat in the chairs near the window. Then followed a <u>wonderful</u> conversation.

I asked E if she ever got unpleasant feeling if alone on a country walk—& E said, very strongly so, especially if she meets another person, she feels afraid; once when E saw someone coming towards her, she turned, & went back. That amazed & thrilled me—fancy E of all people, of such courage & nobility, having such a weakness, the same unwarranted feeling I would get in the circumstance. I could hardly hide my joy and exaltation over having E being so sweet to me, & saying such lovely things. Felt the happiest girl in the world. What is more, E's beauty acted like a flame on me; adored her, with her wonderful eyes, curly hair, flower-delicate face, and black gown. Felt all the more thrilled as this mingled in my mind with the film of Oscar —"posing as a sodomite."

June 11th: I adored E madly, and liked myself, too.

THERE IS NO MORE NEWS OF CHARLES & DI, 1981 (TWENTY-
ONE YEARS LATER)

Aug 3rd: There is no more news of Charles & Di. Read that she did some hoovering on the plane.

Aug 3rd: "Charles & Di," the couple I feel I know almost like neighbours. The wedding was a thing of great beauty and refinement, & seemed to have the most universal appeal. Mozart would have liked it, written lovely music for it, and coarse common people like it, because it was a wonderful show, & sentimental. Tolstoy would have written about it so well.

Aug 3rd: Thinking how happy they must feel now, on their honeymoon; feel sure they are enjoying it very much.

Aug 3rd: Am curious as to how much good the cruise will do them, though of course it should do them a lot of good, it is a rest, & lovely weather all the time.

Aug 3rd: Don't expect to be worshipped by a man, such as Di, but would like a <u>little</u> admiration.

Aug 4th (bedtime): Can imagine Charles is not a very good lover.

Aug 4th (bedtime): Should think Di is sensible enough not to be too disappointed.

Aug 6th: Charles & Di's wedding presents, & her dress, go on show at St. James Palace tomorrow. They have been given three pianos.

Aug 6th: Find this rather the limit, they already have everything. They never will have the technique to play those pianos. The ship is reported to be somewhere near Sardinia.

Aug 7th: Phoned for more cider.

Aug 12th: Think holidays can be over-rated.

Aug 13th (small hours): Wish E had lived long enough to know about Di.

Aug 17th (bedtime): Seem, since E's death, to be the only rootless person I know.

FEEL VERY SADDENED BY CLOTHES, 1974–77

1977: Feel very saddened by clothes.

May 10th, 1974: Got brick-coloured working trousers from M&S yesterday, which are passable, but perhaps I should change them for a large size, in case they shrink when washed.

May 10th: Today, bought M&S cotton ones in a sort of gun-metal colour, but I am not sure if they are nice.

May 11th: Bought myself another pair of trousers from M&S. Feel vexed that I can never get quite what I want; want the dark brown denim ones in size 18. Today got a navy-blue pair with white stripes, "French cut." Rather a risk. I don't like to ask E. She thinks I've got too many trousers already.

May 13th: Monday, & the shops open again. Still not the right trousers in M&S.

May 15th: Swoot [my sister] didn't like my new striped trousers. I don't suppose E will like them either, & I'll have to take them back.

May 16th: Went into town as usual in the p.m. Managed to get the red-brown trousers in size 18, so must take the size 16 ones back. Undecided about the striped trousers.

June 1st: Tried on all my trousers this evening, trying to decide which to wear for better, & which for everyday. Almost feel in tears with frustration & vexation over the clothes—not being able to find things I like. Not even got the corset organised yet, or know where I can get long enough stockings. And I do so long to look nice!

June 3rd: Took back the white M&S trousers, got two crimplene ones in navy blue & dark green.

June 13th: Sick of my blue working trousers with a belt already—they refuse even to get dirty, so I can't wash them to see if they shrink to the right size.

June 14th: Bought a different kind of M&S trousers today, more expensive—but they are still no good.

June 15th: Took back yesterday's pair, and got three more pairs to try. Got a pale green pair despite myself. They are cheerful, for summer. Got a white pair too. Got another gun-metal pair. Intend to take both pairs back in that colour. Think I'll keep the cheap crimplene pairs for working in the house, & bicycling.

June 17th: E vetoed the white trousers, & the green ones yesterday. Really none are any good. Can't take them all back at once.

June 18th: Wore the beige skirt Puddin' had made me, and I thought Peter looked at it rather approvingly. I wonder if in fact he doesn't like me in trousers. Prefers me to look like a girl. If that is the case, then I am off trousers.

June 18th: Took back the four trousers to M&S in the afternoon—it a long drawn-out ordeal, of endless waiting about; & I didn't get my money back (£17)—they said they'll post it. The whole thing a punishment for my stupidity over trousers.

June 21st: Changed the crimplene M&S trousers for a size 18 pair, in brown. Think I'll keep them, and the green ones. Like the sky blue pair, but afraid they are too loud.

June 29th: Dreamt the night before last that I was going to marry Peter. I woke up feeling warm and happy. The dream gave me some hope. E dreamt of me marrying him, too. Wonder if he himself has dreamt it yet? I am not in love with him at all, but that probably doesn't matter.

Three weeks later: Went to M&S to enquire re the £17 they owe me.

July 12th: Went all the way to Mill Road to try "Barney's Superstores" whose sale has been much advertised in the local press. It an exciting-looking sale, but proved entirely disappointing. Tried some jeans in a nice soft material, but the fit bad. The store a lower-class one.

Ten days later: <u>Still</u> not got my £17 back—gnash.

1977: My lovely clothes cheer me a little; that I never wear them is beside the point.

I AM UNDER MUCH MORE STRESS THAN THE QUEEN, 1974–1977

1977: I am under much more stress than the Queen.

1977: The Queen not burdened with an Elf.

Three years earlier:

May 19th, 1974: And it does seem disloyal to E, as these feelings rightly belong to her. But due to E running me down so often, belittling me and making me feel a fool, my feelings for her have cooled rather.

Did the watering, and I put my arm in Elf's for the walk back through the garden. My love for her made me feel thrilled and excited. My mind not really on the plants, and I forgot to turn the tap of the hose off this evening . . . she herself reminded me.

May 19th: Dreamt about getting into a swimming bath with Elf, and woke feeling very sexually aroused.

May 19th: Felt v. thrilled to be re-united with her; aware of a disturbing depth and strength of love for her. Do love her so <u>very</u> much.

DATE? Wish I could love her less. I feel quite ashamed of myself. Of course worry about my health and ability to cope, in view of being in charge of something so precious. My little love, my little jewel, my little flower. She is 99.

May 28th: Things have gone from bad to worse—quarrelled with E on the phone. E really noticing now the lessening of my love, and beginning to complain of its manifestations. E obviously wondering why it is, and I even don't know myself, only her beastly criticisms have a certain amount to do with it. One can hardly be fond of someone who makes one feel like a crushed worm.

June 29th: Feel in duty bound to stay until Elf has her hundredth birthday.

Jan 6th, 1976: The little darling old woman's 101st birthday—to my surprise, hardly anyone noticed it, after last year's great palaver of telegrams and flowers.

Jan 6th, 1977: Elf's <u>102</u>nd birthday, what an achievement, yet all the same, I groan inwardly.

June 7th: Elf is a terminal case.

June 7th: Depressing for anybody who has anything to do with her. Taking her to the lavatory, her incontinence, all the washing. This strain has been going on for <u>months</u>. Yet E said, Elf may not wish to die!

June 27th: Elf just got us up, with some complaint about constipation.

c. 3 a.m.: Elf clutching the bedclothes, which I gather is a sign of approaching death.

c. 3 a.m.: Her eyes staring & frightened.

4 a.m.: Light, birds, & traffic start. Elf sleeping now, but breathing fast.

c. 5 a.m.: Elf still sleeping.

c. 5.30 a.m.: Elf becoming restless again, & obviously beginning to surface to pain.

June 28th: Anti-climax. Elf a bit better.

THE EVENING VIEW OVER THE FIELD FROM MY ROOM IS VERY BEAUTIFUL, BUT EXTRAORDINARILY ELFLESS, 1977

July 9th: My emotional pain is as constant and sharp as a knife. It seemed she didn't die in her sleep. Had asked for breakfast, then suddenly died.

July 9th: A subdued lunch. I sought consolation in sugar, and had two helpings of the syrup steam pudding.

July 11th: My pain still worse this morning. A most beautiful picture of my lovely little Elf in the *Times*. Rushed out, and bought four *Times*. I would not let the newspaper girl touch the *Times*. The papers must be absolutely clean and sacred.

July 13th: Almost felt happy excitement, as I went up to put on my dress, because I was "going to see Elf." The black car, which I had dreaded yesterday, also gave me a kind of keen, childish excitement at the occasion. Enjoyed the slow stately drive out into the country.

July 13th: After a short wait in our car in the drive of the crematorium, the hearse appeared. I had surprisingly a rather non-reaction to the coffin. It did not look touchingly small, like Aunt Maude's did; just Elf's size, & little Elf lay inside the yellow wood, with a pile of flowers on top. I wanted to touch it, as if touching Elf, but did not like to. Did not even know which was her feet end.

July 16th: I recall the subterranean roar of the furnace at the crematorium, and on my way home, pictured for the first time the flames beginning to lick Elf; and Elf as always patient, accepting, not resisting. Would have lain completely still, as the furnace blackened and devoured her. Had always pictured here "ashes" as white, but perhaps after all, they will be black, with the odd shard of bone or tooth.

(*July 10th:* The casket containing her ashes will be brought back and stored in her bedroom, next door to mine! It will contain the most innocent & basic of elements only—mostly chalk, iron, potassium.

July 10th: Elf had borrowed these elements, & now they will be returned. Would even be good fertiliser to thriving plants.

July 11th: Of course, Elf's minerals may not be her original ones, as the body renews its cells all the time.)

July 12th: Optician has just rung up, to inform me cheerfully that Elf's glasses are ready, and must be paid for.

HANIF ABDURRAQIB

■

On Future and Working Through What Hurts

FROM *They Can't Kill Us Until They Kill Us*

MY MOTHER DIED at the beginning of summer. What this meant, more than anything, was that I didn't have school or some other youthful labor to distract me from the grieving process, which during the summer felt long, and slow. In past summer months, when I would be home from school, my mother would be the one who would often come home from work first. It took a while, after she died in June, to get used to not hearing her car pull into the driveway, the tires kicking the gravel along the glass windows of the basement, where my friends and I would be camped out, spending time watching TV or shooting on imaginary hoops. She was a naturally loud woman, so her arrivals were often loud, anchored by some warming noise: a laugh, or a shuffling of groceries, or a walk that echoed through the old hallways of our old house. The real grief is silence in a place where there was once noise. Silence is the hard thing to block out, because it hovers, immovable, over whatever it occupies. Noise can be drowned out with more noise, but the right type of silence, even when drowning, can still sit inside of a person, unmoving.

By the time I started high school in the summer after my mother's death, I was so wound up from sitting largely stagnant in my own sadness for three months, I didn't know how to re-enter a world in which I had to sit and face people on a daily basis. I fought, I found myself consistently suspended, I was the student that teachers threw their hands up about, confused. It was very out of character for me, but I was rebelling against the feeling of anything but grief. When you allow something to grow a shadow at your back, anything that distracts you from it is going to need severing. I think, perhaps, that the key is never letting the sadness grow too large.

In 2014, Future began a run of production that rap had rarely seen. Starting with *Honest*, he released three studio albums and five mixtapes in the span of two years. The start of the run coincided with the crumbling of Future's personal life. The first album of the stretch, *Honest*, was released in April of 2014, a month before Future's son was born with singer Ciara, and four months before Ciara called off their engagement, separating Future from his son, also named Future. Allegations of cheating followed, and within months, Ciara was removing a tattoo of Future's initials from her hand, tattoos that the couple had gotten together shortly after falling in love. It was an intense and public collapse, with Ciara and Future both responding subtly, and then not-so-subtly to the relationship's end. Ciara, less than a year after the split, was in a public relationship with Seattle Seahawks quarterback Russell Wilson, while Future, it seemed, was growing increasingly frantic, detached, and brilliantly productive.

The crown jewel of Future's run is 2015's *Dirty Sprite 2*, which serves as the perfect companion to *Honest* and stands as one of rap's darkest breakup albums. On the surface, it's simply haunted and paranoid: the artist stumbling through descriptions of various drug-fueled exploits. The title itself derives from the mix of clear soda and codeine cough syrup, Future's drug of choice. But it is more than simply several odes to a vice; it's a discussion of the vice as a way to undo memory. There is still the boastful Atlanta hustler persona that Future cultivated on his past albums, but there's also an exhaustion present. On the song "Groupies," he groans through a chorus of "now I'm back fucking my groupies" in a way that sounds like he'd rather be anywhere else.

The reason *Dirty Sprite 2* is such a brilliant breakup record is that it doesn't directly confront the failing of a relationship, but intimately details the movements of what that failure turned an artist into. It is misery as I have most frequently seen black men experiencing their misery, not discussed, pushed into a lens of what will drown it out with the most ferocity. Future, in a year, watched a woman he loved leave him with their child, and then find public joy with someone else, while he wallowed, occasionally tweeting out a small bitter frustration about the newfound distance. There are as many ways to be heartbroken as there are hearts, and it is undeniable that it is exceptionally difficult to be both public-facing and sad. Future's golden run was born out of a desire to bury himself. Rather, a desire to be both seen and unseen.

All of the albums released from 2014–2016 were released to both critical and commercial success, which made the run even more stunning. Future wasn't just creating throwaway works to help forget about his sadness. *Dirty Sprite 2* went platinum. *What a Time to Be Alive*, a 2015 collaborative mixtape where Future outshined Drake at every turn, also debuted at #1 on the *Billboard* chart. 2016's *Evol* also topped the charts. In between, there were the mixtapes: *Beast Mode* and *56 Nights* in 2015, *Purple Reign* in 2016.

All of them ruminated on the same handful of emotions, reveled in the same methods of darkness and escape. I guess, when you work so hard to dodge the long arms of grief, it is impossible to allow all of grief's stages to move through you. It is difficult to talk about Future's run without also talking about what the end looks like, or if it will end. He seems to be reaching toward an inevitable collapse. All of us can only outrun silence for so long before we have no option but to face it. I think of this as I turn the volume up on *Evol* the week after it comes out, an album that deals in all of the various and dangerous forms that love can take. It seems like a small shift in a different direction for Future, who seemed to be sliding back in a more confident, recovering persona. A month after the release of *Evol*, Ciara and Russell Wilson announced their engagement.

What often doesn't get talked about with real and deep heartbreak after a romantic relationship falls apart is that it isn't always just a single moment. It's an accumulation of moments, sometimes spread out over years. It is more than just the person you love leaving; it's also seeing them happy after they've left, seeing them beginning to love someone else, seeing them build a life that you perhaps hoped to build with them. Sometimes it isn't as easy as unfollowing a person on social media to not see these moments. When it is present and unavoidable, there have to be other ways of severing emotion from memory. In a 2016 *Rolling Stone* interview, Future tells the interviewer that he spends most of his days in a dark recording studio, hours with codeine and a notebook, until he loses track of time. It walks a line between punishment and survival, like so many tools of escape do. So many of Future's songs since Ciara left him are about how much excess he can absorb until everything around him rings hollow, and I suppose this is maybe a better option than albums directly attacking Ciara's new life. It strikes me as Future understanding that, in some ways, he deserves where he ended up, and the work, the codeine-fueled brilliance, is how he is delivering his pound of flesh while also trying to never be caught by any single emotion.

It is easy to think of anything that makes you feel better as medication, even if it only makes you feel better briefly, or even if it will make you feel worse in the long run. In my high school years, after my mother was gone, I watched my father run himself into the ground. In part, due to necessity: two high school–aged children, active in sports, caused him, as a single parent, to be in several places at once. But he was (and is) also, by nature, someone who takes immense pride in labor, and this heightened when he seemed to be coping with the death of his wife. At a traffic light on the way home from a soccer practice in 1999, two years after my mother died, my father fell asleep in the driver's seat of the car. The light turned green, and cars behind us honked, eventually jarring him awake. I remember staring at him, the glow of the red light bleeding into the car and resting on his briefly sleeping face. I remember thinking that, instead of waking him up, I should let him rest. That maybe, what we see when we close our eyes is better than anything the living world could offer us in our waking hours. I imagine this is why Future has become obsessed with losing track of time. It is hard to keep missing someone when there's no way to tell how long you've been without them. When everything blurs into a singular and brilliant darkness.

POSTSCRIPT

It is February 2017 and I am crying in the John Glenn Columbus International Airport in my hometown of Columbus, Ohio. It could be the lack of sleep. I just got off of a plane from San Francisco, a city I flew out of at midnight after flying in less than twenty-four hours earlier. I am back in Columbus for less than twenty-four hours to do a reading, and then I am flying back to Los Angeles. It is a wretched schedule, one that has caused many of my friends to put their hands on my face and ask me if I'm doing okay, and I am not really, but I smile and shrug and tell them I'll see them soon. I'm holding a newspaper with my face on it. It is the *Columbus Dispatch*, my hometown's biggest newspaper. I learned to love reading at the feet of this newspaper. As a child, I would unravel it on Sundays and hand my brother the comic section while I read the ads, the obituaries, the box scores. I am in it because I answered questions to a kind interviewer about a book of poems I wrote. It seems almost impossible to measure the amount of work (and luck, and certainly privilege) that allowed me to end up here, but that isn't the entire reason that I'm crying. It is my mother's birthday. If she were living, she'd be celebrating sixty-four years today, and I am in an airport holding something in my hands that she might have been proud of, and I can't take it to her and place it in her living hands and say *look. look at what I did with the path you made for me.* And states away, someone still living has decided that they aren't in love with me anymore, and so I am flying thousands of miles for weeks at a time and staying up staring at computer screens until there is nothing rattling in my brain but a slow static to ride into dreams on.

Headphones are around my neck as I cry in this airport newspaper shop, blaring the second of Future's two new albums, released in consecutive weeks: *Future* on one Friday, and *HNDRXX* on the next. *HNDRXX* is startling in approach and execution. It is Future both unapologetic and unimpressed with himself, all at once. For the first time, he seems truly sad, made plain. It's an album of broken crooning, finally slowing down enough to undo the vast nesting doll of grief. From denial to acceptance, and everything in between. It seems like this may be the album that ends Future's run.

Both are projected to go #1 on the charts, making *Billboard* history. *HNDRXX* is the logical bookend to *Honest*, which started his run in 2014. *Honest*, with its performed depth, offered nothing of emotional substance. *HNDRXX* ends on "Sorry," a nearly eight-minute song where everything comes apart. It's Hendrix apologizing for Future, or Future apologizing for himself, or regret piling on top of regret until the whole building collapses. At the opening of verse two is the line, "It can get scary when you're legendary," delivered in Future's signature throaty drone. The endless work, the hiding from that which hurts, maybe leads to some unforeseen success. And the funny thing about that is how it won't make any of us feel less alone. That's how running into one thing to escape another works. Distance has a wide mouth, and I haven't slept in a bed in 48 hours, and the people who miss me are not always the people I want to be missed by, and the last time I stood over my mother's grave, the weeds had grown around her name so I picked at them with my bare hands for a while before giving up and sitting down inside of them instead. Still, I am in a paper because I chose work over feeling sad for three months, and now I don't have the energy to feel anything but sad. The woman who works at the newsstand taps me on the shoulder, and asks me if I can turn down the music in my headphones because it's distracting other customers. She walks away, never saying anything about the fact that I was crying in the middle of her store.

SOUVANKHAM THAMMAVONGSA

■

The Universe Would Be So Cruel

FROM *NOON*

MR. VONG STRETCHED HIS NECK to look over the tops of the heads of the wedding guests, trying to take in a good view of the bride and groom. When he spotted them, he made a bold prediction: "Ah, lovely. Too bad it isn't going to last." Mr. Vong had been invited, not because he was a relative or because he was well acquainted with the parents. He was the one the young couple turned to, being the only printer who offered Lao lettering on wedding invitations. He was highly sought after for his Lao fonts and his eloquence with the language, his knowledge of how little things can shape and affect outcomes. Sure, his clients could download fonts and print them out at Kinko's, but that kind of lazy effort could signify a lazy marriage, one where at the first sign of trouble divorce would be the answer. And anyway, most of his clients didn't know how to write in Lao, having been born here. They needed him to impress their parents.

Mr. Vong took great care, made his own paper, every fiber dried and flattened in his shop, taking several months. He understood more than anyone the superstitions Lao people had about getting names and dates exact throughout the entire process, how a spelling error during the proofing process could foretell an error in marriage, could change the fate of the couple. He regarded himself as the gatekeeper of their good fortune.

Mr. Vong printed their wedding invitations and charged a very small price in hopes that word would get around about his good printing shop. He didn't make much money on his services. Most of his clients were the ones the bigger businesses didn't want to deal with—men and women working for themselves, who didn't buy in bulk, who didn't have much time to be on the Internet, who didn't speak English but somehow, through some signals of hands and sounds, something could be understood about what they wanted. He took the time to talk to each person and spent many hours helping them pick out material and paint. These clients he liked best. They reminded him of himself—farmers coming into his shop with dirty fingernails because they worked out in the field all day, or butchers who didn't have time to change out of clothes stained with blood from a fresh kill. All of them, doing the grunt work of the world.

The clients he didn't like were the salesmen dressed in fine business suits—the ones who always asked for things to be cheaper so they could get a larger cut of the profit. He chased these men away. He spotted them the way you spot danger. The crease of their pressed suits, the leather briefcase, slicked-back hair, perfect English. They called him "buddy," corrected his spelling. It all made him yell, "Fuck you!" Sometimes, when he was in a good mood and had time to spare and felt like humoring them, he would allow them to be in his shop for fifteen minutes, allow them to talk on and on, to show him their graphs. But he'd eventually get back to yelling the same thing he'd yell at the others like them who had come before. The world treated men like this well. They had offices in towers, and secretaries, but in his shop, one he owned and operated alone, he was boss! And he wasn't going to give them the same treatment others had given them. Of course this didn't make much for him in terms of dollars, but that wasn't the point. The point was to be free, to own a thing you had all to yourself, and to be able to say, "Fuck you! All of you all! Fuck you into hell!" Whatever that really meant, Mr. Vong didn't know, but it was fun to say, something that had been said to him at one point. Fun indeed to see these men lose their smooth talk and make their quick, fumbling exits.

Above all, it was the wedding invitations. They were what gave him the most joy in his work.

This wedding couple had anticipated a very high price for Mr. Vong's care and expertise—but that was not at all. They were so happy, they instantly invited him to their wedding, both of them smiling with their even, bright teeth. With teeth that white, that well-cared-for, there was no reason they could not have offered to pay more than he had asked. But instead they accepted the price like those salesmen, eager for the bargain. No marriage would last where two people didn't recognize what would be the right thing to do.

Now, it was at this point in the night—after the guests had been served papaya salad, spring rolls, minced chicken with fresh herbs and spices, sticky rice, and sweets wrapped in banana leaves—when the bride and groom were having their first dance, as husband and wife, that Mr. Vong made his bold prediction.

"Ai, why are you saying this? Keep your voice down!" Mrs. Vong, his devoted and loyal wife of twenty years, urged, slapping him on his arm and looking around at the people seated at their table, wondering if they had heard. It did not seem so, as everyone else seemed to be busying themselves with their food or in their conversations with each other.

"Just you mark my words: Less than a year. That's my prediction. Less than a year." He returned to his meal, gathering up the minced chicken with a flattened ball of sticky rice.

Mr. and Mrs. Vong's daughter listened. She was amused and curious about the accuracy of his prediction. Her father tended to be right about these things.

"Dad, you know for sure?"

"I know. I know these things," he said.

True enough, in less than a year the bride and groom were divorced.

Later that year, Mr. Vong made another one of his predictions. This time he made it the minute he opened the wedding invitation. He said, "Ah, not even going to happen."

The wedding invitation had not been printed by Mr. Vong. One could presume that the prediction was the result of some petty competition or his hurt pride. It was printed at a fancy shop, downtown on a street called Richmond, whose only specialty was printing invitations. There was no Lao lettering to be found anywhere on the invitation. It was fancy and had raised print. The little silver-sparkled bumps could be felt, running a hand across the lettering, forming the names, addresses, dates. And yes, Mr. Vong's prediction came true. The groom married someone else, named Sue. Phone calls were made: Canceled. Called off.

"Dad, seriously, *how did you know?*"

"Look, I know these things. You just can't have a Lao wedding without Lao letters on the invitation. And you have to have your real name in there. Yeah, it's a long name—but that's *your* name. Why would you want to be Sue if it's really Savongnavathakad? Because, you know, the real Sue will end up marrying the guy if it's there in the invitation."

* * *

Now, when it was time for Mr. Vong's daughter to get married, he spared no expense. He ordered sparkled paint from Laos, made out of the crushed wings of a rare local insect. The gold specks were real and not artificial—real shine and shimmer for a real marriage. He printed the invitations and put each one out to dry on a metal rack. Four on each rack, a total of four hundred invitations, an even number. He did everything he could possibly do to ensure that his daughter's wedding invitations were perfect and ready to be sent out into the scrutiny of the universe. But on the day of the wedding, the groom was not there. He was on the coast of France, vacationing with family. "Look, my family has been planning this for a long time," the boy said. "I just couldn't get out of it. So . . . yeah. Sorry, babes." If the boy's parents even knew about the wedding, Mr. Vong didn't know. They had never met. At the time, Mr. Vong thought nothing of it, didn't question, wasn't curious. And now, thinking of it, there was always some excuse and it was always something coming out of that boy's small mouth. It was as if Mr. Vong's plans were of no value, or of lesser value, or not even up for consideration. It didn't occur to him to ask questions. He believed what he was told. There had been a proposal, and that's all he needed to know about that.

Mr. Vong's daughter threw the phone on to the floor and it stayed complete and solid in its protective case, invented for such situations. Then she ran. She ran and opened the first door she saw, but it turned out to be a closet. She folded herself in there and cried. He let her cry and shooed away everyone who tried to comfort her. A woman ought to cry, he thought. She ought to be allowed to bawl it all out.

And after, she said, "Dad? Dad . . . are you there?"

"Yes. I am right here," he said.

"It's all your fault, isn't it? The invitations . . . something must have gone wrong."

Mr. Vong thought of an answer—one he could use to explain, to reason out what had happened to the day—how the wedding had come to this. "I . . . I found one invitation behind the door." He talked to his daughter as if he were a small schoolboy who had stolen an eraser to win the affections of his friend, and had now been summoned by the head master to explain. "I must have missed it. The one. All invitations must go out. It was just one. I didn't know the universe would be so cruel. I am terribly sorry. I am trained to know, to predict, and to ensure these things." It was not true at all, of course. He had accounted for everything! But this was no time for his own pride. No amount of *fuck-you-to-hell*s could make a difference to that boy. How could you tell her that the boy wasn't kind or good, that she wasn't loved by that boy, that sometimes what felt like love only *felt* like love, and wasn't real. And that even if it had been real, sometimes love can stop spinning like a top you set in motion. You couldn't do anything about that, but, you could say, *Yes, yes, an invitation behind the door. That's what it was.*

SAMANTHA HUNT

■

A Love Story

FROM *The New Yorker*

"A COYOTE ATE A THREE-YEAR-OLD NOT FAR FROM HERE."
"Yeah?"
"My uncle told me."
"Huh."
"He said, 'Don't leave those babies outside again,' as if I already had."
"Had you?"
"Come on." An answer less precise than no.
"Why's he monitoring coyote activity up here?"
"Because."
"Because?"
"It's irresistible."
"Really?"
A wild dog with a tender baby in its jaws disappearing into the redwoods forever. My uncle's so good at imagining things, he makes them real. "Yeah. It's just what he does, a habit." Or a compulsion.
"I don't get it."
But I do. Every real thing started life as an idea. I've imagined objects and moments into existence. I've made humans. I tip taxi-drivers ten, twenty dollars every time they don't rape me.

* * *

The last time my husband and I had sex was eight months ago, and it doesn't count because at the time my boobs were so huge from nursing that their power over him, over all men, really, was supreme. Now, instead of sex with my husband, I spend my nights imagining dangerous scenarios involving our children. It's less fun.

* * *

"Watch out," my uncle says. "Watch out," taking refuge in right-wing notions, living his life terrified of differences.

* * *

Once, I was a drug dealer, back when pot was still illegal here. I'm a writer now. I haven't made any money writing yet; still, that's how I spend my days, putting things down on paper. People continue to come to my house to buy pot and I sell it to them even though I'm no longer a drug dealer and they could get this shit legally, even though I'm sick of the people who pop their heads in my door, all friendly-like: "Hi. How you doing?"

"Fine," I say, but I mean, *Shut up and buy your drugs and stop thinking you're better than me.*

* * *

When I was young, I shopped at the Army-Navy with the thought that if I bought these clothes and wore them I would prevent some beautiful young man from being killed in the garments. I'm romantic like that.

I'm telling you about the coyotes, the kids, the taxi-drivers, the drugs, the writing, and the romance because I want to be as honest as I can here. As I said, thoughts become material. I'm not hysterical or crazy. I'm laying the groundwork for real honesty.

* * *

I had great hopes that the threat of Lyme disease would revitalize our sex life. "Will you check me for ticks?" You know, and things would go from there. Grooming each other as monkeys do. In that way, at least for a while, I got him to touch me again and it felt good, but then Lyme disease never really took off in California like it did on the East Coast.

* * *

The men I know speak about sex as if their needs are more intense or deeper than women's needs. Like their penises are on fire and they will die if they can't extinguish the flames in some damp, tight hole. Through high school and college, I believed men when they said their desires were more intense than mine because they talked about sex so much. They developed entire industries devoted to their desire. The aches! The suffering of the boys! The shame and mutual responsibility for blue balls. The suffering of the boys. *Poor boys,* I thought. *Poor boys,* as if I were being called upon to serve in a war effort, the war against boys not getting any.

* * *

The only desire I have that compares to the way men talk about sex is my fervor for rehashing the past. I relive the exquisite pain of things that no longer exist: my father's jean jacket, my father, Travolta's 1977 dark beauty, how it felt to be alone in the house with my mom after my siblings left for school, the hypnotic rotations of my record-player spinning the Osmonds and Paper Lace, the particular odors of a mildewed tent in summertime. Memory as erogenous zone.

Then I realized that men think they are special because someone told them so.

Then I realized that I, too, have begun to burn lately, and, while no one wants to hear about middle-aged female sexual desire, I don't care anymore what no one wants. There are days I ache so badly, the only remedy beyond a proper plowing would be a curved and rusty piece of metal or broken glass to gouge out my hot center from mid-inner thigh all the way up to my larynx. I'd spare my spine, brain, hands, and feet. I'm not irrational.

The list of potential reasons that my husband and I no longer have sex wakes me up at night. If I'm not already awake thinking about the coyotes. The first reason, and the wildest, craziest reason, is that maybe my husband is gone. Maybe one night a while back I kicked him out after a fight and maybe, even if I didn't mean everything I said, he went away and didn't come back. That would certainly explain why we don't have sex. Maybe I'm just imagining him here still. It can be hard to tell with men, whether they are really here or not. Especially a man with a smartphone.

The second reason I develop to explain why my husband and I no longer have sex is that my husband is, no doubt, gay. A faultless crime, though not without its heartache and deceit.

The third reason I concoct to explain why my husband and I no longer have sex is that he must be molesting our children when he puts them to bed each night. This reason does double duty for me, cultivating worry about both my marriage and my kids at the same time. Such efficiency.

The fourth reason is that I must look like a chubby English maid: bad teeth, mouth agape, drooling ignorance and breast milk. This reason sends me onto the Internet for hours, researching various exercise regimens and diets hawked by self-tanned women with chemically bruised hair. In the middle of the night, it's easy to hate myself as much as the world hates me. A few years ago, my husband bought me a short black wig as part of a sex-toy package. His ex-girlfriend has short black hair. I know the chemistry of other people's desire is not my fault, but the wig, so fucking blatant, really hurt.

Finally, the last reason I imagine for why my husband and I no longer have sex comes almost as a relief, because it requires very little imagination or elaboration and after I think it I can usually go back to sleep. My husband must be having an affair.

I have a friend from college. She's a real New England Wasp, with a fantastic secret. Her family pays for all those Lilly Pulitzers, summers on Nantucket, and boarding schools from a fortune made manufacturing dildos and vibrators. I love that secret. One of the biggest sellers is a set of plastic prosthetic monster tongues, some forked, some spiky, most of them green or blue, all of them scaled for the lady's pleasure, especially a lady with a lizard fetish.

This friend once asked me a greasy question that returns on nights like this one: "Are you the kind of woman who would want to know if her husband's cheating on her?" And she left the question dangling. Her mouth may have even been slightly open. People cheat because they are no longer running away from sabre-toothed tigers. I get that. Adrenaline insists on being taken out for a spin. But there was an indictment inherent in either answer I could give my friend, so I stayed silent and wondered, Was she asking because she knew something?

We moved out of the city because there's no room for non-millionaires there anymore. In the country, life is more spacious. We bought a king-size bed. Some nights we snuggle like baby snakes, all five of us. Those nights, our giant bed is the center of the universe, the mother ship of bacterial culture, populated with blood, breast milk, baby urine. A petri dish of life-forms. Like some hogan of old. Those nights I know we are safe. But when our children sleep in their own room my husband and I are left alone on the vast plain of this oversized bed feeling separate, feeling like ugly Americans who have eaten too much, again.

* * *

The plague of perfectionism on parenting blogs is rancid. Alice in Wonderland birthday parties; Spanish-speaking nannies; healthy children harvesting perfect blue chicken eggs from the back-yard coop; homeschooled wonders who read by age three; flat, tight bellies; happy husbands; cake pops; craft time; quilting projects; breast pumps in the boardroom; tenure; ballet tights; cloth diapers; French braids; homemade lip balm; tremendous flat pans of paella prepared over a beach campfire. What sort of sadist is running these Internets? And, more important, how do these blogs not constitute acts of violence against women?

I glimpsed a huge beyond when I became a mother, the immensity of an abyss, or the opposite of an abyss, the idea of complete fullness, small gods everywhere. But now all that the world wants to hear from me is how I juggle children and career, how I manage to get the kids to eat their veggies, how I lost the weight.

I will never lose this weight.

When we encounter a mother doing too many things perfectly, smiling as if it were all so easy, so natural, we should feel a civic responsibility to slap her hard across the face and scream the word "Stop!" so many times that the woman begins to chant or whimper the word along with us. Once she has been broken, we may take her in our arms until the trembling and self-hatred leave her body. It is our duty.

I once thought motherhood loosened a woman's grasp on sanity. Now I see it is the surplus and affluence of America. Plus something else, something toxic, leaking poison, or fear. Something we can't yet see.

I'd like to post some shots from my own childhood, a version of my parents' parenting blog, if such an abomination had existed back then. In these photos, through the fog of cigarette smoke filling the living room, across the roar of Georges Moustaki blasting his sorrow from the record-player at midnight, it would be difficult for a viewer to even locate the children in rooms so thick with adults acting like adults.

* * *

I've been thinking about drafting a manual for expecting mothers. An honest guide to a complex time of life for which no one's ever properly prepared. After I became a mom, I asked an older friend, "How come you never told me I'd lose my identity when I had a kid?"

"'Cause it's temporary. They give you a new one. And I kind of forgot."

"Really?"

"No."

When I sit down to begin my manual, I realize how specific my guide is to one demographic. So then, O.K., a mothering guide for middle-class, heterosexual women who went to college and are gainfully employed. But once I've arrived there, my pen raised and at the ready, I realize I actually have very little wisdom. So: a brochure. Pen in hand. Until I realize that what I've learned about being a middle-class, hetero mother who went to college could actually be boiled down to one or two fortune cookies. I write, HORMONES ARE LIFE. HORMONES ARE MENTAL ILLNESS. I write, EQUALITY BETWEEN THE SEXES DOES NOT EXIST. And then my job is done.

A few days ago, I was scrubbing the rim of the upstairs toilet because it smelled like a city alley in August. My phone dinged. I'd received an e-mail. I pulled off my latex gloves to read the message. Who am I kidding? I wasn't wearing gloves. Real honesty. I was scrubbing the toilet with bare hands. I was probably even using the same sponge I use on the sink, that area right near the toothbrushes. The e-mail was from my husband. "Thought you might like this," he said. It was a link to a list of life hacks, simple tricks designed to make one's life easier: use duct tape to open stuck lids, keep floppy boots upright with pool noodles, paper-clip the end of a tape roll so you can find it easily.

I wrote him back. "Or you could marry a woman and make her your slave."

He never did respond.

* * *

I'm not saying that men have it better or women have it better. I don't ever want to be a man. I'm just saying there's a big difference between the two.

* * *

When I swim at the public pool, I wear sunglasses so I can admire the hairless chest of the nineteen-year-old lifeguard. I love it that he, a child, really, is guarding me, fiercest of warriors, a mother, strong as stinky cheese, with a ripe, moldy, melted rotten center of such intense complexity and flavor it would kill a boy of his tender age.

* * *

Once, I woke Sam in the night. That's my husband's name, Sam. "Honey," I said. "Honey, are you awake?"

"Uhh?"

"I think I'm dying."

"Yeah," he said. "Uh-huh." And then he went back to sleep.

Presumably my husband likes stinky cheese and the challenge of living near my hormones. Presumably that's what love is.

* * *

Another night, also in bed, I woke Sam. I do that a lot. "I want you to agree that there is more than one reality."

"Huh?"

"I want you to agree that if I feel it, if I think it, it is real."

"But what if you think I'm an asshole?" he asked.

"Well. Then that's real."

"Really?"

"What does that word even mean, 'really'?" I started to scream a little.

"What?"

"The word 'really' suggests that we all see things the same way. It suggests one reality. Right?"

"Sure. Right. Really," he said. *Really.*

One huge drawback to my job as a drug dealer is that, while I grow older, passing through my thirties and into my forties, the other drug dealers stay young. They are almost all in their twenties. Normally, I don't socialize with the other drug dealers, but one night a group of the twenty-year-olds asked if I wanted to join them for a drink. I almost said no, but then decided, why not.

All the motions at the bar were familiar. It's not as if I forgot how to go out for a drink. I know what kind of wine I like. I had no trouble finding a seat. After our first drink, some of the young drug dealers disappeared to play pool, some wandered off to greet other friends. Halfway through my second drink, I was holding down the fort alone, a couple of purses, packs of smokes, and cocktails left in my charge. No problem. I didn't mind a moment of silence.

But then a young man—handsome, long hair, strong hands—joined me at the table. I started to panic.

This, I suddenly thought, is what it means to go out for a drink. This is the entire purpose. Have a drink, meet a stranger, have fantastic sex all night long. But I didn't want to blow up my life. I love Sam. I love our life. Still, there was this young man beside me, interested in me, nervous even.

"Hi," he said. "I'm a friend of Alli's." One of the twenty-year-old drug dealers.

"Hi." I tried not to, but I imagined him naked, me naked. I imagined him accepting the way my body has aged naturally, despite the near-certainty that that would never happen. Very few bodies this close to San Francisco are allowed to age naturally.

"Alli told me you're a mom."

"That's right." It wasn't the sexiest thing he could say, but maybe, I thought, this is how it will work, how he'll appreciate the lines and rolls of my abdomen.

"I was thinking, since you're a mom, you might have some snacks? I'm really hungry. Like, is there anything in your purse?"

After a short excavation, the highest humiliation. He was right. I found a bag of baby carrots and a granola bar in my purse. I passed my offerings across the table to the young man.

"Thanks," he said, disappearing with the food. "Thanks." Some mother's child, some mother who had at least taught her son to say thank you.

"Can you check me for ticks?"

Sam switches on a light, picks me over, stopping at each freckle. How lucky I am to know such love, to momentarily remember what it means to have the body of a child, ignorant of age's humiliation. "O.K.," he says. "You're all clear."

"Thanks. Should I check you?"

"Nah. I'm good. There's no Lyme disease in California. Not really." He switches off the light and now it's night.

* * *

What's the scariest sound a person can hear?

In a quiet country house where the closest neighbors are pretty far away, the scariest possible sound is a man coughing outside at night. Because why is there a man standing in the dark, studying the sleeping house, licking his lips, coughing? Why would someone be so near to my home, to my children, in this place that is not the city?

I know the sounds of this house intimately. I know the difference between the mailman and the UPS man, the garbage truck, the school bus, the washer-dryer in the basement. I know each door. I know the sound of a man outside coughing.

"What was that?" But Sam is already asleep. "Wake up." I whisper so that the coughing man won't know we're onto him. "Wake up, hon. Someone's outside."

"What?"

"Sh-h-h. I heard something."

"What?"

"There's someone downstairs. Someone's outside."

"Who?"

"A guy. Please."

"Please?"

"Go see."

"See?"

"Yeah."

In the dead and dark of night, I send away the only man who has sworn an oath to protect me. I must be an idiot. I must be really scared.

Sam disappears in his underwear and bare feet, leaving behind the retired baseball bat he once thought to stow under the bed for just this sort of occasion. The soft pads of his feet go down the top few steps and then there's no more sound. He's so gone I have a sense our entire downstairs is filled with stagnant black pond water through which he's now wading, swimming, drowning, trying to stay quiet so the bad guy, whoever he is, doesn't hear him, find the staircase, and tear our tiny world apart.

* * *

The uncertain position we all maintain in life asking when will violence strike, when will devastation occur, leaves us looking like the hapless swimmers at the beginning of the *Jaws* movies. Innocent, tender, and delicious.

"Sam?" I call softly, so the bad guy won't know we're separated.

There's no answer from downstairs. Why is it taking him so long to come back?

* * *

I hold the night the way I would a child who has finally fallen asleep. As if I were frightened it will move. I *am* frightened it will move. I am scared my life will suffer some dramatic, sudden change. I try to hear deeper. I try not to shift at all, not to breathe, but no matter how still I stay there's no report from downstairs. What if Sam is already dead, killed by the intruder? What if the bad guy, in stocking feet, is creeping upstairs right now, getting closer to my babies, to me?

Part of me knows that he is. Part of me knows that he always is and always will be.

* * *

Where we live there are squirrels, rabbits, all manner of wild birds, foxes, mountain lions. There are rednecks getting drunk at the sports bar three miles away. There are outlaw motorcycle clubs convening. There are children dreaming. Other living things still exist in the night. Sometimes it's hard to remember that.

Sam is probably fine. He's probably downstairs on his computer. Barely Legal, Backstreet Blow Jobs.

Night ticks by.

"Sam?" There's no answer and the quiet becomes a dark cape, so heavy I can't move my legs. I can't move my body. I am only eyes, only ears. The night asks, *Who are you? Who will you become if Sam has been chopped to bits by the guy downstairs?*

This is a good question. Who am I? Who will I be without Sam? Without kids? I can hear how well-intentioned people at Sam's funeral will say, "Just be yourself." But there is no self left. Why would there be? From one small body I made three new humans. I grew these complex beauties. I made their lungs and noses. It took everything I had to make them. Liver? Take it. Self-worth? It's all yours. New people require natural resources and everyone knows you don't get something for nothing. Why wouldn't I be hollowed out? Who can't understand this math?

The strangest part of these calculations is that I don't even mind. Being hollow is the best way to be. Being hollow means I can fill myself with stars or light or rose petals if I want. I'm glad everything I once was is gone and my children are here instead. They've erased the individual and I am grateful. The individual was not special in the first place. And, really, these new humans I made are a million times better than I ever was.

* * *

The bedcovers look gray in the dim light of chargers, laptops, and phones scattered around our bedroom. In this ghost light I am alone. The night asks again, *Who are you? Who will you be when everyone is gone?* My children are growing, and when they are done I'll have to become a human again instead of a mother, like spirit becoming stone, like a butterfly turning back into a caterpillar. I'm not looking forward to that.

Who are you?

The answer is easy in daylight. But the night's untethering almost always turns me into someone I'm not. I spend nights thinking about the different women I become in the dark. Where am I keeping these women when the sun is up? Where do they hide, these women who have breached the sanctity of my home, who know things about me so secret even I don't know these things? Maybe they are in the closet. Maybe they are hiding inside me. Maybe they are me trapped somewhere I can't get to, like in the DNA markers of my hormones, those proteins that make me a woman instead of something else.

You may ask, Are these women who bombard me at night real, or do I imagine them? You may eventually realize that is a stupid question.

I think about fidelity. To Sam, to myself. The light is still gray. The night is still so quiet. I let the women in, an entire parade of them, the whole catalogue, spread out on the bed before me. Sam is gone and these women keep me company. Even if they terrify me. I let the other women in.

An author lived for a time in a modern house behind mine, on the other side of a eucalyptus grove. She had recently divorced. She is a great writer, though she has written only one book. The book takes a frank approach to sex and bodies. I try to copy her writing. Her book is about prostitutes, so I assume she was once a sex worker. Or maybe she just wants her readers to believe that, for street cred at book parties, in university settings.

I could kind of see into the rear windows of her house at night with a pair of binoculars. These voyeur sessions never lasted long, because all she ever did was sit there. Maybe once or twice I caught her walking to her kitchen. It was boring. She was alone all the time, and while she was no doubt thinking amazing, fantastic thoughts about the nature of art, my binoculars could not see those thoughts.

The town we live near is so small, it was inevitable that we would meet. We did, many times. We once even shared the dance floor at the local bar, a Mexican restaurant, really. We momentarily danced together like robots from outer space. But then each time we met again it was, to her, as fresh as the first time. "Nice to meet you," she'd say. Once, I had to deliver a piece of misdirected mail and she invited me in for a glass of wine. In an instant, I developed a fantasy of the famous writer and me as best friends. I dropped that fantasy quickly, because it was clear that her alien-robot routine back in the bar had not been an act.

When I mentioned that I had three children, her jaw came unhinged. "Oh, my God." Her hand rose to her face as if I'd said I had three months to live. Maybe that was what children meant to her.

I went to hear her read at the local library once when I was very pregnant. During the Q & A, she spoke of child rearing with great disgust. Likening motherhood to a dairy operation. She said that children murder art, and though it was easy for me to dismiss her comments as ignorance—she'd never had a child, she'd never made a life or a death—I could not prevent the other people in the audience from looking at me with pity. "How did you like that?" a number of my neighbors asked me afterward.

"I enjoyed it very much, thanks."

When I was at her house she dismissed me after one glass of wine. "I have to eat my sandwich," she said, as if that sandwich were something so solidly constructed it would be impossible to divide, impossible to share. I left.

The next time I saw the famous writer, she was in the grocery store. Once again, she didn't recognize me or acknowledge the four or five times we'd already met, the wine we had drunk together, so I was able to freely stalk her through the aisles of the store, to spy the items of nourishment a famous writer feeds herself: butterfly dust, caviar, evening dew.

I stood behind her in line at the fishmonger's counter, my own cart bulging with Cheerios, two gallons of milk, laundry soap, instant mac and cheese, chicken breasts, cold cuts, bread, mayonnaise, apples, bananas, green beans, all the flabby embarrassments of motherhood that no longer embarrass me. I heard her order a quarter pound of salmon. The loneliest fish order ever. I stepped away without ordering, scared her emaciated loneliness might be contagious. She kept her chin lifted. Some people enjoy humiliation. Maybe I used to be one of those people, but I don't feel humiliation anymore. The body sloughs off cells every day, aging. After all that, what is left to feel humiliated? Very little indeed.

* * *

The commuter bus that runs between here and the city is one small part of America where silence still lives. It's a cylinder of peace moving through the world swiftly enough to blur it.

Once, on a return bus, there was a woman seated in front of me. People do not speak on the bus. At least, no one who rides with regularity. We understand that this hour of being rocked and shushed is the closest we'll get to being babies again. But this woman was not a regular. She'd gone down to the city for the day. She was ten to fifteen years older than me, mid-fifties, though I never saw her face. I could feel she was buzzing. She'd taken a risk travelling to the city by herself, such a risk that accomplishing it had emboldened her to try other new things, like the voice-recognition software on her smartphone, that newfangled device purchased for her by an older child who'd grown tired of having a mother who lived in a technological backwater.

There was nothing wrong with her hands, but she wanted to demonstrate that even though she was middle-aged and less loved now than she'd been in the past, she could be current with the modern world. She could enjoy the toys of the young. So, on the quiet bus, she began to speak into her phone as if recording books for the blind, loudly and slowly. Everyone could hear her. There on the silent bus, the woman shouted multiple drafts of an e-mail to a friend, laying plain her regret, fumes of resignation in the tight, enclosed area.

Hi. Just on my way home. I spent the day with Philip and his glamorous wife. He had a concert at the conservatory. I hadn't been back in years. It was great to see him. His wife is gorgeous. They live in Paris. Ouch. I just

The woman paused and considered. She tried again. Her voice even louder, as if it were another chorus, a building symphony of mortification.

Hi. I'm on the bus back from San Francisco. What a day. I saw Philip. He had a concert at the conservatory. His wife is gorgeous, glamorous, everything I'm not. They live in Paris and their kids

She paused again. Take three. Loud and utterly desperate. Words falling apart.

Saw Philip and his gorgeous wife. Conservatory. Paris. Kids. I just

I turned to the window, which, although sealed, at least reminded me what fresh air meant, what it was to breathe without the toilet leaking air freshener, without having to hear that woman's echoing regret.

* * *

People should be more careful with their language. People shouldn't infect innocent bystanders with their drama.

There's a man I hardly know, an academic. He began sleeping with a graduate student when his wife was pregnant, but everything was cool, because, you know, everyone involved read criticism and all three of them really wanted to test the boundaries of just how much that shit can hurt.

I imagine that shit can hurt a whole lot.

Every time I hear about another professor with a student, I think, *Wow, that professor I know is way more messed up than I ever thought. Stealing confidence from eighteen-, nineteen-, twenty-year-olds.*

Nasty.

This professor, he cleared the fucking of the graduate student with his pregnant wife, and for reasons I don't understand the wife allowed him to dabble in younger, unwed women while she gestated their child, while her blood and bones were sucked from her body into their fetus.

Though the wife is an interesting part of this triangle, it's neither her nor the husband I'm thinking of here in bed while Sam bleeds out his last drop of life on our living-room floor. I'm thinking of the poor, stupid graduate student.

She and the academic attended a lecture together one night. After the lecture, there was a party where she was in the insecure position of being a student among people who were done being students. And though everyone was staring at her—they knew the wife—no one wanted to talk to her or welcome the grad student into the land of scholars.

This was not acceptable. She liked attention. She liked performance. She cleared her throat—and the noise from the room—as if readying for a toast. She stood on a low coffee table. Everyone stopped drinking. In a loud, clear voice, one that must still reverberate in her ears, the academic's ears, everyone's ears (it even managed to reach mine), she said, "You're just angry because of what I do with my queer vagina."

On my living-room wall I keep a photo of my Victorian great-grandmother engaged in a game of cards with three of her sisters. These women maintained a highly flirtatious relationship with language. "Queer" once meant strange. "Queer" once meant homosexual. "Queer" now means opposition to binary thinking. I experience a melancholy pause when meaning is lost, when words drift like runaways far from home. How did "queer" ever come to mean a philandering penis and vagina in a roomful of bookish, egotistical people? How did common old adultery ever become queer?

I feel the grad student's late-blooming humiliation. How she came to realize, or will one day soon, that her words were foolish. I remind myself there in bed, *Don't talk. Don't say words to people, because words conjure images.* Her words created a likely unwanted idea of an organ that, like all our organs, is both extraordinary and totally plain. Some flaps of loose skin, some hair, some blood, but, outside the daily fact of its total magnificence, it is really not queer at all.

* * *

I am alone with these thoughts, these women.

What is taking him so long to come back?

"Sam?" I climb out of bed. "Sam?" I call from the top of the stairs, placing my hand against the window in the hall. There, I hear that awful sound again. A man outside coughing in the night. "Sam?" Each step down the stairs takes years. I'm frozen by terror. The photos lining the stairwell don't anchor me. Pictures of my girls at birthdays, the beach, riding ponies. "Sam?" I call from the bottom stair. The front door is locked, but the knob begins to turn against the lock and I can't move. Someone is trying to get inside. He's here, the man who has come to chop us into bits. The lock holds, but I am petrified. The man tries the doorknob again. "Sam? Where are you?"

"I'm out here." He turns the locked knob.

"You?" Sam is the man. "How'd you get locked out?"

I grab a corner of the kitchen table.

"Are you kidding?" He coughs again. It is Sam. He's at the door. I see him through the glass, coughing. Sam's the man who's come to chop us to bits. No wonder I kicked him out. No wonder I changed the locks. Sam cannot save me from death and I am so angry. If he cannot stop me or my babies from dying, what good is he? Why is he even here?

"Open the door."

I look at the night that absorbed my life. How am I supposed to know what's love and what's fear? "If you're Sam, who am I?"

"I know who you are."

"You do?"

"Yeah."

"Who am I?" I ask. *Don't say wife*, I think. *Don't say mother.* I want to know if I am anyone without my family, if I am anyone alone. I put my face to the glass, but it's dark and I don't reflect. Sam and I watch each other through the window of the door. He coughs some more.

"I want to come home," he says. "I want us to be O.K. That's it. I'm simple and I want to come home and be with my family."

"But I am extremely not simple," I tell him. My body's coursing with secret genes and hormones and proteins. My body made eyeballs and I have no idea how. There's nothing simple about eyeballs. My body made food to feed those eyeballs. How? And how can I not know or understand the things that happen inside my own body? There's nothing simple here. I'm ruled by elixirs and compounds I don't even know. Maybe I love Sam because my hormones say I need a man to kill the coyotes at night, to bring my babies meat. But I don't want that kind of love. I want a love that exists outside my body also. I don't want to be a chemistry project.

"In what ways are you not simple?" he asks.

I think of the women I collected upstairs, how they're inside me. I'm thinking of molds. I'm thinking of the sea and plankton. I'm thinking of my dad when he was a boy, when he was a tree bud. "It's complicated," I say, but words aren't going to be the best way here. Don't talk. How can I tell him something that's just coming into existence?

"I get that now," he says. "But you're going to have to try to explain it."

We see each other through the glass. He lifts his hand to my face. We witness each other. That's something, to be seen by another human. Sam's seen me since we were young. That's something, too. Love over time. Love that's movable, invisible, love like a liquid or a gas, love that finds a way in.

"Unlock the door."

"I don't want to love you because I'm scared."

"So you imagine crazy things about me? You imagine me doing things I've never done to get rid of me? Kick me out so you won't have to worry about me leaving?"

"Yeah," I say. "Right." And I'm glad he gets that.

Sam cocks his head the way a coyote might, a coyote who's been temporarily confused by a question of biology versus morality.

What's the difference between living and imagining? What's the difference between love and security?

"Unlock the door," he says again.

This family is the biggest experiment I've ever been part of, an experiment called: How do you let someone in?

"Unlock the door," he says again. "Please."

I turn the knob. I open the door. That's the best definition of love I can imagine.

Sam comes inside. But when I go to shut the door behind him he tells me no. "Leave the door open." As if there were no doors, no walls, no houses.

"Open?"

"Yeah."

"What about skunks?" I really mean burglars, gangs, evil.

"Let them in if they want."

If they even exist. If I didn't make them up. "Really?" I ask.

"Really," he says, and pulls the door open wide, as open as it can be.

Hanif Abdurraqib is a poet, essayist, and cultural critic from Columbus, Ohio. His first collection of poems, *The Crown Ain't Worth Much,* was released in 2016 and was nominated for the Hurston-Wright Legacy Award. His first collection of essays, *They Can't Kill Us Until They Kill Us,* was released in fall 2017 by Two Dollar Radio.

Annie Baker's other plays include *The Flick* (Pulitzer Prize for drama), *John, Circle Mirror Transformation,* and an adaptation of Chekhov's *Uncle Vanya.* Honors include a MacArthur Fellowship, Guggenheim Fellowship, Steinberg Playwriting Award, American Academy of Arts and Letters Award, New York Drama Critics' Circle Award, and the Cullman Fellowship at the New York Public Library. She is a resident playwright at the Signature Theatre and cochair and master-artist-in-residence of the MFA Playwriting Program at Hunter College. All of her plays are available from TCG Books.

Jesse Ball (1978–) is an absurdist whose works appear in many languages the world over.

John Batki is a kilimologist, writer, translator, and visual artist. He was born in Hungary and has lived in the United States since age fourteen.

Peter Bush is a translator of works from Catalan, French, Spanish, and Portuguese into English and has received numerous awards. He has translated Quim Monzó's novel *The Enormity of the Tragedy* and two short story collections, *Guadalajara* and *A Thousand Morons*. He lives in England.

Lilli Carré is an interdisciplinary artist working primarily in experimental animation, sculpture, comics, and drawing. She is codirector of the Eyeworks Festival of Experimental Animation, which is held annually in Chicago, Los Angeles, and New York.

Chris (Simpsons artist) is an anonymous artist and storyteller who is known for his surreal artwork and stream-of-consciousness writing. He is a regular contributor for both national and international publications, and has gained a cult-like following on social media, with many touting him as the voice of his generation.

Seo-Young Chu also goes by "Jennie." She teaches at Queens College, CUNY. Her publications include *Do Metaphors Dream of Literal Sleep?: A Science-Fictional Theory of Representation* (Harvard University Press, 2011), "CHIMERICAL MOSAIC: SELF TEST KIT IN D# MINOR," "Hwabyung Fragments," "Postmemory Han," "I, Stereotype: Detained in the Uncanny Valley," "Welcome to The Vegas Pyongyang," and "After 'A Refuge for Jae-in Doe': A Social Media Chronology." Much of her writings can be found on Facebook, Twitter, YouTube, and Instagram.

Daniel Clowes was born in Chicago in 1961. In 1989, he published the first issue of his seminal comic book, *Eightball*. His graphic novels include *Ghost World, David Boring, Caricature, Like a Velvet Glove Cast in Iron, Ice Haven, Mr. Wonderful,* and *Wilson*. His latest book is *Patience*. A major retrospective of his work, The Art of Daniel Clowes: Modern Cartoonist, debuted at the OMCA in Oakland, before traveling to the MCA in Chicago, and the Wexner in Columbus. He lives in Oakland, California, with his wife Erika and son Charles.

Kari Dickson was born in Edinburgh, Scotland. She has a B.A. in Scandinavian studies and an M.A. in translation. Before becoming a translator, she worked in theater in London and Oslo. Previously a teaching fellow in the Scandanavian Studies section at the University of Edinburgh, she is now an occasional tutor in Norwegian and translation.

Tongo Eisen-Martin is the author of the critically acclaimed poetry book *someone's dead already*. He is also a movement worker and educator whose work in Rikers Island was featured in the *New York Times*. He has been a faculty member at the Institute for Research in African-American Studies at Columbia University, and his curriculum on extrajudicial killing of Black people, "We Charge Genocide Again!" has been used as an educational and organizing tool throughout the country. He is from San Francisco. His latest book of poems, titled *Heaven Is All Goodbye*, was published in the City Light's Pocket Poets Series and won the 2018 California Book Award.

Brian Evenson is the author of a dozen books of fiction, most recently *A Collapse of Horses* and *The Warren*. He is the recipient of three O. Henry Prizes, an NEA Fellowship, and a Guggenheim Fellowship. His new story collection, *Song for the Unravelling of the World*, will be published in 2019. He lives in Los Angeles and teaches at CalArts.

Kathy Fish teaches for the Mile High MFA at Regis University in Denver, Colorado. She has published four collections of short fiction: a chapbook in the Rose Metal Press collective, *A Peculiar Feeling of Restlessness: Four Chapbooks of Short Short Fiction by Four Women* (2008); *Wild Life* (Matter Press, 2011); *Together We Can Bury It* (The Lit Pub, 2012); and *Rift*, coauthored with Robert Vaughan (Unknown Press, 2015). Three of her stories have been chosen for the annual *Best Small Fictions* (Braddock Avenue Books) anthology.

Laura Francis is the coauthor of *A Life Discarded* and writer of all the words. Born in Oxford in 1939, Francis spent most of her working life as a live-in housekeeper for an elderly professor of IT in Cambridge. She is (or would be, if she would stop throwing her books out) Britain's most prolific diarist. She has written up to 4,000 words a day since the age of twelve.

Roxane Gay is the author of the *New York Times* bestsellers *Bad Femi-*

nist and *Hunger*, which has been nominated for the National Books Critics' Circle Award and received the NBCC Members' Choice Award; the novel *An Untamed State*, a finalist for the Dayton Peace Prize; and the short story collections *Difficult Women* and *Ayiti*. A contributing opinion writer to the *New York Times*, she has also written for *Time*, the *Virginia Quarterly Review*, the *Los Angeles Times*, *The Nation*, *The Rumpus*, and *Salon*, among others. She is the author of *World of Wakanda* for Marvel. She lives in Los Angeles.

Lucy Huber is a freelance writer in Boston. She has an MFA in creative nonfiction from the University of North Carolina, Wilmington. She writes satire, personal essays, sketch comedy, and many impromptu songs about her cats.

Bonnie Huie is a literary translator of Chinese and Japanese, whose books include *Notes of a Crocodile* (NYRB Classics, 2018) and *Hummingbirds Fly Backwards* (AmazonCrossing, 2016). Her work has appeared in *PEN America*, the *Brooklyn Rail*, *Kyoto Journal*, *The Margins* by the Asian American Writers' Workshop, and the visual arts journal *Afterimage*. She was awarded a PEN/Heim Translation Fund grant.

Samantha Hunt's novel about Nikola Tesla, *The Invention of Everything Else*, was a finalist for the Orange Prize and winner of the Bard Fiction Prize. Her first novel, *The Seas*, earned her selection as one of the National Book Foundation's 5 Under 35. Her novel *Mr. Splitfoot* was an IndieNext Pick. Her work has appeared in *The New Yorker*, the *New York Times Magazine*, *McSweeney's*, *Tin House*, *A Public Space*, and many other publications. Her short story collection, *The Dark Dark*, published in 2017, was nominated for a PEN/Faulkner Award. She lives in upstate New York.

László Krasznahorkai, described by James Wood in *The New Yorker* as an "obsessive visionary," was born in Gyula, Hungary. *The World Goes On* is his seventh book published by New Directions.

David Leavitt's works of fiction have been finalists for the PEN/Faulkner Prize, the National Book Critics' Circle Award, and the *Los*

Angeles Times Fiction Prize, and short-listed for the IMPAC Dublin Award. His writing has appeared in *The New Yorker,* the *New York Times, Harper's Magazine,* and *Vogue,* among other publications. He lives in Gainesville, Florida, where he is a professor of English at the University of Florida and edits the literary magazine *Subtropics.*

Andrew Leland hosts *The Organist* (kcrw.com/theorganist), an arts and culture podcast from KCRW and *McSweeney's.*

Carmen Maria Machado's essays, fiction, and criticism have appeared in *The New Yorker,* the *New York Times, Granta, Tin House, McSweeney's Quarterly Concern, The Believer, Guernica, The Best American Science Fiction and Fantasy,* and elsewhere. Her debut short story collection, *Her Body and Other Parties,* was a finalist for the National Book Award for Fiction and won the Bard Fiction Prize and the National Book Critics Circle's John Leonard Prize. She holds an MFA from the Iowa Writers' Workshop and is the writer-in-residence at the University of Pennsylvania. She lives in Philadelphia with her wife.

Christina MacSweeney was awarded the 2016 Valle Inclán Translation Prize for her translation of Valeria Luiselli's *The Story of My Teeth.* She has translated two other books by the same author, and her translations of Daniel Saldaña París's novel *Among Strange Victims* and Eduardo Rabasa's *A Zero-Sum Game* both appeared in 2016. She has also published translations, articles, and interviews on a wide variety of platforms, including *Words Without Borders, Music and Literature, Literary Hub,* and *BOMB Magazine,* and in three anthologies: *México20; Lunatics, Lovers and Poets: Twelve Stories After Cervantes and Shakespeare;* and *Crude Words: Contemporary Writing from Venezuela.*

Alexander Masters was born in New York, and took his degree in physics and mathematics. In 2016 he published *A Life Discarded,* a biography of the anonymous author of 148 diaries that a friend had discovered in a dumpster on a building site. Over five years, Masters pieced together the life of the diarist (whom he originally believed to be a man and dead) and discovered she was alive and living half a mile away.

Katherine Augusta Mayfield is a recent graduate of Columbia University's fiction MFA program, and is the recipient of writing and art residencies from the Vermont Studio Center, Rufus Stone, and Gullkistan. Her writing has been published or is forthcoming in *No Tokens*, the *Virginia Quarterly Review*, *BOMB Magazine*, and others. She lives in Queens, New York.

Qiu Miaojin—one of Taiwan's most innovative literary modernists, and the country's most renowned lesbian writer—was born in 1969. Her first published story, "Prisoner," received the *Central Daily News* Short Story Prize, and her novella *Lonely Crowds* won the United Literature Association Award. In 1995, at the age of twenty-six, she committed suicide. The posthumous publications of her novels *Last Words from Montmartre* and *Notes of a Crocodile* made her into one of the most revered countercultural icons in Chinese letters. After her death in 1995, she was given the *China Times* Honorary Prize for Literature. In 2017, she became the subject of a feature-length documentary by Evans Chan titled *Death in Montmartre*.

Quim Monzó was born in Barcelona in 1952. He has composed scripts for radio, television, and cinema, and adapted texts for the stage. He has published three novels, nine collections of short stories, and nine collections of essays, and has been translated into twenty-two languages. He is a winner of the Premio Nacional de Literatura, the Ciudad de Barcelona prize, and the Prudenci Bertrana award, among others.

Anders Nilsen is the artist and author of nine books of comics, including *Big Questions*, *The End*, *Poetry Is Useless*, and the forthcoming *Tongues*. His work has appeared in the *New York Times*, *Medium*, *Kramers Ergot*, and elsewhere, and been translated into numerous languages. Nilsen has garnered three Ignatz Awards and the Lynd Ward Graphic Novel Prize. In addition, he is a regular participant in and occasional organizer of the experimental collaborative comics residency Pierre Feuille Ciseaux. He lives in Portland, Oregon.

Diego Enrique Osorno was born in 1980 in Monterrey, Mexico. A reporter and writer, he has witnessed some of the twenty-first century's major conflicts in Mexico and Latin America. He has been called one of the region's most important journalists by the Gabriel García Márquez Foundation for New Journalism and has received Italy's prestigious Stampa Romana. In 2014 he was awarded Mexico's National Journalism Prize, which he dedicated to the Zapatista Army of National Liberation. He is the author most recently of *Slim*, a biography of the richest man in the world, which Verso will publish in English. Like many other Mexican journalists, he has been threatened because of his work.

Gunnhild Øyehaug is an award-winning Norwegian poet, essayist, and fiction writer. Her story collection *Knots* was published by FSG in 2017, and *Wait, Blink* was adapted into the acclaimed film *Women in Oversized Men's Shirts* in 2015. Øyehaug lives in Bergen, where she teaches creative writing.

Ben Passmore makes mad comics in his dusty room, including *DAY-GLOAYHOLE, Goodbye*, and the Ignatz Award–winning comic *Your Black Friend*. He's a regular contributor at *The Nib* and *Vice*. He likes to write about politics, monsters, race, sad punks, and narcissism. He is one of the founding organizers of NOCAZ (New Orleans Alternative Comics and Zine Fest). His latest comics collection, *Your Black Friend and Other Strangers*, was published in May 2018.

Catherine Pond's poems have appeared in *Boston Review, Narrative, Rattle*, and many more. She is a Ph.D. candidate in literature and creative writing at the University of Southern California as well as the assistant director of the New York State Summer Writers Institute. In 2018 she won third place in *Narrative*'s Winter Story Contest. She lives in Los Angeles.

Kristen Roupenian's story collection, *You Know You Want This*, will be published by Scout Press in 2019 and in more than twenty other countries. She holds a Ph.D. in English from Harvard, and an MFA in fiction from the University of Michigan, where she is currently a Zell Fellow.

Benjamin Schaefer is a writer and editor from upstate New York. He studied literature and creative writing at Bard College and at the MFA program at the University of Arizona. His fiction has appeared in *Guernica* and *Electric Literature*, and he is the recipient of fellowships from the MacDowell Colony, the Millay Colony for the Arts, and the Virginia Center for the Creative Arts.

C. S. Soong is the coproducer and host of *Against the Grain*, a radio program and web project that highlights progressive and radical thinking and activism. He holds a B.A. in history from Brown University and a J.D. from Cornell Law School. He has also done graduate work in philosophy at San Francisco State University.

Souvankham Thammavongsa's stories have appeared in *Granta*, *Harper's Magazine*, *NOON*, and other places. She is the author of three poetry books.

Alex Tizon, a Pulitzer Prize–winning journalist, was former Seattle bureau chief for the *Los Angeles Times* and longtime staff writer for the *Seattle Times*. He was a professor of journalism at the University of Oregon.

Stacey Tran is a writer from Portland, Oregon. She is the creator of *Tender Table*, a storytelling series about food, family, and identity. Her writing can be found in *BOMB Magazine*, *The Brooklyn Rail*, and *diaCRITICS*. She is the author of *Soap for the Dogs* (Gramma, 2018).

Kara Walker is best known for her candid investigation of race, gender, sexuality, and violence through silhouetted figures, which have appeared in numerous exhibitions worldwide. She is the recipient of many awards, notably the John D. and Catherine T. MacArthur Foundation Achievement Award in 1997 and the United States Artists Eileen Harris Norton Fellowship in 2008. In 2012, Walker became a member of the American Academy of Arts and Letters. She lives and works in New York City and is the Tepper Chair in the Visual Arts at Rutgers University's Mason Gross School of the Arts.

David Wallace-Wells is deputy editor at *New York Magazine*, where he also writes about science and the near future, including his recent cover story on worst-case scenarios for climate change (which was the most-read *New York Magazine* story ever). He is currently working on a book about the meaning of global warming.

Chris Ware is the author of *Jimmy Corrigan—the Smartest Kid on Earth* and *Building Stories*, which was deemed a Top Ten Fiction Book by the *New York Times* and *Time*. A regular contributor to *The New Yorker*, his work has been exhibited at MOCA Los Angeles, MCA Chicago, and the Whitney Museum of American Art, and an eponymous monograph was published by Rizzoli in 2017.

Frank B. Wilderson III is an award-winning writer, poet, scholar, activist and emerging filmmaker. He has received numerous writing awards, including the Eisner Prize for Creative Achievement of the Highest Order, the Crothers Short Story Award, the Judith Stronach Award for Poetry, the Jerome Foundation Artists and Writers Award, the Loft-McKnight Award for Best Prose in the State of Minnesota, and the Maya Angelou Award for Best Fiction Portraying the Black Experience in America. His fiction and creative prose, as well as his critical and scholarly work, have been published internationally.

THE BEST AMERICAN
NONREQUIRED READING
COMMITTEE

Sophia Casey-Stewart's hobbies include reading, writing, baking (only with cheap box cake mix and store-bought cookie dough), and overanalyzing TV shows and movies. In fall 2018 she will be attending Eugene Lang College at The New School in New York City and trying to figure out how to use the subway system.

 Max Chu is currently a senior. He loves to read, loves to write, and loves the "Beth" coffee mug. He would appreciate if anyone reading this not named Beth not try and take the "Beth" coffee mug. He needs it to do proper and top quality *BANR* work. However, if your name happens to be Beth and you would like to claim the "Beth" mug, Max is willing to establish a trade-system. Whatever that means.

Madison DeVry is not sure what she will be doing this fall. She might be going to The New School or taking a gap year. Either way, she will be reading lots of books and drinking copious amounts of coffee. She will also be missing a certain little basement on Valencia Street and the invaluable time that she got to spend there.

Emilia Villela Fernández graduated from Lick-Wilmerding High School and now attends Yale University. Her friends make fun of her for meticulously overplanning things on several mini-whiteboards she keeps in her room. She is really glad to have been a part of BANR and will miss it: the basement, the cool people, and even the bluegrass that seeps in from the bar next door.

Emma Hardison is a freshman at the University of San Francisco. She is known for her quick wit, stunning beauty, startling intelligence, and undeniably humble nature. She will miss *BANR* almost as much as it will miss her, if that is even possible.

Sidney Hirschman graduated from Lick-Wilmerding High School in the spring of 2018, and is now attending Yale University. When they're not reading or in school, Sidney enjoys sewing, painting, metalworking, and eating food with a lot of sodium in it. This is Sidney's last year at *BANR,* and they would like to thank Clara, Laura, Daniel, Sheila, and Tom Hanks.

Colette "Coco" Johnson is a young African-American woman from San Francisco, California. She is currently a sophomore at Ruth Asawa School of the Arts. In her spare time she likes to listen to music, watch YouTube, and play volleyball. Her goal in life is to be a journalist or on-air host for Clevver, an entertainment news source. She hopes you enjoy the book and is proud of the pieces the *BANR* committee selected.

Althea Kriney wanted to turn this in late like she did last year, but management is really cracking down. She is currently a senior at Lowell High School. Hopefully she graduates next year—it's very up in the air. You'll have to pick up next year's *BANR* book to find out.

Sian Laing is a freshman at UC Berkeley. She is currently embracing her Scottish heritage by looking for Nessie, the Loch Ness monster. By calculating how many sips it would take to drink the Loch Ness, she hopes to gather enough mouths to consume the lake, exposing the monster in all its glory. However, she has yet to discover how the Scottish Environmental Protection Agency feels about her plan.

Lola Leuterio is a senior at Tamalpais High School. She has been a member of the *BANR* committee for the past two years and loves the way it gets her thinking, talking, and learning from people with different perspectives. Lola's role model is Donna from *Mamma Mia* and she believes life's ultimate success is being The Dancing Queen. That pretty much says it all. She hopes you enjoy the anthology!

Xuan Ly is a sophomore at Ruth Asawa San Francisco School of the Arts. She is used to people calling her "Juan," but she wants you to know, even if it is completely irrelevant, that her name is actually pronounced, "Swan." This is her first year on the *BANR* committee and she has enjoyed reading and learning from each piece. She loves her dog and at the moment, she and her brothers are attempting to slowly rename him Zucchini, but she's not sure how that will go.

Zoe Olson is a senior at Mission High School and this is her second year on the *BANR* committee. She likes cookies, cats, and arts and crafts. You can't see, because the image is zoomed in, but she's waving at you from the little picture on the right. Hi!

Charley Ostrow is a freshman at Scripps College. She loves to read, write, watch *The Office,* and spends too much time picking her outfits. This is her first year on the *BANR* committee, and she has loved reading the wide collection of pieces. Enjoy!

Annette Vergara-Tucker is a senior at Lick-Wilmerding High School, who hopes that you take the time to seriously reflect on the writing that the committee selected for this year's *BANR* anthology. The pieces they encountered this year were incredibly reflective of the last twelve months and make for a collection that will be relevant and sought after for generations to come.

Huckleberry Shelf is a senior at Ruth Asawa San Francisco School of the Arts, and *BANR*'s resident devil's advocate. He often confers with a cardboard cutout of Tom Hanks in dark corners of the *BANR* meeting space. No one knows precisely what they discuss, and everyone should be worried.

Very special thanks to Dave Eggers, Nicole Angeloro, Mark Robinson, and Tommi Parrish. Thanks also to Daniel Gumbiner, Sarah Vowell, Rachel Kushner, Adam Johnson, Daniel Handler, Laura Van Slyke, Chris Ames, Olga Sankey, Jody Hanson, Justin Carder, Meghan Berckes, Matt Carney, Natalie Jabbar, Colin Winnette, Andi Winnette, Reese Kwon, Daniel Levin Becker, Abigail Ulman, Jose Segura, Catherine Sullivan, Max Ross, Ted Trautman, Alex Holey, Amy Langer, Sunra Thompson, Claire Boyle, Kristina Kearns, Eric Cromie, Chris Monks, Mimi Lok, Laura Brief, Kaitlin Steele, Lauren Broder, Maggie Andrews, Daniel Cesca, Kelson Goldfine, Angela Gasca, Anna Griffin, Yusuke Wada, Cecilia Juan, Okailey Okai, Sierra Swann, Diana Adamson, Juliana Sloane, Hannah Bardo, Kate Bueler, Rita Bullwinkel, Nirvana Felix, Marisela Garcia, Leo Harrington, Timothy Huynh, Cristian King, Jessica Li, Sam Lozano, Monica Mendez, Oliver Pascua, Veronica Ponce-Navarrete, Francisco Prado, Piper Sutherland, Kenia Tello, Jenny Vu, Nicholas Watson, and Alma Zaragoza-Petty.

NOTABLE
NONREQUIRED READING
OF 2017

DAVE HICKEY
  The Last Mouseketeer, *Perfect Wave*

ROSE HIMBER HOWSE
  An Interview with Garth Greenwell, *Dead Darlings*

LAUREN MICHELE JACKSON
  We Need to Talk About Digital Blackface in Reaction GIFs, *Teen Vogue*
LESLIE JAMISON
  The Digital Ruins of a Forgotten Future, *The Atlantic*

ANDREW LELAND
  Self-Portrait in An Open Medicine Cabinet, *McSweeney's Quarterly Concern*

SAYAKA MURATA
  A First-Rate Material, *Freeman's*
WILL MURRAY
  Let the People See What I See, *Salmagundi*

LUPITA NYONG'O
  Speaking Out About Harvey Weinstein, *The New York Times*

ELENA PASSARELLO
  Arabella, *Animals Strike Curious Poses*
WILLIS PLUMMER
  10,000 Year Clock, *Muumuu House*

DEAN RADER
  Still Life with Cacography, *ZYZZYVA*

REBECCA TRAISTER
  Your Reckoning. And Mine, *The Cut*

JAVIER ZAMORA
  Nocturne, *The Poetry Foundation*

ABOUT 826 NATIONAL

Proceeds from this book benefit youth literacy

826 NATIONAL IS A nonprofit organization that provides strategic leadership, administration, and other resources to ensure the success of its network of eight writing and tutoring centers. 826 National's chapters are dedicated to providing under-resourced students, ages 6 to 18, with opportunities to explore their creativity and improve their writing skills. We also aim to help teachers inspire their students to write. Our mission is based on the understanding that great leaps in learning can happen with individualized attention, and that strong writing skills are fundamental to future success. 826 is the largest youth writing network in the country.

826 National amplifies the impact of our national network of youth writing and publishing centers, and the words of young authors. We serve as an international proof point for writing as a tool for young people to ignite and channel their creativity, explore identity, advocate for themselves and their community, and achieve academic and professional success.

Currently, the 826 Network is in eight major U.S. cities and serves nearly 34,000 under-resourced students ages 6–18 each year, thanks to the support of almost 5,000 volunteers. Each chapter has an imaginative storefront that reimagines tutoring as anything but traditional; provides a gateway for meeting families, teachers, and volunteers; and connects students with community members. And of course, sells Canned Laughter and Robot Toupées.

In addition, there are fifty 826-inspired organizations across the globe. We support educators through 826 Digital, our new online pay-what-you-wish platform designed to help teach and ignite a love of writing. 826 National is the hub of the 826 Network: facilitating collaboration and alignment among our chapters, and bringing the 826 Network model and approach to new communities.

Read on to learn more about each 826 chapter.

826 VALENCIA

826 Valencia was founded in 2002 by educator Nínive Calegari and author Dave Eggers. It comprises two writing centers—the flagship location in the Mission District and a new center in the Tenderloin neighborhood—and three satellite classrooms at nearby public schools. The year 2019 will see the addition of a third 826 Valencia center on the ground floor of an affordable housing development in the Mission Bay neighborhood. 826 Valencia offers tutoring and workshops, supports teachers through in-school projects, and hosts field trips from local public schools. This year 826 Valencia will produce 50 major student-written publications, and cultivate wonder, confidence, and an affinity for writing for more than 7,000 under-resourced students all over San Francisco.

826NYC

826NYC's writing center opened its doors in September 2004. Every year, it provides more than 4,000 students with the opportunity to build their writing skills and confidence in their creative voice through a combination of after-school, in-school, and field trip programs. 826NYC operates year-round out of the world famous Brooklyn Superhero Supply Co., the South

Williamsburg branch of the Brooklyn Public Library, and its East Harlem Writers Room located at M.S. 7/Global Tech Prep. In addition, 826NYC runs short-term programs with Title 1 schools throughout the city. 826NYC publishes more than 25 publications each year, supported by a corps of more than 300 volunteers annually.

826LA

826LA serves over 9,200 students each year at its centers in Echo Park and Mar Vista, its Writers' Room at Manual Arts High School, and at high schools all around Los Angeles. Through after-school tutoring, in-school classroom support, creative writing workshops, and bookmaking field trips, 826LA builds connections between its community of students,

families, volunteers, educators, and supporters. Since its founding in 2005, 826LA has served more than 74,000 students. More than 120 public school teachers each year benefit from 826LA's support, and, in 2017, over 1,230 trained volunteers contributed 22,035 hours of their time. At 826LA, students are transported to a world where writing is a form of magic, their voices are celebrated, and anything is possible.

826CHI

826CHI is headquartered in the Wicker Park neighborhood of Chicago and serves over 3,000 students from more than 120 Chicago public schools. Originally opened in 2005, 826CHI moved in 2014 and opened their new storefront, the Secret Agent Supply Co., full of products that unlock creativity and inspire new adventures for agents of all ages. 826CHI believes all Chicago youth should have equal access to high-quality writing and literary arts education. Over 350 active volunteers support 826CHI's programs, which are dedicated to amplifying the voices of Chicago youth.

826MICHIGAN

826michigan opened its doors on June 1, 2005, on South State Street in Ann Arbor. In October of 2007 the operation moved downtown, to a new and improved location on Liberty Street. Today, 826michigan operates Liberty Street Robot Supply & Repair in Ann Arbor, The Detroit Robot Factory in the city's Eastern Market neighborhood, and dozens of writing and tutoring programs in venues across Ann Arbor, Detroit, and Ypsilanti. 826michigan students—all 4,000 of them—write poems and essays, stories and plays, on field trips, in-classroom residencies, drop-in writing programs in public library branches, and much more. The organization has a staff of 11 and a diverse, vibrant volunteer corps of 500+ adults across southeastern Michigan.

826 BOSTON

826 Boston opened its doors to the Greater Boston Bigfoot Research Institute in 2007. Working with traditionally underserved students ages 6–18 out of its headquarters in the Roxbury neighborhood of Egleston Square, as well as through a network of full-time writers' rooms located within Boston

public schools, 826 Boston has served 19,000 students. Its community of more than 2,500 volunteers—including college students, professional writers, artists, and teachers—helped 826 Boston secure a "Best Places to Volunteer" distinction from the *Boston Globe*. Recent collections of 826 Boston student writing include *I Rate Today a –1,000*, inspired by Jeff Kinney's *Diary of a Wimpy Kid* series, and *Attendance Would Be 100%: Student Proposals for High School Redesign Boston*.

826DC

826DC opened its doors to the city's Columbia Heights neighborhood in October 2010. 826DC provides after-school tutoring, field trips, workshops, college essay support, and in-school publishing programs for students in all eight wards of the District. It also boasts DC's only magic  shop—Tivoli's Astounding Magic Supply Company, Illusionarium & De-Lux Haberdashery—in the heart of the city. Recent anthologies of 826DC's student writing include *Spit Fire, Having to Tell Your Mother is the Hardest Part, Delicious Havoc,* and *My Heart Went Beating Fast.*

826 NEW ORLEANS

826 New Orleans was founded in 2010 as a writing project in a single classroom and has since grown into a multi-program nonprofit that serves over 3,000 students annually. Rooted in the historic 7th Ward, the youth writing center is a literary hub for students across the city. The diverse programming allows young people to work one-on-one with volunteers to develop and publish high-quality writing, from professionally bound anthologies of personal narratives to poems printed on pizza boxes. Because of its exemplary work, the center was invited to become the first Southern chapter of the highly-esteemed 826 Network, allowing them to connect their students to 32,000 young writers across the nation and to continue amplifying the voices of New Orleans youth.

ABOUT SCHOLARMATCH

Founded in 2010 by author Dave Eggers, ScholarMatch began as a crowdfunding platform for college scholarships, and has now grown into a full-service college access organization that supports low-income and first-gen students through every point of the college journey. We serve high school students at our San Francisco College Access Center and nationwide through our Virtual Destination College program, and the ScholarMatcher—a groundbreaking college search tool optimized for the needs of low-income students. We support college students nationwide, with hubs based in San Francisco and Los Angeles. From local website to nationally reaching nonprofit, today, ScholarMatch is a nimble 20-person organization that is actively growing and constantly refining programs based on what works. Our services are free for students and available for contract by community-based organizations, corporations, and foundations. To support a student's college journey or learn more, visit scholarmatch.org.

THE BEST AMERICAN SERIES®

FIRST, BEST, AND BEST-SELLING

The Best American Comics

The Best American Essays

The Best American Food Writing

The Best American Mystery Stories

The Best American Nonrequired Reading

The Best American Science and Nature Writing

The Best American Science Fiction and Fantasy

The Best American Short Stories

The Best American Sports Writing

The Best American Travel Writing

Available in print and e-book wherever books are sold.

hmhco.com/bestamerican

34806477R00191

Made in the USA
Middletown, DE
29 January 2019